THE DOGS
OF ROME

CONOR FITZGERALD has lived in Ireland, the UK, the United States, and Italy. He has worked as an arts editor, produced a current affairs journal for foreign embassies and founded a successful translation company. He is married with two children and lives in Rome.

THE DOGS OF ROME

A COMMISSARIO ALEC BLUME NOVEL

CONOR FITZGERALD

BLOOMSBURY

NEW YORK · BERLIN · LONDON · SYDNEY

Published by Bloomsbury USA, New York

All papers used by Bloomsbury USA are natural, recyclable products made from
wood grown in well-managed forests. The manufacturing processes conform to the
environmental regulations of the country of origin.

LIBRARY OF CONGRESS CATALOGING-IN-PUBLICATION DATA

Fitzgerald, Conor.
The dogs of Rome : a Commissario Alec Blume novel / Conor Fitzgerald. — 1st U.S. ed.
p. cm.
ISBN-13: 978-1-60819-015-7 (alk. paper hardcover)
ISBN-10: 1-60819-015-3 (alk. paper hardcover)
1. Police—Italy—Rome—Fiction. 2. Murder—Investigation—Fiction.
3. Americans——Italy—Fiction. 4. Rome (Italy)—Fiction. I. Title.
PR9120.9.F58D64 2010
823'.914—dc22
2009049430

First US edition published by Bloomsbury USA in 2010
This paperback edition published in 2011

Paperback ISBN: 978-1-60819-054-6

1 3 5 7 9 10 8 6 4 2

Typeset by Westchester Book Group
Printed in the United States of America by Quad/Graphics, Fairfield, Pennsylvania

For Paola, and in memory of
Pat Kavanagh and Katherine Breen.

1

A RTURO CLEMENTE PUT down the phone, turned to the woman lying among the twisted sheets, and said, "That was Sveva. You need to go right now."

"Now?" The woman pouted and started pulling her clothes off the floor.

She stood in front of the open window and linked her hands behind her neck, which raised her heavy breasts a little and made Arturo nervous that she could be seen.

"God, it's hot," she said, turning her broad shoulders to catch the slight breeze. The window looked straight into the lower canopy of an umbrella pine that was almost as high as the apartment building. The outside shutters were half-closed, too, so there was not too much danger the people in the apartments opposite would see her.

Thanks to the tree and the small garden in which it stood, the usual Roman smells of dust, car fumes, and garbage were overlaid with a heavy perfume of pine resin. Even the sounds of the streets seemed to be muted from here. It was a private place, more conducive to sleep than to sex. She seemed to be moving in luxurious slow motion.

"You need to go right now," said Arturo. "She's changed her plans. She's on her way back with Tommaso."

He went to the window and peered out, just to make sure no one was looking. He could see the exoskeletons of rehatched cicadas still clinging to the patch of pine bark outside.

Manuela worked her way methodically into a pair of tight white jeans with jeweled pockets, and struggled a bit with the zipper.

It had been Manuela's idea to spend the weekend together in Arturo's house while Sveva was in her constituency center in Padua. He had not been so sure it was a good idea, and now he was being proved right.

Manuela was soon ready to go. Arturo, dressed only in boxer shorts,

1

pulling in his stomach a bit, but not much since there was no point, accompanied her to the door.

In her shoes, she was taller than he was. Just before she left, she laid a hand on his arm, squeezed it hard, and brought her face close enough for him to see the pinched skin over her lip.

"Arturo," she said, "we could be good together. I know we could. But not like this." She waved a large hand to indicate the bedroom, the apartment, him, Rome, everything. "You have a young child. I respect that. But just don't . . ." She paused. "I am really keen for it to work."

Arturo closed the door behind her and strolled back to the bedroom. He felt relief and no hurry. Sveva said she was calling from Padua. Even if the train left right now, she would still take a whole five hours. He stripped the sheets off the bed and then wondered what to do with them. He put them in the dirty laundry basket, and took out others that seemed more or less the same. He did not see how Sveva would notice the difference. Neither he nor she did the laundry.

And even if she did. He no longer cared to hide his loneliness. When Sveva came to Rome, it was to vote in the Senate against Berlusconi, not to spend time with her husband.

It had been a while since he had made a bed. Removing the creased sheets had already tired him. He set the folded fresh linen on the mattress, then abandoned the enterprise, and went for a shower. He stayed in it for a long time, feeling guilty about all the water he was using, to escape the heat and to wash off the lingering tastes and smells of Manuela.

As he turned off the water, the tree's first adult cicada struck up with a rattling of its tymbals just loud enough to drown out the rasping sound of someone downstairs buzzing the intercom.

Within seconds of stepping out of the shower, Arturo could already feel the first traces of sweat gathering in the lines of his brow. Then the invisible cicada stopped as suddenly as it had begun, and the silence was beautiful. He listened to the droplets of water from his body hit the marble floor.

He squinted at the wardrobe mirror, and saw the blurred outline of a naked man whose flesh was expanding and drooping despite conscientious vegetarianism. Three years ago, he had noticed tufts of hair in his ears. Now he noticed, or admitted the existence of, a dangling piece of lobe above his Adam's apple, like those bits on turkeys, whatever they were called. Wattles.

A muffled thump came from the landing outside the apartment as if someone had dropped something soft and heavy. The cicada outside crawled a few inches up the cracked bark, tried a few experimental clicks before striking up again and rapidly increasing the frequency to a level that seemed unsustainable.

Then the doorbell rang.

Arturo glanced around and picked his bathrobe off the towel rack, revealing Tommaso's comically small one underneath. Arturo pictured his son's round head with its exuberant blond curls all wrapped up inside the hood of his bathrobe, his grave eyes looking out. The child's voice was permanently pitched to a tone of perfect astonishment at all the interesting things he saw around him.

Sveva seemed to regard Tommaso as a strategic mistake. He had arrived late, well into the time of life when most estranged aging couples prefer a pair of high-maintenance dogs to human offspring. But it was a mistake Arturo was glad they had made. Now Tommaso and Sveva were beginning to spend time together. Taking him to Padua had been a first, the mother maybe beginning to make it up to her child for the empty early years, warming to him at last, proud of how he had turned out; she had needed to wait until Tommaso could speak and reason before showing affection. Sveva was not one to coo.

The doorbell rang again, and Arturo could not locate his glasses.

"I am not answering that," he muttered aloud to himself, pulling on the bathrobe. The front door to the building was no barrier to vendors. Someone always buzzed them in. Once, in vengeful fun, he kept a heavyset Kirby vacuum cleaner saleswoman in the apartment for two hours demonstrating her clunky useless product before telling her to fuck off.

He heard a scratching outside the front door, followed by four hard thumps.

Ringing the bell was intrusion enough, but banging at his door was an affront. Arturo tightened the cord on his robe and strode down the corridor, a torrent of abuse already running through his head. Angrily, majestically, he flung open the reinforced door and found himself looking at a sagging cardboard box of groceries and two plastic packs of Nepi mineral water.

A smallish man dressed in a white Adidas tracksuit zipped up to the collar, who must have been hugging the wall on the left, slipped into his vision. Arturo peered at him. The man peered back. He seemed to have a light mustache, but it may have been just the slanted light.

"Arturo Clemente?" said the man, cocking his head to one side. He waved a small bony hand at the box and bottles on the floor.

Arturo had completely forgotten about the delivery of the groceries that he himself had bought last night, and his anger subsided. He stood back and held the door open.

The delivery boy slid the box across the threshold, hissing through his teeth from the effort. He used his foot to get the two packs of mineral water inside. He kicked one too hard and it toppled over as it crossed the slight ledge between the outside landing and the apartment floor.

He wasn't the usual delivery boy. He was not really a boy at all, now that he was standing so close. His hair was wispy and light, like a two-year-old's, but thinning in the middle. He was wearing slip-on shoes under shimmering Adidas tracksuit bottoms that had zippers running down the calves. Arturo felt a quick flash of pity. Here was a man trying to fit in with the ugly prole look of his younger colleagues.

Arturo realized that he'd have to go back to his bedroom for his wallet if he wanted to tip the man, who was breathing fast with little grunts. Maybe he should offer a glass of water. The man gave him a crooked-toothed smile and darted his tongue over his slightly pouting lips. Maybe not.

Arturo walked quickly down the hallway, glancing at the shelves on his left on the off-chance he had left a few coins lying about that he could use, but found none. As he reached the bedroom, from behind he heard the familiar soft clunk of the front door closing. He glanced back briefly and saw the white shape of the man squeezed up against the wall at the end of the corridor.

As he entered the bedroom, Arturo felt a twinge of uneasiness, as if someone had tugged on a thin cord attached to the inside of his navel. The usual delivery boy slid the boxes over the threshold, stepped outside immediately and left. This one looked like he wanted to go nosing his way through the apartment, poking his pointed face into nooks and crannies. A second cicada struck up.

Moving quickly, he retrieved his pants, which were draped over a chair,

4

and fumbled about for his wallet. He decided not to waste time looking for coins or his glasses, and strode out of the bedroom, wallet in hand. The man seemed to have assumed a crouching posture, but had not moved an inch from where he had been before, the box of groceries and plastic mineral water packs slightly to his left.

Arturo nodded curtly and slowed his pace as he moved up the corridor checking the contents of his wallet. Now he remembered he had dumped all the spare change into a Deruta bowl that sat on one of the shelves in his study. All he had was notes, and the smallest was a twenty. He could not tip twenty. Nor would he veer off into the study, leaving his visitor to sniff about.

"Look, I'm sorry about this . . ." he began. His voice was louder than he had intended, his tone more pompous.

The deliveryman suddenly held up a hand to cut him off in midsentence. Arturo was so taken aback that he stopped speaking at once. Then, realizing that he had just done the stranger's bidding, he opened his mouth again to protest. The man took a step forward. He did have a light mustache. He pointed meaningfully to the closed front door, as if he and Arturo were in on some significant quest together. Arturo obeyed again, and paused to listen.

Beautiful Claudia Sebastiano on the floor above was playing a Mozart piano sonata, adagio, holding her own against the cicadas' prestissimo clacking. Someone sneezed twice with an exaggerated whoop. It was late August and the city was mostly quiet.

"What is it?" Arturo's voice betrayed anxiety.

"I thought I heard someone outside the door just now . . . let me see." The voice was slightly nasal and complaining, like a Milanese woman's. He peered into the spy hole in the door. Arturo spotted his glasses on a shelf to his right, grabbed them, and put them on his face. The deliveryman snapped his head away from the spy hole and twisted around to catch what Arturo was doing. He scanned the shelf, Arturo's hands, and then his face. Then his quick eyes registered the glasses perched slightly askew on Arturo's fat nose, and he smiled and jerked his head, as if agreeing that the glasses were a good idea.

Arturo resolved to control the situation. He checked a massive desire to hurl himself at the intruder and trample him to death. The important thing now was to make sure his voice did not quaver. He knew his face must be white by now. His bathrobe had opened, but closing it would seem womanly. Everything depended on tone.

"Thank you for the groceries. I am afraid I can't find a tip. I want you to leave now."

His voice had hardly cracked. Perhaps some anger had seeped through, but that was all the better.

The visitor shifted back from the door and cocked his head slightly to study him. From downstairs, Arturo heard the dilapidated door to the apartment block slam. Was that someone going or arriving? The deliveryman's slow wink was followed by an almost imperceptible upward tilt of the face.

Arturo's mind raced back over the years. An old friend. An old enemy. A debt of some sort. He had never had debts. A more recent encounter, then. Manuela? Surely not. He couldn't work it out. A joke. They were filming this? He wasn't famous enough yet.

Not a joke. A theft. This was a house invasion by a robber. Incredible, but obvious, too.

The man was smaller than he was. It looked like a safe bet.

Arturo Clemente's physical instincts drove him into action before his mind worked its way around to a full decision. He lunged forward, concentrating all his 200 pounds of weight into a single fist that aimed to burst the insulting lips. But with a squeal that was either delight or fear, the deliveryman twisted and lashed out at the side of Arturo's head, knocking his glasses flying. Arturo only just managed to land a glancing blow to the bony shoulder.

"You have a violent streak!" His tone was pleased, as if Arturo had just done something immensely clever. "Are you ready?"

"Ready for . . . ?" Arturo broke off. He was not going to be distracted by words.

The intruder shrugged, then brought his right hand over to rub his left shoulder where Arturo had hit him. Then he unzipped, rezipped his jacket. A flash of something caught Arturo's eye, and he tried to bring the arm that had just hit him in the face into focus. It had not seemed like an impressive arm. It reminded him of a chicken bone. The hand at the end seemed small and pink.

They resumed their positions as if it were an arranged duel. Arturo retreated down the corridor to defend his home. He refastened his bathrobe. His bare feet were clammy on the floor and now he was worried he would slip.

Arturo had done some street fighting against the neo-fascists and the police back in the late seventies. His opponent, now a blur at the other end of the corridor, had got lucky. A real fighter would have followed up on his punch and not allowed Arturo to reposition himself. This time, he would pummel, then strangle, and maybe choke the identity out of his attacker. Arturo growled, balled his fists, and lunged down his hall again like a slow old bull.

The blow he received in the stomach wiped every thought from his mind except for a sickening concept of yellowness. He found himself standing in the middle of the corridor, unable to raise his arms. Even lifting his chin off his chest now seemed very difficult. With great effort, breathing heavily through his nose, Arturo edged his hands around his stomach, and folded them there, like Sveva had done when pregnant with Tommaso.

His hands were cold, and the outflow from his stomach felt like hot diarrhea. Except it was blood. He could see that now, just as he could see the knife in the hand with a silver bracelet, tracing an arc in the air. Without warning, Arturo's right leg gave way, and he found himself half kneeling. It turned out to be a good move, because the deliveryman's jab toward his throat failed, and the knife tip punctured only the air. But the clumsy backhanded thrust that immediately followed, which should have missed him altogether, went straight in under the left collarbone. The attacker then pushed downward with the tempered metal, and transfixed him. Then, for reasons Arturo could only dimly grasp at, he pulled it out again. Arturo raised his infinitely heavy hands upwards to fend off the next blow, but he couldn't see anything now. So he decided he should talk. If he could get the words out, the deliveryman might stop in time. Something thudded against his chest, and he felt the floor, solid, straight against his back. A froth rising in his throat so softened the words as he spoke them that they came out as gurgles. He tried to swallow down the froth but it rose and rose like overboiling milk. Arturo jerked his legs like a baby on a changing mat. The pain signals from each wound were all traveling inward now, all converging on one tiny bright point in the very middle of his body. He didn't want to be there when they merged. He sent the darkness behind his eyes racing down his body, hoping it would get there first.

2

THE KILLER STOOD up. The blood seemed to have gotten everywhere. It had spurted up the walls, some of it even to the ceiling. He
spat into Clemente's clouding eye.

"I win," he said.

Stepping over Arturo Clemente, whose thrashing had quickly decreased
in intensity to become no more than brief jittery movements, the killer
made his way down the corridor. After opening a few doors he found the
bathroom, and came back carrying some white towels. Perhaps he would
not need them. Clemente's powder blue bathrobe had soaked up the mess
below him and turned imperial purple.

The killer crouched down, balancing four towels on his left arm, the
galvanized rubber grip of the knife nestled comfortably in his right fist.
Clemente's face presented itself in profile, though most of his body was
turned upward, set quite correctly for the morgue position. After a moment's consideration, he pushed the point of the knife in hard at the temple,
and deftly twisted it with a flick of the wrist as he withdrew. Almost at
once the twitching stopped. He half wiped the blade on the top towel,
then stood up, and walked over to the door and drew a deep breath. He
was all right, but he had not expected blood to smell so strong. His hands
reeked as if they had been holding fistfuls of dirty coins. He placed the
towels on the floor, then took one from the top of the pile, rolled it up and
pushed it against the bottom of the door. He repeated the operation with
the second.

Returning to the bathroom, he closed the toilet seat and placed the knife
on it. He noticed it still had stains near the grip. He took off his white tracksuit and examined his clothes underneath. The front of his V-necked soccer
shirt had caught a few flecks, but it just looked as if he was a messy eater. His

gray pants seemed fine. He stripped down to his underpants, and enjoyed the relief from the heat. He dropped the stained tracksuit on the tiled floor, which, he noticed, was already wet. Running the water in the sink, he delicately dabbed at dark patches on his short-sleeved shirt. Cold water for chocolate and blood, his mother used to say. When the stains did not wash, he allowed himself more water and a little ordinary soap. Even if he ended up wearing a visibly wet shirt, people would just assume it was sweat, or that he had deliberately soaked himself at a drinking fountain to stay cool.

He started sliding the belt out of the loops in his pants, removed the Kydex sheath, then relooped the belt. He was disappointed with the cheap sheath, which he had bought separate. But the knife, a Ka-Bar Tanto, was magnificent. He picked it off the toilet and brought it to the sink. As he rotated it under the running faucet, the stream of water struck the flat of the blade and spray shot out sideways and backward. Cursing, he leaped back, turned off the water, and checked to see if his clothes had been hit. He resheathed the knife and dropped it on the tracksuit on the floor.

He splashed water all over his face, hands, arms, neck, and chest. He found a patch of blood on the side of his neck, but it wasn't his. Bending his head further down into the sink, he allowed the cool water to wash over his head. When he felt relaxed, he stood up, eyes closed. When he opened them, he saw that his wet hair was dripping bright pink droplets onto his face, lips, and shoulders. He hunted around for shampoo. He had to scrabble his way through the whole medicine cabinet on the wall behind him before he found some, though it was a brand he had never even heard of. He double-checked the bottle to make sure it was shampoo, then poured some onto his palm, and sniffed at it suspiciously. It smelled like expensive face cream. He touched it with a finger, then held up his finger and examined it. Satisfied, he rubbed it into his hair, and used the hand shower in the bathtub to rinse. Then he took off his socks and shoes. He balled his socks and rinsed his shoes thoroughly. They would be wet on the inside, too. He got dressed again, leaving his tracksuit, shoes, and wet balled socks on the floor. He needed something to put them into.

He took his knife and padded out of the bathroom barefoot, victorious but unsure what to do with the freedom of the house. The kitchen was off to his left, and he entered it. A high window looked directly across over the courtyard and afforded a clear view of Building D to the right. No more than seven yards away, standing on a balcony, a woman, taking a break from housework, was leaning on the rail smoking. Her eyes seemed fixed on him as he stood there in his underpants staring back, but she registered no interest or surprise.

Taking some money struck him as a good idea, but the kitchen was an unlikely place for cash, so he moved to the bedroom. As he entered, his reflected self walked toward him, causing him to freeze in midstep until he realized he was looking at four full-length mirrored doors on a built-in wardrobe.

He slid open a mirrored door and was confronted with a row of dresses, skirts, and dress suits hanging on a rail. He was about to move on to the far side of the wardrobe door when curiosity got the better of him and he pulled open one of the drawers fitted into the lower half of the compartment. It was filled with women's underwear, mostly silk and expensive, but some of it ordinary cotton. He stretched an arm into the drawer and ran his hand between the piles of silk. He pulled some of them out, pulled down a handful of summer dresses, and buried his face in them. Some of them smelled like his mother's had. Others were different.

It was a pity the wife was away. He liked the idea of having a woman at his mercy now, begging, sobbing quietly. But he would not take advantage. He would be magnanimous.

He opened Clemente's side of the wardrobe, located the sock drawer, emptied it, did the same with the next drawer and the next, but found no cash. He selected a nice fresh pair of socks, clambered onto the bed, lay on his back, feet in the air, and pulled them on.

He pushed the pile of sharply folded sheets off the bed, and pulled the mattress off the bed to reveal a lattice-wood frame, unsuitable for hiding anything. Then he slit the latex mattress right down the middle. It split like a mozzarella, but the inside was like the outside, and gave up no treasures.

He negotiated his way up the corridor and over and around the corpse. He spotted Clemente's wallet lying on the floor. He hunkered down, stretched out a hand, and took the wallet, only to find it was sticky with blood underneath. He stuck it into his pocket anyhow.

He checked out the living room, threw the sofa cushions about a bit. They had an old TV and a VCR. He didn't think anyone used VCRs anymore. The room had three windows and was bright. He was unimpressed by the modernist paintings on the walls.

He went into the next room, which turned out to be a child's bedroom. The bedspread had a picture of Winnie the Pooh. The child's books were neatly stacked. He sat down on the bed and looked around him, then stood up, smoothed the bedspread flat, patted the cushion, and left, closing the door gently behind him.

Moving past the corpse down the corridor, he entered the room opposite the front door. It was a study. The first thing he noticed was Clemente's Acer flat-screen monitor. Sleek, black.

The glint of coins in a bowl caught his attention. He took a handful and was about to stick them in his pocket when he noticed many of the coins were foreign, and included an American silver dollar commemorating the bicentennial. Heads or . . . eagles. He flicked it once. It came down wrong. He flicked it again. Heads. Good. Then he pocketed it.

A gray Champion backpack sat on a chair. He unzipped it, emptied the contents on the sofa. A book on flowers, a brown apple, crumpled cartons of juice, a sweatshirt. He went back to the bathroom, retrieved his bloodied tracksuit and socks, stuffed them into the backpack, and slipped on his shoes, then returned to the study.

Behind the desk was a gray steel filing cabinet, on top of which stood two plants in terra-cotta jars. Judging by the stains on the top of the cabinet, Clemente had watered them where they were. He opened the cabinet. Clemente's life had been ordered. He checked under the letter *A* in the top drawer, and found five folders marked "Alleva, Renato" filed after "Allergies."

He spent another ten minutes hunting in the study. He found two cards for restaurants in the town of Amatrice, both claiming to make the best *amatriciana* in the world, but did not find any money.

He left the study and went back into the hall. Using the knife again, he sliced through the masking tape holding the grocery box closed and foraged inside for booty. He came out with a jar of Nutella, which he loved. It went into the backpack. He found a jar of strange brown paste. Peanut butter. It might have an interesting taste. He dropped it into the backpack.

He kicked the towels away from the base of the door, peered through the spy hole to make sure the stairway was clear, opened the door, and crept down the stairs, out the main door across the courtyard and away.

Five hours later, Sveva Romagnolo, tired from a train journey and unenthusiastic at the prospect of a few days with her husband, turned the key in the apartment door. Tommaso ducked under her arm and pushed in through the gap, anxious to show off his new shoes with Velcro straps to his father.

3

COMMISSIONER ALEC BLUME received the call on his cell from head-quarters at 17:15, while he was having a late lunch in Frontoni's. Dressed in a T-shirt with paint stains, shorts, and running shoes, Blume was enjoying a white pizza overstuffed with bresaola, rocket, and Parmesan and drinking a beer. His intention was to eat a lot, then run a lot. He was alone in the restaurant, and almost alone in Trastevere. An overheated tourist family stood for a while staring at him through the window, like he was a tropical fish, then moved on, only to be intercepted by a North African hawker selling socks.

Blume picked off a salt crystal from the pizza and crunched it between his teeth. His phone on the table peeped and shook a little, and he pressed at it with an oily thumb. They had texted the address to him.

The street name on the display meant nothing, but the efficient sovrintendente at the desk had very usefully included the zip code. Blume saw it was in a nearby area, so he had time to finish his lunch and knock back a thimbleful of coffee before returning to his car. He called Paoloni, told him they had a case. Paoloni said he knew and was already on site.

Blume drove at a stately speed beneath the plane trees, not wishing to spoil the quietness of the streets. He took just ten minutes to reach the top of the Monteverde hill. He glanced at a Tuttocittà map to find the street. Five minutes later, he swung his Fiat Brava around a corner and parked. Three squad cars blocked the road, their lights flashing. A forensics van had been slotted in at a right angle in the narrow space between two parked cars, its front wheels and nose blocking the sidewalk, the back section creating a bottleneck on the narrow street. As he arrived, Blume saw an ambulance, unable to squeeze behind the forensics van, start executing what would probably be a twelve-point turn. The coroner's wagon had not arrived yet.

Apartment building C, one of four around a pebbled courtyard, was guarded by a uniformed officer who did not even ask for identification. Blume gave it anyway, told the officer to note it down, check who was going and coming, and generally do his job. Then he went in.

The building had no elevator. When Blume arrived, puffing, on the third floor, the apartment door was shut, and the landing outside crammed with far too many people.

Inspector Paoloni was wearing a billowy Kejo jacket despite the heat, low-slung jeans, and bling-bling bracelets. His head was shaved bald, his face was gray.

"I went in, but they told me to leave," he said when he saw Blume.

"Who did?"

"The head of the Violent Crime Analysis Unit. He wants only the most senior officer or the investigating magistrate in there. He's raging, says the scene has been totally compromised with all the people walking around."

"What people?"

"D'Amico was here. Then he went, only to be replaced by the Holy Ghost, of all people. Also it appears the wife who found the body touched it, walked all over the place."

"D'Amico. As in Nando? What's he doing here?"

Paoloni shrugged. "Beats me. Anyhow, he's a commissioner now. Same rank as you."

"I know." Blume did not like to be reminded of D'Amico's promotions. "The thing is, he's not an investigator anymore. So he has no reason to be here. And the Holy Ghost, was that a joke?"

Paoloni adjusted his crotch, sniffed, scuffed the wall with a yellow trainer, and looked vacantly at his superior. "No, he was here, and says he'll be back."

"But Gallone never comes to a crime scene," said Blume.

"Yeah, well, he did this time."

Vicequestore Aggiunto Franco Gallone was Blume's immediate superior. Everyone referred to him as the Holy Ghost, but nobody could say for sure where the name came from. It stuck, because he was invisible when the hard work was being done, but somehow always present with a pious demeanor whenever the press or his superiors invoked his presence. There was a story that he got the name back in 1981, when, a mere deputy commissioner at the time, he was found weeping in the station, devastated after the attempted murder of Pope John Paul II.

Blume looked around. There were four policemen standing on the landing. There was one other apartment on the floor, he noticed, and its door was firmly shut. "Is the officer who first arrived on the scene here?"

"Yes, sir," said one of the uniformed policemen, coming out of a comfortable reclining position.

"What are you doing now?"

"I am logging the names of people coming in and out."

"You get my name?"

"I know who you are, sir."

Blume looked at the officer. He was in his thirties, and would have seen his fair share of scenes.

"On a scale of one to ten, how bad is it in there?"

"A scale of one to ten? I don't know—two, three?"

"That low?"

"No children, no rape, just one body, not even that young. Corpse fresh, so not much of a smell, no wailing relatives, no animals, no public, no reporters yet."

"Who was here when you arrived?"

"A woman. The wife of the victim. She found him like that. She called 112."

"Why did you let the witness leave?"

The policeman's gaze flickered, and he shifted his weight onto the other foot.

"There was a kid, short thing, with long blond hair. It seemed best to let them get out of here. They left when the ambulance men arrived."

"We have female officers and psychologists for these things."

"That wasn't all."

"What else?"

"I got a direct order, from the vicequestore. He told me the technicians from UACV were on their way, said I was to let the witness leave."

"The Holy Ghost spoke to you directly?"

"Yes, Commissioner." He grinned at Blume's use of the nickname.

"Beppe, did you get the name of this officer?" said Blume.

Paoloni nodded.

"Right," said Blume. "Let's go in."

He bent down and stepped through the barber-pole-colored crime-scene tape around the door. His foot caught on a lower strand and snapped it.

The head of the Violent Crime Analysis Unit team came down the corridor and pointed to Blume. "Come in, come in, join the trample-fest. So now you're the officer in charge? Not, who was it—D'Amico? And not Gallone? Or are you all in charge? Maybe you'd like to invite a few friends over?"

Blume looked at the technician in his pristine white suit with the yellow and black UACV symbol on his breast pocket. The man was at least fifteen years his junior.

"I picked up the sarcasm from the start. There's no need to keep going."

The young UACV investigator shrugged and walked away without offering any walk-through.

Blume wondered again about D'Amico. D'Amico had been his junior partner for five years, and had been pretty good. Two years ago, he had moved to a desk job in the Ministry of the Interior. Blume regretted the wasted training, but D'Amico had other plans for himself. Every few months Blume would hear news of how D'Amico had widened his political base, increased his leverage.

As Blume and Paoloni entered, the medical examiner, Dr. Gerhard Dorfmann, was already packing away his things. Blume nodded amicably at Dorfmann, who stared back with loathing, his default demeanor. Blume waited until Dorfmann recognized him and finally conceded a curt nod.

Upon first seeing Dorfmann's name on a report, Blume had felt a slight thrill at finding another foreigner. He had briefly wondered whether Dorfmann might be another American. That was a long time ago. Even then Dorfmann had seemed old. Blume wondered what age he had now achieved. His hair was gleaming white, but there was a lot of it. His eyes were hidden behind thick gold glasses that had gone in and out of style several times since he first bought them. His face contained thousands of wrinkles, but was free of folds or sagging skin. It was finely fissured like old porcelain.

Dorfmann was from the Tyrol and spoke heavily accented Italian. He would not accept being mistaken for a German, though he allowed that people might think he was Austrian. Dorfmann soon revealed a low opinion of Americans. He was not very fond of Italians either.

Blume no longer felt offended. Essentially, Dorfmann disliked people who were still breathing.

"Knife attack," said Dorfmann, completely ignoring Paoloni.

"Very well, thank you, and you?" said Blume.

Dorfmann continued. "Four wounds. Stomach, lower abdomen, throat, head—behind the orbital lobe. All of them potentially fatal. He was probably dead when the last blow came. The knife hand-guard left a sign in the lower abdomen, so it went in with some force. Probably right-handed. What are you doing here? I don't see why I should repeat what I just told your dandy colleague. No evident bruising elsewhere, nothing sexual that I can see despite the open robe, though we'll wait for the autopsy. No mutilations in genital area."

"My dandy colleague?" The ME had to be referring to D'Amico.

"D'Alema."

"D'Alema? You mean D'Amico?"

"Yes. That's the one. Not that fool D'Alema. D'Alema is far from dandy. Or intelligent, or politically literate . . ." Dorfmann was about to express some deeply held political opinions, which Blume did not want to hear.

"OK, doctor, but here we're talking about Nando D'Amico, not the political failure that is D'Alema."

"Yes." Dorfmann was pleased enough at Blume's choice of terms to overlook the fact of the interruption. "Your colleague, D'Amico. He was walking about polluting the crime scene, then left, possibly to shine his teeth."

"So what sort of person did this?" asked Blume, trying to hunker down to examine the body but finding his knees were having none of it.

"I would not describe the stabbing as frenzied. Nonetheless, the person who did this was not serene."

A small pool of blood had gathered on either side of the neck, and there were impact spatters on the walls to the side and behind the victim, but the blood spillage on the floor was contained. Paoloni was walking up and down, head bent, staring at the floor, then the wall. Blume saw from the way he was moving he was describing a grid pattern around the body. The forensic team ignored him.

"Time of death?" Blume asked Dorfmann.

"This is an unpleasantly hot and dirty city, and the apartment is warm," began Dorfmann. "When I woke up this morning, I thought we might be in for some refreshing rain, but a hot wind arose and blew the clouds over to Croatia."

Blume clicked his tongue sympathetically. Damned Croats.

"The liver temperature, however, is warmer even than this place. Loss is just under eight degrees. First signs of rigor around the mouth. The body was almost certainly not here early this morning."

"Can we say midday?"

"You can say it."

"Eleven?"

Dorfmann shrugged.

"Nine?"

Dorfmann looked very doubtful. That was as good as he would get.

Dorfmann turned away and pulled off a pair of latex gloves, picked up a clipboard, and made a slight flourish with his hand to emphasize that he was signing off on the case already. "Lividity on back, buttocks. I don't think anyone moved the body. This seems to be where he died. If you want pinpoint accuracy about the time, it will be up to you or your dandy friend to give me some markers."

Blume was looking at the towels over by the door.

A photographer in a white jumpsuit stooped and took a shot of the box of groceries, against which he had propped a photographic scale ruler. Blume noticed that he was alternating between an ordinary thirty-five mm. Canon and a digital Nikon SLR. He removed the ruler and took two more shots of the box, once with the ordinary camera and once with the digital. Then he turned on Clemente's halogen lights overhead and repeated the process. He was doing a conscientious job.

"Get those towels over there. Photograph them, I mean," said Blume.

The photographer looked Blume up and down, assessing his authority, then scowled and continued to photograph the box. Blume went for the friendly angle.

He said, "I've got a Coolpix. It's only a small Coolpix. Wouldn't be much good here, I suppose."

The photographer stood up and stared at him, then, without a word, returned to his job.

Blume dismissed a fleeting image of himself plunging his cheap little Coolpix down the photographer's throat. The technicians were moving through the apartment in white suits, acting under their own orders and initiative. He stopped one, asked for and got a pair of latex gloves, and pulled them on. He had left his own in the car. Everything was going very smoothly.

"My mentor and master," declared a voice in a Neapolitan accent.

Blume lifted his gaze from the stained body on the floor, which did not have a name yet, and turned around to see Nando D'Amico, resplendent in a golden silk suit, step through the front door, breaking another strand of tape.

"Close your vowels, Nando. You'll never make it into the political elite till you learn to close those Camorra vowels," said Blume.

"Elocution lessons from a non-EU immigrant. The shame of it," said D'Amico. "But of course, you are from the deep north. Superior to every last Leghista in Lombardy."

"So are you. We're the same rank now."

"So we are. We'll have to do something about that. Now here's a fact not a lot of people know," said D'Amico. "Naples is slightly north of New York. Check it out next time you're near a globe."

"My people were from Seattle."

"Where's that?"

"Far away from here. Listen Nando, what are you here for? Who's been assigned?"

"You."

"And you are here because . . . ?"

"The departmental top dog himself sent me. He said the dead guy was important. I reminded him I no longer run a murder team and told him I needed a superior officer."

Blume said, "I am not your superior anymore."

"I meant morally."

"How long have you been here?"

"About half an hour." He held up a hand as if in admonishment to objections Blume had not yet made. "I am here in an official representative capacity, not as a detective. That needs to be made clear."

"Gallone is here, too."

"Yes, all those atheists who doubted his existence look like fools now, don't they?" He made a show of looking around. "But he seems to have dematerialized again."

"I see a Violent Crime Analysis Unit doing plenty of good work, policemen outside, a medical examiner finishing up his job. It looks to me like we are already under the direction of an investigating magistrate, am I right?"

"Yes. Public Minister Filippo Principe."

"That means I was informed late," said Blume.

"That happens. Happened when we were partners, too."

"How long were you here before me? Be precise."

"Forty minutes."

"The forensic team was here already?"

"About five minutes after that."

"Did you enter the apartment?"

"What, am I under suspicion?"

"Well, did you?"

"In the company of Gallone and the first reporting officer, yes. The door was open. The wife had opened it."

"Where is she?"

"I don't know. She wasn't here when I arrived."

"Weird, isn't it? You, a representative from the Ministry, and Gallone of all people, being the first to arrive."

"After the patrol unit, you mean. All I know is I was sent, and I arrived. If there was a delay finding you, it's hardly my fault."

"OK," said Blume.

D'Amico plucked at his tie. "I forgot how aggressive you get."

"I'm not being aggressive," said Blume, and patted him on the shoulder. "And I'm happy to hear the investigation is under Principe's control. I like him. He'll give us room. He listens, thinks."

"Except he's not here," said D'Amico.

"He'll get here. He knows it's best to let the forensic team work the scene first before he sees for himself."

"If you say so," said D'Amico.

"I do, Nando. Where were you just now?"

"Getting these keys duplicated." D'Amico held out and jingled a bunch of keys in front of Blume.

"Those are the keys to this place?"

"Yes. They were on the shelf there, near the door. The technicians gave me permission. Seems like, despite their complaining, they've got plenty of other material here."

"Meaning?"

"Fingerprints, footprints, saliva, hairs. The killer, whoever he was, left traces of himself everywhere. We may even have footprints. That is to say, bare feet."

Blume looked at the corpse in the hall. Paoloni had put on latex gloves and seemed to be intent on pulling back the lips of a stab wound in the head. "The bare footprints will be his."

"Not unless he got up and walked about in his own blood, which he could have done, but it doesn't seem likely. Also, they are small footprints," said D'Amico.

"A woman's?"

"Who knows?" D'Amico shrugged. "Here, want a key?" he offered Blume a large H-shaped key for the quadruple deadbolt lock to the front door beside which they were standing. "I didn't bother getting copies of the key to the front gate. But this one"—he handed Blume a blue aluminum Yale key—"opens the front door to the building. Not that you'll need it."

"Why?"

"It's not secure. Just give it a shove, it opens by itself."

Blume took the key anyway.

D'Amico reached over and switched off the lights in the hall. His shining suit and white shirt seemed to dim slightly, but his tanned, handsome face continued to glow.

Blume had several questions. He picked an easy one.

"That cardboard box there?"

"It's full of groceries from the SMA supermarket. Apparently Arturo Clemente here bought them himself yesterday evening, and ordered a delivery for this morning."

D'Amico pinched the top of his pants to make sure the crease was still sharp. Blume wiped his brow with the back of his hand. "Arturo Clemente's the name of the victim?" he asked.

"Yes."

"So what? You think the grocery boy killed him?"

"Looks like it, doesn't it?" said D'Amico. He checked a wafer-thin watch, straightened his shirt cuffs. "We get the grocery boy, leave him with Ispettore Zambotto for an hour, we'll have the case resolved before supper. That would be nice."

D'Amico snapped open a shell-shaped cell that he must have been already holding in his hand, found the number he was looking for, and held the phone to his ear. With his free hand, he smoothed his shining black hair and murmured into it. A technician down the hall cursed and dropped a cyanoacrylate fuming wand. One of his colleagues, who was stretching a cat's cradle of threads from bloodstains on the floor back to the corpse, laughed. Paoloni, who was sketching the scene in a notebook, joined in.

D'Amico was nine years Blume's junior and for five years had been two ranks below him. In those days, he had been a neat young man in clean shoes and a polo shirt. Every time he went up a level, he upgraded his clothes style. If he ever made questore, he'd have to dress like Louis XIV.

D'Amico clapped his cell phone shut without saying who it was, but announced: "It seems we have a political murder on our hands."

Blume looked at the bloodied body in the loose bathrobe. He noted the splatter patterns on the wall and floor, the cardboard box and the packet of cornflakes visible on top. He said, "It doesn't look very political to me."

"Well it is—which explains why Gallone was here."

"Explains why you are here, too," said Blume. "That's a politician?"

"No. He was an animal rights activist of some sort. It's his wife who's the politician. She's also the one who found him. She made the call at 16:05."

"The forensics complained you had been looking through the apartment already," said Blume.

"I looked in, is all. Gallone was with me. He's still my superior, so I did what he wanted."

"What party? The wife I mean."

"The Greens," said D'Amico.

"So we're looking for an environmentally unfriendly errand boy."

D'Amico smoothed his hair and looked doubtful. "We can't rule out anything. On my way back from the hardware store with the keys, I had a chat with the porter. I must have been with him when you arrived. The porter says he saw nothing."

Blume stayed silent.

D'Amico continued, "He doesn't strike me as being a very reliable witness. Judging from his breath, either he was drinking in his cabin, or he had just spent some time in a bar."

"The porter is going to be defensive as well as eager to please. He'll be trying to give the sort of answers he thinks you want to hear," said Blume, unable to break his teaching habit.

"He has already been doing some finger-pointing at various residents."

"He could be right. We're going to have to check up on them, too."

"Gallone has been appointing uniforms for the house-to-house visits. He's suspended leave, called in for a few extra recruits from around town."

"Gallone the coordinator. That's new, too," said Blume.

D'Amico slid his hand into his jacket, and from his inside pocket extracted four sheets of paper, neatly folded and stapled together. He thumbed through the sheets, then handed them to Blume.

"This is a list of all the residents in this and the other three buildings in the complex."

Blume glanced through the pages. "Some of the names are circled."

"Those are the ones about whom the porter has grave misgivings. He circled them himself."

Blume turned to the next page. "There are more names circled than not."

"He is a very suspicious porter."

Blume said, "How can he sleep at night being surrounded by so many murderous residents? Little wonder the poor man drinks. And you, you've been very busy for someone sent to represent the Ministry."

D'Amico looked offended. "I was just trying to be useful."

"You entered the crime scene, spoke to the medical examiner, had keys duplicated, and spoke to the porter. Either you're a judicial investigator or you're not," said Blume. "You were once, now you're not. From now on, you stay here at the doorway."

"Fine," said D'Amico.

Blume walked toward the body in the middle of the corridor. The photographer had vanished into the adjoining rooms.

"I got the impression from the medical examiner that this has nothing to do with queers, despite the bathrobe," said D'Amico from his post by the door.

"Despite the knife, too," said Blume. "Knives are surrogates, remember?"

"You think it could be sexual?"

"Could be anything. Except I trust Dorfmann. His autopsy will tell for sure."

A technician walked out of the victim's study, carrying a plastic-wrapped computer. They would find out more about Arturo Clemente when they pried into his files, followed the trail he had left all over the Internet like an unwitting snail.

Paoloni was examining the shelves along the corridor. The technicians had moved away from the area immediately around the body. Blume waved at one of them and asked for permission to explore. The technician shrugged, nodded.

Paoloni shuffled over and stood beside Blume, looking more like a snitch with privileges than a law enforcer.

"OK, let's start. Beppe, you finished your sketch?"

Paoloni showed it to Blume. It looked like it had been done by an ungifted five-year-old, but it included measurements, and would do until the technicians supplied their version.

"Slight grazing on the knuckles," said Blume. "Dorfmann might be able to tell us more, but it looks like he didn't manage to put up much of a struggle."

Paoloni asked, "What do you think? The killer was handy with his weapon?"

"Not necessarily. The victim looks as if he wasn't expecting this."

"I think that, too. He didn't know what hit him," said Paoloni.

"I wonder did he know who hit him," said Blume.

"No sign of forced entry," said Paoloni. "Someone delivered the groceries and someone killed him before he had time to put them away. Makes sense to presume it was the same person."

They stared in silence at the corpse for a while longer. Paoloni said, "I see the assailant being alone."

"I agree."

"If there had been a second person, he would have gripped the victim in some way, pinned him down, tied him up. Something that we would be able to see."

"Yes," said Blume. "Two people come at you with knives, you run, barricade yourself in a room. Maybe not get very far, but at least some of the wounds would be in your back. This guy looks like he thought he was in with a fighting chance. Stabbed in the front of the body each time. What do you make of those towels over by the front door?"

Paoloni pushed his thumb into his nostril to show he was thinking.

Eventually he said, "No idea. Like the killer wanted to clean up or something, but then didn't bother. One was streaked, like he cleaned the blade on it. The others are clean."

Blume said, "It's as if he wanted to stem the flow of the blood, like he was scared it would run under the door."

Paoloni made a dismissive click with his tongue, tilted his chin up, and said, "It would never have run that far once the heart had stopped beating."

"Maybe our killer didn't know that," said Blume. "Which would make him a first-timer."

Blume went over and looked at the towels. They were pure white and fluffy. He thought of his own towels, multicolored strips of sandpaper. Two of the towels were still folded and pristine; the other two had been unfolded then rolled into a snake shape and left near the door.

"Nice towels," offered D'Amico, who was standing near to the door. "By the way, I forgot to mention, the wife spoke to the victim at ten thirty this morning. On the phone. From Padua."

"You forgot to tell me?"

"The Holy Ghost knows this already. He was the one who told me. He got it from the wife."

"Did you tell Dorfmann?"

"No, I just heard, like I said."

"Phone Dorfmann now. Tell him you're the dandy one, and you've got a marker for him."

"The dandy one?"

"Yes."

Blume went back to Paoloni at the body. "Can we roll him over?"

They rolled Clemente's body over. There were no wounds behind, but Dorfmann would have said if there were. As Blume had expected, Clemente's bathrobe had soaked up most of the blood.

"Not much blood," said Paoloni. "Considering. His heartbeat must have slowed down pretty quick."

Blume turned around as he felt a presence behind him.

Inspector Cristian Zambotto had arrived, heaving and gasping and cursing after his trip up the stairs. Zambotto was dangerously overweight and had flat black hair that stopped suddenly somewhere high up on the middle of his head, leaving room for a wide rim of pocked skin that eventually merged with his thick neck.

After D'Amico left to pursue a political career, Zambotto was assigned to him. Blume did not know much about Zambotto except that he almost never contributed anything to anyone's conversation, as if at some point in his life, Zambotto had decided it was too difficult to turn calories into words.

"Cristian, spend about half an hour here, OK? Get the scene into your head. Then I want you to find out who delivered those groceries, and bring him, or them, in for questioning. I want to be able to leave here, go interview the suspect. Take backup if you need it."

"Right," said Zambotto.

"Paoloni, take a few minutes here, then catch up with me in whatever room I'm in, OK?"

Paoloni nodded.

"Then you can go back and requestion the people in the apartment block. I want you to draw up a timeline using the reports from the police officers that Gallone appears to have assigned. We have a ten thirty call from the wife, an estimated time of death not long after, and now we need to find out about when these groceries were delivered. Also, you'll be doing the paperwork on this."

Paoloni gave him a dirty look.

"You can get Ferrucci to help you."

"Oh, great," said Paoloni.

"Why, you'd prefer to do the paperwork with Zambotto?" Blume looked at Paoloni, who shook his head quickly, more as a warning to Blume not to forget that Zambotto was still standing there. "Yeah, I thought so."

Paoloni was making life hell for an officer-class graduate called Marco Ferrucci, but Blume saw a lot of raw talent in the young man. He figured Paoloni did, too, which might explain why he was so intent on humiliating him. Ferrucci had the potential to outshine them all.

Blume was about to say more in Ferrucci's defense when he caught sight of Gallone, who had appeared at the doorway. Blume positioned himself next to the body, like a guard.

Gallone had an agente scelto remove the rest of the crime scene tape from the doorway, then walked in, head bowed. He raised sorrowful eyes and looked at Blume, then held his hands aloft. "Everything in order? Commissioner D'Amico?"

"Yes, sir. All under control," said D'Amico.

"We shall manage this well," he told D'Amico. "This is not being announced. No appeals for information, not yet. The rewards for clearing this one up will be high. I have that on good authority." He turned his attention to Blume. "Commissioner, although you are not suitably dressed—"

"I had some leave, and it's the weekend."

"Although, I repeat, it seems almost irreverent for you to be standing in running shorts, you are assigned to the case under my aegis. The investigating magistrate is Filippo Principe. I believe you and he are old friends."

"I respect him," said Blume. "So, if Principe has charge of the investigation, and you and I are reporting to him, where do D'Amico and the Ministry fit in?"

D'Amico spoke up. "Stop referring to me in the third person, Alec. You're hurting my feelings."

"Sorry, Nando. I'd expect you to do the same in my position."

Gallone said, "D'Amico has coordinating responsibilities. The investigative work is our responsibility. The investigating magistrate is on his way. We have arranged a meeting of the investigative team tomorrow morning at nine. Now, if you'll excuse me."

Gallone was gone.

"Nando, I need your cell number, if it's changed," said Blume.

"No, same as it always was."

Gallone was among them again. "I forgot to mention an important detail, Commissioner. It's about a cell phone. Sveva Romagnolo, the poor widow, left her cell phone behind, and wants it back. It has important government and political contacts and names on it. I was wondering had you seen it."

Only Gallone could not know a cell phone at a murder scene was one of the first things to be taken by the technicians.

"The UACV will have removed it."

Gallone clicked his tongue in irritation. "I know that they would have if they found one, but they say they never found one. It's not on the list of items removed from the scene."

"Well if they didn't find one, why should I?"

Gallone nodded slowly as if accepting a doubtful proposition. "It's hardly that important. What is important is that I personally shall be interviewing the widow. In this case, I shall report to you. You are not to importune the widow. Understood?"

Gallone was gone. D'Amico stood for a whole minute, sulking but splendid in his golden suit. Then he too left.

4

AFTER GALLONE AND D'Amico had left, Blume and Paoloni went over to examine the grocery box. The masking tape that had held the flaps closed was slit neatly down the middle. Blume looked through the contents. Cornflakes, organic apples, fair trade cocoa, bananas (one of them becoming spotted), jam, basmati rice, toothpaste. At the bottom, he found the receipt. It showed a total of €113.23, and thirty-seven items, each listed by name. The time and date stamp showed Thursday, August 26: 17:23.

Blume started removing the contents and setting them out on the floor. He counted thirty-four items in all.

"How many did you get?" he asked Paoloni.

"Thirty-five."

Blume went into Clemente's study and found a Staedtler felt tip, and came back with it. As he returned the groceries back to the box, he marked them off against the receipt. Paoloni had been right: thirty-five items. When everything was back in, he discovered that two listed items seemed to be missing: one jar of Nutella (1 lb.) and one of "*Crema arach*" (8 oz.). Peanut butter! So they sold peanut butter in the stores up here. Maybe he'd buy some. His father had been a great believer in the goodness of peanut butter. Sometimes the three of them would make a special shopping trip to Castroni on Via Cola di Rienzo and stock up on peanut butter, Hershey bars, marshmallows, Jell-O, rice pudding, maple syrup, Paul Newman salad dressings, Mexican tortilla chips and taco shells, shortening, root beer, mincemeat. His mother used to be outraged at the prices, but in those days it was the only store in Rome that sold what his father always called "luxury western items," making the same joke each time they went.

Zambotto appeared and announced he was ready to go. Blume told him to get five uniformed officers to help him and work in three teams of two. As Zambotto was leaving, the Investigating Magistrate, Filippo Principe, entered. Principe paused to salute the departing policeman, who gave a half grunt of acknowledgment.

The magistrate, fifteen years Blume's senior, had a tanned, healthy look. He was dressed in a lightweight beige suit and a sky blue shirt open at the collar. Behind round glasses, his eyes were wrinkled as if he was looking into the sun.

He came over, and he and Blume shook hands, something they only ever did at the opening or the closing of a new case. Principe nodded courteously to Paoloni who appeared behind Blume. Blume told Principe what he had found out so far, which did not amount to much.

"You're looking well," said Blume. "For an old man."

"I managed to get away," said Principe. "Two weeks in Terracina. Three days on the beach in the company of my daughter's son. What do you say, is it wrong not to like your grandson?"

"I wouldn't know."

"I never thought excessive coddling could produce such monsters. He pretended to drown, you know. Just to get attention. Screamed from the sea. I stayed under the umbrella, and now his mother thinks I'm . . . Well, never mind."

"For some reason, Vicequestore Franco Gallone and my old partner Nando D'Amico, now Commissioner D'Amico, if you please, were here before you," said Blume.

"It's a political case," said Principe. "Gallone is taking direct orders from the Questura, which is responding to the Ministry of the Interior, which has already sent your former partner D'Amico. I may have control of the investigation, but the Holy Ghost responds only to the prayers of the hierarchy, you know that. Relax."

"This political thing . . ." said Blume. "This mess here is the work of an amateur."

"The victim's wife is an elected MP. It's automatically political because of the wife."

The investigating magistrate walked down the corridor and paused above the sprawled body. He stood there in silence for a few moments, then, with a rapid hand movement that almost looked as if he was brushing away a fly or parrying a smell, made the sign of the cross. "You and Paoloni carry on," he said. "I'll get more details from the technicians."

The bathroom was a mess of damp towels, talc on the floor, footprints, a bar of soap with a hair on it that the technicians had decided to leave. An embarrassment of forensic riches. A small teak cabinet was attached to the wall. Blume opened it and examined the toothpaste, mouthwashes, bandages with pictures of crocodiles, junior vitamin pills, a jar of aspirin tablets from the USA, Vic's menthol rub, handing some of the items to Paoloni, who squinted carefully at their labels then handed them back, like an old woman checking prices in a supermarket.

A wickerwork laundry basket stood in the corner. Blume pulled up the lid. A set of sheets lay on top. He pulled them out and wrinkled his nose slightly against the light gust of urine and sock sweat. He went into the bedroom.

The umbrella pine outside the bedroom window filtered the sun. The white walls were cool to the touch and left a chalky dust on his gloves as if slightly damp. He looked at the split mattress, the clothes scattered on the floor.

"Women's underwear," said Paoloni, still following him.

"Call the investigating magistrate in here," ordered Blume.

"What do you think of that?" asked Blume when Principe and Paoloni appeared at the bedroom door. He pointed to the bedsheets on the floor.

"The doer was looking for something, messing with women's underwear. We'll probably get samples off them," said Principe.

"I was referring to the sheets."

"What about them?"

"They're still folded, or almost. Look." Blume went over, picked up a sheet, smelled it. "Fresh." He unfolded it. The fabric was ironed flat, the creases sharp. "Someone was changing the bed."

Blume continued to search. The doors of the wardrobe were open, clothes scattered here and there.

Blume pulled out a Staedtler pen and used it to lift a pair of silk underpants. He lifted them up to his face. They smelled very faintly of woman, but they also smelled of conditioner, dry-cleaning fluids, and soaps. None of the items had been discarded there by a woman undressing. Everything else about her side of the wardrobe suggested order, cleanliness. She would not be the person responsible for strewing her clothes on the floor.

Blume put the underpants down again and ducked his head under the bed. Nothing. Not even a dust bunny.

"Why would you change the bed?" he asked Paoloni and Principe.

"Dirty sheets?" suggested Principe.

"This place is perfect," said Blume. "They definitely have a housekeeper. Looks to me like she's here almost every day."

"Everyone in this neighborhood has a cleaner," remarked Paoloni, a hint of bitterness in his voice.

"The housekeeper would change the sheets, wouldn't she? Once, twice a week, whatever."

Principe picked up Blume's line of reasoning. "So why was he changing the sheets himself? If it was him."

Blume nodded, "As you said, dirty sheets."

"So you think our man was up to something in this bed."

"If so, it wasn't with his wife, who was at the other end of the country," said Blume. "The used sheets are in the laundry basket."

"OK. I'll make sure forensics is planning to bag one, though I think they would have anyway."

Paoloni and Blume left Principe in the bedroom and moved into the kitchen. Blume liked the room. Each brushed steel unit would cost him two months' wages. He pulled a drawer, which slid out with millimetric precision from between the drawers above and below it. He looked inside and saw wooden spoons, an egg whisk, a shining bottle opener, and place mats. The counter was black granite, shining and clean, with thick edges. A juicer and coffee grinder looked as if they had been made by the same German engineers responsible for the perfect drawers. A blue LED display on the oven told him it was 18:15. The fat refrigerator clicked and started humming. He opened it. The lettuce and fruit were still bright and fresh on the lower shelves. They had yogurts of every conceivable flavor. A bowl of green beans with plastic wrap over them sat on the top shelf, looking like it was meant to be lunch. A jar of peanut butter was wedged between two jars of capers in the door. Blume opened the jar. It was almost finished. How did they expect it to spread properly if they kept it in the refrigerator?

They moved into the study. Again, the room was dustless, apart from a thin grayish patina on the floor where the computer had been before the technicians took it away. A pile of glossy animal rights leaflets lay on the floor. He picked one up. It showed a baby fox with large eyes, and the caption read, "Does your mother have a fur coat? Mine used to."

Blume felt the accusation did not apply to him. He noticed a few things dumped on a Japanese-style sofa with black cushions. He walked past the sofa, not pausing to consider the objects. He did not want to influence Paoloni.

"Anything look out of place to you here?" he asked.

Paoloni looked around the room. "It's pretty neat. Not much out of place. Maybe that stuff on the sofa?"

"Good," said Blume. "Let's wait till Principe catches up."

The investigating magistrate arrived a few moments later.

"Anything?"

"We haven't started," said Blume. "We were about to look at this pile of things on the sofa."

Blume went over to examine it. A book on flowers, an apple, crumpled cartons of juice, and a sweatshirt were heaped together.

"What does this seem like to you two?"

Paoloni was writing down a list of the objects in his notebook. When he had finished he looked up and said, "I don't know. Even neat people dump things in a pile sometimes."

Principe's brow furrowed, but he had no suggestions to offer.

"A book on flowers," said Blume.

"Yeah, well he was one of those Green types," said Paoloni.

"But it's the sort of thing you might take outside with you. Same goes for the sweatshirt. I'm not sure about the apple, but those empty cartons of juice. You wouldn't drink them in here, then put them there on the sofa. They were removed from a bag," said Blume.

"Why would he have empty cartons in his bag?" asked Paoloni.

"He's one of those Green types, like you said. Probably didn't want to throw them on the street like most . . . Italians."

"Like most Romans," corrected Principe, who was from Latina.

"Apple's a bit wrinkly," observed Paoloni.

"Clemente was a man," said Blume. "What sort of bag would he carry?"

"I don't carry a bag," said Paoloni.

"I carry a briefcase," said Principe. "A backpack? That would fit what he seems to have been like."

"Yes," said Blume. "Let's see if we can find it."

They searched the study, but found nothing. Then they went through the other rooms of the house. Eventually they found a black Invicta back-pack folded away in the back of the wardrobe.

"It wasn't this," said Blume. "If he had taken the trouble to fold it up and put it away, he would have cleared the mess from the sofa in the study."

"Maybe the wife took it?" said Paoloni.

"Good point. Go find out. The first reporting officer is at the door. Ask him."

Paoloni left.

Blume turned to Principe. "If the wife didn't take the bag, then the killer probably did."

"If he's stupid enough to keep it, it will be strong evidence against him," said Principe.

"Why would you empty out and remove a backpack?" asked Blume.

"To put stuff in?"

"Right. Which means the killer did not work out what he needed be-forehand. He was not properly prepared. More evidence of amateurish behavior. Real amateur, not feigned."

Blume sat down on the floor beside the leaflets. He slid open the filing cabinet, leafed through at random, pulled out a file folder marked *G-L*. It contained another folder marked *Galles*. The first document inside was headed *Plaid Werdd Cymru*, which meant nothing to him, and contained a list of names and telephone numbers in the UK. The next document folder was marked *Die Grünen/Verdi Austria* and contained more names. Under *L* he found a brochure on lemons. Other files mentioned bird-ringing, bike lanes—after a while he stopped opening the folders to see the contents. *C-Camorra/Crimine* looked promising, but the papers were political leaflets, a printout of a conference speech by the head of the Green Party: no names or numbers. A folder marked *Cani* was noticeably thicker, and contained some disturbing photographs of bloodied dogs. He turned them over to see if the photographer's name was on the flipside, but found only a few dates. One of the ugliest images had "web campaign?" scrawled on the back. Blume laid that one aside. Nothing was filed under *H*. He opened the top drawer: ACP countries, Attivisti (more names), Alleanza Nazionale, Ambiente, Animali.

He needed to get the head of the forensic team to give him a list of ob-jects removed from the scene.

"Alè?" Paoloni often romanized his name.

"What?"

"The wife wasn't carrying a bag when she left. The officer was certain of that."

"OK."

"Also, the coroners are here."

Blume left the study. The head of the forensics team who had let him in earlier had vanished, leaving his deputy, a personable overweight youth, in charge.

"Hey," said Blume. He had worked at least seven times before with this guy and liked him.

The man turned around and Blume immediately forgot his name.

"Did you find a wallet?"

"No."

"A cell phone?"

"No."

"Are you looking for a cell phone?" asked the young man, who, maybe, was called Fabio.

"Not so much me as my boss . . . It doesn't matter. Still, it's a bit unusual. No cell phone at all?"

"I can check," said the young man. "But I don't think so."

Flavio, not Fabio.

"Thanks," said Blume. "Maybe we'll have a secondary scene, too. Clemente probably had an office somewhere."

No way was the guy called Flavio. Flavios were always thin. Francesco was a better bet.

"OK, Commissioner Blume. You just let us know."

"Thanks, Flahvrwb."

Blume began another tour of the house. He opened the door to a child's bedroom, which he found depressingly neat.

Principe came in, then stood in the middle of the room. "Doesn't look like our killer even came in here," he said.

"What makes you say that?"

"Well, you can see. Nothing in here has been touched. He made a mess of the other rooms."

"Yes. I was just thinking about that," said Blume. "The door to this room was closed, too, wasn't it?"

Principe thought for a bit, then said, "Can't say I remember."

"I noticed it," said Blume. "I'll need to check with the people first on the scene to see if it was closed when they got here. Then we can check the photos."

"Supposing it was closed, so what?"

"The killer seems to have looked into every room in the house, and every door is open, except this one. It doesn't make sense to think he didn't come in here."

"OK," said Principe. "Then he closed the door on his way out."

"Also, he left this room neat. Didn't mess it up like the others. To me that looks like a choice. It looks like the sight of a child's room brought out something in him. Mercy, respect, whatever."

"There is such a thing as overinterpretation," said Principe. "I need to talk to the coroner's team. I'll send Paoloni in here; you can run your idea by him."

Paoloni arrived and stood in the middle of the room. Blume repeated what he had said to Principe.

"So he decided not to mess up a child's room," concluded Blume.

"Oh, you mean he was being thoughtful?" said Paoloni coming out of a long yawn. "I would have missed that. Are you saying he has his good points, likes children?"

"Yes. I think it could be important for profiling," said Blume. "He didn't mess up the child's room, but he left the father dead in the middle of the apartment. That's . . ."

"Not normal?"

"I suppose," said Blume. "There's something going on there. Maybe he suffered as a child, something along those lines."

"You're not beginning to feel sorry for him?"

"God, no," said Blume. "I'm always pleased when I find out an assassin had a lousy childhood. It means they got what they deserve, even if they had to pay in advance."

From the corridor outside, Blume heard Principe discussing the removal with the men from the coroner's team.

Blume looked at a row of Disney DVDs between two bookends made to look like trees with happy faces. They stood lined up beside a DVD player, beside which was a small black television set. *Aladdin, Aristogatti, La Bella Addormentata, La Bella e la Bestia, Biancaneve*, all in alphabetical order.

The only books were maps of the sky at night, atlases, an English picture dictionary. They looked unopened. He bent down and looked underneath the bed, where, as if in hiding from the organizing agency that ran the rest of the house, lay a crumpled Batman suit and cape.

5

A T HALF PAST ten in the evening, after repeating his alibi for the umpteenth time, Leonardo Ulmo told Inspector Paoloni that he could no longer take it. Paoloni nodded as if he understood, said he would see what he could do.

But they kept him there.

Leonardo said all he had done all day was deliver boxes of groceries in the Monteverde neighborhood. Blume nodded appreciatively and wrote this down. Leonardo became more specific about his day. Blume asked about his delivery to the apartments at No. 7 Via Generale Regola.

Leonardo explained he had had two deliveries to make at this address. Two boxes of groceries to Block C, Apartments six and ten on the third and fifth floors. Also two packs of Nepi mineral water for Apartment six. Block C had no elevator. Most of the deliveries he made were to apartment buildings with no elevators.

"Yeah? How's that?" asked Blume.

"The people who live in buildings without one often have their groceries delivered. That way they don't have to carry them up the stairs. I do."

Blume peered at him from over the tips of his fingers. "OK," he said finally. "That makes sense. Go on."

"So I'm taking up the boxes on the . . ."

Blume held up a hand. "What's with this getting right into the middle of things? First of all, who sent you?"

"My manager at the supermarket," Leonardo explained.

"Described by my colleague as a sweaty bastard who wears a striped shirt and white belt?"

"That's the one."

"Did you deliver anything before Via Regola?"

"Yes. To Via Regnoli, Carini, Quattro Venti."

"And after?"

"Piazza Cucchi."

"You can give me the exact address?"

Leonardo could. Blume wrote it down, then said, "Are you thirsty?"

"I'm dying of thirst," said Leonardo.

"Be right back," said Blume and left the interrogation room. He got the number from the address Leonardo had given him and called. A woman answered, and was quickly able to confirm her groceries had been delivered at precisely eleven o'clock that morning. It was just before her favorite comedy DJs came on Radio 2.

It was not a total alibi, but it was close. Blume went up to the ground floor, bought two bottles of water, drinking his own on the way back, cursing himself for being fooled yet again into paying a euro for stuff that ran free from the faucets. He stuck the empty bottle into his pocket. He would use it for refills.

He handed the other bottle to Leonardo, who drank it in a single draught.

"Thanks."

"You're welcome. So, after the delivery to Piazza Cucchi, you went back to the supermarket?"

"Yes. My arrival time is logged, so you can check that."

"OK. Let's go back. What time did you get to Via Regola?"

"Must have been half past ten."

"Must have been or was?"

"Was, must have been. I don't know. A bit later. Ten forty, OK?"

Blume drew three circles around ten forty on his pad.

"I parked the Iveco alongside a row of cars, opened the back doors, took out the porter's trolley and two boxes and the water."

"A porter's trolley?"

"For carrying the boxes and the mineral water."

"You pull the boxes all the way up the stairs using this metal trolley thing, bouncing from step to step all the way to the top? Wouldn't it be quicker just carrying them yourself?"

"Maybe, until my back caves in."

"OK."

"So I got to the apartment block, pulled in the trolley with two boxes and two packs of mineral water."

"Who let you in?"

"I don't know. The front door was open, anyway."

But Blume had not reached the front door yet in his mind's eye. He was still standing on the street outside the apartment lot. "The front gate to the courtyard was open?"

"Yes," said Leonardo.

"Was the porter on duty?"

Leonardo thought about it for a moment. "No. I don't think he was. No. It was very quiet. Hot. A lot of shutters closed because they're all on holiday."

"So you get to Apartment Block C. And the front door is already open. Why is that?"

"It's got a faulty lock. It doesn't always snap shut."

"So in you go."

"No. First I buzz on the squawk box to announce I'm on my way."

"Which intercom?"

"Both. Top apartment, which is number ten and the one on the third floor, which is number six. I pressed both buttons together."

"Who answered?"

"I don't know. When I heard the intercom being picked up, I just yelled 'groceries.' I was already half in the door by then."

"How come you remember the numbers of the apartments?"

"I've been doing the job for eighteen months. These guys are regulars."

"Do they always get deliveries on Fridays?"

"One of them does. The other is more irregular. I suppose I remember them also because they're both men. Most of the deliveries are to women."

Blume placed his fists on the table and leaned in closer. "Can you remember the names on the door? Relax, close your eyes, think about it calmly."

"I'm not calm."

"No reason not to be, Leonardo. You're being really helpful. Ten more minutes here is all, I promise."

Leonardo closed his eyes. "The upstairs buzzer has one name only. It's German or English. The downstairs one has two names. On the top is Romano, or Romagna, Romagnolo or something. The other name . . . No. Begins with an *L*. Or is it a *C*? That's why I'm here, isn't it? Something happened to the guy on the third floor?"

Blume ignored the question and looked at his pad. "You're in Block C, at the bottom of the stairs. What then?"

"I went straight to the top floor first."

"You carried all the boxes up to the top floor?"

"No. Way I do it, I drop off the box of groceries and the mineral water for the apartment on the third floor landing on my way up to the top. I get to the last floor, deliver the other box. Then, on my way down again, I ring, guy opens the door, I push it in, he gives me a tip."

"The apartment on the third floor. Is it always a man who answers?"

"Usually. Sometimes a housecleaner."

"How do you know she's a housecleaner?"

"Old. Older than him. Also, you can tell."

Blume picked up his pen again, and said, "OK, what about the man? What's he like?"

"Sometimes he chats, sometimes he pretends I don't exist. I prefer it when he pretends I don't exist, because then he usually tips. When he chats, he doesn't tip."

"And today, how did he behave today?"

"I never saw him today."

"You never saw him?"

"Not today. I got to Apartment ten at the top, rang the doorbell, this skinny German guy who lives there answers, all dressed up in sportswear, like you."

Blume looked down at his hairy legs. "Then the guy downstairs, can you tell me what we said his name was?"

"We didn't," said Leonardo.

"Right, we didn't. Well, the name is Arturo Clemente."

"I go back down the stairs with the trolley, and when I reach the landing outside Apartment six, the box and the water six-packs are gone."

"Gone?"

"Gone. I figure he must have opened the door, pulled them in by himself, and closed the door so as not to give me a tip. Stingy bastard."

"You didn't ring the bell to check?"

"What's to check? Only reason would be to ask for my tip, but I've got some dignity."

"Did he ever do that before?"

"Not tip? Yes, like I told you. But I don't remember him ever pulling the groceries in off the landing."

"How did he know they were there?"

"How the hell do I know? He opened his door, saw them. I just know they were gone. I rang the intercom downstairs, remember?"

Blume tapped the pen against his front teeth. It was a metal pen, and clacked as it hit the enamel.

"What then?"

"Nothing. I left."

"What time was this?"

"I don't know. Like I said, twenty to eleven, a quarter to."

Blume asked, "Could anyone have come into the building without you hearing?"

"Sure they could."

"So did anyone?"

Leonardo closed his eyes again. Then he opened them again. "I can't remember."

"Just think of the sounds you heard," said Blume. It was almost a gentle invitation.

"Wait. Someone was playing piano." Leonardo grinned, pleased with himself.

"Fast? Slow? Good playing? Maybe it was a CD?"

"Slow—but fast bits, too. It wasn't a CD. The person went back and played the same piece a few times."

"Just piano music?"

"Yes."

"Can you hum the tune for me?"

"No."

"Try."

"I can't. It was classical music."

"OK. Any other sounds?"

"It's was kind of a quiet, sleepy morning. I can't remember any more sounds. Apart from the cicadas. Wait, there was another sound, like someone hitting woodwork." He hit the table with the base of his palm. "Sort of like that. Three, four times."

"From where?"

"From below, when I was sliding the box into the apartment upstairs."

"OK, Leonardo. That's good."

6

INVESTIGATING MAGISTRATE Filippo Principe was waiting when Blume came out.

Principe nodded at the door to the interrogation room. "No defense lawyer present, so his statements are legally worthless."

"I know that," said Blume. "But he's not our man."

"Is he likely to cause trouble about this interrogation?"

"No. He's a nice guy."

Blume went up to the ground floor where he found Zambotto leaning against the jamb of a door halfway down the corridor, staring at a vending machine like it was a TV screen. He called, and Zambotto came lumbering down the corridor, unhappy to be wanted.

"What?"

"I want you to prepare it as a voluntary witness statement. Did you ask the supermarket manager about pilfering?"

Zambotto looked at him without a hint of comprehension. Blume motioned him to follow him back downstairs. "Paoloni and I discovered some of the items in the grocery box were missing. I just thought we should ask the manager if the delivery people ever lift out items from the boxes—you know, pilfer."

"What items?" asked Zambotto.

"Peanut butter."

"What is peanut butter?"

"American food," said Blume.

Zambotto stuck out a wide flat tongue in disgust.

"We found a list in the box of groceries," said Blume. "There were two things missing. Peanut butter and Nutella."

"Uh," said Zambotto.

"I'm not saying it's important. It's just a fact. But if the killer took them, then it's relevant. If he didn't, then it's not."

"All deliverymen steal stuff," said Zambotto as if quoting a well-known proverb. "But the supermarket's never going to admit that."

"Depends how you ask, I suppose," said Blume. "Did you ask?"

"No."

Blume nodded. "No reason you should have. Did you get the supermarket manager's home number?"

"I got his cell phone number. I have it here," Zambotto unbuttoned his orange and brown jacket, fished out a notebook from his inside pocket. "His name is Truffa."

"Truffa, you say?" Blume pulled out his cell phone, pressed the numbers as Zambotto called them out. He dismissed Zambotto with a nod of the head. Zambotto went into the interrogation room.

"You going to call him now?" asked Principe.

"Why? Think we should wait?" Blume dialed the number, identified himself to the man who answered and apologized for calling so late, paused for a second, then made a weak joke about bad television. Two minutes later he hung up and shrugged.

"Well?" said Principe.

"OK. This supermarket manager—Truffa—just told me customers almost never try to pull a fast one or complain about missing items," said Blume.

"Is that a breakthrough of some sort?" Principe wanted to know.

"Not at all," said Blume. "Hardly makes any difference. But it means stuff doesn't go missing. Customers would complain if it did. It doesn't make sense to lose a job, even a lousy one, for the sake of a can of beans."

The door to the interrogation room burst open, and Zambotto appeared, breathing heavily, his enormous head hanging down as if he had just completed a round in the ring. "Had to get out of there, stop myself from strangling the fucker."

"Why, what did he do?" said Principe.

"He denies everything. So maybe he didn't do it, but he's using this tone of voice, you know, like he was calling me stupid."

Blume said, "You know what, Cristian? I think we can leave it there."

"What?"

"He's not who we're after. Also, I want a break. Maybe you want one, too?"

Zambotto nodded.

"Fine," said Blume.

Blume left the basement and went up to the serious crimes section on the second floor of the station in search of Paoloni, who was supposed to be setting out the investigative chronology. But instead of Paoloni in the office, he found the young deputy inspector, Marco Ferrucci, tongue out in concentration as he tapped something into his police computer on the desk. Blume had not intended to use Ferrucci until the following day.

"When did you get in?"

"About an hour ago, sir."

"There was a reason I didn't call you. I wanted at least one wide-awake officer on the job tomorrow. Who told you to come in?"

"No one."

"So what, you just dreamed there was a case, woke up, and came in?"

"I wasn't asleep. It's not late."

Blume cut him off. "So where's Paoloni?"

"He said the computer hurt his eyes, sir."

"He went home?"

"I don't think he went home. Anyhow, he's been working very hard until now."

The phone on Blume's desk in the next room began to ring. Almost all the calls to his desk now came from within the building, and the only person he could think it might be was Gallone.

"Are you going to answer that, sir?" asked Ferrucci.

The phone stopped ringing.

Blume said, "Answer what?"

But then it started up again. Blume banged his way into his poky office, grabbed the receiver, brought it up to his ear, but, just to provoke Gallone, said nothing.

"Alec?"

It was D'Amico, not Gallone.

"Nando."

"Yeah, it's me. So you're in the office. I called this number because I know it by heart. I was about to call you on your cell."

"Where are you?"

"In my office in the Viminale," said D'Amico.

"Aren't we supposed to coordinate or something?"

"That's what this is: coordination."

"Have you got something for me, Nando?"

"Yes. The widow, Sveva Romagnolo, did not make an emergency call when she found the body. Not at first."

"No?" said Blume.

"OK, picture this," said D'Amico. "Romagnolo finds her husband's bloody corpse on the floor, her kid is presumably suffering psychological trauma so she whips out her cell like any normal person would do and she calls—get this—not 112, 113, or 118 but 1240—directory inquiries. She made that call at three fifty-five. That's nine minutes before we logged the emergency call."

"Wait. Go back a bit. She whips out her cell phone?"

"Sure."

"The one that went missing from the crime scene?"

There was silence from on the other end of the line.

"Nando? Did you lift Romagnolo's phone from the crime scene?"

"It wasn't part of the crime scene. She left it there after the fact. It's irrelevant to the murder. Unless she did it, which is out of the question."

"Is it?" asked Blume.

"Pretty much, yes. She was traveling with her son. She was in her constituency in Padua. Hundreds of people saw her. She's a senator, for God's sake."

"When the Holy Ghost started talking about the cell phone, you didn't think to explain? Maybe even give it to him?"

"He didn't ask nicely. And he'd just have given it back to her, without checking the calls and the numbers on the contacts list. And I want to know why the Holy Ghost is suddenly so visible."

"You ever hear of a chain of evidence, Nando?"

"You could ask the same of Gallone. He was happy to hand over an important piece of evidence. Do you want to hear what I phoned to say or not, Alec?"

Blume realized he was pressing the receiver too hard against his ear. He put his free hand on his solar plexus and tried to measure his feelings. He was tense, but not angry. D'Amico was presuming complicity, but he was also sharing information. Blume knew D'Amico's interest in the case was political, that's why they had sent him down from the Viminale. For some, including D'Amico, evidently, it was more urgent to find out who the widow knew and who she had called than who killed her husband.

"Romagnolo calls directory inquiries, you say?"

"Yes," said D'Amico. "If we get a warrant, we can maybe find out who she was looking for, but I don't think we need to. She was looking for the Collegio Romano commissariato, where you are."

"Here? This station?"

"Yes," said D'Amico. "A few minutes later, she phoned the desk downstairs there and asked to speak to the vicequestore aggiunto. So it looks to me like she got directory inquiries to give her the number for your offices, or tried to get Gallone's number, which is not listed. They wouldn't connect her, so then she said it was an emergency, and they asked what sort and she told them. When I say 'they,' I mean the officer who took the call."

"She called directly?"

"Yes. I just spoke to the desk sergeant who took the call. He remembers she then told him she was a personal friend of the vicequestore aggiunto, and demanded to be put through. He patched her through to Gallone's cell number."

"So she wanted the Holy Ghost in particular, not just any old police."

"Funny, that. Someone wanting Gallone," said D'Amico.

"She can't know him all that well," said Blume, "or she'd have had his number already."

"Gallone's the sort of person whose number you cancel from your phone first chance you get. I did. Anyhow, after talking to Gallone, she called the central switchboard here at the Viminale. I don't know where that call went to, if anywhere. Probably to someone more important than Gallone."

"And after that?"

"After, maybe because no one had come yet and she was beginning to freak at what was in front of her in the apartment, she called 113, where she spoke to the dispatchers. They routed the call to Via Cavalotti, but they had no one available, so it was rerouted back to you. The same desk sergeant took the call, got the address, dispatched a unit, then called the Holy

Ghost to inform him. But Gallone said a team had already been sent to that address, and called the poor bastard on the desk an incompetent."

"So, first Gallone, then you people at the Ministry, then an ordinary emergency call, in that order?"

"Yes," said D'Amico. "Which is why I heard about it first, and you last."

"So where is she now? The wife, or the widow as she now is."

"She told the first unit—the one sent by Gallone—that she was removing herself and her child to her mother's house. She gave an address. But didn't Gallone say he was dealing with that?"

"He did say that, yes," agreed Blume. "You can tell he's handling it by the way he let the wife walk away like that. OK, Nando. You coming around here to coordinate with me anytime soon?"

"I was thinking of going home. I'll stay on call if there's anything you need me to do," said D'Amico.

Blume thought about it. For now, he didn't want D'Amico to do anything.

"Just be here tomorrow morning. Before the meeting with Gallone," said Blume, and hung up.

Blume walked out of his office. "Ferrucci, what have you got for me?"

Ferrucci, who had been bobbing up and down in his seat from enthusiasm, and showed no signs of tiredness, said, "I got a list of addresses, sir."

"Whose?"

"Romagnolo's mother's place. Clemente's office and . . . I got two so far. You need any more?"

Blume wondered if he had been overestimating Ferrucci. "That's all you got?"

"Yes, sir." Ferrucci went bright red.

"You could have used a phone book for that. What's with the computer?"

"I was looking up Clemente, sir. I hadn't finished."

"Tell me what you know."

"He worked for LAV—that's the League Against Vivisection. He is the chairman of the Lazio section. Was the chairman. He sort of specialized in protecting dogs."

"Meaning?"

"He campaigned against illegal dog fights. He's been at it for a while. There are newspaper articles dating back at least as far as 1998. He did a documentary on it. Remember the operation last year against a dog fighting ring in Tor di Valle?"

Blume did, though it had involved the Carabinieri, not the police.

"He was behind that. Kicked up a big media fuss. His name's all over the papers in that period."

"Good. So we have a motive. Who did he do the documentary with?"

"Taddeo Di Tivoli. He's the host of a TV show."

"I know the name," said Blume. "But I don't really watch TV. What else did you find out about Clemente?"

"He was thinking of going into politics, joining the Greens. That's his wife's party."

"Right. Anything else?" Blume was beginning to believe in his young colleague again.

"No. But I heard the vicequestore was . . ."

At that moment, Paoloni came in and belched.

"Broad beans don't agree with me," he said and rubbed his stomach. "It could be the beginning of Favism. Go on, Ferrucci, you were saying: Gallone was what?"

Ferrucci, his voice rising a little from tension, continued: "I heard he had taken charge of questioning Romagnolo."

"Or so he thinks," said Blume. "Go on."

"Well, I know Vicequestore Gallone doesn't like becoming entangled . . ."

"You can't entangle the Holy Ghost, Ferrucci. Knotty problems just pass right through him," said Paoloni.

"Well . . ." Ferrucci looked unhappy. "I realized it was unusual for him to, you know, work a case personally, and so I looked for a point of convergence between him and Romagnolo, see if there was some special connection that would explain his interest."

"You ran a check on Gallone?" Blume thought his voice conveyed warmth and admiration, but Ferrucci flinched.

"Yes, sir."

"Well?"

"I found one. They were at college together studying jurisprudence."

"You looked up university records," said Blume. "What made you think of that?"

"First I looked up police files, sir. Clemente, Romagnolo, and the vice-questore were tagged because they were members of a revolutionary group called Prima Linea at La Sapienza University."

Blume and Paoloni both burst out laughing. Ferrucci looked worried, thinking it might be him they were laughing at.

"Comrade Gallone," said Paoloni. "Who'd have thought it? I always figured him for a spoiled priest. Maybe he was one of those Catho-communists you used to hear about."

Prima Linea was an echo from a distant past when the Communists really thought they might just make it. Blume was a child in another country when they were active, and Ferrucci had not even been born.

Blume tried to imagine Gallone in a combat jacket hurling Molotovs at the police he was later to join. Plenty of right-wing politicians and administrators had been in far-left movements in their youth. Even so, if he had kept it quiet, Gallone obviously felt vulnerable. What Blume found funniest of all was the idea that the vicequestore might ever have had an ideal. Or been young.

"Right. I'm filing that in my head for next time I need to compromise the bastard," said Paoloni.

"Good work, Ferrucci," said Blume.

"Alè?" said Paoloni.

"What?"

"I need to go for a drink in Trastevere, see who I can meet. You coming?"

Blume looked at his watch. It had just gone eleven. "You think?"

"You decide," said Paoloni.

Blume had never had much street credibility. D'Amico had told him once it was because he would not compromise, but he knew it was his voice. His accent, acquired in the schoolyard, was perfect Roman, but a hint of something else lay behind it, a watchfulness, a lack of spontaneity, or a slight reticence in his movements. Whatever it was, he put people on their guard.

"I think I'll pass," he said.

"Are you staying here?"

"I don't know. I might try to steal some sleep, a few hours. Here or at home, I haven't decided. But I'm on call if you need me."

Ferrucci's relief at Paoloni's departure reached Blume like a softening in the air.

Blume said, "I want you to get in contact with Zambotto, give him the address to Clemente's office, tell him to get over there, find a way of getting in. I'll meet him there later. Tell him to wait for as long as it takes."

"Yes, sir."

Blume scribbled down the address of Clemente's office, shoved it in his pocket.

"Then finish retrieving the essentials—car registration, relatives, friends, telephone numbers, Internet providers, name of bank, credit card transactions, all that sort of stuff. Also, see if you can get a copy of the Carabinieri report on that dog-fighting raid, first thing tomorrow. Go straight to the Court Records Office tomorrow morning. Let's not waste time. Get the investigating magistrate to help you with it. It's Principe. He's good. He'll help you if the Carabinieri decide to be unhelpful. And then go back home and go to bed. You get all that?"

"Bed?"

"Yes. Tiredness leads to oversights. People who don't sleep make stupid mistakes."

7

BLUME SAT IN his car in the underground garage and couldn't sleep. He had climbed into it with the intention of driving home, napping ninety minutes, and changing into proper clothes before going to Clemente's office to join Zambotto. But he didn't feel comfortable going home while Paoloni was still working his contacts.

He decided to put his phone on the dashboard and try to fall into a doze while he waited for it to ring. The oily smell of the dark garage and the soft seat of the police Brava, which he had pushed back into maximum recline, seemed to invite sleep. But Blume stayed awake.

Again he checked the signal strength bars on his cell phone, even though he had received and made calls from the basement countless times in the past. The phone was showing a signal at full strength, but he could not rid himself of the idea that the tufa walls and concrete pillars were somehow blocking his communications with the outside world.

After half an hour, Blume drove the car up the ramp, out through the electric gates, and into the piazza. He got out, breathed in the warm night air, and phoned Paoloni, but got no reply. He was not surprised. Paoloni often went offline when he was doing his thing. Incoming calls made confidential informers and potential witnesses nervous. Fine. Time to join Zambotto. He pictured the bulky policeman with his drooping eyelids waiting without acting.

Clemente's office was located near the zoo, or the Biopark, as it liked to call itself now that almost all the large animals in it had died or been poisoned by disgruntled keepers. Blume double-checked the address in his pocket and turned on the engine.

The traffic on the northbound quays was still heavy. Small cars with young people wove in and out, cutting him off over and over. Blume did his best to keep calm and drive carefully, but he still found himself doing more than sixty as he came out of the tunnel leading to Ponte Risorgimento. As he slowed down to turn right, his phone rang. He was surprised to see Zambotto's name on the screen. Zambotto did not usually take the initiative of placing a call.

"The office was being searched already," said Zambotto without even checking to make sure the right person had answered.

"Clemente's?"

"Yeah, that one. Your colleague D'Amico was here with two uniforms. They've just left."

"Stay there. I'll be there in three minutes."

Blume ran the traffic light and headed down Viale delle Belle Arti at high speed. He raced up Via delle Tre Madonne, and almost lost control as the wheels lost their grip on tram tracks. A police car was coming up in the opposite direction and Blume bore down on it. The police car whooped its siren, and swerved across the road to block Blume. An officer jumped out of the passenger side, pistol already in his hand. Blume got out, his police ID held high.

Nando D'Amico, wearing a white shirt, stepped carefully out of the backseat of the car and unfurled a dark jacket.

He put on the jacket and became less visible. "Alec! What's going on?"

Slowly, the policeman lowered his weapon.

"That's what I want to know, Nando. What's going on?"

"I don't follow."

"What were you doing at Clemente's office?"

D'Amico ran his hand over his chin, then stooped a little as if to examine his stubble in the car side mirror. "Who says that's where I was?"

"What were you doing there?"

"Helping. It's not as if you've got so much manpower you can do without help, is it?"

"You are not a judicially appointed investigator."

"This attention to rules, Alec. Is it something new? Because I don't remember you being averse to closing an eye now and again."

"If it helped a case to progress, sometimes. This is different."

"No. It's not. Anyhow, your grunt Zambotto was there. He seemed surprised to see me. I can tell you right now, there's no point in considering the place a secondary crime scene. Nothing there."

"How did you get in?"

"We picked up the keys from Clemente's secretary on the way. Ferrucci found her address for us."

"Is she still there?"

"No."

"Where is she?"

D'Amico consulted his wrist. "In bed I suppose. It's almost one in the morning. We brought the keys, not her. We'll question her tomorrow."

"We?"

"You, then," said D'Amico.

Blume pulled out his cell and called Ferrucci.

"Who are you calling?" said D'Amico.

"Shut up." Blume let it ring until the young man's voice came on the line. "You gave D'Amico the address of Clemente's secretary?"

There was a pause as Ferrucci worked out the tone of the question. Blume repeated it.

"I shouldn't have?"

"Answer yes or no."

"Yes."

"When?"

"About half an hour after you left."

"And why didn't you tell me?"

"Commissioner D'Amico told me not to."

"And you did what D'Amico said?"

"He's a superior officer . . ." Ferrucci's voice trailed off.

"Did he say why you weren't to tell me?"

"He said you had enough on your plate already. He wanted to do you a favor, not force you halfway across town."

"That was thoughtful. From now on, Ferrucci, everything, and I mean everything, filters through me first. Got that?"

"Yes, sir."

"Where are you now?"

"Almost home."

"Go to bed before you do any more damage. Give me her name."

Ferrucci did so, and Blume hung up.

"Satisfied?" said D'Amico.

"No. I am the opposite of satisfied."

"That is part of your character. Now I think we should be going."

"You will go when I say."

"Alec, I think you're forgetting I am not your junior partner anymore. You can't order me. If anything . . ."

"Shut up, Nando. I want you to go and get that secretary. Go back to wherever she lives, drag her out of bed, bring her straight here. If she protests, threaten her. Just get her here. Then I want you to promise me you'll keep out of my investigation."

"I'm sorry, Alec. Really. But I can't keep out . . . I see you haven't changed yet."

"What do you mean *yet*?"

"You're still dressed for jogging."

"Oh, that."

"You should bring a change of clothes into the station. Almost everyone else does. Come here."

D'Amico hooked his elbow under Blume's arm. Blume felt his entire body stiffen in response. Italians touched too much. Especially southerners like Nando.

D'Amico led him out of earshot of the two uniformed policemen.

"It comes all the way from the top. I have to monitor the case. I was just hoping I could be useful to you while I did it."

"Was taking the wife's cell phone your way of being helpful?"

"Yes, as a matter of fact it was." D'Amico's handsome profile went from black to blue and back again as the light bars on the police car flashed. "You know why they sent me?"

"Because you are my former partner and I'm supposed to trust you?"

"You can trust me, but that's not what I meant," said D'Amico.

One of the policemen came over to ask D'Amico's permission to move the cars off the middle of the road.

"Fine," said Blume. "And turn off the flashing blue on your vehicle, too. It's pointless."

The uniformed officer hesitated, awaiting a nod from D'Amico.

"Move it, for God's sake," ordered Blume.

D'Amico gave a quick nod of sanction. When the policeman had left them, he said, "I didn't mean why they sent me in particular. Why do you think they assigned someone to monitor the case?"

"The wife is a politician. She's got contacts," said Blume. "She's applying pressure to some important people."

The flashing lights went off. D'Amico spoke into the darkness. "I was worried you hadn't grasped that fact."

"It's not that hard."

"No, it's not, but sometimes you act as if you didn't know how things work here."

"Here where?"

"Here in Italy."

Blume laughed. "Like I haven't lived here? I've been on the force for longer than some of the recruits have lived. Or almost. People who vote weren't even born when I came here."

"The Ministry doesn't want talk about a proper investigation not being done into the murder of an opposition MP's husband. She has friends everywhere. Did you know her father was an MP, too?"

"No."

"Christian Democrats. And she's got an uncle who helped found Forza Italia, and a cousin who's something big in local politics in Mantua. It doesn't matter that her own particular political party is small. She'll change when it suits."

"So she is piling the pressure on," said Blume. "What does she want?"

"We're not sure. For now, it looks like she wants as little publicity as possible. She was estranged from her husband. At least that's what I heard."

"Sounds to me like she could have something to do with it."

"I doubt it, but that's why I took her phone. To check the records on it, see who she called, what numbers she has, what numbers she deleted."

"That was my work."

"Or Principe's. Anyhow, the work has been done for you. The Ministry has to know if there is any likelihood of her turning out an embarrassment. Nobody wants to be found out doing favors for someone who had her husband killed."

"The phone isn't evidence enough," said Blume.

"No, but she was a pretty damned unlikely suspect to begin with. Her husband didn't even have any money of his own."

"She doesn't want publicity. Is that all?" asked Blume.

"Far as we can tell. Thing is, she's calling in favors. It's important to find out anything compromising about her in case she calls in too many. Or starts threatening scandal."

"And what about the victim, Clemente? What do you know about him?"

"Nothing. That's up to you."

"I don't believe you know nothing."

"I am sorry to hear you say that."

"Nando, go get that secretary. Bring her here."

"It could take an hour, maybe more," said D'Amico.

"I'll wait."

"OK," said D'Amico.

"Give me the keys to the office."

"I left them with Zambotto."

Blume had almost forgotten about him.

"OK. One other thing, Nando."

"What?"

"Don't try to brief her about what to say. I'll know if you do. I taught you, remember?"

"I remember," said Nando, disappearing into the darkness.

8

ZAMBOTTO WAS WAITING, leaning against a curving white marble wall smoking a cigarette. Even from twenty yards away, the smoke found its way into Blume's sinuses and made him feel sick, but from somewhere near the pit of his stomach, he also felt a craving. As Blume walked over, Zambotto ground his cigarette out on the wall.

"That was a long three minutes," said Zambotto.

"I needed to talk to D'Amico."

"Clemente's office is on the second floor," said Zambotto.

"What will I find there?"

"Nothing much."

"Did it look like D'Amico had been there long when you arrived?"

Zambotto did not seem to understand the question.

"You know, was he finishing off, or did he continue looking around when you arrived? That sort of thing."

"He arrived twenty minutes before me," said Zambotto.

"How do you know that?"

"I asked the patrolmen who brought him."

"Well done."

"Sure."

Blume sat down on the doorstep. It was dirty, but pleasantly chilly against his bare legs.

"What time is it?"

"One fifteen."

"You can go home if you want, Cristian. Get some sleep. There's a meeting tomorrow morning at nine."

"You want the keys?"

Blume held out his hand, and Zambotto handed him a ring with two heavy and one light key on it before ambling off, like an incurious ox.

Blume took out his phone and called Paoloni. This time he got an answer.

"I got nothing," said Paoloni picking up on the second ring.

"Were we expecting anything?"

"No. I was ninety percent sure it was no gangland slaying, now I'm one hundred percent sure. No one knew what I was talking about."

"Make that ninety-nine percent," said Blume. "There is nothing certain in life, except death and taxes."

"I've heard you say that before. I don't get the bit about the taxes."

"Who did you ask?"

"I used an Albanian guy I know as my main source," said Paoloni. "He owes me a lot. Owes me more than a man should be able to live with. But I got nothing. Not even a suspicious blink. The other people I met this evening either know nothing at all about this Clemente or they're keeping very quiet. I'll talk to some more people tomorrow, but I don't see this going anywhere."

Blume said, "Either they know something but are scared of speaking, which suggests professional gang involvement, or this was a haphazard event from someone outside the loop, and they really know nothing."

"Weren't you listening? They know nothing. Tomorrow I'm going to meet more know-nothings. This is a dead end."

"OK," said Blume. "You know what you're doing. You saw the apartment. Give me an adjective for the crime scene."

"An adjective?"

"Just the one, mind you."

"Haphazard," said Paoloni.

"I just used that," said Blume, "but it's a very good adjective. By the way, did you know anything about D'Amico visiting Clemente's office?"

"How should I know what he gets up to nowadays? Is that where you are now? Clemente's office?"

"Yes."

"With D'Amico?"

"No, D'Amico's gone now."

"Want me to come around?"

Blume considered. "No," he said at last. "I'll do this myself."

Blume hung up and looked at the clock on his phone. It was nearing two in the morning.

There was nothing to do but wait. Blume fished in his shorts pocket and pulled out his badly dented Transcend MP3 player. The headphones were in the other pocket, and they took a while to disentangle. He had been planning a soft run, and had loaded the player with precise but sleek and laid-back music, the stuff his father used to listen to, a frictionless quality sound that no one in Italy knew anything about.

The first track was "I.G.Y." by Donald Fagen. Clear, forward-looking, optimistic music. His mother, from the East Coast, never quite got it.

She had bent down over his bed, early on a Friday morning, when he was half-awake, kissed him, and told him to behave while they were gone. She left a scent of Marseille soap and oranges, her European smell, as she straightened up. There was an art historians' conference in Spoleto. They were staying overnight. His father had stroked his forehead. All he had to do was open his eyes and sit up, smile, and bid them a proper good-bye. They could have exchanged an embrace, if he had still been doing that. But he lay there, a stinking, useless, lazy teenager, irritated at having been woken.

Fagen segued into Boston, who told Blume to lose himself in a familiar song, close his eyes, and slip away, and from Boston to Clapton, to "Horse with No Name," Creedence Clearwater Revival, the Doobie Brothers, Kansas, "Dust in the Wind," Van Morrison (whom his father knew all about before they discovered him in Europe), Linda Ronstadt, James Taylor, Neil Young, and "Blinded by the Light," which he never understood.

His parents never made it out of the city. Both were shot dead, along with a third customer, during a heist on the Banca Nazionale del Lavoro on Via Cristoforo Colombo. They had not even mentioned they were going to the bank. One of the bank robbers had been shot dead, too. The one who didn't do the shooting.

The police came to his school to find him, but he had skipped out with five friends and spent the afternoon smoking weed on an embankment in Villa Borghese, flicking butts and roaches on the cars passing below on Viale del Muro Torto. The police went to his apartment building and left word with the neighbors to call when they heard Blume return. They posted a policeman outside his apartment to wait, but pulled him out to deal with a reported assault.

When Blume and his loud friends came back at nine in the evening, nobody was there waiting for him. It was the woman in the apartment below who called.

When the police came, Blume and his buddies were crammed into the apartment, getting buzzed, listening to the Clash. He opened the door and saw them there, a policeman and a policewoman. Some of his friends lounging on the couch saw the uniforms.

- Wooo! Heavy!

- Pigs on the loose!

- Fascists!

Blume played it punky and hard, and started closing the door on them before they had even spoken, saying yeah, yeah, the music would be turned down.

"Fuck this," the policeman had said, and stuck his foot inside the door, bouncing it back open, almost slamming the edge against Blume's temple. Blume looked up in surprise and straight into the policewoman's dark eyes brimming with pity.

It was past two when the patrol car returned. D'Amico was not in it. He had evidently got himself a lift home while Blume sat waiting.

One of the patrolmen waved to Blume before opening the back door to deposit a young woman in the middle of the road. Then he drove off.

Blume stood up. "Over here."

She hesitated, then turned in his direction and walked over.

She was young, with thick glasses. Blume might have found her attractive had she been a little older.

"When they arrived the first time, they didn't tell me what happened," she said. "Then they came back."

"I know. I sent them."

"I refused to cooperate till they told me," she paused and looked at him. "Is it true?"

"What did they say?"

"That Arturo has been killed."

"Yes. It is true."

"I need time to process this."

"I'm sorry, but there isn't time. We have to move as quickly as we can. There will be follow-ups. For now, I want you to lead me into the office, and tell me what if anything is out of place to you. If nothing is out of place, then I want you just to show me around. Do you think you can do that?" Blume held out the keys.

The office was on the second floor. They used the broad, winding staircase instead of the elevator, almost as if they had silently agreed not to make more noise than necessary.

"Who else is here?"

"All offices. Lawyers, a museum ticketing company, a travel agency, and, on the top floor, an accountant."

They walked into the office. She switched on fluorescent lights, which cast a fizzy whiteness that Blume found unpleasant after the dark street.

The office was matte gray and characterless. Some of the IKEA-style furniture was garishly colored to give a faux ethnic or northern European bohemian look, but the room they were in was dominated by an outsized photocopying machine whose wheels and multiple paper trays made it look like a robot with fins. The wall behind contained white shelves lined with green binders.

On top of a white desk sat a graceless Apple computer made with see-through plastic.

"Is this where you work?"

She nodded.

"Anything out of place?"

She shook her head.

Blume took one long step into a truncated corridor with two doors on the right.

"Clemente's office is behind one of those doors?"

She nodded again.

"And the other?"

"Bathroom."

"Right." He walked down, opened the first door. The bathroom was long and narrow. It looked unused. To the left was a shower. Blume imagined the pleasure of stepping under it.

"Boot up your computer, then show me his office."

"You haven't even asked my name."

"I'm sorry. I must be more tired than I thought. I am Commissioner Alec Blume. I already know your name. It's Federica. Right?"

"I didn't even ask to see your identification."

"Want to see it now?"

"No, it's OK. I trust you. You look . . ."

"Tired. I look tired."

Clemente's office was small and almost entirely blank. In the daytime, he would have had a nice view of plane trees and a stretch of parkland. In each of the four corners sat piles of white cardboard boxes.

"Anything out of place here?"

"Not that I can see."

"What about those cardboard boxes?"

"Posters, flyers. Animal rights. To help change the laws on animal mistreatment, strays, dog fighting," explained Federica.

Blume picked up a beige folder lying on Clemente's desk and opened it. It contained flyers, a few typewritten sheets, some handwritten notes.

"This folder on his desk?"

Federica frowned. "I don't know. Usually he leaves his desk clean, but not always."

Blume picked up a few sheets and read them. They seemed to be notes for a campaign against the idea of giving children puppies for Christmas. If he were dictator, Blume would ban all dogs from the city. Big ones that bit children and fouled the streets, small ones that yapped at him from the arms of childless women, and every type in between.

One neatly handwritten page had some names, numbers. In the middle of the small pile of papers were several sheets with the name "Alleva" handwritten in block capitals on top.

"Come here a minute, Federica."

Blume sat down and started reading, handing each sheet over to the secretary as he did so. Some sheets were typed, others handwritten. It took twenty minutes. He waited for her to finish looking at them, for she did not seem to be reading them, then asked, "What do you make of it?"

"It's a description of a dog-fighting ring. The breeds, what he saw, the number of dogs killed—it was our main campaign recently. After the campaign against Christmas puppies, which is annual. I thought you would know that."

"No, I know very little so far." Blume picked up the file folder. "Let's go back into reception, your room, and you can fill me in a bit. Sit down there, in the chair you usually use, in front of the computer. Like that. Good."

Blume discovered that Federica had seen Clemente leave the office at four o'clock on Thursday afternoon. He had not said where he was going. Home, she supposed. She could not believe she would never see him again. Her chin wobbled.

Blume gave her some weep time. He watched her shoulders shudder and her head shake, and decided to ask, "Did you ever sleep with him?"

She stopped crying and flashed him a look of disgust.

"Lousy question. It's my job," said Blume. "But seeing as we're on the subject, what about other women? Do you think he might have had other women, or another woman?"

She looked at him as if not understanding.

"Other than his wife," he added, just to be clear. He watched her lips tighten, her arms fold over her chest.

"You're not betraying him if you talk, only helping us catch whoever killed him."

She shook her head, but it was a gesture of defiance rather than negation. Blume now felt she might have an idea, after all. He thought of the bedsheets in the dead man's apartment, and ran a small risk.

"We already know there was a woman. What I need from you now is a bit of confirmation. Can you give me her name?"

This time she stooped a little as if to hide behind her computer.

"OK. Not her name. But you need to help me here. Did she visit this office frequently?"

Federica crumpled a perfectly good blank sheet of paper on the desk, turned away from him as she dropped it into the wastepaper basket, then shifted the basket with her foot to a slightly different location. Blume gave her time to complete the operation. As she looked back up at him, he caught a hint of a nod.

"Great." He still needed a name, but he wanted to give her space. "Tell me, who's the record-keeper here? You?"

"Yes."

"Names of members, subscriptions, mailing lists, that kind of thing?"

"Yes."

"What else do you do?"

"Campaign news, press relations, arrangements with printers for publication of posters and flyers."

"Are you responsible for the money side of things?"

"No, that was Arturo."

"You've no complaints about the way you're treated?"

"We believe in what we do here. They were completely honest with me about everything. At least, everything to do with money."

"Where do you keep the files?"

She pointed to her computer.

"All of them in there?"

"We upload to the computer in Milan. Some stuff gets printed out, but we never use the printed-out stuff."

"Where is it?"

She got up, walked over to a wall, and pulled open a white sliding door to reveal yet more fat green binders, neatly arranged alphabetically.

"Member lists, invoices, utilities, campaigns, press cuttings," she explained. "But it's better organized on the computer."

"What did Clemente use his office for?"

"Working."

"Working means different things to different people. Did he file, type on the computer, write with a pen, make calls, meet people, drink coffee, play Internet games?"

"Arturo was hopeless with computers. He never used his. He didn't even have a cell phone."

"So what did he do all day?"

"He wasn't here all that much. He'd write out campaign projects, get me to put them into flowcharts, PowerPoint, that sort of thing. He made phone calls, received visitors."

"What sort of visitors?"

"Usually people who wanted to donate, become members, offer voluntary work."

"Including the woman we were talking about?"

She looked at him almost with a pout, as if he had no right to return to the same uncomfortable theme of a few minutes ago.

"Well?"

"Yes."

"I know this is hard for you, but you won't have to talk about this to anyone other than me," said Blume.

It was a lie. If her evidence turned out to be important, she'd find herself telling it several times to the investigating magistrate, the preliminary

64

judge, about ten more policemen, a court judge, and finally the press. "How do you know they were having an affair?"

"I never said they were."

"But we already know it. Don't worry about what you said, just tell me how you knew."

She stared at the desk.

"This is nothing to do with you," said Blume. "I just need to know how you could tell, just so . . ." He searched for a convincing bluff, but came up empty-handed. "Just so we can be sure," he said briskly.

She stared at her desk, and spoke to it accusingly, "The way they moved, looked at each other. Also, she was pretty open about it."

"Did you like her?"

"No." This time she made no silent head movements.

"Is her name on the records here?" Blume leaned forward and patted the computer monitor.

"Yes. She was a big donor."

"Find the name in there, will you?" Blume stood up and went behind her to look at the screen. It showed a spreadsheet scrolled down to the last few names. The cursor was blinking beside a name. Manuela Innocenzi, she had joined LAV six months previously.

"That her?"

A sad nod.

Blume found a piece of paper and pen and took down the address and telephone number.

"These files on the dog fighting," he tapped the folder in his hand. "Did you prepare them, collate them, whatever?"

"No. Not those ones. They're not from here. They have no reference number. All our files have LAV reference numbers. Nothing gets filed till it has a number, and we get the number from the computer. That way the computer has at least a trace of all hard copies."

"So what are these?"

"They must just be his own files. Just notes."

"But they're not from this office?" Blume turned the beige folder in his hands. It was the same kind magistrates used, the same kind Clemente had had in his study.

"Maybe he wrote them here. They're not in the system yet, that's all. He'd have to give me them first, then I'd organize, assign numbers to them."

"You'd copy out his longhand?"

"Only if he asked me to. Sometimes I'd just scan handwritten notes, but not often. Usually he'd do most of it on the computer, even though he found it hard. He isn't like a boss who expects his secretary to do everything."

"I see. So these were his personal notes? They were a draft or something?"

"Yes."

"Maybe he did them at home?"

"Maybe. He does a lot of stuff at home."

"Can you remember seeing them on his desk? On Thursday, before he left?"

She thought for a while, then said, "No. I don't think they were there. Like I said, he keeps his desk clean. He brings stuff back and forth from his house. He goes around with a backpack all the time. I mean he used to."

"A backpack?"

"A gray one. He bicycles to work. It is the best way to carry things."

Cycling in Rome, thought Blume. Another good way to get killed.

9

BLUME CALLED A patrol car and had her taken home, and he asked for someone to be sent over to control access to the office until the magistrate decided what needed to be done. But he did not see it as a repository of evidence, and did not wait to see when, or if, someone arrived.

What interested him more, far more, was the person Clemente had been in bed with. And the possibility that D'Amico was trying to fuck up his investigation. It was time to find out for sure.

Blume drove through the sleeping city, taking just twenty minutes to get back to the crime scene at Monteverde.

The porter was not in his cabin, but the gate to the courtyard was open. When he reached the door of Block C, he pulled out the aluminum Yale key D'Amico had given him and opened the front door. He extracted the key from the keyhole, allowed the door to swing closed again, then gave it a hard push with the flat of his hand. It resisted. He used his shoulder, and with a sharp click the door burst open. Blume held the door open with one foot and examined it. The strike plate was bent and recessed into the woodwork where the latch connected with the jamb. The faceplate on the door was also bent. They looked as if they had been like that for years. Getting by the porter and into Block C did not pose much of a problem. Nothing about getting into the building required planning.

Carrying the file folder from Clemente's office, Blume made his way up to the third floor. A young policeman stood in front of the door. His efforts to set a wide-awake look on his face gave him the panicked air of a child being found out in a lie. Blume showed his ID.

"When did you come on duty?"

"Midnight, sir."

"Who was here before you?"

"When I arrived, there was no one here."

"Figures," said Blume.

Taped crookedly to the door was a typed notice prohibiting entry pursuant to Article 354 of the *Code of Criminal Procedure*. Police tape was stretched in an X from cornice to threshold, and in five lateral strips from jamb to jamb. Blume peeled back as little as he could, put the H-shaped key into the deadbolt. It opened after one turn. He stepped inside the dead man's apartment and turned on the light.

The first thing he did was look at the space from which the corpse had been removed. The rusty stains on the floor showed where the body had lain. Blume stooped down and looked. He considered the thin strands of red and brown on the wall. The white and blue strings set out by the technicians to fix the source to the third dimension ran down the wall, across the floor. Wispy red and brown lines marked the white wall, like a Schifano canvas. Thin-edged weapon, right-handed assailant. The blood patterns strongly suggested the assailant had been standing more or less in the middle of the hall. He had cleaned himself up in the bathroom, leaving traces of himself everywhere. He must also have changed his clothes, carried the dirty ones out in a bag. Probably the bag he took from the study. The one the secretary said Clemente used to bring to the office?

The towels by the door had gone to the lab for examination. Blume stepped back down the hall to where he estimated they had been, and thought about the towels.

The killer had placed them there because he thought the blood might run under the door. Someone who watched horror flicks or played video games might think like that. If the killer was someone who watched those movies and thought he'd have a go at it in real life, then Clemente was just a random victim.

Blume did not like the idea of total randomness. Yet he did not believe there was anything professional or political in the murder, either. The truth lay somewhere in between.

The grocery box had gone to the labs along with its contents. Food for a dead man. The killer had used his knife to open the box, Blume was sure of it. And then, on impulse, he had stolen chocolate paste and peanut butter, kids' food. He had left the house with a bag of some sort, since he had to hide his bloody clothes. He had probably stolen the wallet.

The uniformed officers yesterday had reported that the neighbors next door were away on vacation, as were those above, and the one below worked all day in his store on the other side of town. When Clemente was killed, there had been people in the two apartments of the top floor where the delivery boy had gone with another box, while a girl had been playing the piano.

Blume returned to the study and, as he had done exactly twelve hours earlier, slid open the dangerously heavy top drawer of Clemente's filing cabinet and thumbed his way to the back files under *A*. He pulled out Allergie, Alleva, and Animalisti, and dropped them on the desk, then dropped the file he had picked up from Clemente's office on top. The file folders were identical. Some of the handwritten notes in the folder from the office seemed to continue in the Alleva file on the desk.

It was quite the worst case of evidence planting he had experienced for some time. He almost felt embarrassed for D'Amico. It did not reflect well on himself either: D'Amico had been his pupil.

Blume gathered all the papers he could find with the name Alleva on them, returned to his car, and drove across the city again to his apartment.

His original plan had been to sleep for an hour, but he slept for five and was woken by his cell phone ringing.

"Where are you, Commissioner?" said Gallone's voice. "You are already a quarter of an hour late for the coordination meeting."

"I was just in the middle of a . . . I am in the middle of something. It's important. I didn't have a chance to phone," said Blume.

"Where are you now?"

Blume looked at his bedroom clock. Jesus. How had that happened? "I'd prefer not to talk now. I'll tell you later, sir."

"What's wrong with your voice?"

"Nothing. I just have to keep it down. The person I'm interviewing, a C.I., is a bit cagey. I need to hang up now."

"Who's your C.I., Blume?"

"That's confidential, sir."

"You don't have any confidential informants. That's what Paoloni does. Where are you?"

"I really had better go. I'll explain later." Blume hung up. He got out of the bed and suddenly the floor seemed to tilt. He sat down quickly again as wave after wave of nausea rolled over him. He had skipped dinner. Ever since he was a kid, skipping a meal had sent him into some sort of glycemic crisis. His mother used to worry about it and had been about to take him to the doctor when she got back from the short break with his father. The day after, as he had sat in the wreckage of an abandoned teenage party, a policewoman sitting on the sofa opposite him, the doctor's secretary had called up and spoken in icy tones about there being no excuse for skipping appointments. So he had never gone back to the doctor. Every year, he underwent an obligatory medical, during which he folded his arms over his chest and spoke in monosyllables. The previous year, the doctor had taken out a beak-shaped metal instrument and pressed a piece of fat from his flank between the blades.

Doctors.

After some toast and an apple, he felt a bit better. He had always had problems oversleeping. Once he was down, he was out. He had to skip the coordination meeting, but he'd make it up with an investigative breakthrough.

10

A T A QUARTER TO TEN, showered, gelled, fresh, and reinvigorated, Alec Blume walked out of his apartment block, properly dressed in beige chinos and a soft, dark blue cotton shirt with an ample breast pocket containing his notebook, pen, and phone. He wore heavy Clark casuals and carried a leather briefcase, still supple thanks to his careful application of Leather Balm with Atom Wax once a month. It was a wide and deep bag, large enough for the art books his father used to carry in it. He carried no weapon.

Blume decided to go straight to visit this Manuela Innocenzi that the secretary had fingered. If she was the person in bed with Clemente before his murder, she might have a lot to tell, and he would drag her in for questioning.

He plugged his phone into the cigar lighter below the dashboard to recharge, and phoned the office. He expected the youthful, bright voice of Ferrucci to answer. Instead he got Zambotto.

"Cristian? It that you? What are you doing answering phones?"

"It was ringing."

Blume explained where he was going.

"Manuela Innocenzi?" said Zambotto. "Some name."

"What do you mean some name?" asked Blume, beginning to see the answer as he asked the question.

"You know, Innocenzi," said Zambotto.

"Innocenzi, as in . . . Innocenzi?" said Blume. It had not even entered his thoughts, yet it had been the first thing Zambotto's anvil-like mind had come up with.

"No way."

"OK. No, then," said Zambotto.

Blume felt butterflies in his stomach, a feeling he used to get in school and during his presentations at college. It was the bad-dream feeling of being visibly stupid in front of other people. Innocenzi was the name of the clan that controlled the entire south and south-west of Rome, most of the Agro Romano to Fiumicino and Ostia, with pockets of influence in the Agro Pontino, Foggia, Circeo, Latina, even Campania.

He pulled over to the side of the road and switched on his warning lights. "No way," he said.

Zambotto seemed to have hung up.

"No," repeated Blume. "It's just a coincidence of surnames."

Zambotto was still there. "Innocenzi has a daughter. No wife, no brothers or sisters. Just the daughter."

"Not one that sleeps with a do-gooder like Clemente. They'd never move in the same circles."

"What have circles got to do with people fucking?" said Zambotto.

"Innocenzi's a pretty common name," said Blume.

Zambotto seemed to be considering the idea. Eventually he said, "I can't think of anyone I know called Innocenzi except for that bastard. You want, I can ask Ferrucci. He's good at research. He'll be here in a minute."

Blume hesitated, then pulled out the piece of paper he had copied out in Clemente's office earlier, and read off the address to Zambotto.

"OK. Tell Paoloni, tell Ferrucci, but let's keep this close. It's probably nothing. As for this woman, I'll go there myself now. You give this address to Ferrucci, check it out together, then call me immediately. It's probably only a coincidence."

"In some ways, it'd be pretty good if it wasn't," said Zambotto.

"How?"

"It settles the case. Boss's daughter sleeping with married guy, married guy gets whacked. Not too many problems with motive."

"You think that would be a good thing, us having a run-in with Innocenzi?" said Blume.

Zambotto relapsed into silence.

"Let me know as quick as you can."

The woman in silk pajamas who answered the door twenty minutes later had probably once had strawberry-blond hair. Time had faded it, and she had retaliated against time by turning it carrot-orange. She glanced at

72

Blume wearily as if he were a well-known and unwelcome acquaintance. She stepped back to allow him in and did not even glance at his badge, from which a younger version of himself gazed out intently.

He knew immediately he was not going to have to be the one to break any bad news to her. Tears had already washed away all pretence of youth.

"Manuela Innocenzi?" asked Blume. She had let him into the building without a question as soon as he said police. Neither Zambotto nor anyone from the office had got back to him yet.

She nodded, loosened her hair, let it fall over her shoulders. She was barefoot. She led him into the living room. Blume glanced around, half hoping to see an unequivocal picture of Benedetto Innocenzi, old boss of the New Magliana Gang. She motioned him to sit down. He looked for a piece of upright furniture and found none. Reluctantly, he slid into the embrace of the fat pink cushions of an armchair.

"Enya!" she called, and an Irish Setter edged over to her feet as she sat down on a pink sofa opposite.

He said, "I am Commissioner Blume," and then paused as he watched the shifting weight of her breasts under her loose top and the wrinkling of the V of visible skin as she bent down and stroked the dog, which she kept sleek.

"What was your name?"

"Blume."

"I got that. Your first name, I meant."

"Alec."

"That's a Scottish name?"

Blume had no idea.

"Where are you from?"

"The police."

"Originally."

"America."

"Really? Do you like dogs, Alec?"

"Good God, no. But I know you do," he said. "That's what I want to talk about."

"About dogs? Or about a man who dedicated his life to looking after them?"

"The other. The man, I mean," said Blume. "But if you don't mind, I'd just like to clear up that we're talking about the same person."

"Arturo Clemente," she said. "He was murdered. Knifed to death. That's what you're here to talk to me about, isn't it?"

Blume tried to find some purchase on the yielding cushions. "Yes. Where did you hear about his murder?"

"On the news."

"Radio or TV?"

"Radio."

"It hasn't been made public yet," said Blume.

"Yes, it has. You just haven't been listening to the radio."

This was possible, Blume thought. The news would have got out by now.

"What I want to know is if you have been doing anything at all," said Manuela.

"What I want to know," said Blume, "is how you know about the knife. Was that detail on the radio, too?"

"For all you know it could have been."

She had him again.

"I don't think it was." Blume was now remembering the point of holding morning meetings to coordinate investigations. He needed these details.

"Maybe it wasn't, then," said Manuela. Her indifference to being caught out was total.

Blume's cell rang, and he took the opportunity to struggle off the armchair into a standing position in the center of the room.

"It's her. It's definitely the daughter," said Zambotto's voice. "Want someone to come over?" He sounded pleased, like he couldn't wait to tell all his friends.

"No. Thanks anyhow," said Blume and hung up, and turned his attention to the woman. Her face was tracked and furrowed, as if her tears had been made of acid.

"What were they saying about me?" she said.

"Nothing. That was something else."

"Sure it was."

"Police business."

"That's what I am right now. Police business. I have been sitting here all fucking night waiting for you useless bastards to come here and ask me questions."

"You could have phoned," said Blume.

"If you hadn't got as far as finding me, then you weren't making much progress, so what would be the point? Anyhow, I don't phone the police."

"I'm having a hard time understanding here," said Blume. "Are you planning to help or not? Let's begin with some basic information."

"I slept with Arturo, about twelve times. No, not about. Exactly twelve times. That's what you wanted to know, isn't it?"

Blume settled himself on the broad arm of the armchair. A strand of red hair lay curled on the armrest. "I was going to get to that in a more roundabout way. What about his wife?"

"What about her?"

"Wasn't there a risk?"

Blume casually rolled his forefinger over the fabric and curled the hair between it and his thumb.

"We did it here, we did it in a friend's house in Amatrice. Yesterday was the first time in his house. First time and last time." She looked more angry than upset now.

"Who was this friend in the country?"

"A friend of Arturo's. There's no obligation to answer your questions, is there?"

The idea of bringing this woman in for questioning seemed remote now. "Not yet. How did you hear of the murder? And don't say the radio."

Manuela pushed an unruly curl from her forehead, patted her hair into shape. "A friend of my father's. He phoned."

"And what was his source?"

"Unofficial channels."

"From the police or the judiciary?"

"Next thing you'll be asking me who my father's friend is."

"No, next thing I'm asking is at what time this friend phoned."

"Last night. Late. They phoned up to see if I was OK. It was two o'clock in the morning. I have been awake since, waiting for you. I expected there to be two of you, though."

Blume was not surprised that the information had leaked. If the department and forensics teams had leaks, the judiciary was an open faucet. But the news had traveled too fast to this woman. She knew even before the calls among law enforcement agencies had completed their circuit.

"OK, and now my next question is: Who's the source?"

"This is all irrelevant," said Manuela. "If you're serious, I'll talk to you. If not, then I want you to leave."

"What do you mean serious?" said Blume, pulling out his sunglasses case.

"If you are serious about catching the bastards who killed Arturo, I'll help you. If I can."

It was not so much an offer as statement of intent. Blume took out his sunglasses and a soft blue lens cloth. He polished his glasses.

"Have you ever heard the name Alleva?"

She did not hesitate. "Yes. It was not him."

Blume replaced his glasses, folded the lens cloth over them, placed the strand of red hair carefully on the cloth, and put away the case.

"No?" said Blume. "I hadn't even got as far as suspecting him."

"It would make sense," said Manuela. "But I think I might have heard something by now."

Blume nodded, trying to look wise. He wanted to know where to fit Alleva in, but could not ask. He promised himself never again to skip an investigation meeting before dealing with a witness. He went for a different line.

"When did you last see Arturo Clemente?"

"Friday morning. I left him at around half past ten. We had been together since the previous evening."

"Where was this?"

"At his house. I just said."

"Were you in bed together?"

"Yes. I just said that, too. No wonder you don't make much progress in your investigations."

"Why did you leave?"

"Because he asked me to, said his wife was returning. She was meant to be away all weekend. I want you to check up on that. What was she doing coming back? Look into her. That's what you should do. She's an icy bitch."

"Did she know about you two?"

"Maybe. Arturo implied she did. He said he was not going to hide our relationship, but I didn't believe him. Sleeping in his house was my way of testing him. We had been planning to go to back to Arturo's friend's house."

"You think you can tell me who this friend was?"

"He works in TV. He used to be on first-name terms with Craxi, De Michelis, Martelli, all those types. Arturo did a documentary with him."

"Taddeo Di Tivoli," said Blume, remembering the name Ferrucci had given him.

"That's him. I never trusted him. I think he wanted to exploit the fact that I am, you know, my father's daughter, get a scoop or something. Anyhow, he has a farmhouse in Amatrice. He told Arturo to use the place whenever he wanted. Arturo had instructions on how to get there in his wallet. The key was under a laurel bush in the front garden. He wasn't with us, of course. I wouldn't have gone if he was. Neither would Arturo."

"Nice villa, is it?"

"It's OK. A bit musty. Full of reminders of Di Tivoli as a spoiled kid."

"How long had you been in a relationship with Arturo Clemente?"

"Since I met him, basically. That's six months ago."

"And why did you . . . what's the connection between someone like him—" Blume stopped, thought about Alleva and dog fights, worked out what he was trying to say, then came up with his question: "Are you an animal lover?"

She caressed the dog with a bare foot. "Ask Enya here."

"Is your father?"

"No."

"He doesn't like animals?"

"That's not what I said. He has other worries."

"Do you feel different from him?"

"Of course I do. I am his daughter, not his clone. But I am close to him, too. Remember that."

"So you are your father's daughter?"

"I am not involved in his business affairs, if that's what you mean." She gave him a half smile with the left part of her face. "Whoever phoned you a minute ago can look it up."

Blume pulled out a bent notebook from his breast pocket and flicked it open. It was completely blank. "You're talking to me now. Already that's something your father wouldn't do."

"Don't start taking notes," said Manuela. "I'll get nervous. And you're

77

wrong. My father talks to plenty of police, always has. He's very open, too. Also, I have a simple reason for talking to you."

Blume put away his useless notebook. "What's that?"

"I need you to find out who killed Arturo. Forget about Alleva, though. It's a nonstarter. If it had been him, that would already be known."

"How do you know he is even a suspect? Perhaps we haven't even questioned him."

"I know you haven't," said Manuela. "You are all moving far too slowly."

"Are you telling me that someone has questioned Alleva? Someone like your father?"

"I am saying nothing in particular," said Manuela.

"OK, let's move away from Alleva."

"Yeah. It's a dead end," agreed Manuela.

"Now, without being too explicit about the sort of man I think your father is, let me say I somehow don't see him supporting animal rights like you. How about that?"

"That's fair."

Blume said, "He'd despise an animal rights sort of person, wouldn't he?"

"Animals are not his first priority."

"Maybe he disapproved of a man who went running to the authorities to report illegal dog fights?"

Manuela gave a short, hard smoker's laugh. "He didn't have Arturo killed, especially like that. That is what you're working your way around to insinuating."

"I wasn't going to insinuate it, I was going to say it straight out. Suppose he felt that Clemente, a married man, was, you know, dishonoring you and, by extension, him?"

She shook her head, "We're not in Sicily here. Even in Sicily they don't behave like that anymore."

"Some of them do, and your father is from a different generation. Maybe he found it embarrassing. Maybe he was worried about your reputation. Fathers can be funny about their daughters."

Manuela shrugged. "That's not the case here. If anyone was embarrassed, it was his politician wife, but not me. I've had other men besides him. Arturo was married and had his faults, but I thought . . ."

Her eyes suddenly filled with tears. She blinked and they rolled down her face, catching Blume off guard. He had not heard any wavering or cracking in her voice. He wondered if they were genuine. D'Amico had never believed in anyone's tears. He used to say it was the one thing Blume had to learn from him. But Blume believed they were always at least a bit true. Sadness was the one thing you could depend on.

Her voice still steady, Manuela said, "Sorry. It's such a waste. I was not expecting to break down in front of you." She flicked the tears off her cheeks with her thumbs. "You asked a moment ago if I was like my father."

Blume nodded.

"Let me tell you about something that happened when I was a child. Then you can judge for yourself," said Manuela. "I always liked dogs. I got my first one, a border collie, or mostly collie with a bit of something else thrown in, on my ninth birthday. I was fond of it, but never got around to naming it, and my parents never suggested I give it a name. When I was ten and a half—maybe you've checked up on all this already?—my mother was killed."

"No," said Blume. "I haven't read—I only just found out who you are."

"In a house invasion," she said. "It wasn't in Rome. They'd gone to Foggia. Why the fuck anyone would willingly go to Foggia is a mystery. Business, I suppose. Anyhow, the house belonged to a great uncle or something of my father's. Look, none of that matters. She got shot dead during a robbery."

"That's what happened?"

"It was an anomalous event."

"Anomalous. That's a strange choice of word."

"It's the one my father used at the time. I remember I didn't know what it meant. Sometimes I still don't," said Manuela. "My father never found out who did it."

"Did the police?"

She looked at him like he was a simpleton.

"I'll take that as a no," said Blume.

"After the funeral, a few weeks after the funeral, I think it was, I asked my father if I could name the dog Eleonora, which was my mother's name. I was a kid. Anyhow, my father freaked. Like I have never seen him do since. Said he was going to kill the beast, how could I dishonor my own mother

79

in that way. He screamed at me. Then he didn't talk to me for weeks. Finally, one day he comes up to me and tells me it's time the dog had a name, a Russian name: Laika."

"That was the first dog in space," Blume said.

Manuela paused and peered at him in search of irony. "Yes, Commissioner. Anyhow, my point is that became her official name only."

She bent down and stroked the dog on the floor with her hand as she continued in a lower voice. "Sometimes, when I was walking her in an open field or on a dark street, and could be sure no one was around to hear, I'd call the dog by my mother's name, Eleonora."

Blume looked at the silky creature flopped on the parquet.

"It's not her, if that's what you're thinking."

"No. I suppose not. Laika would be a few hundred dog years old by now, I suppose."

"Thanks. I must look great today."

"Came out wrong. I'm not very good with dogs and their years. So Laika-Eleonora died."

"She got run over by a car. It was a hit-and-run. The guy braked after he smashed into Laika, then thought better of it and sped on."

"Too bad."

"I was twelve when it happened. It was slightly more than a year after my mother had died."

"Children shouldn't have to suffer such losses."

Manuela did not seem to have heard him. "I remember how my father stood in the frame of the doorway, looking down the corridor at me, his eyes full of pity. I ran to him and he took me in his arms. I remember he was so tender. Then you know what he did?"

"What?"

"He lifted my face gently away from him, and pushed my hair away from my forehead." Manuela imitated the gesture now, as she gazed across the narrow space at Blume. "He looked me in the eye, and he said to me, 'Poor Eleonora.'"

"Ah, so he found out about you using the name."

"He always finds out, always knows. You should remember that, if ever you meet him."

Manuela clasped her knees and closed her eyes. "I felt close to him then, and I've felt close to him like that on other occasions."

"I can see why you feel that way. Sounds like he is a good father," said Blume.

He didn't mean what he said. Roman criminals had too many hang-ups about the sanctity of their own families. It was one of their weaknesses. In Naples, they were less deluded.

Manuela opened her pale blue eyes. She pointed the square white edge of a manicured fingernail at him, and said, "No, Commissioner, you're missing the point again. You asked me if I was my father's daughter. The answer is yes. After he had comforted me, I gave him the car's license number. It took four hours to hunt down that bastard who killed my dog."

11

ON REACHING THE Collegio Romano station, Blume transferred the hair he had taken from Manuela's house to a small paper sachet, labeled it with his name, number, date, place, and time of retrieval, and left it to be delivered to the labs on Via Tuscolana. Without witnesses, Manuela had been happy to tell him she had been with Clemente, but she might change her mind about it later.

On his way up to his office he ran into Paoloni in the corridor.

"What was said at the meeting?" asked Blume.

"You mean besides the Holy Ghost lamenting your irresponsible absence? Not much. Zambotto, me, Ferrucci, that's about it for the real people. Gallone's directing the door-to-door, for which we have fourteen uniforms for three days. He's deputized Micheli and Labroca to deal with the crime lab report and autopsy. He's handling media relations himself. D'Amico looking over our shoulder on behalf of the Ministry. That's about it. Gallone is keen for us to look into Alleva, and you seem to have a lead with Manuela Innocenzi."

"I don't think it'll go anywhere," said Blume. "Neither do you. If Innocenzi was involved, you'd have picked up at least a vibe on the street, wouldn't you?"

"Definitely. Same thing for Alleva," said Paoloni. "It doesn't feel right. I'd have heard something. I know who Alleva is. He's got a good thing going."

"Gambling, numbers that sort of thing?" asked Blume.

Paoloni gave him a look. "If he tried he'd have two bullets rattling in his skull in a matter of hours. That's a monopolized area."

Blume held up his hands. "OK, I was just thinking aloud. Alleva organizes dog fights, but doesn't run a book. Where's the money in that?"

"So maybe he's allowed to run a small book, but he would never be the enforcer. He's tolerated. He's a niche player, providing services that the bosses can't be bothered with or haven't thought of doing themselves. He has just one heavy, guy called Massoni. They've been working together for years. Massoni does all the PR."

"PR?"

"Yeah all the intimidation and stuff, plays the bouncer, opens doors, makes Alleva look important. But that's it. I don't think the *mammasantissima* Innocenzi allows Alleva or any other freelancers to have more than one monkey."

"Alleva operates in Innocenzi's territory?"

"Alleva usually stages his dog fights in the Pontina zone, Selcetta, Trigoria, Ponte Galleria, that sort of place. So yeah, he operates well within their territory."

"What's this Massoni like?"

"Standard-issue thug. Big. Spends a lot of time with his arms crossed, feet apart. Crew cut, tattoos. Alleva's the one our Carabinieri cousins raided, the one RAI made that documentary about. Alleva's small-time, but he'd have no problem dealing with a tree-hugger like Clemente."

Blume said, "You have to admit, he looks like a good suspect."

"Sure he does. Also, Clemente was really breaking Alleva's balls over the dog thing," said Paoloni. "You could almost sympathize with Alleva taking him out like that. But not a whisper on the street about Alleva making a move . . . Here comes my predecessor."

Blume turned around to see D'Amico walking down the corridor toward them.

"Catch you later," said Paoloni.

"Sure."

"Hey, Alec. The vicequestore wants a word with us. He's in his office."

Blume followed D'Amico down to the far end of the corridor where Gallone had an office that overlooked the piazza below.

"Where were you this morning, Commissioner?" demanded Gallone.

Blume sat down without answering. D'Amico sat down slightly closer to Gallone's desk, extended a white cuff from his gray jacket, and adjusted a titanium cufflink, then leaned over and tapped Blume on the knee. "What point have you reached in your investigations, Alec?"

It wasn't that Gallone wanted to speak to the two of them. It was D'Amico and Gallone both wanting to speak to him, doing a poor imitation of the good cop-bad cop routine.

Blume went over all the actions taken the night before up to where he had visited Clemente's office and found some papers with Alleva's name all over them. He stopped and looked at D'Amico's perfectly shaved cheek to see if there were any signs of blushing. Nothing.

"As you both know," said Gallone, "the person found murdered in his home yesterday was a certain Arturo Clemente, a member of the Green Party, and had just been chosen as a candidate for the Lazio regional elections. This is already enough to make it a media event. But we could at least have hoped that the murder of a minor Green Party hopeful would not cause an enormous uproar."

Gallone played back his last sentence in his own head, and decided it needed a politic amendment.

"I deplore the murder regardless. But, and here's the thing, his wife is . . . Sveva Romagnolo, an elected member of the Senate of the Republic. It was she who discovered the body of her husband."

"I thought the child did," said Blume. "Isn't that what you told me, Nando?" he said looking over to D'Amico. "The child found the body?"

D'Amico nodded. "That's right. It was the child."

"An underage person does not count," said Gallone. "It was hardly the child that made the call. It is tiresome for me to have to go through all this again. If you had attended this morning's meeting, you would know all this. I hope your so-called confidential informant provided some useful information."

"None at all," said Blume. "But I meant to ask, and sorry if this has all been made perfectly clear in my absence, who did Romagnolo call first?"

Gallone retreated behind his desk and leaned on the back of his chair.

"Who did she call first?" Blume repeated. "Us, the Carabinieri, her mother, the ambulance, someone else?"

"It so happens, I was among the first people to speak to Sveva Romagnolo," said Gallone. "Or perhaps I was the second person. Understandably, she phoned a top-ranking official in the Ministry who is also her friend. The important thing is she informed the authorities immediately. Indeed, she informed the authorities three times. The murder of the spouse of a member of Parliament is terrible news. We are going to be under a lot of pressure, both from the parties allied with the Greens and from the Government parties, which are going to be anxious to be seen not to discriminate. It is better to keep this at as high a level as possible, so it is probably a good thing she phoned a ranking official." He paused, then added a demotic touch. "At least she did not phone the Carabinieri."

"Well, sir," said Blume, "I think whoever did this was not a professional. That's my theory so far. For that reason, the technicians are not going to find the killer's prints on AFIS, and most of the evidence they get will be exclusionary. Same goes for the DNA. I don't think the autopsy is going to tell us much either. That makes Alleva a less likely suspect."

D'Amico pulled his leg over his knee and turned a pointed shoe in Blume's direction. "Are you saying he did not have a motive, Alec?" he asked.

"Maybe he did," said Blume. "But would a professional criminal, even one who is not a killer, have made such a mess as that?" He kept his eyes steady, watching D'Amico's expression.

"In December, the Carabinieri carried out a raid on a dog-fighting ring," said D'Amico. "And the organizer of the ring was Renato Alleva."

"Yes. I know that."

Now it was Gallone's turn. "The victim, Clemente, was campaigning against the dog fights. He had cooperated in the making of a television documentary on it."

"And did this Renato Alleva get arrested as a result of the campaign?" asked Blume.

"Yes," said Gallone.

"No," said D'Amico, then held up a calming hand toward Gallone. "That is to say, not arrested. Just detained. Then released immediately."

"Detained, then," said Gallone. "Point is, Alleva has a long criminal record."

Blume turned back to D'Amico. "Nando, tell me about that raid."

"It was a sort of reality TV thing. The cameras were running, the Carabinieri swept in, detained forty-seven people, took names, charged Alleva and a few others. They sealed off the fight pit. A crew filmed the place, a warehouse out the Via della Magliana, mile 7.1, filmed the dogs, interviewed some of the Carabinieri and a few of those detained. That was it."

"They interviewed some of the detainees?" asked Blume.

"Yes, it's mentioned in the report. It doesn't specify who, though."

"No follow-up?"

"No."

Gallone clapped his doughy hands briskly as if to signal the end of the meeting. "Well, Commissioner Blume, it seems you are ready to follow the most significant investigative vector, which leads directly to Alleva."

"Before we grapple with vectors, I'd like to complete basic first steps. Like interviewing the widow."

"I have done that," said Gallone. "There is no need."

"Have you written a report that we can read, sir?"

"I shall be writing a report after this meeting," said Gallone.

"Even so, I would like to do an interview myself, sir," said Blume.

"Out of the question. This is a case that requires delicacy. I don't want you trampling all over the woman's grief. You don't have the diplomacy. And you don't have my authorization."

"I see. The wife is probably not our main interest, anyhow," said Blume.

"I am glad to hear you say that, Commissioner."

"And neither is Alleva."

"I don't see how you can reach that conclusion."

"You were wondering about my whereabouts this morning, sir? Among other things, I was interviewing a woman called Manuela Innocenzi."

"And who might that be?"

"Her father is a certain Benedetto Innocenzi," said Blume, raising an eyebrow.

"I don't understand. What's her connection?"

"Genealogical. Father-daughter. Couldn't be simpler."

"That's not what I meant, damn it. With the case. What's her connection with the case?"

"Clemente was having an affair with her."

Gallone sank into his green leather chair, almost disappearing behind the desk. He crossed his arms while Blume spoke of the bedsheets, the secretary in Clemente's office, his interview of Manuela Innocenzi. D'Amico shook his head slowly from side to side as if in silent admiration.

When Blume had finished, Gallone brought his fist down on the table, and said, "Just when were you going to break this piece of news about Innocenzi's daughter to us, Commissioner?"

"When? I just did," said Blume.

"We don't need this," said Gallone. He pulled out his cell phone, then stared at it with loathing. Whoever he had to report to was not going to be happy at the new layer of information.

"It complicates matters," said Blume, "but I think I might be able to make you feel a bit better about the situation, Questore."

"And just how do you propose to do that?" Gallone tried to sound scathing, but his question had a note of hope.

"By looking directly at the facts," said Blume. "The victim's wallet seems to have disappeared, but I don't think we're talking about a robbery that got out of hand. Also—you can confirm this, Nando—the killer left prints everywhere."

"Looks like that," D'Amico replied. "It's too early to say for sure, since we've got to get the prints of other people like the wife, friends, and all, but, basically, yes, it seems he even left a perfect 3-D thumbprint on a bar of soap."

"Then he went into the bedroom and messed about with clothes, including the wife's. Dorfmann said the stab wounds showed signs of controlled frenzy. I think we can rule out a professional hit from the very fact it was a knife. We're looking for a person who's probably quite young."

"Why a young person?" asked Gallone.

"Older men use guns. The oldest use other people," said Blume.

At that moment, the door opened. Blume caught a glimpse of a woman with red hair, in a white blouse, blue jeans.

"Oops," was all she said before backing out of the room.

"Who was that?" said Gallone.

"I don't know, sir. Do you want me to call her back in?" said Blume making as if to stand up.

"No. I just remembered. I had an appointment. You've put my whole schedule out for the day, Blume."

"Was she part of your schedule? I am terribly sorry."

"Get on with your theory."

"My hypothesis, sir. The first impression you get when you look at the chronology is that the killer seems to have operated opportunistically. He knew how to get in. He planned, but was careless about his prints and other things. That's a bit contradictory, but it means he knows his prints are not on file. All that forensic evidence is going to waste unless we catch him. But once we do, he doesn't stand a chance. Clemente's wife and Manuela Innocenzi were both out when the killer struck. Maybe it just happened that way. Maybe not. I need to talk to the wife now."

"You are not to interview the wife, Commissioner. Not until I say so," said Gallone.

Blume ignored him and continued. "It seems clear that the victim opened the door. We also found a box of groceries. I think the killer may have posed as the delivery boy to get in. I think he was creative and used the props he found at the scene. The circumstances suggest that Clemente did not know his killer's face. But let's say the groceries were not being delivered. What then?"

"You tell us," said Gallone.

"I don't know. Was the killer following the delivery boy around, waiting for a chance? That seems unlikely. It seems far more likely that he would have got into the house by some other method. In other words, he must have had some other pretext prepared to get Clemente to open the door. And that means there had to be a prior point of convergence between them. So we need to look into Clemente's friends and, sir, we need to ask his wife some questions."

"I don't like this insistence on the wife and friends," said Gallone. "We've already got a prime suspect, Alleva, and now you tell us that there's also a connection with Innocenzi, though I still see Alleva as the most likely candidate."

D'Amico stood up. "No, sir. Commissioner Blume is right. If we rule out Innocenzi on the grounds that the murder was completely unprofessional and leave him far too exposed to suspicion, then we need to rule out Alleva on the very same grounds."

"So you no longer believe in the Alleva hypothesis, Nando?" Blume asked. "In spite of the documentary evidence I found on his office desk? You know what it looked like to me? As if a fastidiously neat person had tried his best to scatter papers about, but could not bear to make too much of a mess."

Above D'Amico's bright white collar the slightest hint of a blush appeared, then almost immediately faded. But he waved a minatory finger at Blume and rolled his eyes in Gallone's direction. So now D'Amico was playing at being back on his side, his old partner and friend, pretending to cut Gallone out of the loop.

As for Gallone, he had retreated into himself and was too preoccupied even to acknowledge that they were leaving his office without being dismissed. As D'Amico closed the door behind them, Blume saw him wince, then pick up his silver cell phone again.

12

BLUME WENT STRAIGHT across town to the investigating magistrate's office in Prati.

"Alec," said Principe, leaning back and stretching his arms behind his head to reveal underarm sweat stains. "We missed you this morning."

"I'm here now."

"You arrive when it's too hot for sane people to think straight."

Blume glanced over at a rusting air conditioner hanging from the lower half of the window. "Does that thing not work?"

Principe shrugged. "I've never tried. Air conditioners give you throat infections, colds, and muscle spasms. I hear you want to take this investigation in a different direction. On a collision course with the second most important crime family in Rome."

"How do you know that?"

Principe waved his hands like a conjurer. "Magistrate magic," he said.

"Who phoned ahead?" said Blume. "Was it the Holy Ghost?"

"Yes, he filled me in on your meeting with Manuela Innocenzi. Now he wants me to block you. Should I?"

"I don't see the point. I doubt that the Innocenzi syndicate had anything to do with the murder. This was a half-botched attempt done by an amateur."

"Or by a professional imitating an amateur," said Principe. "The messier the killing, the dumber the assassin seems, the less likely we are to tie it with a professional like Benedetto Innocenzi."

"We'll talk after I've interviewed the widow."

"Ah. Now that was the other thing he wanted me to prohibit."

"Well, you don't want to block the only two avenues of investigation."

"No. You should go ahead, talk to the widow. It seems you're not convinced by the third avenue—the one leading to Alleva's door?"

"I am not ruling anything out," said Blume. "As for that television documentary Clemente was involved in, we could do with a copy of it from RAI. Maybe also a list of all the people involved in its making. You could maybe send Ferrucci there. Phone ahead, ease his way. It's not as if it's confidential material. They broadcast it to the nation a month ago, or to that part of the nation still up at eleven in the evening and watching RAI 2."

Principe took out a fountain pen. "Fine. Anything else?"

"Not for now," said Blume. "You coming for a coffee?"

Principe shook his head sadly. "I can't. Coffee is full of cafestol. My doctor says there's no point in taking Zocor at night then undoing all the good work during the day."

"I have no idea what you're talking about," said Blume.

"You should pay attention to these things," said Principe. "Stress raises cholesterol. You look stressed."

"I'd be more stressed if I couldn't drink coffee because of . . . whatever that thing was," said Blume.

"Cafestol. I'm allowed to drink filtered coffee, you know, that grayish brew you Americans like. Apparently there's no cafestol in that. But I can't bring myself to. I'd rather die."

Blume retrieved his car from outside the court building and drove back to the station. He parked it in the piazza outside, nodding to the illegal parking attendant, who had hundreds of car keys attached to chains around his waist and jingled as he walked.

Blume walked into the station courtyard. Until recently, it had been filled with police vehicles and a very old Fiat Jeep, but then a decision was made to take over the piazza outside and turn the courtyard back into its original function as an internal garden, with a fountain in the middle. The removal of the cars had not caused flowers to burst through the concrete. And no one had thought to repair the fountain, a slime-covered object, said to be by Borromini, around which squadrons of tiger mosquitoes swarmed.

As he reached the center of the courtyard, he lifted his head up from the ground directly in front of him and saw someone sitting on the dilapidated wooden bench. Even before looking at her directly, Blume had already registered her as the woman who had walked in on their meeting by mistake. The object of her study was the crumbling fountain.

She had a graceful white neck, and her hair was the same copper color as the leaves of the Mirabolan plum tree behind her. She had hooked one leg over the other and rested a board and sketchpad on her knee. At twenty paces, he thought he could detect the smell of white soap and pastel colors, which suddenly reminded him of a moment in playschool in Seattle, long ago.

She was wearing blue jeans and All-star sneakers and a white blouse. Something about the whiteness of the cotton blouse, the brightness of her skin, told him she was American. A few loose sheaves from her sketchbook were fluttering in the wind. Now he noticed that she was only a few years younger than he was. At ten paces, he had resolved to say something to her. She sensed his arrival and glanced up and gave him a smile.

Blume smiled and nodded at the sketch she was doing. She half held it up, almost as if asking him for an opinion. As she did so, a gust of dusty wind pulled some papers from the bench beside her and sent them gliding to the ground. One piece slid over the broken paving, losing its pristine whiteness. Blume picked it up, in spite of her protests of "*Grazie—non importa.*" Holding the sheet with a slightly reverential air, he approached her.

"There you are," he said in English.

"*Non era necessario,*" she said, with a smile that gave him a constricted feeling in his chest. He hoped she would hurry up and notice he had spoken in English.

"No problem," he said. This time the message got through.

"Ah, so you speak English? I was a bit slow in noticing."

"No, not at all." Blume was full of disagreement.

"The wind," she explained.

"Yes, I saw it."

I can see invisible streams of air. I'm gifted that way.

But she didn't seem to notice his phrasing, and gathered the sheets together and, without separating the clean from dirty or even the blanks from those with sketches, bundled them all into a soft leather bag. Now she was packing away all her things, as if the gust of wind had been a sudden order to abandon the field. Her right hand was covered in charcoal dust, yet her blouse remained perfectly white.

"Come on, let's see the last one you did. My parents were art teachers. I know a bit about these things."

Laughing, she flapped her hand around in her bag, eventually settled on one, and held it out to him.

Blume found himself looking at a charcoal smudge. He didn't want to take it in his own hands in case he held it upside down or sideways or something.

"I bet you're wondering why I am in a police station sketching."

In fact he was wondering how to ask her out for a drink. All other inquiries were suspended from his mind, so that when she asked him a direct question, he answered with distracted candidness.

"Is my sketch any good?"

"Not yet."

It's what his father would have said to him. Did say to him.

She said, "You know something? It's good you said that. I could have got all creeped out if you'd done the whole gallant thing."

"I'm not saying you couldn't make it . . ."

"Don't spoil it. Just tell me, could you do any better?"

"No. I was a great disappointment to my father. I get Paoloni to do the crime scene sketches, and you should see his work."

"I am Kristin. It begins with a *K*. I'm just leaving."

"Alec, though my name varies depending on who is talking to me. Most say Alex, Alessio, Alessandro, or Alè. But in all cases it begins with an *A*."

Blume stopped talking, and wished he had thought of stopping before.

She packed away her things and started walking across the courtyard to the front gate. Blume walked beside her. She was almost as tall as he was.

"Where are you from, Alec?"

"I work here."

"Before that."

"Seattle."

Six years ago, he had passed the halfway mark. He had now spent more of his life in Italy than out of it. But Seattle was where he was from.

"I'm from Vermont. Near Plymouth." She paused briefly to see if he had anything to say about that. "You been in Italy long?"

"Yeah, a bit," said Blume. A bit more than a bit. Twenty-two years. He wasn't going to tell her that. He was only beginning to tell himself it. "What was your business with the vicequestore aggiunto?"

"Gallone, isn't it? I just needed to give him a conference invitation."

Blume wanted to know more, but did not want to waste time talking about Gallone. They had already reached the piazza outside, and he was in imminent danger of losing her.

"Are you going to be around later this evening?" There, he'd said it.

Kristin stopped and gave him an appraising look.

"Sure," she said finally. "I'm going for a drink in Trastevere with some friends. You know the fountain in Piazza Santa Maria? We're meeting there around ten this evening."

"I don't want to butt in on any plans or anything," said Blume, wondering who and how many these friends were and, more to the point, what gender.

"I'm going to be there. You're very welcome to come along." Kristin held up her hand to mark the end of the conversation, turned it into a half salute, and walked off before Blume had thought of anything to say.

Even so, Blume was pleased with himself. His last relationship had ended two years ago after a massive row that began over, of all things, his refusal to vote. Elena left him, and three months later married a more participatory member of the electorate.

In his twenties, Blume had had the rare distinction, almost unheard of in Italy, of not living with or even depending on his parents. But he had failed to exploit the full potential of his autonomy. He found flirting and the other preliminaries so excruciating that rather than go through them again, he would stick with the same woman, regardless of how fast the relationship trundled downhill.

This meeting with Kristin had not been too bad. Maybe he was improving with age. He went to the canteen for lunch, ordered coffee, and forgot to eat.

13

Back in his office, Blume looked at a list of names that Ferrucci had gotten from the Carabinieri. Ferrucci had apologized five times so far for helping D'Amico out the previous night without telling him. Blume had forgiven him, but was not going to allow him to know it yet.

The Carabinieri had detained forty-seven people and then released forty-six of them without charge. The one charge was against Renato Alleva, organizer of the event. It was his seventh time to be detained.

On this, as on the last six occasions, Alleva had been charged under Articles 718-721 of the Penal Code. The first set of articles referred to illegal gambling, and Alleva was acquitted all six times because no one had found any money on him. Article 727 referred to the mistreatment of animals, and on five separate occasions in the past he had been found in breach of this statute, which came at the end of a section setting out the penalties for similar crimes, such as cursing in public, insulting God, and speaking ill of the dead.

This time, however, an ambitious prosecutor had also charged Alleva with criminal association. This was a serious charge, and Renato Alleva had hired real lawyers to deal with it in the Court of First Instance. He won. The case was now scheduled to go before the Court of Appeal.

Eight dogs were recovered and put down. A letter of protest from LAV dated October twelfth of the previous year was appended. LAV was Clemente's organization. A reconfirmation that the link between Clemente and Alleva was direct. So maybe Gallone was right to insist on Alleva. But for now Blume was sticking to his own instinct, Paoloni's assurances, and the word of the daughter of a gangland boss.

Blume stuck his head out of his office. "Ferrucci. If Paoloni's about I want him in here."

Ten minutes later, Paoloni entered. He pointed at the Carabinieri report on Blume's desk.

"I saw that. There is a prosecutor who needs to be shunned," he said.

"He's young," said Blume.

"So is Ferrucci in there, but even he knows better than to blunder his way through something like this in the hope of advancing his career."

Blume agreed with Paoloni's analysis. The dog fights made excellent negotiating territories. People made bets, passed information. Deals got made, orders imparted, moods judged. They provided a nice cross section of criminal life in one place. Like boxing bouts but even more so. When Paoloni and other detectives operating the streets needed to send out a warning or a request, a dog fight was a perfect interface point. Sacrificing a few animals for the sake of maintaining the peace was worth it.

Alleva had certainly been in criminal company. Ferrucci had listed the charges against the men detained. Then he had separated them by category, marking out twelve names who had served time for violent crime and twenty-six who had been charged but not convicted. The others had records relating to drug pushing, theft, robbery, vandalism, trading without a license, disorderly conduct, and so on.

Just three of the names had no previous convictions.

"We've got twelve convicted violent offenders," said Blume. "Five of them have done stretches for murder, the other seven for assault. I suppose we can start with these."

"I'll follow these up," said Paoloni. "But I don't see we have a motive for any of them."

"The only one with a clear motive is Alleva," said Blume. "Like the Holy Ghost says."

"Yes, but it wasn't him," said Paoloni. "He didn't order it, either. Are you going to trust me on this?"

"Remind me again why you and I know it was not Alleva."

"Intuition."

"Come off it," said Blume.

"You don't believe in intuition?"

"Sure I do. It's that mysterious gift policeman have for knowing they're right when they're wrong."

"I know Alleva," said Paoloni. "He's too smooth. He doesn't do violence.

That's the prerogative of the Innocenzi gang. He operates because they let him."

"No violence?"

"A little light intimidation is all. It only works on some. Look at the names of the guys on this list—how would you set about intimidating them?"

Blume pointed to the list on the table. "So you think we should prioritize these guys before Alleva?"

"Definitely," said Paoloni. "That already gives us a crossover point where they intersected with Clemente."

"But Alleva has a motive," said Blume. "Now don't get me wrong here. I'm not buying the line that the Holy Ghost is selling, and I don't even like dogs. But the way I see it, a person who does this sort of thing to dumb animals wouldn't have too much of a problem doing the same to a human. Give me a strong reason."

"OK," said Paoloni. "He called me this morning, said he was worried about this Clemente thing."

"Alleva called you? He's a friend?"

Paoloni stuck his fingers into the belt loops of his jeans and pulled them up. "He called me. It's my job to know him, and people like him."

"Go on."

"He said people were mistakenly connecting him with Clemente."

"People like us?"

"More dangerous people. It sounds to me like Alleva might already have had an intense little talk with some Innocenzi executives, or the *mamma-santissima* himself."

Blume thought back to Manuela and the way she had categorically ruled out Alleva. "Did Alleva say he had spoken to them?"

"No," said Paoloni. "But he sounded like he had. What I mean is he sounded scared. Innocenzi doesn't like too much private initiative. Alleva is tolerated, but if he wants to break wind, he has to get permission. And now you say the victim was messing around with Innocenzi's daughter. Why would anyone do that?"

"Maybe he didn't know. No reason Clemente should make the connection, not if he was honest. I didn't make it," said Blume.

"And you are as honest as they come," said Paoloni.

Blume ignored the sarcasm. "Alleva wouldn't have dared touch a person Innocenzi's daughter was sleeping with, no matter how bad that person was for business. He would have gone through Innocenzi. And that puts Innocenzi back in the picture, except for the nature of the hit. But let's suppose Alleva didn't make the connection. Suppose he decided Clemente's activism was getting too expensive. Suppose he had Clemente eliminated without knowing anything about his sex life."

"I thought you were not convinced by the Alleva angle," said Paoloni.

"I'm not. But I can't rule it out just to spite Gallone, D'Amico, and whoever's pushing the agenda."

"They don't buy it any more than us—at least, your ex-partner D'Amico doesn't. He's just following orders, and the order is to close down the case as quick as possible with the minimum of fuss."

"The widow won't want that. She'll want whoever killed her husband," said Blume.

"Maybe," said Paoloni. "Then again, maybe not."

"Why would she not?"

"She's a politician."

"That's pretty cynical," said Blume.

"Politicians are all the same," said Paoloni. Suddenly he lowered his voice and put his hand on Blume's shoulder. "Has Alleva got something on you? Something that might make you want to defend him?"

"No," said Blume, moving out of Paoloni's reach. "He does not. What about you? Does he have anything on you?"

He expected Paoloni to react with anger to the counterattack, but Paoloni simply said, "He might. Maybe on others, too."

"Something big?"

"I wouldn't go to jail for it, but it wouldn't help my career any. Tell you something, though: what Alleva's got on me is nothing compared to Innocenzi's leverage over half the department and just about all the local politicians. He's got some pretty convincing political mentors in Parliament, too. So no matter what, this investigation is going to flow right around Innocenzi, like he was a hidden rock. If we lower our sights and move against Alleva, then Alleva is going to get his revenge on people like me."

"You and others."

"A few others. I'm not going to advance the case against him, because I don't think there is one. But I think you'll help me."

"What makes you think that?"

Paoloni pulled out a soft pack of MS, extracted a crumpled cigarette, and lit it. Smoking was banned in the offices, but no one had ever reported anyone for breaking the rule. "Two reasons," he said. "First, you're my superior officer and it's up to you to look after my interests, just like I look after yours."

"I hope the second reason is more convincing than the first," said Blume. "And put out the cigarette."

Paoloni dropped the cigarette, still lit, on the floor. Its smoke streamed upward toward Blume's nostrils. He went over and trod on it.

"Second," said Paoloni, "you don't believe Alleva had anything to do with it either, so it's not as if I'm asking you to look the other way."

"No," said Blume. "But neither are we going to pretend Alleva isn't there. He's going to get detained and questioned. I want to talk to the widow, but, basically, Alleva is our next move."

14

Y OU WERE ABSOLUTELY right from the start," said D'Amico. He had folded his arms on the roof of a gray sedan outside the station. "We can't even build a time frame without the help of the widow, politician or no politician. The Holy Ghost appears to have got her to give up her fingerprints and a DNA sample, but we need her testimony. She could even be a suspect."

"I see you've decided you're coming with me to the widow's."

"I brought a car. We may as well go now. We can talk on the way."

"It's not the widow I want to talk about," said Blume. "I'll drive."

"That's not possible, Alec. This is a Ministry car. Insurance thing. Sorry."

"Fine. While you drive, you can tell me about that pathetic attempt at evidence planting."

D'Amico opened the door and climbed into the driver's seat. "What are you talking about?" he asked as Blume climbed in beside him.

"You're not going to start the game again. I'm talking about you slipping into Clemente's office and placing files from his home there, just to make sure I saw the name Alleva."

D'Amico waited till Blume had closed the car door, then said: "You're right, naturally. But there is no need to shout about it in a public piazza."

"How wrong of me," said Blume.

D'Amico calmly reangled the rear-view mirror by a degree or two as he pulled out of the crowded piazza. "It was the obvious connection. The victim campaigned against dog fights, the man who organized the shows has the victim killed. Sorry if I was heavy-handed. They are nervous at the Ministry, in case someone starts thinking this was a political assassination or something."

"That's unlikely."

"I know," said D'Amico. "But they want the case closed as fast as possible. I thought I could speed things up. That's all."

"That is evidence-planting, Nando."

"You taught me."

Blume slapped the dashboard with his hand, making D'Amico jump slightly. "I never planted evidence. I never taught you to plant evidence."

D'Amico changed gear, accelerated on the straight stretch along the Circus Maximus. "I remember, four years ago, that case we worked together, the one with the girl battered to death by her student boyfriend because she tried to break up with him. Do you remember?"

"Sara," said Blume. "I remember her. I can recall every particular."

"So can I," said D'Amico. "Just to make sure he stayed where he belongs, we tried to pin a rape conviction on him, too, even though it was probably consensual sex first, before he killed her. Do you remember that, too?"

"I remember," said Blume.

"And do you remember how there was a copybook with lecture notes belonging to him lying on the bed, next to her body," continued D'Amico, "and you told me to remove it, and I didn't understand, because I thought you wanted to help the murderer by removing a piece of evidence that helped put him at the scene?"

"I remember all this," said Blume.

"Then you explained to me that the copybook was there because they had been in bed studying together, and that not only undermined our rape charge but humanized him."

"Yes, it would have," said Blume. "And since we're taking a stroll down memory lane, you'll also remember the bastard confessed, and he wasn't even particularly sorry. He had a problem believing anyone had a right to dump him."

"He confessed afterwards," said D'Amico. "But we removed the copybook first."

"Which is why it worked. And we were working together, police against killer. Your attempt was police, or Ministry, or whatever you are now, against police. And you are introducing evidence. What you did with Alleva's notes was—it was totally unconvincing, and wrong. There is a big difference. The spoiled brat who battered Sara to death was guilty."

"Well, suppose Alleva was guilty? He still might be."

"If he is, your actions won't help gain a conviction, but they could jeopardize one. There is no comparison between the cases. Don't insult my intelligence or Sara's memory. We haven't even brought Alleva in for questioning."

"Which is what you need to do. Take the initiative. Go to Principe, get him to issue an arrest warrant. Principe is going to issue one anyhow, he has to. Stop being so bloody-minded."

"Do you know more about Alleva than I do?" asked Blume. "Has the Ministry been conducting parallel inquiries?"

"Nothing like that."

"So why the insistence?"

"I'm not sure why," said D'Amico. "It's coming down on me from above. I get the idea it might be the widow who wants it like that. It makes sense, if you think about it. Her husband murdered on a point of ethical principle, trying to save dogs."

"You lot are so cynical about politicians," said Blume. "If it's the widow, then what could be better than going to see her now?"

"I'd prefer to have Alleva in custody before seeing her. That would cover us if she kicks up a public row."

"As you say, that's up to the investigating magistrate, not us."

The temperature had climbed to over 86°. The humidity was stifling, but D'Amico preferred to keep the windows down and the AC off. He drove with his arm hooked out the window, one hand on the steering wheel. His only concession to the heat had been to remove his jacket, which he had smoothed, folded, and laid on the backseat, having first brushed the seat clean. As they started off, he glanced back at his jacket, almost as if he wanted to tell it to fasten up. As always, D'Amico was carrying his Beretta, snugly attached to his side in a minimalist leather holster.

"Nando?" said Blume.

"What?"

"Don't try to plant evidence in one of my cases ever again."

"OK."

15

Sveva Romagnolo's mother's house was in EUR, a Fascist-era development of linear, white marble-clad monumental buildings to the south of Rome, built in the 1930s to impress international visitors who never came to a Universal Exposition that never was.

By the time they arrived, Blume felt as if he had been in a Turkish bath in a woolen coat. D'Amico parked the car, stepped out, and stretched. His armpits were perfectly dry, as was the back of his shirt. His forehead shone, but did not glisten. This had to be a racial thing, Blume decided. Blume had now sweated so much that his entire shirt had simply become a darker shade of blue.

The courtyard contained five short umbrella pines and a circle of squat date trees reaching no higher than the lowest balconies of the four-floor buildings around them. The buildings were new. D'Amico nudged him and pointed to the modern security cameras, then nodded approvingly.

After being challenged by a sober and shaved porter in a tinted-glass cabin at the front gate and displaying their credentials, they followed a pathway that traced a figure eight across the well-tended grass. At the midway point, an automated sprinkler emerged from beneath the ground and squirted a jet of water at them across the path, wetting their pants and shoes.

"*Cazzo!*" exclaimed D'Amico, staring at the bright water on his shoes as if it was liquid manure. Blume walked quickly ahead in case D'Amico noticed he was laughing.

Examining the names on the intercoms and the brass letter-slots, he realized that each household had an entire floor to itself. Thinking of the thirty intercom buttons on the front door of his six-floor building in San Giovanni, Blume reckoned that the apartments here had to be around five times larger than his own. The name tags showed that the Romagnolos lived in Apartment four, at the top.

"Who is it?" challenged a male voice from behind the intercom. It reminded him of someone.

"Commissioners Blume and D'Amico," announced Blume in his most officious manner. "Open, please."

Whoever was there was either having difficulty in finding the open button, or had gone away. In either case, the door remained closed. Blume closed his eyes and listened to his empty stomach gurgle. He would count to thirty before putting his finger on the buzzer and leaving it there while he counted to thirty again.

He had got to fifteen when, without further communication from the intercom, the door clicked. D'Amico pushed and Blume stepped in ahead of him.

When they had stepped into the courtyard, the brightness of the afternoon, which had been trying Blume very much, became suffused with the green of the garden and the cool shadow of the buildings around. Now, as they stepped into the atrium, the intensity of the light dimmed so much that they both immediately took off their sunglasses. Through flat tinted glass windows, the garden outside was dulled to deep brown. The air was cool, deionized, and dry, like the inside of an airplane.

D'Amico, who was softly whistling "Il Fannullone," called the elevator, which turned out to be surprisingly small, like an upended zinc coffin. They squeezed in together.

As they came out of the elevator on the top floor, Blume mopped his forehead and D'Amico patted his cheeks. There was just one apartment, and the hallway was filled with plants. An expensive bicycle, unlocked, was parked behind a small ficus tree.

Blume reached out and pressed the doorbell. Instead of a ding-dong, it made a soft cooing and cheeping sound like a jungle bird.

"What's with the bell that makes zoo sounds?" said Blume.

The door opened, and he found himself standing in front of Gallone.

"Vicequestore," said D'Amico, stepping forward into the space left by Blume, who had fallen back a pace. D'Amico extracted a large-screen cell phone from his pocket.

"This belongs to Romagnolo, sir. You specifically asked for it to be returned to her, I remember."

"That's her phone?" Gallone sounded suspicious. "Where was it?"

"In the apartment, after all. It had not been logged properly. They've cloned the SIM and whatever else they do with it, so we can give it back."

Gallone nodded slightly, but then his face darkened as he reregistered Blume's presence. "I specifically told you to leave Sveva alone."

Blume said, "Sveva? You mean Senator Romagnolo?"

"Franco?" It was a woman's voice. "Who's there? Why don't they come in?"

"Just a minute," said Gallone, but the woman had already appeared behind him.

"Oh, colleagues." She sounded disappointed, and sounded tired. "I suppose this is funny in its own way. Franco was just promising me that I wouldn't have to face too much questioning, yet here you are."

"They are not here to question you," said Gallone. "They are returning the phone you left behind in the apartment."

"I do not mind being questioned if it helps the case," said Romagnolo. "Well, come on in. Don't stand there at the door all three of you."

"I shall monitor the interrogation, Sveva," said Gallone.

"No, Franco, I'd really prefer it if you didn't."

"In that case . . ."

"You're quite right," said Romagnolo. "In that case there is no need for you to spend any more time with me here. I really appreciate what you have done." Lightly, she placed her hand on the small of Gallone's back, murmured something polite to him, and ushered him out the front door and closed it behind her.

Blume felt like clapping.

She turned to him and said, "Do you always smile so widely when interviewing the recently bereaved?"

Blume straightened his face. "I am sorry," he said. He felt like his favorite teacher had just scolded him, and he felt irritated at the effect she was having on him.

The contrast with Clemente's mistress was striking. It was partly a question of class and looks, but it was not just that. Where Manuela Innocenzi had been red, raw, angry, talkative, and corrosive, Romagnolo just seemed downcast, but composed and reticent.

Sveva Romagnolo made a gesture with her hand that Blume took to be an unenthusiastic invitation into the spacious apartment. She had a high oval forehead, and long, straight brown hair fell down on either side of a dead-straight parting, giving her the look, Blume thought, of a 1960s university radical. Her nose was slightly upturned and, compared with her wide mouth, a little too small, perhaps the result of plastic surgery. She wore a thin, flat silver necklace and a raw silk blouse. When she moved, the silk rustled against her breasts and seemed to change color from green to blue and back. Admiring her long legs and the light, loose-fitting black pants that ended just above the ankles, Blume noticed she was wearing a pair of simple Birkenstock-style sandals. It went fine with her image, but it still felt strange to be meeting a senator of the Republic in sandals.

She led them across a large open-plan room, as large as Blume's entire apartment, and out through a sliding door onto a large terrace overlooking the garden they had just walked through. The high trellises covered with shiny Chinese privet leaves interlaced with jasmine formed an effective barrier twice as high as the original wall on which they rested. Potted orange and lemon trees did sentry duty along the outer wall, and ivy climbed up the wall of the house. In the middle of the terrace was a small but fully functioning fountain made of four stone turtles supporting a basin, from the center of which three smaller basins rose, like stacked champagne glasses. It would be fun to play football up here, Blume thought.

"Please, do sit down," she was saying, indicating a circle of wicker chairs with brightly colored maroon and purple cushions.

Even in the act of sitting, he asked his first question: "How long have you known our vicequestore aggiunto?"

"The *vicequestore*. God, what a title for Franco." She let out a long breath. "I have known him for . . ." She scrunched up her face, thinking, and finally Blume saw the creases of age in her face, "He was at La Sapienza with me. God, almost thirty years."

"Old friends?"

"And nothing else. Absolutely nothing else." Romagnolo gave her shoulders a small shudder as if shaking off a repellent image of Gallone touching her. "We grew apart. Met again sometimes. There was a group of us. It's also where I met my husband."

The woman did not look her age. When he had been little more than a child in Seattle; she had already been a political activist at the university. He suddenly felt babyish in front of her. To compensate he added gruffness to his tone.

"So Gallone also knew your husband?"

"Not really. When they were younger their paths crossed a few times."

D'Amico said, "Excuse me interrupting. We found this in the apartment." He handed Romagnolo the cell phone. "This is yours, isn't it?"

"Yes, thanks. I need this." She immediately started thumbing at the buttons, consulting the menus.

Blume reached into his leather bag, pulled out a pad of paper, and opened it. "First of all," he began, "may I express my deepest condolences for your loss. It must be a terrible shock."

It was a stock phrase and he had used it or variants of it many times before, but it was not bereft of meaning. It was terrible losing a loved one. It went beyond words, which is why he had reconciled himself to using more or less the same phrase repeatedly. He also liked the covert accusation it contained. It must have been a terrible shock; it better have been a terrible shock.

Romagnolo finally laid her phone aside. Blume found himself looking hard at the widow's hands, which were long-fingered and, he noted, showed the early wrinkles and spots of middle age that her face had yet to acquire. Whenever he was meeting the first of kin after a murder, he checked out the hands and wondered if they could have struck the fatal blows, pulled the trigger. Often they had, but so far the hands had belonged to men only.

Sveva Romagnolo thanked him for his kind words, and lapsed into silence. D'Amico had taken out a notebook, too, and was staring at it sullenly as if he had forgotten how to read or write.

As they sat in momentary silence, Blume became aware of the irritating trickle of the fountain behind him. Far in the distance, someone was trying to start a motor scooter, or a lawn mower. Blume was wondering about the child. Should he ask? He decided he shouldn't, but his mouth betrayed him: "How old is your son?"

"Six." Romagnolo enunciated the number very clearly, to underscore its pathetic smallness and warn him away. She fixed her eyes hard on him as she said it. They were dark brown, almost black, and, he realized, a little too small. She didn't have such nice eyes.

"How is he?" inquired Blume.

"Traumatized. Destroyed. Inconsolable. He's been so hard to deal with. I've hardly had a chance to take it in myself."

Blume nodded sympathetically. He was calculating her probable age when she had the child. She must have been at the very limit.

"When you entered the house, did you notice if the door to your son's bedroom was open or closed?"

"No."

"No which?"

"No, I didn't notice. How the hell would I notice something like that with Arturo lying in . . ."

She brought her hand to her throat.

"You didn't maybe close it yourself, then. You know, sort of protectively."

"No! Is this normal, for the questions to be so irrelevant?" Romagnolo directed this question at D'Amico, who gave her his most fetching helpless smile.

"Do you eat peanut butter?" asked Blume.

"Are you serious?"

"Well, do you?"

"No. That was my husband. For the protein. He doesn't eat meat. Didn't eat meat."

"Did your husband have a bag?"

"A bag, like a handbag?"

"Any bag."

"A backpack. He usually went around with a gray backpack. He rode his bicycle a lot."

"We didn't find your husband's wallet. The killer probably took it, but just in case, do you have any idea where it might be?"

"He usually kept it lying around the house, or in his pocket. No, I have no idea where else it might be."

"His secretary says he didn't have a cell phone."

"He thought they were bad for his health."

Blume allowed a few beats of silence to pass.

Romagnolo said, "Franco was talking about a man called Alleva. He tortures animals. My husband and a friend made a documentary about this. I would have thought this Alleva would be in custody by now."

"He will be, soon," said Blume. "Apart from Alleva, did your husband have enemies?"

"Arturo campaigned really hard against illegal dog fighting. And that earned him a lot of enemies from the criminal underworld. People like this Alleva, I presume. He was responsible for Rome and the Lazio region. I remember he said there were three different gangs in the business, Gypsies—sorry, Roma—Albanians, and Italians. He said he was dealing with the Italians, because he felt he had some chance of success, but . . ." she opened her palms to display her ignorance of the details.

"Can you tell us where these places were?"

"I can probably remember a few of them. But, given that my husband reported every encounter he discovered, the police should have detailed records. Unless, that is, they got trashed as soon as he made them."

Blume ignored the barb, which applied more to the Carabinieri anyhow, and not the state police. What interested him was how little interest Romagnolo had had in her husband's activities.

"Did you receive any strange phone calls recently?"

She glanced upward and leftward as she sought to remember.

"No."

"Anyone new arrive at the house?"

She hesitated. "Not that I know of."

"Did your husband mention any new friends?"

"My husband would not mention his latest friends to me."

There. He had hit something. "What do you mean?"

"By what?"

Blume said, "He wouldn't mention his latest friends. Are you talking about girlfriends?"

To her credit, she did not waste time on pretences. She said: "You can't say girls. They were older women. They fell for what they thought was his big soft heart. A man who likes animals that much can't be bad."

"And was he—bad, I mean?"

"Oh no. Poor Arturo. He was a good man. He was just a bit vain. Vain and lonely, I suppose. Maybe not even vain considering the old *babbione* he chose."

"He knew you knew?"

"I guess he must have. We never talked about that side of things. Could one of these . . . women have anything to do with what happened?"

Seeing no point in pretending otherwise, Blume said: "That's just what I was wondering." Then he added, "Did you notice any change in his daily schedules?"

"He did not have a regular working day like other people. And I'm so busy myself I could hardly notice. I am often in Padua."

"Your electoral district."

"Yes."

"So you are often away from home?"

"I would go so far as to say I am mostly away from home. I spend far more time in Padua than in Rome."

"I see," said Blume. But he didn't see. If you were married to someone, he reckoned, you should live with them. If you weren't willing to live with them, then it was going nowhere.

Blume was not sure what to make of the woman he was talking to, and he had a feeling he would not have been too keen on Arturo, either. She cared for politics and the environment, he for animals, neither of them for the other. That left the child as their common moral center: the child with the books in alphabetical order and the image of his stabbed father in the middle of his home.

"So you wouldn't notice if he, say, had been coming in later than usual?"

"Not immediately, but I would probably have heard about it from Angelica or Tommaso."

"Who's Angelica?"

"Our babysitter—nanny, I suppose. She's there most days." Sveva Romagnolo allowed a note of bitterness to creep into her tone. "Or was. She seems to have been scared off. At any rate, she's vanished."

Blume glanced quickly at D'Amico. This could be significant.

"Vanished? The babysitter has vanished?"

"Well, no. Not vanished exactly. She phoned this morning, as a matter of fact," said Romagnolo. "She said she needed time off to recover from the shock. As if I don't—oh, never mind." She brushed invisible dust from her arm, and thus dismissed the useless Nanny Angelica from the conversation.

"And what age is Angelica?" Blume wasn't so sure he wanted the subject dropped so quickly.

"Oh, let me see . . . sixty-five, seventy. It's rather hard to tell with those fat southerners."

Nando broke his silence. "I am a southerner," he announced.

"Indeed?" said Romagnolo. Blume had rarely heard a word that conveyed less interest.

D'Amico crossed his arms and relapsed into silence.

Blume continued to ask her about new friends, changes to schedule, strange phone calls, and she continued to tell him that she had nothing to report.

"You were in Padua with your son."

"Yes."

"And the idea was to spend the weekend there?"

"Yes, but I got called back for an emergency vote to be held on Monday. Berlusconi is threatening to use a confidence motion—you read the papers."

Blume did not. He hated politics. "So you came back on Friday afternoon. Why not Saturday?"

"My son was getting bored. He's still too young."

"Arturo was not expecting you?"

"I made sure to phone ahead, tell him I was on my way back."

"At what time did you phone?"

"Half past ten from Padua station."

"OK," said Blume. "Now, this nanny person who looks after the house. When does she come?"

"Every other day."

"And she does all the cooking, cleaning . . ."

"Sometimes she cooks, but Arturo did his own cooking, too. She cleaned, looked after Tommaso."

"She did the washing? Made the beds, changed sheets, that sort of thing?"

"Yes. She did that sort of thing."

"Always?"

"Always."

Blume looked back over his notes, and started asking the same questions again. When he asked her again about Arturo's enemies, she said, "What? Weren't you listening before? I've already told you all I remember."

"Just in case you forgot someone."

"I'm not going to repeat myself. If you weren't listening, maybe your colleague was." She nodded at D'Amico, who bowed his head slightly lower.

Blume stood up. D'Amico did the same and, a moment later, so did Romagnolo.

"Frankly, the political aspects are outside my competence," said Blume. "All I can say is that I shall be vigilant and keep you completely informed."

Blume stuck out his hand, which she took very lightly and briefly. "I am sorry for your loss."

"Thank you."

She accompanied them back in silence through the spacious living room, empty of grieving relatives and friends.

16

WHEN THEY GOT downstairs, D'Amico opened the door and they walked out into a blare of cicadas. Blume looked at the cars parked on the road outside and asked D'Amico, "The Holy Ghost was not transported here by an official car, was he?"

"I hope not, because if he was, we're not the most observant policemen in the world. He can't have used a car from the carpool, either, or you'd have recognized it."

"You'd have recognized it, too," said Blume, pulling out his cell phone. "I think they've replaced maybe two vehicles since you left . . . Ferrucci?" he said into the phone. "Yes, it's me. I need you to get me the address of Di Tivoli, Taddeo—yes that's the one, the guy on TV . . . Hold on, I've got D'Amico here, he can write it down for me. Via Alcamo, six. Yeah, I know the street. Thanks."

D'Amico was looking at the address he had just written down. "Can't say I know this street."

"I only know it because it's near where I live," said Blume. "It's a short street. A dead end, if I remember right."

It occurred to Blume that in the three years D'Amico had been his junior partner, not once had he invited him back to the house. D'Amico was married, had two kids of indeterminate age.

They climbed into the car.

"So now we go to Di Tivoli?" asked D'Amico.

"He's the one who made the documentary with Clemente about the dog fighting," said Blume. "He seems like an obvious person to talk to. Unless you can think of something better."

"Maybe we should report back to the vicequestore first," said D'Amico.

"Sure. You do that. But first drop me off at Di Tivoli's."

"If I take you there, I may as well stay."

"So stay," said Blume, without much enthusiasm.

D'Amico drove all the way down Via Cristoforo Colombo with his brow furrowed as if he was trying to remember something. As they passed Via Appia Antica, his countenance cleared and he said, "I know who Di Tivoli is."

"I just said, he's the guy made the documentary—"

"No. Before that. I remember Di Tivoli got kicked off the air around 2001 because . . . I don't know, he was annoying or something."

Blume said, "Yeah. It's good the way there are no annoying people left on TV anymore. You sure he didn't get kicked off air because Berlusconi and his minions came to power?"

"No, he slapped a guest or something. It's probably on YouTube."

"I think I might remember," said Blume, who never watched television. "He was gay or something, wasn't he?"

"Who? The guest? I can't remember. Good reason for hitting him, though."

"I meant Di Tivoli," said Blume. "Maybe not gay, but a bit camp. Used to march around the studio trying to be outrageous."

"No," said D'Amico. "You're thinking of that curly-haired queen on Canale 5. The one who's an expert on everything. Di Tivoli is the one with the sexy girl co-host."

"That hardly narrows it down."

"Sexy girls with glasses," amended D'Amico. "Leftists."

"By leftist you mean they have brains?"

"Just glasses. Myopia, money, and attitude. But there was something else . . . This is it." D'Amico parked in front of a No Parking sign attached to automatic gates.

"He's got a garage," said Blume. "Jesus, I'd give my right arm to have one of those."

The main door to the building was open, and they went straight in, nodding curtly to a porter who almost challenged them. The man who answered the apartment door had ginger hair fading to gray, but a lot of it. An unkempt tuft fell over his forehead, and he kept pushing at it with the palm of his hand, as if checking it was still there. He was wearing a blue linen suit, such as only a slim person should ever wear, and it looked good on him. The frames of his glasses were white. He wore suede desert boots.

He was not the host Blume had been thinking of, but he was camp enough, thought Blume. It was probably a job requirement.

He did not invite them in, merely walked away leaving the door open.

Blume did not like the lifeless beige and grays, birch, pine, and cork in Di Tivoli's apartment. But it was no doubt a classy place in a glossy-magazine sort of way. Di Tivoli picked up a remote control, pressed a button, then shook his head and put it down. He picked up another, did the same, and Blume heard the soft whistle of an air conditioner start. A few seconds later, he felt cool air waft by his face. He could do with one of those almost as much as a garage.

"This heat is killing me," Di Tivoli said.

Blume looked around. Di Tivoli had brought the trappings of his trade into his home. A bank of high-tech and hi-fi equipment occupied two built-in shelves. A boom microphone stood on a stand. Behind it was an expensive but outmoded reel-to-reel recorder from the 1970s. A higher shelf held a wooden bust of a very ugly old man.

Blume sat on a sofa, put his bag down, unclipped the flap, unzipped the top, and pulled out a notebook. Di Tivoli perched on a matching armchair opposite.

"Nice place you've got here," said Blume.

Di Tivoli scowled.

"You know, we're practically neighbors. I live on Via La Spezia. Know it? On the corner of Via Orvieto, the one with the fish market?"

Di Tivoli continued to scowl.

D'Amico made himself comfortable on a sofa with square cushions speckled like a sparrow's eggs. He stretched his legs out and examined the fit of his socks over his tibia. It would be up to Blume to do the talking.

"Tell me, how well did you know Arturo Clemente?"

"Since university days. Off and on over thirty years," said Di Tivoli.

"Did you also know Sveva Romagnolo back then?"

"Yes. And Questore Gallone," said Di Tivoli.

"Vicequestore Aggiunto," corrected Blume.

"The minor gradations of rank in the police are not of great interest to me. All I know is that he's your superior."

"He most certainly is," said Blume. "So you've always known Clemente?"

"No, we fell out of touch until this dog-fighting campaign."

"Did Clemente come to you with the idea for a documentary?"

"Actually, it was Sveva's idea. To help his campaign and my career," said Di Tivoli. "Part of being a journalist in Italy is you go in and out of favor. I had been out for a while since, well, it was a famous moment on TV when I slapped that hick from the Northern League. I'm sure you've both seen it."

"No," said Blume. "I don't watch TV."

"It's on YouTube now. Millions of hits," said Di Tivoli.

"Told you," said D'Amico, and nodded, pleased with himself.

Blume shook his head. "Don't visit YouTube either."

"Well, perhaps you should learn to," said Di Tivoli. "Anyhow, this documentary was a comeback. I'd secured a commitment from the director of RAI 2, who's a friend of Sveva. The idea was to make a documentary with a thesis everyone agreed with, regardless of political persuasion."

"Everyone loves a dog," said Blume. "Except me, perhaps."

"I can't stand the filthy creatures, either, but, yes, that was the idea. Hard-hitting, tough scenes, good investigative journalism, scandalous discoveries, but no political party feels alienated. Do you follow politics?"

"No," said Blume.

"You don't seem to have many interests, Inspector."

"Commissioner," said Blume.

"Commissioner, of course. You were quite right to correct me," said Di Tivoli.

"Titles are important."

"Accuracy is important," said Blume. "Words are important."

"Commissioner, I could not agree more," said Di Tivoli. "Which is why I want you to look at that box over there."

Blume looked at what he had taken to be an ordinary stereo. He now saw it was a small black computer box with the letters *XPC* printed on it, sitting next to a wide flatscreen TV.

D'Amico looked even more uncomfortable, and half made to rise, as if to switch the machine off, but Blume caught his eye and shook his head. It was probably a bluff. Surely the guy didn't have microphones planted around the room. Then he looked again and realized that the microphones were not hidden. A great big boom mike was standing there right in front of them. He had assumed it was a fashionable retro prop, like the 1970s reel-to-reel next to it. Then he remembered how Di Tivoli had picked up a remote control, then put it down again before turning on the air conditioning with a second one.

"That's fine, Di Tivoli," said Blume, opening his pad and taking out a pen. "Nothing bad has been said by anyone here. I am assuming that what I say now is going on to a tape?"

"A hard disk, Inspector. Sorry—Commissioner. You're not very knowledgeable about these things, are you?"

Blume looked across at the black box, which winked an orange light in his direction. "Let's move on," said Blume. He stood up and began walking around. He went over to the bookcase where the machine with the orange light was humming. On the shelf above was the shining old wooden bust of the bald middle-aged man that he had noticed as he came in.

"Who's this, Buddha on a bad day?" Blume reached out his hand and lifted the head from the shelf. The lips were carved into a snarl, the nose was large and bent. A missing section from the top of the forehead added to the belligerent effect. It was heavier than he had expected, and he had to grab hold of it with his other hand.

"Leave that alone!" Di Tivoli showed surprising speed in getting up and across the room. "No one touches that."

"OK, OK," said Blume. Di Tivoli stroked the top of the bald wooden head before returning it reverentially to its shelf, then going back to his seat. Blume wondered if he talked to it.

"It's very old," said Di Tivoli.

"A museum piece?"

"Etruscan. From Veio. More than two thousand years old."

"And why isn't it in a museum?" asked Blume.

"Because it's ours. Legally. The question was settled a long time ago."

"Ours? Yours and whose?"

"Ours. My family's. My great-grandfather, who was from Veio, bought it in London in 1902 and brought it back to where it belongs."

"This isn't Veio," said D'Amico from the sofa.

Blume leaned against the shelves, inches from the black box with the orange light.

"Don't even think of touching the computer," said Di Tivoli.

"I wouldn't dream of it," said Blume, then leaned down and pressed the off switch.

17

For a moment, it seemed that neither Di Tivoli nor D'Amico had quite realized what Blume had done.

Di Tivoli leaped up quickly and banged his leg against the corner of the Indian teak coffee table in the middle of the room, causing a slight tingling from the silverware in the dresser on the far side of the room.

The sudden flash of fear Blume saw in Di Tivoli's face had already resolved itself into pious outrage once he realized Blume was not about to attack him physically. Then, he pulled out a thin black phone, and the look of outrage was slowly replaced by a smirk. Blume heard his name mentioned twice.

D'Amico meanwhile pulled out an even thinner phone and went to stand by the front door, murmuring something. Blume stood there in the middle of the room between them, watching one, then the other.

Moments later, Di Tivoli was back, a swagger in his step. He stood in the middle of the room, adjusted the gray curls on his head, and smiled at Blume.

"Look at the computer, Inspector."

Blume looked. The orange light was still winking away.

"You need to hold the button for five seconds before it shuts down."

"You mean like this?" But before Blume could make a second attempt, his cell phone rang.

"Here we go," said Di Tivoli.

Blume fished it out of his pocket. "Yes?"

It was Gallone. He had just received a call from the Questura informing him that a certain Commissioner Blume, in the company of Commissioner D'Amico, was attempting to intimidate Taddeo Di Tivoli. He hoped for Blume's sake this was not right.

"We're not intimidating him, sir," said Blume.

"You will leave that house now. Both of you. You will then report directly to my office, Blume. Understood?"

"Yes, sir." Blume looked at Di Tivoli's smug face, and felt the muscles of his arm tighten. He imagined smashing something heavy into Di Tivoli's womanly lips, the bright flash of joy, and the gray ashes of his career afterward.

"Nando, we're leaving," said Blume.

D'Amico slipped his phone into his jacket, and said, "I think we'll stay a little longer."

"I don't think you realize how high I can reach if I have to," said Di Tivoli.

"I know you move in exalted circles," said D'Amico. "It's fun up there, I imagine."

"Yes, it is," said Di Tivoli.

"Lots of swimming pool parties in Sardinia, Ischia, Elba, Portofino, lots of girls, lines of coke. Oh, and boys."

"I don't know what you're talking about," said Di Tivoli.

Blume loved hearing that phrase. People who suddenly declared they no longer understood the words being spoken to them were people who had been cornered.

D'Amico had discovered a mirror near the door and groomed himself a little before returning to the living room. "It's all part of the privileges you enjoy," he said. "The thing with boys, though. That's more awkward."

Di Tivoli whitened and sat down. "No charges have been made against me."

"I know," said D'Amico soothingly. "It's just one of those silly-season stories. So far, you have been interviewed merely as a person informed of the facts. Am I right? Public Prosecutor Bernard Woodruff is conducting the inquiry. Another awkward bastard with a foreign name, like Blume here. Always a bit harder to know exactly where they're coming from, these half-foreign ones."

"This is still being recorded," said Di Tivoli.

"I'd erase it, if I were you," said D'Amico. "Here, let me give you a sneak preview of something even you might not know about. I hear the villa owned by that Sicilian reporter, Nicotra, is going to be sequestered by the Finance Police acting under the direction of the DIA. Nicotra has the odor of Mafia about him. Now you and Nicotra, apparently . . ."

"All right, all right, that's enough," said Di Tivoli.

D'Amico looked over at Blume and said, "I knew I'd heard this idiot's name recently for some reason."

"So you know stuff," said Di Tivoli. "But it's not as if you can do anything about it."

"You're probably right that I can't make it go away, nor would I want to; but I think I could make it worse. Look, all we need is a nice, short, friendly interview, then we're out of here. How about a little bit of mutual understanding? No more filing complaints about my colleague, that sort of thing."

Di Tivoli nodded.

Blume clapped his hands together. "Excellent. Now, where were we? Sex—boys? *Che combinazione.* That reminds me, do know who your friend Clemente was sleeping with?"

Di Tivoli tapped the hollow of his cheek with his thumb, still weighing up his options. Finally he said, "I know he had another woman. She came with him to my country villa in Amatrice. Her name was Manuela. She was very plain. Ugly, even. Aging, vulgar-looking, though surprisingly educated in speech. But I don't know who she was. Why, was she somebody important?"

"Well, yes. She's daughter of Rome's second biggest criminal. It'll be fun mixing this fact up with Woodruff's investigation."

"I didn't know anything about that!"

"We believe you. Don't we, Nando?" D'Amico nodded solemnly. "It's the fickle public you need to worry about. The Italians love a good conspiracy theory. Now I want to talk to you about the dog meets you saw."

Around a month before the documentary filming began, Di Tivoli could not say exactly when, Arturo Clemente and he had gone down to the very end of the Via della Magliana, beyond the warehouses selling building materials and bathroom fittings to where the road, after two miles of potholes and crumbling embankments, gives up pretending to be fit for ordinary cars. Out to the place where all the bushes had strips of plastic shopping bags clinging to them, but even further than that, past the gypsy encampments nestled under the bridges carrying the beltway that marked the end of the city boundaries.

"Where out there?"

"To a field, about a mile and a half beyond the beltway. Off the Via della Magliana, to the north. There's a fence with two, no three, strands of barbed wire. Clemente stopped at the corner, pulled up the last post, walked into the field with it, making a gap, drove in, got out, closed it again. At the far end of the field were a few rotting sheds, a row of things that look like chicken coops, except turns out they're for dogs, and off to the right, a bit uphill, a warehouse or distribution shed with tarmac and parking."

"Wait, that doesn't make sense," said Blume. "You cross an open field to get to a distribution warehouse?"

"Yes, a warehouse with tarmac parking and no connecting roads. Totally invisible to the authorities. Great country we live in, isn't it?"

"Would you be able to find this place again?" asked Blume.

"Yes, I should think so."

"The cars in the parking lot, how many?"

"I'd say about thirty."

"What sort of cars?"

"Almost all of them SUVs and Jeeps, but I remember seeing one or two really old white Fiat Unos."

"The vehicles, they were clean or dirty?"

"They were dirty. Everything was dirty," Di Tivoli shuddered at the memory. "It had been raining a few days before."

"So what happened there?"

"Clemente parked the car, we went in."

"You went in, just like that?"

"We were undercover, obviously. What I mean by that is we weren't there as an activist and a reporter."

"OK, so these guys have never seen you on TV, or YouTube. I can believe that, but the people there must have known Clemente if he had been busting their balls."

"He was disguised."

Blume glanced sharply at Di Tivoli, but the man was apparently being serious.

"Disguised as what?"

"Not as anything in particular. He had on this little blond mustache; he'd dyed his hair, and was wearing a long leather coat, a Roma AC cap, and hide ankle boots. The outfit almost did his head in."

"He supports Lazio?"

"Not the soccer cap—the hide boots and the leather coat. He wouldn't even wear leather shoes in real life. Never ate an egg. He was deadly earnest."

"Never ate an egg?"

"No. He had no limits. Or too many, depends how you look at it."

"Going back to the meet, no one checked you two out?"

"It's not as if anyone was really that bothered. People would look at you a bit, but no one was checking. People milling about and dogs snarling and . . . Jesus." Di Tivoli shook his head.

"What?" Blume leaned forward.

"The smell. The smell of that place is something I'll never forget."

"What was the smell?"

"Mud, blood, alcohol, cigarette smoke, but most of all dogs, dog shit and fear."

"Sounds heavy."

"You've no idea."

Blume said, "The two of you just walked into this den of horrors?"

"There was a thug of some sort at the door, but I don't know if he was supposed to be a bouncer. I thought he might try to stop us, but he didn't."

"How many fights did you watch?"

"Two, but I wasn't really watching them, I was looking at the locale, working out the lighting, and figuring where to put cameras for when we filmed the raid."

"Did you take notes about the place, the events?"

"Nothing that will be of any use."

"Let me decide," said Blume. "Do you have them here?"

Di Tivoli left the room and came back minutes later with two file folders. He handed them to Blume who glanced inside. Each contained a few typewritten sheets.

"These are typed," said Blume.

"I can certainly see why you became a detective."

"Don't start, lover boy. You typed them up afterwards—from memory?" He laid them aside. He doubted they, or Di Tivoli himself, were going to be of much value.

★ ★ ★

As they walked out of the apartment building into the searing heat, Blume gave D'Amico a pat on the back.

"Glad I came with you now, aren't you?" said D'Amico. "You wouldn't believe the compromising shit we've got on people in the Ministry. The thing is, a lot of the people we got shit on are also the people who run the Ministry."

"I've got to admit it, Nando. Sometimes you have your uses."

18

D'AMICO LEFT HIM at headquarters and went on to the Ministry. On his way to his own office, Blume knocked on Gallone's door.

"In! Ah, it's you, Commissioner. I am very disappointed, and very angry too, I don't mind saying."

"I think there have been a few misunderstandings, sir," said Blume. "The investigating magistrate instructed me to go straight to Sveva Romagnolo. I'm going to write up the report now and deliver it to him. I can't ignore a specific instruction from a prosecutor."

"You could have informed me," was all Gallone said. Blume waited for more, but there seemed to be no more talk about defending the privacy of the grieving widow, and Blume got the feeling Gallone was not keen to recall the image of himself being unceremoniously bundled out of Sveva's apartment.

"And I think if you call Di Tivoli, you'll find he has no complaints to make of us. I am going to write up the report on that interview, too. Will you sign it off before I forward it to the prosecutor?"

Gallone seemed to have lost interest in the incident, too. Responsibility weighed heavily upon him. Blume doubted he had ever done so much paperwork in his life. And the widow was not even thankful.

"Blume, I am very busy. I have to write up some reports myself. I got the autopsy report, and now I discover that Romagnolo had appointed her own medical examiner to attend the autopsy. She did this without informing me."

"Anything interesting in the autopsy?"

"What? No. No. Confirmed cause of death was multiple stab wounds. Stomach contents—breakfast. Clemente had eaten high-fiber spelt. Which is basically cardboard, if you ask me. And an apple. Brown rice the night before. You'll get a copy. Oh, and we're going after Alleva. Making a move tonight—or maybe tomorrow morning, at this rate. Don't miss the next meeting, Commissioner."

"I won't. What about the house-to-house calls?"

"Nothing. Nothing at all. And still I have to write a detailed report on all this nothingness," said Gallone.

Blume's tiny office was preceded by a larger room that Paoloni, Zambotto, and Ferrucci shared, though only Ferrucci was ever to be found there. It served as a sort of antechamber to his office and even lent it a slight air of authority. Right now, it contained Ferrucci, who was sitting at his desk, staring at the computer screen.

Blume went into his office and phoned the investigating magistrate.

"I said you told me to visit Sveva Romagnolo. You did, didn't you?"

"Yes, that's fine," said Principe. "Anything?"

"I would say she is sufficiently grief-stricken, but you can't always judge these things. Who am I to say how sad a person should be?"

"Or show themselves to be," said Principe. "I've issued a detention warrant on Alleva."

"Yes. So I heard. Gallone's supposed to be coordinating, so you'll be lucky if it's executed this side of Christmas. The poor man has never seen so many forms."

"Damn. I better make sure he manages to organize an arrest by tomorrow at least," said Principe. "I'll phone him now."

Blume hung up and called in Ferrucci.

"Have you still got that list of names of the people the Carabinieri detained after the dog fight?"

"Yes. Zambotto and Paoloni are checking them out now."

Blume looked at Ferrucci's hopelessly frank face. The day would come when even Ferrucci would be tough enough to talk to the bad guys, but not for a long time.

"They are looking into the bad guys?"

"Yes. Working backwards: from the worst offenders to the least."

"All the way back up to Alleva and his helper, what's his name?"

"Massoni. Some of these guys have even worse records," said Ferrucci.

"I've been thinking, Marco: maybe we have been doing this the wrong way around."

"Doing what the wrong way around?"

"The list."

"You mean going from the most to the least likely is the wrong way to do it?"

"Yes," said Blume. "That's exactly what I mean."

"But . . ."

Blume waited. He wanted to see if he had been right about the young man's intelligence. For a moment he doubted it. Ferrucci seemed to stare stupidly at the window, but then his eyes darted sideways as if he had glimpsed a quick-moving animal on the rooftops outside.

"I get it," he said.

"Let's hear it, then."

"OK. Your theory is that the victim was killed in a random or semi-random attack."

"Let's say semi-random," said Blume.

"Now we have a list of names, and the first ones we are looking at are those who have killed before, those who are connected, have previous convictions, and so on. But that would make the killing less random, and more organized."

Blume nodded encouragement. He was pleased with his protégé.

"So," continued Ferrucci, "when the Carabinieri carried out the raid on the warehouse, they detained only three people with no criminal records. Three people who are not crime professionals."

"The ones we were planning to question last. Where are they?"

Ferrucci ducked into his office and was back with a sheet. "These three here." He quickly circled three names with a pen.

"When's the next meeting of the investigative team?" asked Blume.

"At seven this evening. The Holy Ghost wants to know who's doing overtime after eight."

Ferrucci, trying to sound nonchalant as he used Gallone's nickname for the first time. But he'd just earned himself the right.

"So we've got about one hour. How about we check out these three. Right now. You pick one name, I'll pick another."

"And the third?"

"We've got one hour. Neither of us has time to interview more than one person. I'll get the third after the meeting, or maybe tomorrow. Go on, pick a name."

Ferrucci pointed at the first of the three names. "Gianfranco Canghiari. Hairdresser, salon near Parioli, house in Trullo." He glanced at his watch. "He should still be at work. Should I go now?"

"Yes."

"What do I ask him?"

"I don't know. Ask him why he likes seeing animals tear each other apart, whether he declares all his earnings, whether he has a clear conscience about how he uses the computer—anything. Hassle him a bit. Get a feel for what sort of a person he is."

Blume indicated the next name on the list, Dandini, a car salesman. "I'll talk to this guy, see who he is. Then one of us will check out the third guy tomorrow morning, or whenever. What's his name?"

"Angelo Pernazzo. Perl scripting programmer."

"I don't even know what that is," said Blume.

Dandini turned out to be a man with black curly hair who looked like he was on the verge of bursting into a Puccini solo. Despite himself, Blume liked him almost immediately. He sold fat, ecologically criminal cars from a lot situated off the beltway next to Casale Lumbroso, and was just finishing off a sales pitch to a couple interested in a Volkswagen Touareg when Blume arrived. Blume allowed him to see them off, then he and Dandini went into a prefabricated hut, where Dandini loosened a wide yellow necktie and placed his bulk in front of a roaring air conditioner. He put his hand in his jacket, pulled out what looked like a sheet from a child's bed, and dabbed his forehead with it.

"I heard thunder earlier. Rain would be nice, but then we have to wash all the cars, especially if it's got sand in it."

Dandini seemed genuinely pleased to meet Blume. Even when Blume pulled out his police identification Dandini continued to beam at him, and offered Blume a business card, as if completing a fair trade.

According to Dandini, being caught up in a swoop by the Carabinieri was quite the best thing that had ever happened to him.

He paused, a big expectant smile on his face as he waited for Blume to pick up the cue.

Blume obligingly expressed wonderment at the paradox.

Because—here Dandini clenched his fist—it brought it home to him that he had a serious gambling problem. He opened the top drawer, pulled out a white cardboard box, opened it, and offered Blume a puff pastry.

Blume declined. Dandini helped himself to one. The very next day, he and his wife sought help. They found a place on the Via Casaletto.

Some dry flakes of pastry and a cloud of sugar escaped his mouth, and he stopped talking for a bit until he had things under control.

The people there were kind to him about his problem, but a bit harsh with his wife, who they said needed to change her superficial attitude. He didn't get that bit, but they were doing much better. He hadn't gambled in months. He had totally given up drinking, too, except on weekends and after a sale.

He thanked Blume for the interest shown by the police in these things. If it were up to him, there would be no more poker machines or lottery scratch cards either.

Blume wanted to know why he went to a dog fight. Did he not know it was cruel and inhumane and illegal?

"The odds," said Dandini, shaking his large head slowly. "They had such great odds."

Dandini said he had been in the office all day on Friday.

"Can anyone else confirm that?"

"Giovanni."

"Who's he?"

"My junior business partner. He's gone to a customer's to get some papers signed. He'll probably go straight home after."

"OK, maybe I'll talk to him. Anyone else?"

"I made three sales yesterday. Well, I made one sale and signed the contracts of sale on two others. Maria, our secretary, was there. She draws up the ownership papers. She goes home at four."

Blume took her number down. "When did you make the sales?"

"All morning. It takes a while, you know. The paperwork, showing them the car, putting on the license plate, waving them away. I was doing that from nine until lunchtime, then after lunch I made the third sale. It was a good day."

"And you have the names of these customers. They can say you were here?"

"I hadn't thought of that. Sure." He pulled open a lower drawer and pulled out two folders. "These are the names, if you need them."

A group of moneyed youngsters appeared in the forecourt, and Dandini looked at Blume longingly for permission to leave. Blume had not even begun to ask questions, but Dandini had solid alibis. In any case, he knew Dandini was not the man he was looking for.

19

BLUME MADE IT back to the station just in time for the meeting. He went to his office. Someone, probably Ferrucci, had left two file folders tied with ribbon on his desk. He opened them, saw that they were profiles of Alleva and his henchman, Gaetano Massoni. He dropped them into his bag and went up to the conference room.

The furniture inside was minimal: no telephones, nor even telephone jacks in the walls. A projection screen, usually left open, was set against the wall flanking the door. To minimize the opportunities for the installation of permanent bugging devices, all the audiovisual equipment, including an extremely expensive projector, was set on a wire-framed cart that could be wheeled out of the room when not in use. It was a room designed for deniability.

He sat down, opened his bag, and read the files.

Renato Alleva, born 1966, in Genoa. This was already odd. The Roman underworld, like Rome itself, was provincial. Alleva was an outsider, and operated on sufferance. Alleva's early career seemed to be that of a thwarted confidence trickster. Arrested in 1982, '86, '88, '91, and '95 for impersonating an insurance salesman, area manager for a supermarket, charity worker, business investor, and realtor, he was unmasked each time by his intended victims, who had called the police. As he never actually managed to take any money off anyone, the sentencing was light. In 1995, Alleva spent two months in the hospital with multiple fractures inflicted, it seemed, by relations of the old woman to whom he had tried to sell a temporarily unoccupied apartment on the Via Marco Sala. He spent the next eight months in Marassi prison. Blume looked at the mug shots of Alleva's flat face with its cubic nose and pig eyes and wondered how its owner came to think he should try a career based on winning trust. But

Alleva had learned from his mistakes. Going from confidence trickster to dogman had been a smart move.

Blume memorized Alleva's charge sheet like he used to learn poems in school. He would remember it for as long as he needed to, then forget it. Sometimes faces, their crimes, and, most often, their victims, got stuck in his mind's eye, along with fragments of school poetry.

> *Lontano, lontano*
> *Come un cieco*
> *M'hanno portato per mano.*

As for Massoni, the criminal record dated back to 1980, when Massoni was thirteen. The details of the charges brought against him in the years 1980 to 1985 were absent, "pursuant to the terms of Article 15 DPR 448/88" relating to the protection of juveniles. The comment was marked with an asterisk, which, Blume saw, referred to a footnote to the effect that Article 52 of Law 313/02 had since repealed this provision. But not before Massoni's youthful exploits, whatever they were, had been deleted.

Massoni didn't let his eighteenth birthday slow him down. He had started out with arrests for criminal damage to a vehicle, resisting arrest, dangerous driving, and assault, for which he received noncustodial sentences and a suspension of his driver's license. He was back eight months later after being caught driving, and the suspension on his license was extended. From 1990, Massoni seemed to be specializing in assault. He was arrested for inflicting bodily harm on would-be clients of a nightclub where he worked for a while as a bouncer, but the victims did not press charges. In 1991, he was arrested and charged with beating up a thirty-five-year-old woman called Elena, with whom he had been living. He got seven months for this, his first taste of jail. Released after three months, he was picked up again for another assault, this time on a twenty-year-old girl and her five-year-old son, but the charges were dropped. He was back in Rebbibia in 1993–94 after slashing the face of a Juventus supporter. He was also charged with being part of a gang of Roma Ultras who hurled a Vespa scooter from the South Curve stand of the Olympic Stadium onto rival supporters below. In 1995, he and four others were acquitted for insufficient proof on charges of a racist attack on a certain Francis Mi-anzoukouto, a technician for Radio Vatican, who lost the use of his left hand after being savaged by dogs on his way home from work.

In 1998, Massoni's record became slightly more interesting, with arrests for tax evasion, illegal gambling, and extortion. No charges for maltreat-ment of animals were made against him until 2002, but that, Blume fig-ured, had more to do with the absence of specific legislation until then. It looked as if Massoni's interest in animals dated to around 1997–98.

He was about to start reading the sheets he had taken from Di Tivoli when Ferrucci walked in and sat down quickly at the far end of the desks, where Blume had put himself at the last meeting.

"Well?" demanded Blume. "How did it go?"

"Fine," said Ferrucci. "I'm not sure what you wanted me to find out, but I don't think this guy had anything to do with it."

A pale orange beam of light lit up the area where Ferrucci had chosen to sit. Blume looked out the window and saw the sky directly above was whitening, while farther away it darkened. He turned his attention back to Ferrucci, who looked different somehow. It wasn't just the strange light of the coming storm.

"Am I imagining it, or have you just had your hair cut?"

Ferrucci touched his hair, hesitated as if considering a denial. His short-cropped fair hair looked yellow.

"Yes."

"Yes I am imagining it? Or yes you've just had your hair cut by a person you were sent out to interview on suspicion of murder?"

"You never said he was a suspect."

"Did you pay him for the haircut?"

"He would not talk to me otherwise."

"You let him shave you, too?" Blume heard the sound of voices com-ing up the corridor. If he continued this line of questioning he'd end up humiliating Ferrucci. "OK, forget that. What was your impression?"

"I don't think he makes a good suspect," said Ferrucci. "I'm not sure, though."

"What makes you think that?"

"Fat," said Ferrucci just as Paoloni and Zambotto walked in. "Fat, soft, short arms, perfumed . . ."

"You talking about your boyfriend?" asked Paoloni, taking a seat near but not next to Ferrucci.

Zambotto looked at Ferrucci and said, "You got a haircut since I last saw you. Me, I was working."

"Chatty, fussy, busy, knows everyone," continued Ferrucci. "Gay, I think."

"You *are* talking about your boyfriend," said Paoloni.

Blume said, "Shut up, Beppe." To Ferrucci he said, "Like gays don't kill?"

"He says he was in his salon all morning. Showed me an appointment book, invited me to call up any of the names there. He's got six alibis for the morning, five for the afternoon. Also, there's a bar opposite. The bar tender brings in orders for the customers. He says he was in and out at least four times on Friday."

"OK. Good work."

"Also I asked in a few other stores. The ones who remembered, remembered him there."

D'Amico arrived next. In a concession to the fact that it was Saturday night, he was dressed in a combination of Lacoste and Zegna instead of the suit he had on earlier. He must have a wardrobe in his office, thought Blume.

D'Amico came and sat next to Blume, as if they were still partners. Finally, Gallone marched in. He stared at Blume seated at the top of the room and seemed about to say something, but finally settled to sit off-center and began the meeting.

Blume glanced through the few pages he had taken from Di Tivoli. For a journalist, the man wasn't much of a speller. There was not much in the notes, either. Blume circled the names he found: Alleva was there, along with Clemente and several other names and numbers, which seemed mostly to do with production fees. Blume noted down these names, too. He recognized some of them as being "front-line" RAI reporters. Real reporters. Not like Di Tivoli. But the notes were not going to help much. There was nothing there.

"Have you quite finished your reading, Commissioner Blume?"

Blume put the papers carefully back into his bag, zipped the compartment closed, fastened the closure in the flap, put the bag on the floor, and then said, "Yes, sir."

With each of Blume's exasperatingly slow movements, Gallone had jutted his chin a little further, so that now his neck tendons looked ready to snap.

"We are here to map out a plan for Alleva's capture," said Gallone. "I demand your undivided attention."

"You have it, sir."

"We have a detention order from Principe, and about time, too. The press knows almost everything now, and we have reached twenty-four hours since we got the alert. Any delay and it'll look like incompetence. We get Alleva into custody now. Also, it's what the family expects."

"The family?" asked Blume.

"The widow, Sveva Romagnolo."

"Right."

"Well," said Gallone, "there's nothing in the autopsy that we did not already know. Death by a single-edged knife partly serrated at the end, almost certainly an assault knife. No hesitation wounds. The killer went straight to it. He was either skilled or got lucky."

"What about other evidence?" asked Paoloni.

"So far, we have nothing from the fingerprints. No match of any sort," said Gallone. "They started with the ones in the bathroom and one on a piece of masking tape on the cardboard box. The DNA is going to take longer. The crime scene manager's report is almost ready. Clemente was murdered where he was found. Not much else to it."

"Ok," said Blume. "But all the evidence continues to point in the same direction, which is not toward Alleva."

"Commissioner, you wasted an entire afternoon importuning the widow and a media personality. You disobeyed a direct order to report to me. Let's not make it any worse now."

"No, indeed," said Blume.

"Back to Alleva," began Gallone. "We can get backup if we need it. I want him in custody tonight."

"Not a good idea, Questore," said Paoloni.

Everyone turned round to look at him.

"I don't remember asking for an opinion on this," said Gallone.

Paoloni had his arms folded and head tilted back as if he was talking to someone hovering just above his head.

"It is going to be hard to get to him tonight. I heard that he was last seen, on his own—in the sense of without Massoni—in the company of some of Innocenzi's *scagnozzi*. It is therefore possible that we will never see him again. But the point is, he is not on his own. We don't have the manpower to go in and lift him. Even if we did, it could be complicated."

"I can order the manpower," said Gallone.

"We don't want to go in there," said Paoloni. "Everyone in this room understands that." He lowered his head and looked at Gallone. "You understand it, too, sir. We can't just walk in and pick him up if there is a chance of others intervening, especially if they are Innocenzi's crew. It could spiral. All deals would be off. We'd lose months, years of intelligence and contacts. Also, these people know a lot of secrets and pull a lot of strings. These things need to be negotiated. I don't think we really want this general aggravation in the Magliana area. All we want is Alleva. Let's wait till we can get just him."

Blume was surprised to see Gallone take all this backtalk. He even seemed to be listening.

"OK. How do we get Alleva, then?" he asked.

"We get him tomorrow morning when he's visiting his mother's," said Paoloni. "He always visits his mother on a Sunday. Brings her pastries. Sunday's a quiet day."

"It's also an overtime day," said Gallone. "So where does the mother live?"

"Testaccio area. He goes there at around ten. We can follow him from his house or wait for him at his mother's."

"We could do both," said Gallone. "Just to be sure."

Gallone, getting back into his old habits, assigned Paoloni the task of setting up the stakeout for the following morning. This was not what Paoloni did best, but Blume wasn't going to waste his breath.

As the meeting was breaking up, Ferrucci suddenly announced, "I've got a DVD of Di Tivoli's documentary for RAI. I forgot to say. I picked it up at Viale Mazzini on my way back."

Blume looked over. Ferrucci held a DVD in his hand. The RAI butterfly–talking heads symbol was printed on the cover.

"What time is it?"

"Seven thirty," said Ferrucci.

"OK, let's watch it," he said.

"Not everyone, Commissioner. That's hardly necessary or efficient," said Gallone. "I suggest you pick one of your men to watch it with you."

Blume massaged his temples. "I wasn't going to—never mind."

"I'll watch it with you," said Ferrucci.

"I'll get the popcorn," said Zambotto.

Paoloni left the room and returned wheeling the wire rack with the DVD player and TV on it. Ferrucci put in the disc, turned on the TV, and sat down next to Blume. Zambotto and Paoloni had gone.

The documentary was pretty much as Ferrucci had said. Plenty of midrange shots of Di Tivoli himself in profile, his chin pointed slightly upward as if he were gazing ahead into an uncertain future.

The dog fights were filmed with a hidden camera, and there was a lot of wobble and confusion and sometimes too much darkness for it to be clear what was going on. The sound editors had overdubbed some of the fights with a frantic dance track.

Go-go-go-go-go-go-go-go-go-go-go-go-go-go! went the track, and Blume leaned forward with enthusiasm. Two pitbulls circled, then tore into each other, head to head, and the track burst into a manically repetitive refrain.

Blume found himself marking out the beat with his feet. He felt like punching the air and saying, "Fuck yeah!" Now that's what dogs are for.

Later, to make up for it, the sound editors spliced in a few shots of bloodied, staggering, and dying dogs, and played Fauré's *Requiem*.

Clemente was interviewed. He appeared sitting in the office Blume had been in early that morning. He used a lot of statistics, possibly to keep calm, because when he started talking about the way dogs were trained, he seemed to be struggling to stay in his seat. He seemed like an earnest type, dressed too young for his age. He did not resemble the corpse Blume had seen, but live people never looked like their dead selves.

The Carabinieri raid was well filmed. The reporters had set up a long-range camera at the end of the field that could pan across the whole scene as the Jeeps came roaring up to the warehouse. A large skinhead bouncer seemed about to put up some resistance as the Carabinieri stormed the door he was standing beside, but knelt down with his hands behind his head when a shotgun was pointed at him.

"Stop the tape," said Blume.

"It's a DVD," said Ferrucci, but stopped it.

"Can you go back a bit to that guy kneeling?"

It took Ferrucci a few attempts to get a picture frame that had some readable detail in it, and even then it was hard to make out faces.

"That there must be Massoni, Alleva's enforcer," said Blume, pulling out a file folder from his bag. "You leave these folders on my desk?"

Ferrucci nodded.

Blume opened the profile of Massoni. There were two sets of police pictures. One, in color, from five years before, the other in black-and-white from eight years ago. He chose the black-and-white one.

"They should never have started using color," he said, holding the photo in front of him, then comparing it to the picture on the screen. "It overwhelms all the essential details." He handed the photo to Ferrucci, "What do you think, is it him?"

Ferrucci looked hard at the photo, then at the screen, and said, "I have no idea."

"Yeah, it's impossible, isn't it? And this is with real cameras, not your usual CCTV." Blume studied the screen image carefully. "Let's just say that this could be the same person. Right, let's get back to the film."

They had sent in two cameramen with the Carabinieri, as well as an extremely righteous Di Tivoli, who came running up to the people as they were manhandled by the Carabinieri, and hurled questions at them. They hurled back abuse that was bleeped out. Worst of all, their faces were pixelated.

"I didn't think to ask for the master tape or whatever it is," said Ferrucci apologetically.

"Doesn't matter. We've got the names of the people, anyhow. We can gaze at their faces anytime we want."

More Carabinieri in white overalls were shown bending over mutilated animals, trying to gain control of an enraged taupe beast using two control poles with restraining loops.

"That's a Tosa Inu," said Ferrucci.

"Ugly beast," said Blume, watching the slavering black mouth trying to snap the restraining pole.

"No, they're nice dogs, really," said Ferrucci. "We need to go and rescue them. Or send someone there. I'll deal with it, if you want."

Blume glanced over to see if Ferrucci was trying to be funny, but he seemed to be intent on the scene in front of them.

A sudden whoosh of wet air slammed open a window, and Ferrucci paused the documentary again as Blume went over to close it. As he arrived at the window, a flash of white lightning seemed to envelop the whole building, and left him with a taste of aluminum in his throat. The thunderclap that followed shook the building, and then the rain came crashing down. Ferrucci joined him at the window. There was no point in trying to watch the DVD as long as the storm was directly overhead.

Looking ahead to his date, Blume began to worry that Kristin wouldn't turn up in this weather. But after a few minutes, the storm moved away, toward the Castelli Romani. The lightning flashes now had a yellowish tinge, and the thunder rolled as well as crashed.

Now the screen showed Di Tivoli back in the studio. He talked a bit about the organizer being known to the authorities, but did not mention Alleva by name or show any picture.

The reporters were waiting for some of the detainees as they came out of the Carabinieri station to which they had been taken. More obscenities, but three did agree to be interviewed. Again, their features were obscured, though not their voices. One, who sounded drunk, defended dog fighting as the same as greyhound racing. Another was defiant and spoke of the free market and the right to free speech. A younger voice that seemed to come from a throat filled with mucus drew historical parallels with bear-baiting, then laughed and said sure, when the reporter asked him if he thought bear-baiting could be defended. Cut to Di Tivoli, trembling with barely suppressed rage, pretending he had just heard the interviews at the same time as the viewer. Di Tivoli then summed it up with hints of political complicity and the need for further acts of courage by the media. Clemente had got about thirty seconds.

Blume wondered if he had time to interview the third name on the list, Pernazzo, before his meeting with Kristin. Probably not. He should not have tried to get a date in the middle of an investigation.

"Someone had to watch it, I suppose," he told Ferrucci. "I'm going to interview that third person on the list, Angelo Pernazzo."

Ferrucci ejected the disc without replying. His jaw seemed to be quivering, but whether it was a trick of the thunderstorm light, Blume could not tell.

20

A T THIS TIME of the evening on a Saturday, Via di Bravetta was clogged with cars full of people from Corviale determined to celebrate Saturday night anywhere that was not Corviale. The house in front of him was done in yellow stucco that looked like dried vomit, but behind him a stretch of undeveloped fields still glittering from the rain an hour before rolled down to the Portuense area and gave the illusion of grassy slopes stretching all the way to the mountains behind. Blume pressed the intercom button next to the name Pernazzo.

"Pernazzo?"

"Yes?"

"Angelo Pernazzo?"

"Yes. What do you want?"

"Police."

The pause that followed was long enough to make Blume press the intercom button again.

"I'm still here, fuck it," said the voice.

"Did you hear me? I said police."

"OK."

The buzzer sounded, and the lock to the front door clicked open. Blume held it open with his foot and pressed the buzzer for a third time.

"What!"

"Which floor?"

"Third."

"OK. On my way."

Blume took the elevator and stepped out onto a narrow landing with three chocolate-brown doors, each of which had a brass plaque showing two different surnames. The plaque on the middle door looked new. The first name was T. Vercetti and the second A. Pernazzo. Below the doorbell was a paper tag covered in adhesive tape. This displayed only the name A. Pernazzo. Blume hooked his fingernail under the tag and eased it back to see what name had been there originally. S. Pernazzo. He flattened the new tag back into place and rang the bell.

Blume thought he must look tired, but the person who opened the door was evidently in a worse state. He looked as if he had been dipped in nicotine, then rolled in clay. His small nose twitched slightly. It was slightly upturned, a bit pink, the sort that plastic surgeons put on so many women. He jerked the door open, then retreated into his apartment, leaving the door ajar.

"*Permesso?*" said Blume, and taking the sullen silence as permission, walked over the threshold. Angelo Pernazzo was waiting for him in the middle of the hallway, in a slightly crouched position as if ready to leap. Blume tensed for a brief moment, ready to parry, but Pernazzo turned around and entered the last door on the left.

Blume followed Pernazzo down a short corridor, past a kitchen in which he glimpsed a table covered with a plastic cloth, on which sat an open tin of butter beans, a glistening fork, a torn piece of bread smeared with something brown. He walked into a small living room. The marble composite floor was so sticky that it snatched at the soles of his shoes so that each step was accompanied by a short clack of release as his foot broke free.

The shutters were down, closing off the remaining few minutes of evening light. The main source of illumination in the room was a large computer screen in the corner. The picture on the screen showed a detailed fantasy landscape as seen from above. Blume was fascinated by the level of detail. There seemed to be hundreds of characters doing battle below.

Pernazzo pointed at the screen, revealing a woman's silver bracelet on his arm. He indicated the level he had reached and asked, "You into World of Warcraft?"

"Me? No," said Blume. "I'm an adult."

He moved away from the computer and sat on a chesterfield sofa that smelled of yeast and dust. A Mars Bar wrapper lay on the floor at his feet.

Pernazzo picked up a pair of balled-up mauve socks from the floor. Blume could smell them from where he sat. Pernazzo bent down and put them on, then straightened up and asked, "What's this about?"

"You were detained at an illegal dog fight. Remember?" said Blume.

"That? Is that what this is about?"

"Why? Is there something else it should be about?"

"No. It's just it was a while ago, you know. And it was the Carabinieri, not the police." Pernazzo licked chapped lips.

Blume settled into the brown velvet chesterfield. He thought he could smell fish from his left. He brought his hand up to his nose to block the smell, then turned his gesture into a yawn, which became real.

"You are tired," said Pernazzo settling into a plastic-covered club chair opposite Blume. "I never am."

"No?"

"If you sleep, you lose," said Pernazzo. "I follow the Uberman sleep schedule. It maximizes my REM sleep and minimizes non-REM sleep, which is just a waste of time."

"I see," said Blume, and yawned again.

"What you have to do is take six twenty-minute hyper-sleeps, every four hours. When you close your eyes, you go straight into REM, skipping four unnecessary phases. It's called polyphasic sleeping."

"And you do this?"

"Yeah, it's raised my productivity."

Foul air seemed to be seeping up from inside the brown cushions. Blume leaned forward. A gray Champion backpack sat beside Pernazzo's computer desk.

"You work in computers," said Blume.

"I write scripts for Web sites. Some of the companies I work for are big names, but I am paid fuck all, and the work's never regular. No stable income. You think that's fair?"

Blume had no opinions on the matter.

"Nobody pays for quality, either. I do quality work. High intelligence doesn't pay."

"Depends on your unit of measurement," said Blume.

"Euros," said Pernazzo. "I did day trading for a while. Naturally, I was good at it, but you can't do much with the Italian stock market. The MIBTEL gained, what, five percent over the year? In the same period, the Dow Jones Industrial was up twenty-three percent."

"You lost money?"

"Of course I did. You can't make money in this fucked-up country."

"So you started gambling."

"I have always gambled, as you put it. Usually I win."

Pernazzo seemed to have sunk down into the chair so that its arms were higher than his.

"So you're a winner. Tell me, is this apartment yours?"

"Of course it is."

"Did you buy it?"

"No. It used to be my mother's. She died last year."

Blume ignored the opportunity to express his condolences. "And your father?"

"He abandoned my mother before I was born. Makes me a bastard."

"I see. Your mother's name was?"

"What? You don't believe I had a mother? Her name was Serena."

"Serena Pernazzo. You took her surname," said Blume.

"Yes. This was her apartment. Now it's mine because she's dead."

"What did she die of?"

"Old age."

"Is that what is says on the death certificate?"

"The death certificate says she died of heart failure."

"Where did she die?"

"In her room."

"In this apartment? Mind if I take a look?"

Pernazzo sprang out of his chair. "Of course I mind. What's this got to do with dog fighting? Have you got a search warrant?"

"No. Do you think I need one?"

Pernazzo went over to his computer, moved the gray backpack toward the wall, and started shutting down programs, turning his back on Blume. "If you're not going to ask me any more questions about the dog fight, then I have no reason to speak to you."

"You're very nervous."

"That's your fault."

"So, have you given up on illegal dog fighting?"

"Yes."

"You're only saying that because I used the word illegal. Have you thought about looking for help for your gambling problem?"

"I don't have a gambling problem. I usually win."

"So you have plenty of money?"

"Enough."

"But not enough to afford your own apartment until your mother died."

"That's because I only play small amounts." Pernazzo's voice went up. "I am not a dupe. I read systems. I studied form for horses, but there are many other factors, which I couldn't know about. Dog races have better odds. Ask anyone. Anyhow, it's all fixed."

"So why play if it's fixed?"

Pernazzo looked at Blume as if he were an idiot. "Because if you learn how they're fixing it, then you bet the same way."

"That's what you did?"

"For a while, but then they notice, and you have to stop. Those Neapolitans that run the greyhound races in Valle Aurelia, they don't like people winning."

"So you moved from greyhounds to illegal dog fights," said Blume. "Doesn't look to me like you're much good at any of this."

"That's because you know nothing about it!" Pernazzo writhed with frustration in his chair at Blume's stupidity. "I study tactics. I was learning Alleva's system. It was just a question of time."

"Ah, so you know Alleva. What about his helper and enforcer, Massoni? Ever heard of him?"

"I might know the name," Pernazzo said to the screen.

"Angelo, turn around. It's rude to talk to people like that. Did your mother teach you nothing?"

Pernazzo twisted around in his seat.

"It looks to me like you could do with more REM sleep," said Blume.

"I'm fine."

"Your eyes are moving rapidly now," said Blume. "Did you owe Alleva money?"

"I did once," said Pernazzo. "But I paid him."

"Just once. Where did you pay him?"

"Not him. That guy you mentioned. I can't remember his name."

Blume looked at Pernazzo's feet. They were both pointed directly toward the door. A fat yellow toenail protruded through a hole in one of his socks.

"Massoni."

"Yes, him," said Pernazzo

"Did Massoni come here?"

"I think so. Yes."

"When?"

"A year ago. I can't remember."

"Was your mother alive then?"

"Yes."

"Wasn't she alarmed?"

"She never even saw him. I deal with my own shit."

"Earlier on I was talking to a man called Dandini. Do you know him?"

"No." Pernazzo shook his head.

"He is troubled by his gambling. I think you should be, too."

"Well I'm not."

"OK. What's in that bag?"

"What bag?"

"The one at your feet."

"Oh, nothing."

"Can I look?"

"No. No, you cannot. I'm not sure I even have to answer your questions."

"Why can't I look?"

Pernazzo picked up the bag, tossed it to him. Even as he caught it, Blume realized it was empty.

"OK, I won't look if it annoys you. Angelo, I'm very thirsty. Can I trouble you for a glass of water?"

For a moment, Pernazzo seemed to freeze. He jerked out of his chair and sat down again. Then he picked up the gray backpack and carried it out of the living room.

"I'll just take my personal belongings away," he said. "You're not allowed to look at anything, you know."

"I know the rules," said Blume.

As soon as Angelo had left, he stood up, went over to the computer desk. He saw a silver dollar, and picked it up, turned it over in his hand. Nineteen seventy-six. He had been in grade school? He called tails, tossed it, got tails. Sitting next to the mouse were two empty plastic tubs of a yellow crème dessert. Three black curled half-moon fingernail tops sat on top of an open page of a programming manual.

Angelo came back into the room with a glass of water. He scanned his desk, Blume's hands, and then his face.

"You were spying into my computer."

"Great graphics," said Blume. "That's one of those online fantasy games, isn't it? I've heard of them. Are you any good?"

"I am one of the best. Possibly the best in the country, certainly in Rome," said Pernazzo.

"You ever been out of Rome?"

"Sure."

"Ever been to the States?"

"No."

"I see you have a silver dollar."

Pernazzo said nothing.

"So you're good at this game?"

"One of the best. Level seventy."

"Really? And how many levels are there?"

"Sixty."

"If there are sixty levels . . ." began Blume.

"Sixty levels for most people. But when you reach the top, there is a higher plane."

"Sounds very frustrating," said Blume.

Pernazzo handed him a glass. It was greasy around the rims, and caked with lime scale inside.

"I can't drink from this," said Blume. "It's filthy."

"Do as you fucking please."

"Very well, I'll do it myself," said Blume and walked quickly out of the living room into the kitchen.

Blume placed the glass on top of a pile of unwashed dishes and pizza cartons. He opened a food cupboard and peered inside. Potato chips, Pavesi chocolate drop biscuits, Rice Krispies, UHT milk cartons, Nutella, pasta in the shape of wagon wheels, Knorr mixes, and a single jar of Skippy peanut butter.

Pernazzo appeared in the doorway behind him, panting a little.

"I see you have peanut butter," said Blume.

Pernazzo pulled a piece of kitchen towel from beneath a toaster, dislodging a shower of crumbs. He wiped the side of his mouth with the towel, balled it up, put it on the counter.

"So?"

"Where did you get it?"

"Supermarket, I suppose."

"Really? You see, I like peanut butter, but it's hard to find in this city. Not as hard as it was once, but still. Which supermarket?"

"I can't remember."

"A local one?"

"I can't remember, OK?"

"OK. Do you get the supermarket to deliver? Some supermarkets, they put your shopping in a cardboard box, bring it to your house. Ever hear of that?"

"No."

"You never heard of it? I think they all do it now."

"Well, I never heard of it."

"There's nothing clean in here, Pernazzo. Can't you afford a maid?"

"I'm not interested."

"Do you have a girlfriend, Angelo?"

"None of your fucking business."

Blume looked again at the peanut butter. "You know what?" he said. "That has a bar code on it. Now that could be useful." He picked up the jar, which had no top. It was slippery in his hand. "Mind if I borrow this?"

"Of course I mind," said Pernazzo.

"You're right, of course," said Blume. "I have no right to deprive you of food." He ripped the label off the jar and pocketed it.

"You can't do that!" Pernazzo's voice rose to a squeak.

"I just did," said Blume. "I'm interested in seeing if this came from a certain supermarket. That can't worry you, can it?"

"Chain of evidence!" said Pernazzo. "You can't just—you need other police in here, search warrants. You have to log evidence."

"You've been watching too much television, Pernazzo. And this is just personal curiosity on my part. I don't see why you should be so worried."

Pernazzo seemed to have entered a sort of trance. "You can't use that type of bar code for the exchange of information keyed to a unique identifier without referential integrity."

"I'm afraid I wasn't quite following you there," said Blume. "What I want to find out is whether this label got beeped through a checkout at a certain supermarket. If you want, you can have the label back afterwards."

Pernazzo opened his eyes wide, like Blume used to do when trying not to sleep in the classroom.

"Angelo, your whole setup here. You know what it says to me? It says loser."

"Well, you're wrong. You're the loser."

"How much money did you lose to Alleva?"

"Who says I even lost? Maybe I won."

"You said you lost. You said it yourself. You paid off a debt to Massoni last year."

Pernazzo brought a finger up to touch what seemed like a very faint mustache. "You always lose at the beginning. That's how it works. Then you get better at it. You get knowledge, skills, weapons, you move up. Eventually you become the best there is."

"Maybe in your games. Not in real life, Angelo. You never win gambling with criminals."

"That's just where you're wrong. I have it hacked. I know how it's done."

"How the dog fights are done?"

Pernazzo touched his nose, licked his lips, scratched his crotch. "It's valuable knowledge."

"I won't tell," said Blume. "Promise. Let's go back into the living room, and you tell me about it."

Blume had been breathing shallowly while in the kitchen, which was worse than the living room. He was lusting after the idea of drawing a deep breath of air as soon as he got out of the building. When they returned to the living room, he remained standing. Christ, he needed to get out of there.

"So tell me. How have you hacked it to make such a success of your gambling?"

"I know their underdog trick."

"The underdog trick. How does that work?"

Pernazzo moved away from Blume and stood by the shuttered window. It was dark outside now. The storm rumbled in the background.

"It works like this," said Pernazzo. "They get the meanest animal, some big as fuck Rottweiler, stick him in a cage with other dogs. They give the dogs water, but don't feed them for about three days. Any longer than that, the animals lose strength permanently. Then they throw in a hunk of meat. Total frenzy. The meanest dog fights the others, wins. But every time he tries to eat, the others set on him again. Any time one of them tries to get the meat, the others go for him. You following?"

"Yes."

"But sometimes there is a dog that doesn't attack. He hangs back, lets the others do the fighting, and when the top dog is defending his place, he sneaks in and grabs a small piece of meat. A nibble, retreat, a nibble, retreat. That dog became the hidden champion. The underdog."

"I get it. So they create the underdog, then get people to bet against it?"

"They build up a bit of a record for the champion big dog, the Rottweiler or whatever, get the clueless gamblers to lay bets on him, and he wins a few fights. Then one day, they bring out the underdog, which they've been training to be really fucking mean. They file his teeth, too. Make them real sharp. So now it's mean as well as clever, pumped full of hormones, fed on raw meat, milk. No grains. Throw him in against some big dog, clean up on the fight. Except next time, I'll have my money on the underdog."

"Angelo, did you just make up that bullshit?"

"It's not bullshit!" Pernazzo's voice became shrill.

"You didn't make it up, then?"

"No!"

"OK, so who told you? Who explained the underdog strategy to you?"

Pernazzo brought a pink hand up to his mouth and nibbled at a fingernail. Blume repeated his question.

"I don't have to tell you my sources."

"No, you don't have to tell me, because I know. Only two people could have told you that. Alleva, who, by the way, was a con man before he became a dog man, or else his helper, Massoni, whose name you couldn't remember. I wonder how much they were going to take you for? You are a loser, Angelo," said Blume. "And you are a lousy liar, too. You have been in close contact with Massoni and Alleva. Close enough for them to feed you a line of bullshit."

Pernazzo hunched his back and took a step toward Blume. Pernazzo was small, but Blume's instinct made him take a step backward.

"Get out of this apartment," he said.

Blume ignored him. "Have you ever heard of Arturo Clemente?"

"No."

"You never heard of him?"

"Never."

"Even though he was the man responsible for bringing television cameras and the Carabinieri to one of Alleva's dog fights?"

"No."

"Even though you were detained that evening?"

"No."

"Even though you said a few words to the television cameras. Even though just before coming here I watched you giving your opinions on bear-baiting."

Silence.

"Did you not even watch the TV documentary when it aired? You must have wanted to see yourself on TV."

"Leave my apartment now or I will call the Carabinieri."

"No you won't. But if you don't want to see me again, I don't suppose you'd mind giving me some fingerprints and saliva samples?" said Blume.

"What for?"

"To exclude you from our inquiries."

"Inquiries into what?"

"The murder of Arturo Clemente."

"I have no idea what you're talking about."

"Ah. There's that phrase again. Where were you yesterday morning?"

"Here at home."

"Can anyone else confirm that?"

"No. But I was online playing Texas Hold'em poker."

"Really? If I remember correctly, that's illegal in Italy. Did you win at that, at least?"

Pernazzo shrugged.

"A bit. The pot wasn't big."

"Help me here, Angelo," said Blume. "How can I be sure you were online like you said?"

"That's your problem."

"No, Angelo. I think it's yours."

"What? Because it's illegal?"

"Because it's not much of an alibi."

"I was playing from seven in the morning until the early afternoon."

Blume went over to the computer. "Show me," he said.

Pernazzo wiped his nose with the back of his hand. Blume tried not to look at the silver gleam between Pernazzo's knuckles as he pressed the keys on his keyboard, making the fantasy landscape dissolve.

"This is the program," he said.

Blume watched as the name "Full Tilt Poker" appeared on-screen. A virtual felt table appeared. Four avatars sat around a table. A busty woman, a frog, a dog, and a cowboy. "Which one is you?"

"None of these. We're just observing others. You think all of a sudden I'm playing there and talking to you? I have to sign in, join a table. You don't get it, do you?"

"No. I don't," said Blume. "So when you join, what are you? A woman, a dog, an insect, what?"

Pernazzo closed the program. "That's my business."

"And you were playing this game all Friday morning?"

"Sure. You can get your IT department to check my IP. I know they spy on us anyhow."

The fantasy landscape reappeared on-screen. Blume moved the mouse to pop up the Windows taskbar, but nothing happened.

"Hey, what are you doing?"

"I was trying to pop up that clock thingy, check the time."

"This isn't a Windows system. The clock's on the top."

"Ah, so it is." It showed nine thirty. He had to meet Kristin at nine thirty. He was not going to make it.

"OK. I'm going to go away, have someone check your IP address like you said. I'm going to check that label, and I'm going to think a bit about Angelo Pernazzo the underdog, the loser. This will take me up to two days. For two days, therefore, we will be watching you. Any attempt to leave Rome will result in your immediate arrest, and then we'll come in here and tear this rat's nest you call home apart. So just sit there and play your computer games until I knock. Think you can do that?"

Blume took out a card with the station number and his name and rank on it, and held it out. Pernazzo plucked the card from Blume's large hand, skimmed it toward the computer desk. He missed and the card fluttered to the floor.

"You might want to engage the services of a lawyer or"—Blume pointed to the computer—"enlist some elves and wizards to help you."

21

IT WAS TEN fifteen when Blume, hungry and beginning to suffer from the exhaustion of the past thirty or so hours, reached Piazza Santa Maria. The rain, heavy as he left Pernazzo's, had eased off. Young tourists, obediently following the instructions in their Lonely Planet guidebooks, sat huddled on the soaked steps of the fountain surrounded by pigeon shit, leering drunks, and drug addicts, and waited for something cool to happen.

He saw Kristin immediately. She was standing slightly off-center, away from the fountain, hands by her sides. Although she was clearly American, and clean-cut and female, no one was bothering her.

"Kristin," said Blume, sticking his hand out, as if it were a business meeting.

"Hi," said Kristin, taking his outstretched hand briefly. Her hands were dry, and sturdier than he expected.

"I am late. I'm sorry. Something came up . . ." said Blume. He tried to think of some non-idiotic words, but thoughts seemed to slip down from his brain into his neck, leaving his mind empty and his voice thick. "Here we are, then."

Kristin said, "Yes. Here we are. Glad you could make it."

"Me, too," said Blume. He'd think of something clever to say in a minute.

"Have you any particular plans?" asked Kristin. "I'm hungry."

"Aren't we going to wait for your friend—your friends, I mean?" asked Blume.

"They're not coming. Marty called me earlier, said they couldn't make it."

"Ah, no?" Blume decided not to bother feigning disappointment.

He looked at a bar opposite where a waiter was swiping raindrops off shining tables. "Maybe a drink?"

Kristin looked at the bar and seemed to dismiss it with a shake of her head, then said, "Do you like Roman cuisine?"

"You mean *pajata*, and tripe and pigs' trotters, horsemeat, liver, and all that stuff?" asked Blume.

"Yes. I love that stuff."

"You do?" Blume had had to learn to cook for himself very quickly, and had remained unadventurous.

"Yeah, come on." She almost took his arm. If he had moved the right way she might have taken it. But he wasn't quick enough.

Blume followed Kristin down Vicolo del Moro behind Piazza Trilussa, and from there into a narrow lane with wet black cobblestones that bulged and swelled as if barely holding down a future seismic event.

The lane led to a two-story, ocher-colored medieval house, so small that it looked like a scale model. A wooden veranda had been attached to the front of the building, forming a porch that was fenced off by a palisade of rush mats supporting clematis and jasmine creepers. The porch area had enough room for five tables, four of which were occupied. No signage indicated that this might be a restaurant, and from a distance, the diners looked like an extended family having a private meal outside their front door. No more than thirty yards away, the quays of the Tiber boomed and raged with traffic on wet asphalt, which was here toned down to white noise.

By a series of hand signals and gesticulations, Kristin managed to secure the one remaining table, and she and Blume sat down facing each other. Only now that he was seated could he see the name of the restaurant, Mattatoio Cinque, inscribed above the narrow doorway, out of which an agile waiter made a curving backward step, and emerged bearing menus, bread, and water on outstretched arms.

Kristin ordered *rigatoni alla pajata* and, displaying her American impatience, directly ordered the second course as well, choosing *frattaglie*.

"*Frattaglie?*" echoed Blume, holding up a hand to stop the efficient waiter from writing down the order in his pad. "You know what they are?"

She shrugged happily. "Sure."

Blume wasn't convinced. "It means the insides of animals," he told her.

"Better than the outsides, I'd say."

"Stomach lining and livers, kidneys, testicles, windpipes, and . . . stuff?"

The waiter smiled and addressed himself to Kristin. "Today the cook has prepared veal heart with artichoke and carrot cooked in lard with white wine and white sauce."

Blume glanced at the finely shaped woman in front of him. She was going to consume the heart of a calf cooked in the rendered fat of a pig?

The waiter tossed a glance in Blume's direction. "I'll just have the osso buco," he said. "And a bottle of the house red."

"And before that? The pasta?" asked the waiter.

"I'll go for the *amatriciana*," said Blume.

The waiter noted down their orders, nodded, and went indoors. Before they could strike up a conversation, he was back again bearing a three-quarter-quart carafe of dark red wine, then with two long steps withdrew to the next table, occupied by a German couple.

"Would you like some wine?" Blume offered.

"Sure," she said. "Half a glass will be plenty."

Blume poured himself a half glass as well.

The pasta came, and they ate in a bubble of silence, which Blume tried to pierce with an occasional jab at finding out more about Kristin's past. But she was more interested in her veal intestines.

Kristin started asking about him. Blume overfilled his mouth and chewed hard on the fatty bits of the diced bacon wondering how much he wanted to reveal. He limited himself to saying he had been in Italy for many years.

She asked about his parents. He had been waiting for this question, and decided he wanted to come across as terse and uncomplaining, maybe a bit gruff.

"Both shot dead in a bank raid on Via Cristoforo Colombo."

Kristin nodded, twisted a glistening strand of pasta on her fork.

"Mmm," she said. "Now that is good."

Blume gave her pasta a look of hate, and added some graphic detail. "Some stupid bank guard tried to play hero and pulled out his weapon to defend a bank's money. Bank guards. Can there be a more pathetic job than that?"

She looked slightly bored as he told her this. She had not even said she was sorry to hear it. The tragic death of his parents had always guaranteed at least sympathy, if not sex.

Kristin had a question: "Did they catch the guys?"

"One was killed there. Not the one who shot my parents. He got away.

Obviously, there was a third waiting outside, probably a fourth doing look-out."

"Did you have to identify the bodies?"

"Yes. My mother had been shot through the breast."

"They showed you that?" Kristin's voice rose in disbelief.

"No. They told me. It was supposed to be a comfort. Straight to the heart. Death would have been instantaneous. They showed me her face. My father's face, too. The first bullet hit him in the mouth. It looked like he was grinning at me. The second and third in the abdomen. It wasn't instantaneous for him."

"So you decided to become a cop and hunt them down for the rest of your life?"

"No. It wasn't like that. And the shooter is dead anyhow."

"So he did get caught," said Kristin. "In the end."

"No, he just died in the end. It was summer 1987, and I had just finished an exam in political economy. I came home, there was a letter waiting for me, postmark was local. I opened it and inside was typed 'Verano Riq. 57 no. 23-bis.' Nothing else.

"Verano. As in the cemetery?"

"See? You'd make a good detective, too," said Blume. "The cemetery is walking distance from where I live."

Kristin interrupted. "So you still live in the same apartment?"

"Yes."

"Are your parents buried in the same cemetery?"

"Yes. Do you want to hear this or not?"

"Go on."

"So I went straight to the cemetery, to Section fifty-seven, found the tomb number. *In our hearts forever*, it said. *Pietro Scognamiglio 17 October 1961 to 19 May 1987.*"

"And who was this Scognamiglio?"

"I didn't know. I ran the name, found out he had spent more time in Rebbibia than out of it, had a list of violent crimes attributed to him. Kept getting released, though."

"That's it?"

"That's it."

"So you don't actually know this Scognamiglio is the guy who pulled the trigger."

"No. But someone knew, and that someone sent me a message."

Kristin soaked up the oil from her plate with a piece of bread, and put it in her mouth, then pushed her plate away. "That was excellent. So did it make you feel better, seeing that tomb?"

"A bit," said Blume. "Not much. I'd like to be absolutely certain that's what the message meant, and I would prefer to have put Scognamiglio in his tomb myself."

"I guess the death of your parents is the reason you're still here."

"Yes. I was just seventeen. It was hard to survive on my own in a foreign country."

"And yet here you are."

Blume tried to determine her tone. It was not quite mocking, or maybe it was.

"I had already been living here for three years. I thought I was going into freshman class at Franklin High, but they brought me here and put me into the first year of a *liceo* in Parioli. I was fourteen then."

"Why did they come here?"

"They were art historians. My father was also an illustrator. I did not take after him."

"So you lived on your own after seventeen?"

Blume nodded.

"That must have been interesting. How many other kids had a free house every night?"

"It wasn't my apartment," said Blume.

"You were next of kin. There's no way the house could have gone to anyone else."

"It was a rented apartment. It never belonged to them. It belonged to a guy called Gargaruti, some fucking character, he turned out to be."

"Yeah? Tell me about him."

Blume allowed a look of great sadness to wash over his countenance and said, "Maybe some other time."

"OK."

"Unless you want to hear now . . ."

"No. That's OK. Some other time will do."

"Yeah, because, he was . . ."

Kristin interrupted him, "So tell me, how did you survive?"

"The police helped me. First of all, they tried to get in contact with my relatives in the States. My mother had a sister in L.A., kind of a failed actress. She didn't reply to any letters. Nothing. So then they had to send me to an orphanage."

"That's very Dickensian. You don't mind me saying that, do you?"

"I don't care. Also, I didn't really live in the orphanage. I continued in school, then the nuns gave me some freedom. I even got lifts back and forth from the police, spent some nights in the apartment, which was paid for until the end of the year. Also, it took the City of Rome three months to complete the paperwork, and so by the time I went in there for my first day, it was only weeks before my eighteenth birthday."

"How did you survive for money?"

"I taught English, then started giving Latin and French lessons, too."

"You were good enough at Latin and French to give lessons?"

"Yes. I'm good at languages. Very good. I find them easy to learn."

"What else do you speak?"

"Spanish—obviously. Basically, it's Italian with a lisp. My German's quite good. That's all. A bit of Albanian. Some Romany. Greek."

"Ancient Greek?"

"No. Modern. I used to go to the islands in June and July with college friends. I can order food in Greek, read a menu."

"You pick up languages just by listening to them?"

"No. I need to study them. What I am good at is picking up accents. I can tell accents."

"Who were these police who helped you?"

"A policewoman, the one who came around to tell me. Marina. She came around the following day, and the day after that, and then her partner arrived, and after him, another, and they all started checking up on me, seeing if I was OK. Five cops on rotation for a year and a bit, all looking out for me. I still know them all."

"Did your parents leave money?"

"No. They weren't planning to die. And they were both part-time university teachers, with a lifestyle above their means. No properties, no assets, some savings from my mother eventually emerged. My father left a debit card in his drawer, and after a long search I found the PIN hidden as a telephone number. So I started drawing money out of his account. But it didn't last. After six months, the bank found out my father wasn't alive.

I'm not sure how. Not only did they block the account, they also called in the Finance Police and denounced 'persons unknown' for theft."

"So you have a criminal record?"

"No. I get this visit from the Finance Police, and they give me grief for a while. Then I get a lawyer's letter from the bank, saying they want all the money back plus interest plus legal fees and so on. And then in comes Gargaruti, my landlord, doubles the rent there and then."

"A landlord can't just double the rent like that."

"He can here, if the apartment is let to a non-Italian. Gargaruti had other apartments, and a take-out restaurant, a *rosticceria*. He worked there all day. He always smelled of roast chicken. Anyway, he tells me to turn up for work in the restaurant on Monday. I did. The pay he gave me didn't cover my rent, and he said he was charging interest. Then he gets all kindly uncle again, tells me to eat all the roast chicken I want. I told Marina, the police-woman, about him. She spread the word and the police sort of leaned on him. My rent went back down, I left his kitchen. Three years later, I used my mother's savings to buy the apartment from him. He needed persuasion about that, too."

He lifted his glass to drink some of his wine, and kept the rim of the glass against his mouth and narrowed his eyes until all he saw was the red wine. When he put down the glass, he picked up his napkin, and pressed it against his mouth, leaving a purple stain like a bruise on the linen.

"A few days after I had identified my parents, they asked me to bite on a piece of gauze, and put it with tweezers into a plastic tub. Mitochondrial DNA testing. It wasn't necessary. This was the early 1990s. The police labs were developing a training program for technicians, and this was a good opportunity."

"Don't you resent that? The police using you like that for training their technicians?"

"No." Blume was emphatic. "The police did everything for me. They took care of me. They kept coming back to check. I'd have ended up on the street if it hadn't been for them."

"Or back in America."

They were interrupted by the arrival of the second course. Kristin tucked in with relish to a red and pale yellow mess of pieces in a bowl. Blume couldn't help but wonder at the incongruity between her talc-scented freshness and this voracious appetite for slaughterhouse leftovers. He thought of Clemente lying on the floor, the blood congealing around him. Dorfmann dipping a blood-soaked swab on a Hemastix strip and turning it green.

"You're supposed to eat the marrow," said Kristin, jabbing a fork in the direction of his plate, where he had hardly touched the osso buco. "That's the best bit."

Blume looked without appetite at the cross section of leg-bone with strings of gray flesh attached to it. He reached out for more wine, but discovered the carafe was already empty.

"I did go back to America. A year later, as soon as I was eighteen and could travel alone. There was no one there. I found out where my aunt lived. I watched her house in Los Angeles for a day, and I think I saw her. I have two cousins."

"You went all the way over to the USA, then just looked at your aunt from a distance?"

"I didn't see what I could say to her. Anyhow, it was just one day out of my vacation."

"You considered it a vacation?"

"I was there with Valentina, my girlfriend. We did a coast-to-coast. Two months traveling and working. She got a J-1 visa, so she could work, too. It was fun. My life has not been a total wreck, you know."

"Did you hang out with students or cops in those days?"

"Both. A lot of people studying law and economics were thinking of joining the police."

"What about the expat community? Did you have much to do with them? Other Americans?"

Kristin's voice seemed to echo as she said that, and Blume realized he was slipping into a half-dream state, battling wine and sleepiness with adrenaline. The sensible thing would have been to go to bed, get a proper six hours at least before the Alleva operation.

"Not much. I never got on with visiting Americans." He was tired of talking. "But what about you? Tell me what you do. I haven't managed to get any information from you."

"Well, I was a lawyer until recently. I worked for Merck Sharp and Dohme. Pharmaceuticals. What I couldn't tell you about rizatriptan benzoate ain't worth knowing."

"What does that do?"

"Gets rid of headaches."

"Does it work?"

"I don't know, I've never had a headache," said Kristin.

"Shit, I get them all the time," said Blume.

"Well, you could try drinking less," said Kristin, timing her comment with the arrival of the waiter with another carafe brimming with red wine.

"Why did you quit your job?"

"Ethical stuff. They do too many experiments with dogs. Cats, too—more cats than dogs, actually, but I had some real issues with the dog experiments. I made some ill-advised comments in an in-house magazine."

"You like dogs?"

"Sure. Don't most normal people? Apart from the experimenters, and even some of them feel pretty lousy sometimes."

"I don't like dogs in the slightest," said Blume. "Filthy noisy stinking creatures."

"You're a cat person, then?"

"Isn't that code for gay when applied to men? I don't care—look, I never even think of cats. They live in my courtyard, piss on the motorbikes, that's all I know about cats. Dogs, on the other hand, are creatures I actively dislike."

Kristin seemed annoyed to hear this, and to distract her attention he asked the waiter what was on the dessert menu.

"*Torta mimosa panna cotta frutta fresca crème caramel torta all'arancio cassata siciliana—molta buona questa—la prenda,*" replied the waiter, not wasting more than six seconds of his life in listing false alternatives before telling him what to order.

"Oh yes, the *cassata,* I'll have that," said Kristin.

Blume ordered the same.

The waiter ambled off toward another table, with the air of having decided not to give them anything, after all.

"Where are you from?"

"Vermont. I already told you that in the courtyard."

"So that's what your accent is," said Blume.

"I lived where there are trees, big gardens. Cold, rich, middle class. Very comfortable. My closet at home is about the size of my apartment here. Dad is an anesthetist, or was. Retired. Now he just bores people to sleep."

"I don't get the connection between Merck and whatever and you wandering through the corridors of a police station in Rome," said Blume.

"I don't work for a pharmaceuticals company. I used to. But I quit. Now I work as a legate with the embassy on Via Veneto."

"What's a legate?"

"A legal attaché."

"You don't say more than you have to, do you? Must be part of being a lawyer."

"Must be."

"What exactly are you legally attached to?"

"The FBI."

Blume considered this. "The FBI works from the embassy? I thought they operated through Europol. I've heard of cooperation, but it's always been very specific. I suppose I don't know much."

"Your rank doesn't help there," she said, and pushed back a strand of hair that had fallen across her forehead. "I am an FBI legate to the Embassy of the United States in Italy. I report here to a regional security officer, and back home to the Office of International Operations."

"And you draw bad pictures of fountains in courtyards in your spare time."

"Bad pictures, huh? You didn't like the reference to your rank. I'm sorry, Alec."

"No. I don't care about that. But seeing that this is more an interview than an evening out, it occurred to me your sketch might have been a prop, to allow you to sit there waiting for me."

"I couldn't think of anything better."

"So you're here talking to me, finding out things about me because . . . ?"

"I maintain contacts in the Polizia, the Carabinieri, the Finance Police, and even—would you believe it—the traffic police," said Kristin. "These contacts are official, unofficial, diplomatic, confidential, open, private, public—whatever. They tell me whatever they feel like telling me. I don't ask them to tell me more. It's all very aboveboard and friendly."

"What's the point?"

"Helps us get a feel of the place. Keep an ear to the ground."

Blume gave her his skeptical-cop look.

"I do work a little with people who may have special operational remits. We pool information and work together in what is called a country team."

"You have contacts up high?"

"I've exchanged a few pleasantries with the prefect at embassy dos."

"What were you doing at my station?"

"Handing out invitations to a conference on terrorism. Before you say it, almost everyone knows the conferences don't resolve anything, but that's not what they're for. Attendance is always total. Know why?"

"Free food? Cops love free food."

"Yes, they do. But it's not just that. The top brass is there. That way, lowly commissioners get a chance to have a private word with questors and prefects. We provide a little private court where the vassals get a chance to ask favors of the barons. All played out in front of us. They know we're watching, but they don't care. After all, we're all allies."

The waiter came out of the tiny doorway with two plates and a winning smile.

"There we go," he declared, placing desserts in front of them, then standing back as if planning to watch them, like a proud mother feeding her two children. Blume gave him a look that sent him off with a scowl to the next table.

The *cassata* was something special. Blume had not tasted a *cassata* so good since he had been in Palermo. Blume now regretted sending the waiter away like that. Excellence and beauty should always be acknowledged and publicly praised. Italians were good at that, and he was not.

"Good, isn't it?" mumbled Kristin, breaking the reverent silence that had descended as they allowed the candied fruits, chocolate, cheese, and sponge cake to quietly dissolve in the heat of their mouths.

"It's more than good. People should come here just for this," agreed Blume.

All too soon, it was gone. Blume rubbed his thumb in the sweet white trail left on his plate and stuck it in his mouth. Kristin was intently cleaning off all residues with her middle finger.

"We could order another," suggested Blume.

Kristin giggled, which he found disconcertingly out of character.

"Marcello!" called Kristin.

The waiter responded like an eager cocker spaniel, and bounded over to the table, radiating smiles solely at Kristin.

"*Il conto, per piacere.*"

Annoyingly, very annoyingly, when Marcello came with the bill, he handed it to Kristin, and before Blume could protest, she had put a gold American Express on the platter.

"How much was it?" he demanded, trying to read her surname on the card. It was upside-down to him, and seemed to spell out Holmquist.

By way of response, she handed him the check: 126 euros. "The wine was particularly dear," she said.

Kristin signed the stub. Blume went to the bathroom. Kristin was waiting for him on the street outside.

His alcohol-fueled policeman's swagger was slightly more pronounced as he walked down the lane toward the brighter, noisier, and dirtier streets ahead. He'd make a move on Kristin before they reached the intersection.

But he delayed a fraction too long, and when they reached the end of the lane, a large group of young people and two motorcyclists, conscientiously not going against the one-way signals on the road by driving on the sidewalk instead, caused them to separate for a moment, and when Blume turned around again, she had moved as if to go left and he as if to go right.

"I'm going this way," she said, in a tone that excluded all possibility of invitation.

"How am I supposed to pay for the dinner? Can I see you again?" There, that was unambiguous.

"I'll phone you," she said, with a smile that suddenly and very briefly revealed where future years would etch themselves into her face.

"You don't have my number."

"You're in the book, aren't you?"

"No, I'm ex-directory." He started hunting his pockets for a pen and paper. He always, always had a pen when he was working. Now he didn't. His bag was in his office, damn it. "I'm not in the book," he repeated in case she had missed the danger of the situation. He had given Pernazzo his last card. What a fucking waste. He pulled out used Kleenex, plastic wrappers, scraps of paper no good for writing on, and dropped them on the wet ground.

"Calm down, Alec. Just tell me your number. I'll remember it."

Blume gave her his number. She repeated it.

"OK, I've got that memorized. I have a great head for figures." Without waiting for him to reply, she turned and walked off. She went through the noisy crowd like a white-sailed boat cutting through a darkening lake.

It was only as he took off his jacket at home that Blume remembered the peanut butter label from Pernazzo's kitchen. With a mounting sense of dread, he began searching his pockets. Surely he hadn't thrown it away when he was looking for . . .

Gone.

22

THE FOLLOWING MORNING, Blume sat with Paoloni in a metallic-pink Fiat Punto on the sidewalk outside the PAM supermarket in Magliana. It was a ridiculous color. The idea, apparently, was that it didn't look anything like a police vehicle, which would be the case if it had a woman with shopping in it. Instead, it contained two grumpy grown men watching traffic.

Blume was still thinking about the label he had dropped on the street. Pernazzo's squealing about chain of evidence had been right insofar as it probably would not be admissible in court, but if the label had been traceable back to Clemente's supermarket, the case was as good as closed. Why had he not placed it in an evidence bag when he got back to the car? Too much of a rush to get to Kristin, and then he had drunk too much wine, talked too much, and literally thrown a piece of case evidence on the street.

It was time he quit drinking.

Theirs was just one of hundreds of cars jutting out at all angles from the sidewalk as if thrown there by a bad-tempered child. Wedged in between an Iveco flatbed truck and an off-white, massive 1970s Mercedes that may have been abandoned there for good, they had a clear view of the street, the supermarket, a bank, a bakery, and a newsstand, and a twelve-story apartment block in which, Paoloni promised—and Ferrucci had confirmed from his computer—Alleva lived. They were waiting for Zambotto, who was accompanying a junior officer, and Ferrucci, who had apparently had difficulty persuading the superintendent-mechanic that he had a legitimate need for a car. Or was old enough to drive.

Blume wondered if Pernazzo had been fooled when he said they would be watching him. Hardly likely if he ever listened to the police unions and hierarchy complaining on the radio about their lack of resources.

Blume pulled the Motorola Tetra radio handset out of his jacket pocket and studied it. It looked like it was on. He handed it to Paoloni. "I can't turn this thing on."

"You needed to rekey and switch to DMO," said Paoloni.

"Right," said Blume. "You do it."

The door to the front of the apartment block opened, and a man with a pink top of some sort came out. Blume couldn't make out the features from where he was, and had not thought to bring binoculars. The man walked quickly.

Ferrucci's voice came out of the Motorola again. He had apparently decided to speak excitable Greek. "I have Alpha One quitting Charlie One. Alpha One out of Charlie," he said.

Before Blume could ask him to talk properly, Ferrucci began to make sense: "Subject does not appear to be carrying any object. Light yellow pants, pink polo shirt, baby blue pullover knotted over chest, soft brown shoes. Wallet in his back pocket. No visible weapons. Hand in pocket."

Ferrucci had only seen pictures of Alleva. So there was always a chance it was the wrong person.

"That'll be Alleva," said Paoloni. "He likes pastel colors, baby blue sweaters, that kind of stuff. It's sort of his trademark."

Ferrucci came back on the radio. "I have subject going right, right; no hesitation, unaware; right turn number one not taken, number one is not taken; subject proceeding straight. Right turn number two taken."

As Ferrucci finished his commentary, Alleva lifted his face and Blume recognized the piggy features.

"Subject checking road. Now scoping back toward six o'clock," continued the radio commentary.

"What do you think?" asked Paoloni. "Is Ferrucci high?"

"Leave him alone. He always gets landed with the paperwork. This is all very exciting for him," said Blume. "Even if it is a total waste of time."

"What was the name of your suspect again?"

"Angelo Pernazzo."

"And you think we should visit Pernazzo after this?"

"Yes. Before he figures out he's not being watched."

Ferrucci's happy voice interrupted them. "Crossing road, committed to turn, now unsighted to me, unsighted to me."

Blume handed Paoloni the Motorola. "Why don't we just get out and grab the bastard now?"

"Better not try it in this neighborhood," said Paoloni. "We don't want to draw much attention to it anyhow."

Ferrucci said, "Our man got into a black Land Cruiser."

Blume turned on the engine.

Paoloni held the radio to his ear and reported. "Zambotto and his partner have picked up the target. Zambotto agrees it's Alleva. They've taken up the eyeball on the Land Cruiser. We'll come in as backup and Ferrucci can be tail-end-Charlie." He put the radio down between the two seats, hooking a strap over the handbrake. "I'm putting this on hands-free now."

Blume moved onto the road, almost taking out a motor scooter that was overtaking an Opel station wagon that was overtaking a bus. Their car was now perpendicular to the traffic lane, blocking all vehicles coming from the left. The motorists on the right started speeding up to prevent them from completing the maneuver. The cars to their left started up a horn concerto.

Paoloni said, "That was subtle." He picked up the Motorola. "Zambotto, tell us where to go."

"Via della Magliana, north—go up to the intersection, hang a right."

Two minutes later, Zambotto confirmed that Alleva's Land Cruiser was continuing due north on Via Oderisi da Gubbio.

Blume reached the same road about thirty seconds later, and slowed down. Then Zambotto reported that the target had turned right and was moving east toward Piazza Fermi and Via Marconi.

"Something's wrong," said Blume.

Paoloni seemed to be trying to get a cigarette out his pants pocket. He stopped struggling long enough to say, "Why? What's wrong with that route?"

"Too roundabout. Don't like it," said Blume

"He has to turn right once he's on Via Marconi, which is southbound only at the intersection, but then maybe he'll take the first left, double back, and continue north. That's where his mother's house is. It's OK."

A light blue Nissan Micra cut in front of Blume, flashed its warning lights, and sped off.

"That was Ferrucci," said Blume.

"I got the eyeball," came Ferrucci's voice. Blume could hear his delight. "Piazza della Radio," continued Ferrucci. "Looks like he's trying to find parking. I'm pulling over. Wait. Subject is making another round of the piazza. Maybe he's looking for parking. What do I do?"

"Stay there, Ferrucci. Don't follow him out of the piazza, though he's probably made you already." Blume said to Paoloni, "Alleva's mother's house is farther away down toward the river. What's he doing circling that piazza?"

"It's Sunday morning. Porta Portese market is on," said Paoloni. "It's one of the last places available for parking."

"I still think he's circling because he knows he's being followed," said Blume.

Zambotto's voice came on the radio. "We've reached the piazza, too."

"OK," said Paoloni. "If Alleva leaves, you follow. Ferrucci, you stay."

Zambotto replied almost immediately, "He's leaving the piazza, headed back where he came from. We're following."

"I should stay here?" Ferrucci sounded disappointed, and no one even bothered answering him.

A few seconds later, Blume saw the Land Cruiser speed past him on the opposite side of the road. Following at a safe distance was Zambotto. The central island prevented Blume from making a U-turn and following.

"OK, Zambotto, we've lost him. You may as well follow him wherever he's going now."

"He's stopped at the intersection. Either he's turning left or . . . no, he's done a U-turn. He's coming up behind you now."

Blume watched his rear-view mirror. The Land Cruiser was coming down the road at high speed, weaving in and out of the traffic. He let it pass him, then accelerated into its slipstream. No point in subtlety now.

"This is like a chariot race in the Circus Maximus," said Blume. "Let's end it. When he gets back to the piazza at the bottom of the road, move in and stop him Ferrucci."

Paoloni cracked open his window and tried to slot the cigarette end through it. Blume pressed the accelerator to the floor to close the gap on Alleva's vehicle.

"Jesus," said Paoloni, as the wind blew the cigarette end back into the car.

Blume pressed the palm of his hand on the top of the steering wheel and twisted it leftward and rightward as he weaved between a Smart and a number 780. "Tell Ferrucci to stand by."

Paoloni stopped hunting for his burning cigarette. "Stand by for what?"

"To head off the target."

"Stand by, Ferrucci," Paoloni said. "Target headed back your way. We are now in pursuit." Paoloni bent down to see what had happened to the remains of the cigarette.

Putting his hands at a eight-and-four position on the steering wheel, Blume accelerated again and came racing up behind a blue van. The van driver began to move over to block them, Blume put his hand on the horn, kept it there, then began to pass. The blue van moved farther sideways.

"Motherfucking cunt," said Blume bursting into English. "Get the— the FUCK out of my way."

"I understood almost every word of that," said Paoloni. "He's not moving over."

"We're going to arrest that bastard in the van," said Blume. "Get his number."

"Closed his exit!" came Ferrucci's voice. "Looks like he's going to— no, wait, there's a person here wants . . . Motorbike helmet."

"Ferrucci. What . . ."

But Blume never finished his question.

Behind his ear, he heard a thick metallic clunk as the pre-tensing mechanism in his seatbelt engaged, and he felt himself being lifted upward. The very front of his mind seemed to snap a photographic still of the rear end of Alleva's vehicle, which had come to fill the entire windshield. The bumper on the Land Cruiser was higher than the front of the Punto and was everywhere to be seen, rising in front of him, massive. He noticed that Paoloni was tilting forward, head first, toward the floor. The spare wheel on the back of the Toyota was like a silver target. It had a black bull painted on it.

Then, with a violent convulsion, the seat spat Blume toward disintegrating squares of glass in front of him. The seatbelt did its job, and angrily snapped him back down, wrenching his shoulder, cracking his collar bone, slicing into his waist like a violin string, jerking urine out of his bladder. It was only after the tremendous noises had passed that Blume realized how loud they had been.

He did not remember closing his eyes, but he seemed to have missed the moment when the car in which he was traveling turned into something else. He was sitting in the open air, and could hear the wind ringing in his ears. He was free above, but below, the car was clutching him tightly around the legs, reluctant to let him go. Struggling, but not as much as he had feared, Blume managed to free his right leg, then his left. Both were still attached to his body. He was completely free of the car. Looking back in, he could see Paoloni's glistening, upside-down, angry face. The Toyota in front of him throbbed. Its engine was still running, but the smoked glass and height prevented him from seeing inside. He limped over to the passenger door and yanked it open. Even as he did so, he realized how foolish this was, and braced himself to receive a bullet point-blank through the head. He had not even pulled out his own weapon. But the driver's seat was empty. Reeling with relief overladen with a sense of enormous frustration, Blume moved with exquisite muscular pain toward the front of the vehicle, trying to get a line on the fugitive.

Then he heard three cracking sounds. At first he thought they had to be in his head, the aftermath of the accident, but the sounds had a definite locus that was outside the rush and roar of his own thoughts. There was something in the sound that was mechanical, powerful, and full of death. Blume now identified them as pistol shots, and he instinctively began to crouch as he tried to move toward them. He moved his right hand across his body as he sought his service pistol, but as he did so, he felt his left knee beginning to buckle. To stop his stumbling from turning into a fall, he sought to balance himself by throwing his arms out, like a tightrope walker caught in a gust of wind, and forgot about going for his weapon. He concentrated his eyes on the ground. Moving from the black tarmac of the road to the white concrete of the sidewalk, he noticed that what he had thought was sweat dripping from his forehead was a steady red stream of blood. He held his hands out and kept his eyes on the ground, staggering on. Footsteps were thundering behind him, and several figures overtook him, shouting as they went. All in Italian, he noticed. He could remember clear American voices making gleeful shouts in the long evenings after school. Now he found himself here, like this.

Blume continued to move forward, though he no longer knew why. At one point, his knee had given way, and, as he fell, his body swung around, and he saw the Fiat Punto in which he had been traveling smashed into the back of the Land Cruiser like a crumpled rose.

Paoloni and Zambotto had appeared from nowhere, passed him, and now seemed to have reached their destination, for they were standing perfectly still side by side like two communicants waiting for the priest to arrive with the host. Blume, staggering, retching, dripping, and moaning, felt like a drunk at a baptism as he came up behind them. They were contemplating a Nissan Micra whose passenger side window was shattered.

Inside, slumped sideways, head in the driver's seat, lay Ferrucci, his hand outstretched in what seemed to be a self-deprecating gesture. Don't mind me, I'll just lie here with my white face on this darkening seat.

Ferrucci's temple was pierced by a star-shaped wound. On the way in, a single soft-nosed bullet had tunneled a concave point of entry like the withered black sepal at the base of an apple.

Blume joined the silence. In the lull, he recalled the sound of a motorbike, which he had been listening to as it raced away. Only now that the sound was gone did he realize he had been hearing it at all.

Paoloni turned around to say something, and Blume saw fury in his eyes. He felt his legs buckle, and the sidewalk, sensing its chance, rose up and gave him a merciful blow on the back of the head.

23

BLUME LISTENED TO the clump of nurses' shoes across the hard hospital floor. The noise level increased as the door to his room opened, then decreased with a puff of air that smelled of antiseptic and mold as it was closed again.

A sigh escaped from someone nearby. Slyly, Blume opened an eye to see who it was, but all he saw was the ceiling. He tried to move his head sideways, but it would not budge. He opened both eyes wide in horror at the realization that he was paralyzed from the neck down. The door opened, closed as someone left, and he found himself alone in the room.

A strangled cry welled up from his chest, and he clenched his fists in rage. He kept them clenched for around ten seconds, then thought about that for a while. Slowly he unclenched them. Clenched them again. It hurt a bit, especially the left arm. Fine. He waved his hand, bent his knee, wiggled his toes, and flexed his elbows. Then he fell asleep.

When he next awoke, it was evening. Someone had turned on the television in the corner of the room, which he could hear but not see. A contestant who wanted to be a millionaire was taking her own sweet time about deciding whether Beethoven had written three, seven, nine, or no symphonies at all.

He remembered every particular of the operation he had fouled up: right from the moment he left his house in the small hours of the morning to the time he climbed into the Fiat Punto with Paoloni to when he had seen his junior colleague's martyred body. The Land Cruiser had stopped dead, they had driven straight into the back of it. The target had made his getaway, probably on that motorbike he remembered hearing. Someone had shot Ferrucci.

Blume turned his mind to his injuries. Memory served him better than present sensation in this case. He realized his neck was in a whiplash collar. He remembered hot metal folding around his heels before he pulled himself out of the car, and the way he had found it hard to walk. While standing looking at the dead Ferrucci, he had become aware of a fierce constriction in his rib cage. His nose, now bandaged, had hit the windshield, and he had heard his jaw crack. He ran his tongue over his teeth, and felt a fissure ending in a sharp point in his back molars.

The commercials segued into a news update.

Pain was filtering back into his legs, ankles, head, chest, arms. He was definitely coming off some sort of medication, and he wanted back on it. He dozed off and slept in fits and starts all evening and night. No one fed him.

WEDNESDAY, AUGUST 31

On Wednesday morning, he found himself wide awake. Certainly awake enough to worry if he had been knocked permanently stupid by the crash. Pain had dulled his powers of recollection, and the detailed reconstruction of events that he had been able to manage so easily the day before now seemed an impossible task. He was aching for a visitor and thirsting for knowledge of what had happened.

At ten in the morning, five hours after he had woken up, a doctor arrived.

"Ah, you're awake."

A nurse would have said, "We're awake." The doctor, more detached and fundamentally not caring one way or the other if he ever opened his eyes again, said "you." Blume couldn't say which annoyed him more.

"And hungry, and thirsty," said Blume. "I think I may die of thirst. Can I get fruit juice?" For hours he had been thinking of how fresh apple juice would feel in his throat.

"Yes, yes," said the doctor, as if to himself. He placed his hands, pudgy, white, on Blume's ears and stared into his eyes for a few moments. Then he took a penlight out of his breast pocket and shone the light directly into Blume's pupils. Blume couldn't turn his head away or grab the doctor by the lapels and head-butt him in his face, so he lay there looking at the doctor's nostril hair. Besides, he had an urgent question to ask.

"How long have I been here?"

"Boh." The doctor shrugged his shoulders, then consulted what Blume surmised was a chart on the wall behind him. "Admitted Sunday lunchtime, Monday, Tuesday, Wednesday. That makes three days."

"Three days?" Blume was outraged. He remembered bits of the journey in the ambulance, being rolled onto a stretcher, sharp pains inside his body that seemed to move outward, decreasing in intensity until they floated off his skin like cologne, and then sleep. This was surely only a few hours ago.

"Is this Intensive Care?"

"No. How could it be Intensive Care if you've had a visitor in here with you?" He patted his hands together.

"What visitor? What's his name? Or her name?"

"Why on earth would I know that?" said the doctor. "A colleague, I believe. Another policeman, who looks pretty beat-up. He got admitted shortly after you. He's asked to be informed when you're properly awake. I'll get a nurse to call him now. He left his name and number with the nurses. By the way, did you enjoy the morphine?"

"I was on morphine?"

"Oxycodone. Tiny dose. But no longer," said the doctor with a touch of relish. "I'm putting you on Celebrex, and then nothing, because, as I say, there's nothing wrong with you."

"Can I have some juice, please? Apple if it's available."

"I'll see about that when I've finished this examination. Now, can you move your feet in opposite directions?"

He could and did. The doctor frowned, as if Blume were pulling some silly stunt.

"You really are perfectly all right," he said. "When you came in, your pressure had dropped very low, and we suspected a ruptured spleen, but that was not the case."

His tone implied it should have been.

"Also, you had a head trauma, but the pressure in your skull remained manageable. Let me see, we also suspected broken ribs, but again, it was just bruising, so lucky again. Your left arm, now that is badly sprained . . . But," he concluded sadly, "not broken."

Blume had a hairline fracture in a kneecap and lacerations in the groin. The doctor seemed to enjoy the effect of this revelation, but eventually, and with some regret, revealed that they, too, were minor. Brightening

173

up a little, he remembered that Blume had managed to misalign his nose and, if he planned on breathing normally again, would require septorhino-plasty.

Blume asked again about getting some juice, and the doctor left, saying he would see what he could do. But he must have been thwarted in his efforts, because the juice never arrived.

After waiting for forty minutes, Blume turned himself around in the bed to see if he could find a button or something to call someone. Halfway through his movement, his ribs seemed to break again and his body locked itself into an agonizing position from which he dared not move. He started groaning and cursing. As his position became more painful and he felt his legs cramp up as well, his curses grew in volume and obscenity. A nurse with flagging cheeks and tired eyes appeared at his bedside and shoved him back down. Blume was about to protest when he realized that most of the pain had subsided.

"What was all that about?" she demanded. In humble tones, Blume begged for some apple juice, and the nurse left, also to see what could be done.

Blume dozed off and dreamed of crystal pitchers of lemonade sitting on a picnic table in Discovery Park, and his father pointing to Bainbridge Island. His mother was drinking a Tab, a beautiful drink for beautiful people, and for some reason was poking him painfully on the arm, over and over again. To get her to stop, he opened his eyes, and there was Paoloni, his unhealthy pale face brightened by a swollen combination of blues, yellows, and reds.

Paoloni handed Blume a small room-temperature carton of apricot pulp with a crooked straw in it.

"The nurse said you wanted this."

Blume's arms were heavy, his left hand damaged and his fingers numb. He felt very squeamish about moving his arm with the drip attached to it. It was all he could do to hold the small carton of juice up to his mouth and not dribble too much.

"Here." Paoloni waved Blume's wallet, keys, and cell phone. "I'm putting them in the top drawer here. They tell me your clothes were destroyed." He looked at Blume and said, "Your face didn't come out of it too badly. Your nose looks a bit . . . Ferrucci's dead."

"Yes, I know," said Blume. A clear picture formed in his mind of Ferrucci's exploded head, his pathetic gesture of defense.

"His funeral is later today."

"What time?"

"Four o'clock."

"I need you to bring me some clothes, Beppe. I'm not missing the funeral."

Paoloni received this pledge with such indifference, Blume wasn't sure he had heard.

"Did you hear what I said?"

Paoloni was gazing with an absent-minded air across the room. "Sure. I'll get someone to . . . if that's what you want. I'm not going."

"What do you mean, you're not going? Of course you're going. What sort of cop refuses to go to a colleague's funeral?"

"The sort of cop that killed him," said Paoloni.

Blume disentangled what he could of the events of the past few days, pulling apart the separate strands of thought that probably belonged to his opium sleep. His arrival in hospital, his being wheeled around, pushed, injected, and made to sleep—all that was hazy but everything before was clear. He was certain that Paoloni had been in the car beside him. Paoloni's declaration therefore made no sense.

"You didn't kill him."

"I might as well have, the way things turned out," said Paoloni.

"We all messed up. Me, especially, with my driving."

Paoloni shook his head. "I warned Alleva we were coming."

The realization seemed to hit Blume in the base of the stomach before it had registered in his head. "You told him that? Jesus, Beppe. You tipped them off. You tipped off Alleva, which is why he was ready. He called in Massoni to make his getaway, and Massoni shot Ferrucci."

Paoloni knotted his arms, crossed his feet, and twisted his body as if he was trying to screw himself into place.

"I didn't tell him, exactly. Like I didn't tell him the operation was going down that morning. All I said was we would be picking him up the next day."

"It's not so hard to guess that we'd have made our move in the morning."

"It wasn't supposed to happen like that," Paoloni said. "I figured Alleva might get rid of some merchandise, something like that, to make sure he wasn't caught with anything incriminating. He wasn't supposed to panic and run. He wasn't supposed to shoot. He didn't shoot. Massoni did."

"You informed a criminal about a police operation," said Blume. "That's what it comes down to. And a colleague got shot."

Perhaps it was the result of the bruising, but the fear on Paoloni's face was more yellow than white. His lips were chapped and swollen and dry, and he kept pausing in his speech as if to detach his tongue from the roof of his mouth.

"Alleva was supposed to come quietly. I gave him a heads-up. It was a gesture. He would owe me a favor, which I would cash in as soon as he got released."

"He owes us now," said Blume. "And if he makes trial, then he'll owe us his life."

"I'm going to get some water," said Paoloni.

"I wouldn't do that if I were you," said Blume. "Because I think as soon as you move out of my sight, I'm going to call in your name and order your arrest. Complicity in the murder of a fellow officer. That's what you'll be booked for."

Paoloni leaned over him, and for a moment Blume felt under attack, but then Paoloni's shoulders slumped forward.

"It's all gone to shit."

"Sit down, Beppe."

Paoloni sank into the chair, tucked his legs under it, and began to sway slightly back and forth.

"I liked Ferrucci. So maybe it didn't look like it. But he was a colleague . . . I mean, Alleva wasn't supposed to react. Alleva wasn't Clemente's killer. You know that. We were both agreed on that before all this happened, weren't we?"

Paoloni was right, but Blume was not about to offer easy comfort. "Stop swaying and look at me when you're talking to me," he said.

Paoloni stopped rocking back and forth, but kept his eyes to the floor as he spoke. "I didn't see any harm in making myself seem like an inside informant, since the operation was pointless to begin with. Alleva wouldn't

even have gotten charged. We had nothing on him. The tip-off was supposed to be a cheap favor that wouldn't have cost us anything. It just
went bad."

"And now?"

"I don't know, you're my commanding officer. Tell me what I am supposed to do."

Blume pulled himself upright, registering the pain it caused him only
after he had completed the movement. He turned his head slowly, like a
gracious monarch, to scan the room. Paoloni and he were the only people
there. The door was closed.

"Who else knows?"

"Nobody," said Paoloni. "Nobody except you."

"If I tell you to go and confess to Principe, go and turn yourself in, will
you do it?"

Paoloni looked at Blume in shock. Then he touched his forehead, and
nodded. "If that's what I have to do."

"It's what you have to do, Beppe," said Blume.

"Now? Right now, on the day of the funeral?"

"Yes."

"You won't help?"

"I am helping."

"It doesn't feel like help."

"Just promise me you'll do all I say. Exactly what I say."

"OK, I promise," said Paoloni. "You want me to go to Principe, tell him?"

Blume thought about it, as Paoloni resumed his swaying. "Maybe," he
said. "I need more information. I need to know about what happened after the accident. Where is Alleva?"

"He vanished. So did the shooter, Massoni."

"We know for sure it was Massoni shot Ferrucci?" asked Blume.

"Yes. The getaway was by motorbike. Ducati 999, which was abandoned
in the vicinity of Tor di Valle. Hidden in bushes and trash."

"When was it found?"

"The next morning. Monday, nine thirty-five."

"Just like that?"

"It is an abandoned site, ready for building. A crew of Albanians sent in
to set up prefab huts found it, got into a fight about who saw it first, fore-
man called for help."

Blume tried to picture it. He caught himself checking the story for plausibility. He allowed the building site to fade from his mind, imagined the two fugitives. "They could have made either of the airports. Right?"

"We checked flight manifests," said Paoloni. "All names were checked. Nothing. They would have had false passports."

"What about the bike?" asked Blume.

"It had been reported stolen a month before. It had been resprayed, license plate changed. Previous owner has no record, two kids, job in cell communications. Migali, I think his name was."

"Trace evidence on the bike?"

"Albanian paw prints all over. Also some GSR on the throttle, matches the residues at the scene, so we know the shooter was driving, but we knew that already."

"Shell casings?" asked Blume.

"Yes. Two nine-millimeter shells. Three shots, but we can't find one."

Blume tried to imagine the events. Alleva and Massoni fleeing toward the airport. The police standing in the parking lot like a bunch of shocked schoolgirls. Himself lying on the ground.

"No one went in pursuit?"

"We didn't get the license plate, and we weren't sure at first if there was just one motorbike or a car as well. Still aren't. It seemed like two people were on it. We called in backup immediately. But there was no interception of the bike."

"OK. What about tracing cell phone signals? When was that done?"

"Immediately. A trace was put on Alleva's phone immediately," said Paoloni.

"When you say immediately . . ." began Blume.

"I mean it. Within minutes. More or less at the same time as we called in backup."

"Because you had his cell number," said Blume.

"You can check that," said Paoloni. "My call giving Alleva's number was made before the ambulances came. I did it as soon as I thought about it, which was almost immediately. Within a minute."

"And the result?"

"They located Alleva's phone at home."

"When they check the provider's logs, your number will be there," said Blume.

"I know that," said Paoloni. He started to say something else, but then stopped.

"What?" said Blume. "You're thinking it would be easy enough to justify your call to Alleva without having to admit to tipping him off? Sure it would—but now you're asking me to say nothing. It's a big ask."

"I know . . . But there's something else." Paoloni bent his head down and mumbled something.

"Beppe, is there someone under my bed?"

"What? No."

"Then raise your head so I can hear you. What did you just say?"

"That Alleva called me."

"I thought you called him."

"No. I mean afterwards. After the killing. Alleva called me. He called me the day after."

24

BLUME KEPT HIS voice level. "Where was Alleva calling from?" he asked.

"I don't know. He was being careful. He began by telling me one radio mast was all I'd get. He didn't move position to make it difficult to trace. Also, he obscured the number."

"What did he say?"

"Three things. One, that he didn't pull the trigger. Two, that he never imagined anything like this would happen. And three, that he was sending the killer, Massoni, straight to us. He said to expect Massoni to come up the Via Casilina in an SUV in about half an hour. He also said he would call back when we had Massoni in custody. But surprise, surprise. Massoni never came driving up the road."

"What did you say to him?"

"I said we would get him anyhow. And I told him he would probably not live long."

"Then what did you do?"

"First I put out an alert to get Massoni picked up. I mentioned who the suspect was, just to make sure the cars got there on time. Then I called the Holy Ghost and asked him to take charge of any arrests that might result from the tip-off."

"Did he ask who the tip-off was from?"

"No, he didn't. He never does. Even you don't always ask."

"It's so often better not to know," said Blume. "Then what did you do?"

"I contacted the technicians in the Padua interception center immediately, gave them my number, gave them the time and date of his call, told them it was highest priority."

"And they accepted all that, from an inspector?"

"I told them it was to do with the killing of Ferrucci. They got back to me in two hours. They had not managed to triangulate Alleva's location because he never moved, and the phone number disappeared from the network immediately after, along with the IMEI code for the phone. So he must have removed the battery, probably smashed the device. He's being careful."

"Not so careful that he didn't make a call. They got no information at all?"

"No, they did. I was going to tell you. The call was made north of Rome, near Civitavecchia. It connected to a base transceiver station at the end of the Autostrada Azzurra, just above Civitavecchia. The radius is huge. Too big to work. And it was two days ago. He probably made the call, then destroyed the phone there."

"I see that," said Blume. "And you acted as quickly as you could? You reported contact between you and Alleva to the technical team?"

"Yes. Same as after the shooting. I don't care what happens to me as long as Alleva and Massoni get caught."

"But you do care what happens to you if they don't get caught," said Blume.

"I don't follow."

"Sure you do. I believe you when you say you'll come clean if it means catching Alleva and Massoni, but you'd prefer not to, if possible."

"Only if possible," said Paoloni.

"Right. But there's a corollary. If they don't get caught, then you don't want to get caught, either."

Paoloni was frowning in concentration, as if Blume's reasoning were new to him. "I suppose you're right."

"I need to believe that you put getting them into custody ahead of your career. If news of the tip-off comes out, I don't see how you can continue working with other police."

"The phone calls I made. I came here and told you. I'm doing what I can," said Paoloni.

Blume nodded. "OK. So, you got this phone call the day after the shooting. What time?"

"Morning, eight seventeen to eight twenty. Less than three minutes. That's what the technical report says."

"There's a report?"

"Yeah. They prepared a report. When they called me back to give me the information, they wanted to know who they could send the report to. They need authorization from a ranking officer or magistrate. I was hoping you could see to that."

Blume thought about it. The report was proof that Paoloni had done what he could to find Alleva.

"OK. Maybe I can intercept the report before it lands on the wrong desk. At least we know he was still in the country. Even if he was in a port city."

"It was only Civitavecchia," said Paoloni.

"You don't think Civitavecchia makes a good escape route?" said Blume.

"If you're escaping to Sicily or Sardinia and don't feel like you need to hurry, it's perfect," said Paoloni. "I think it's just sheer chance he called from there."

"Maybe it was deliberate misdirection. Still, there are ships to South America from there. Some ferries go to France, Corsica, Barcelona, or you could board a cruise ship going anywhere."

"Not anywhere fast," said Paoloni.

"Which is why the police don't watch seaports as closely as airports," said Blume. "I don't know. Maybe he sailed away an hour later. Say he got to Corsica or Nice, he could have flown from an airport there, especially if he's changing passports."

"They."

"What?"

"You keep saying 'he,' but there's two of them. Alleva and Massoni. And Massoni's the one who pulled the trigger."

"You're right," said Blume. "But I bet Alleva's escape plan is made for one. Staying together makes them more conspicuous, anyhow. They'll have split up. And if we find Alleva, then we'll find Massoni. Alleva's already shown he'll give up Massoni easily."

"Except he didn't," said Paoloni. "Massoni never came down the road in his SUV. We were watching other roads from the south and east as well. Nothing."

"Again, you're right. But if he can pretend to betray Massoni like that . . . I don't know. I think he could. Maybe he tried, but Massoni didn't fall into the trap. At any rate, I think they are now separated."

Blume peeled back the strip of bandage holding the needle in his arm and started sliding the needle out with his thumb. "Jesus. You'd think they could put a needle in without causing so much fucking bruising."

"Maybe you did that to yourself," said Paoloni.

"What?"

"In the accident."

"Oh, right."

"Like your nose."

"What about my nose?"

"It looks funny."

"Beppe, go downstairs, buy me a razor and shaving cream."

When Paoloni had left, Blume completed the removal of the intravenous feed, and stared at his arm with a look of disgust. He shoved the needle into the side of his mattress, took the keys, wallet, and phone Paoloni had brought him.

Paoloni returned, and Blume handed him the keys. "Go to my house, now. In the bedroom, there's a white cupboard with a sliding door. You'll see a suit wrapped in green plastic, or maybe blue. Anyway, take that. Get me a pair of socks from the chest of drawers and on your way out, next to the door, there's one of those plastic shoe holder things. Open it, take out a pair of black shoes. Bring the lot back here. Shit, a shirt. I need a shirt— and a tie, too. Either you iron me one or you buy me a new one. White, collar size sixteen, and a nice dark blue tie. No designs. There's a big menswear place down at Piazza Re di Roma, near the apartment. It should take you, what, forty minutes to get there and back. Less if you use a siren. Turn it off when you're buying me the shirt and tie."

"Are you leaving here?"

"I'm going to the funeral. We both are," said Blume.

25

WHILE PAOLONI WAS gone, Blume shaved, using the sink in his room. The whiplash collar made it difficult, and he couldn't get rid of some stubble on his chin. He checked his nose, and it seemed fine to him, maybe a little fatter and more off-center than before. Then he sat there in his paper-thin green hospital pajamas waiting for Paoloni. He checked his cell phone and found the battery had died.

When Paoloni eventually arrived, it was with a shirt with a 14½ collar. It would have been too small at the best of times, and did not come close to closing around the whiplash collar. Nor had he reckoned on his left arm not working at all. In the end, he had to forego the tie, which was a fat ugly thing anyhow, and get Paoloni to help him. As for Paoloni, he was now wearing a jacket and an open yellow shirt. His jeans were the same as before.

Blume had to get Paoloni to tie his shoelaces, and it was just then that the nurse with flabby cheeks walked in. He expected a hands-on-hips scene of womanly outrage, but she just glanced down at Paoloni and then at Blume.

"What are you doing?"

"My shoelaces, or he is."

"So you're leaving us. There'll be paperwork."

"Have it sent to me."

"No. You have to sign yourself out. We don't want you dying, then suing us."

Paoloni straightened up. "If he died, then he couldn't . . ."

"Yeah, OK, Beppe. Thanks." To the nurse he said, "Can you get me the forms to sign?"

"Of course. The question is whether you're even capable of pushing a pen."

"It's my left arm that hurts. My right's OK."

"You need to get that left arm in a sling if you're planning on discharging yourself—which, it goes without saying, I am opposed to your doing."

"It's a funeral. I have to be there."

The nurse shook her head. "And then I suppose you'll come straight back here?"

"To be honest," said Blume, "I hadn't really been planning . . ."

"I was kidding. What I'll do is send you down to emergency. They can put your arm in a sling. Then you'll book yourself into outpatients for some follow-up visits. Won't you?"

"Um . . ."

"You will. Because the discharge form will be waiting for you at the desk with a note from me. No return appointments, no discharge papers."

"Thanks, I appreciate this," said Blume. "It might get you into a bit of trouble, mightn't it, me disappearing like this?"

"Trouble with who? The doctors here? Hah!"

Blume thought if she had not been a middle-aged woman and a nurse, she might have spat on the floor at this point.

It took Blume, with Paoloni following him around like a silent dog, more than an hour to get his arm put in a sling, make an appointment to return in two days, and sign the discharge papers. Finally, he walked out of the hospital, expecting a sense of liberation and air, but the heat was so great that he forgot about everything else and just concentrated on not swaying or stumbling. Paoloni lit a cigarette and started across the parking lot, Blume followed.

As Paoloni drove them out of the lot, he lit another cigarette.

"Jesus Christ," said Blume, who was battling down wave after wave of nausea. "Put that out." Somewhere far below the nausea and the shooting pains assailing his body, Blume knew he was hungry. "Close the window and turn on the air-conditioning."

Paoloni flicked his new cigarette out the window, and spun the dial of the AC up to full. He closed his window, blew smoke from his mouth, and said, "We've still got too much time before it starts," then slowed down so much Blume thought he was going to pull in.

Blume was pleased to see they were about to enter the Giovanni XIII tunnel and get out of the sun for a bit. "Where are we going, by the way?"

"Borgata Fidene," said Paoloni.

"Right," said Blume. "So that's where Ferrucci lived."

The area of the city to which they were headed was a densely packed cluster of apartments built on a section of flood plain, hemmed in by a railway line, the beltway and a bend in the river. The area had never been properly paved, let alone cleaned, and there were no sidewalks, just rows and rows of cars parked against apartment block walls. Traffic sped up and down narrow strips of asphalt in the middle, where some children played. If two cars ever met in the center strip, one had to reverse all the way back to the beginning of the street. For this reason, the inhabitants tended to respect the one-way traffic signals, but they were less respectful of other laws. For a small area, it accounted for a lot of police work.

On Via Prati Fiscali, they hit a pothole so large Blume banged the side of his head against the window and wrenched his damaged arm.

Paoloni slowed down again. "Sorry."

"We two should not be in a car together. That's what it is," said Blume.

For the first time since he had walked into the hospital that morning, Paoloni smiled a little.

"You know, Beppe, my driving spooked Alleva. I lost my cool, and Alleva panicked. If he hadn't panicked, maybe Massoni wouldn't have seen any need to shoot Ferrucci."

"Massoni wouldn't have been there if I hadn't tipped Alleva off."

"All this is going to come out when internal affairs starts its investigation."

"I won't be telling them anything about your driving," said Paoloni.

"I appreciate that, but maybe you should."

"Shit, I should have turned off there," said Paoloni. "They put the sign for the Salaria at the exit, not before it . . ."

"Take the next exit, double back," said Blume. "If Alleva knew we were cops because you tipped him off, his actions don't make sense."

"That he fled like that and allowed his thug to kill Ferrucci?" said Paoloni. "I know. Massoni's thick, but I didn't think he'd deliberately shoot a cop. I'm sure Alleva didn't mean him to. That's why I believed Alleva when he phoned me, saying he was sending Massoni to us like a sacrificial bull."

"What do you think happened?" asked Blume.

"I think Alleva or Massoni thought we were someone else."

Blume said, "I think you're right. All it took was a few minutes, long enough to panic. Alleva gets the nod from you, what does he do? He gets rid of a few things, then maybe calls in Massoni to make arrangements, gets him to hide some stuff, prepare for custody, get some alibis, whatever. But they didn't meet to make a getaway. Also, if he was planning a getaway, the first thing he'd do is abandon Massoni."

Paoloni turned left onto a quiet street with trees and less trash than usual. "This way might even be quicker. Not as much traffic. We're almost there."

He rolled down the window, and within seconds the cool air inside the car was swamped by humid heat. "Mind if I smoke?" he said.

"Same answer as fifteen minutes ago," said Blume.

"Can I leave the window down, then? The air-conditioning gives me a headache. Also it gives me an acidic taste at the back of my throat. A bit like tomato skins. Ever get that?"

"No."

Blume had to raise his voice a little above the sound of the car engine echoing back from the building walls through Paoloni's window, "So Alleva arranges to meet Massoni, sees he's been followed, and thinks it is someone else, even though you warned him we were going to pick him up."

"I don't think he was expecting an operation like that, more of a visit from two cops, told to come quietly, like in the past," said Paoloni.

"And then my driving freaked him, he ran to Massoni, who had noticed Ferrucci, thought he was someone else . . . They thought it was an assassination attempt."

"Maybe," said Paoloni.

"Who are they scared of? Who would have them taken out? Innocenzi comes to mind."

"I thought about that, too," said Paoloni. "Suppose Innocenzi thought Alleva had killed Clemente. Clemente was fucking Innocenzi's daughter, which makes him sort of bastard family. So it's like Alleva killed Innocenzi's son-in-law, if you see what I mean. If Innocenzi thought that, then I wouldn't want to be Alleva. I wouldn't want to be anywhere near him. Getting shot would be good compared to getting disappeared, kept alive for days while Innocenzi used you to set an example to other would-be rebels and hopefuls."

"Enough to make you panic and start shooting," said Blume.

They arrived at a brick wall on which someone had painted "Romanians Out" and a backward swastika.

"This is it," said Paoloni.

"This is a church?" said Blume.

26

BEHIND THE PERIMETER wall was a church made of the same brick, surrounded by a parking area full of police vehicles, including a short Iveco bus. At first sight, the numbers seemed impressive, but the people took up far less space than their cars. Around half the police present were in uniform. All of them were wearing sunglasses. Paoloni had his on already.

"Go make yourself seen," Blume told Paoloni. "Tell them we'll get the people who did this, because we will. Relax. Nobody will blame you."

"Ferrucci's family would if they knew."

"They don't know," said Blume. "But even if they did, it's what your comrades think, not them."

Paoloni nodded and moved off.

Blume could feel a lot of eyes turning in his direction, then swiveling quickly away before he could catch them. That was fine. He wanted to be seen. It was important for them to see him there, out of the hospital, in attendance, back in charge. Some would appreciate it.

His new shirt was soaked through with sweat, and the sun was hurting his eyes. At best, he could stand another five minutes out here, waiting for the hearse to arrive. The doors to the church stood open, and the darkness inside seemed inviting. A hand pressed his shoulder, and Blume thought his legs might buckle from the added weight.

"The Holy Ghost wants you to go over to him so he can bless you in public." It was Principe.

"I don't feel like it," said Blume.

"I thought you wouldn't, which is why I'm warning you now. He was on television two days ago saying Alleva's actions and his subsequent disappearance are absolute proof of his guilt. You catch that item?"

"No. I was dead to the world."

"So you're to be congratulated for your brave effort," said Principe.

"He wants to associate my name rather than his own with Ferrucci's death." Blume found he was walking toward the yawning doors of the church, as if they were drawing him in.

"I thought you should know. Also, he's talking about promotion, which is really turning people against you."

"I need to get in there to sit down," said Blume.

"Fine. I'll walk you in. He's also shutting down the Clemente case."

"He can't do that."

"He can. Well, no, he can't. But he's the one who gets to make all the announcements of the decisions made by the big boys. Get this—on radio two days ago he was saying 'absence of evidence is not evidence of absence.' He is very pleased with the phrase. I'm pretty sure someone made him learn it off by heart. D'Amico, probably. The Holy Ghost's theory is that Alleva probably wore gloves when he killed Clemente."

"But there is evidence. Fingerprints, fibers, DNA traces all over the place."

"But they are not necessarily those of the killer."

"That's twisted logic." Blume could not think straight now. He made it to the door. The church seemed to be exhaling bad breath, but at least it was cool. There were plenty of empty pews to choose from. A short woman whose jet black hair showed white roots appeared in front of him, blocking his way.

"I am sorry," she said.

Blume glanced at her, but continued walking. As he passed, he said, "What for?"

"Your injuries."

"Oh, it's nothing. And now if you'll excuse me, I need to sit down."

He walked past her and threw himself into the back pew.

Principe said something to the woman with the dyed hair, then sat down beside him.

"You feeling OK?" he asked Blume, his voice dropping to a whisper as someone a few rows ahead turned around to look at them.

"Not really." Blume lowered his voice, too. "Look, I sent in a sample of hair to the labs. Did you hear anything about that?"

Principe nodded. "Yes, the head of the lab, Cantore—know him?"

"Not really. I've met him, but I can't say I know him."

"Well, Cantore wanted to know what your idea of a joke was."

"I know, I know. There was no chain of evidence, no consent given, no crime scene to justify lifting the sample—I just needed further confirmation that Manuela Innocenzi was in Clemente's apartment."

"So why did you send him the hair of a dog?"

Blume closed his eyes. He could see the funny side of it. There was definitely a funny side. But he didn't feel like laughing. Maybe when the funeral was over.

"They got saliva from the victim's eye," Principe continued. "The killer spat into it. The saliva contained a high quantity of cortisol, which indicates that the person was excited or anxious at the time of killing."

"That's useful information?"

"Cantore told me about the cortisol. I only mention it because it fits in with your idea that this was not a professional killing."

"Jesus," said Blume forgetting to keep his voice down. "We all know that. It was a knife attack. Can't we move on a bit?"

"No," said Principe. "That's just it: we can't."

"You're going to tell me I've been taken off the case," said Blume.

"What are you talking about? Of course you're off the case. You are supposed to be in a hospital bed. A kid was killed, two policemen injured."

"I know," said Blume. "I was one of the two. But you don't need me for the next step. I need you to issue an arrest warrant on a guy called Angelo Pernazzo. He's the one we want. For the Clemente murder."

"Who?"

"Angelo Pernazzo. Just get his fingerprints. That'll do it. I had a label . . ."

"Arrest on what charge?"

"Make something up. That's your job." But Principe was already shaking his head. "What—you mean you won't?"

"I can't," said Principe. He took off his shiny glasses and polished them on his sleeve. "They issued a writ of certiorari. The case, or the remnants of it, is being transferred to a different office."

The nervous woman with the black hair appeared at the end of the pew and gave him a half wave. Blume glared at her until she moved out of his scope of vision.

Principe had produced a sheaf of papers from inside his jacket pocket and was riffling through them. "The prosecutor general has taken me off the case. I am to write up everything on the Clemente case, then give it to them, and they'll incorporate it into a general file regarding possible corruption and abuse of office."

"What's this about?"

"I'm not entirely sure what's going on. This writ is the maneuver they always use when they want to stop us from investigating politicians. You ask me, I think Clemente's widow pulled strings to have it shut down."

"She's that powerful?"

"Her family's been in politics for two generations. She's got uncles, cousins in practically every party."

"Doesn't she want to know who killed her husband?"

"I think she's happy to think it was Alleva. She lived apart from her husband most of the year, is a good-looking woman, has ministerial prospects, and would no doubt prefer their private life not to be the object of police investigation and press speculation."

"What about Angelo Pernazzo?"

"Weren't you listening? I no longer have jurisdictional competence. And even if I did, it would be hard for me to give instructions based on your hunches."

"It's more than a hunch."

Principe sighed. "Supposing I could do something, what would it be?"

"Get his fingerprints. That's all it will take."

"I can't order it. But maybe I can make representation to the prosecutor general. I'm taking it your suspect has no alibi."

Blume hesitated.

"Alec, you're not going to tell me to risk having a run-in with the prosecutor general by betting on a feeling you have against someone who does have an alibi?"

"He has an alibi, only I don't like it," said Blume.

"I don't like a lot of people, but that doesn't mean they're not real, unfortunately."

"It's a computer alibi," said Blume and explained about Pernazzo's online poker, while Principe's impatience made him rock back and forth in the pew as he listened.

At the end he said, "There's nothing I can do with that. Can't you see?"

"Get the technicians to check out his alibi, then," said Blume. "We've got his name and address, they can see if he was online from his home when he said he was."

"Telecom Italia needs a court order to release the names of customers . . . I could do it, bundle his IP with an investigation into file-sharing or something. It's a lot of work."

"Not officially. Just let the computer crimes division know you and I are interested in this IP address. They'll help. Tell you what, get in contact with a guy called Giacomo Rosati. He knows me. Explain the situation, then get him to call me directly if anything turns up."

Principe puffed out his cheeks and shook his head, but agreed. "Do you mind if we get back to the other case? Ferrucci's murder. That's where all the attention is focused now."

Blume tried to nod, but his whiplash collar would not allow it. From the front of the church, a group of six young policemen in dress uniform and white gloves stood up and began walking toward the exit.

"The pallbearers," said Principe. "It looks as if the coffin has arrived."

"We may as well stay here, then," said Blume. "Where's the family? I need to pay my respects after."

Principe nodded. "Down there. Second row from front. He had a sister."

Blume saw the back of the head of a young woman with long dark hair. Beside her sat a bald man who had hidden his face behind a hymn sheet. His shoulders were shaking.

"And the mother?"

"For some reason, she feels she has to greet everyone as they arrive. That was her at the entrance. The one with the dyed black hair," said Principe.

Blume closed his eyes. "I didn't realize that was her."

"You look like death," said Principe. "Are you coming down to the front?"

"No," said Blume. "I'll stay here."

Principe hesitated. "Are you sure you're OK?"

"I am sure I am not OK," said Blume. "I never said I was OK. I feel like shit. Which is why I'll stay here at the back. You go down front. Also, tell Paoloni to meet me here afterwards."

"Fine," said Principe. As he walked down the aisle, the pallbearers arrived, bearing the coffin on their shoulders. All the cops in sunglasses who had been outside followed behind, veering off to fill the middle pews as the coffin continued its voyage down to the front. The last policeman to take his place was Gallone, who came down the aisle with a slow, reverent gait, his face a mask of sorrow, his eyes downcast. Before the altar, he made the sign of the cross, bowed his head, and genuflected, staying there on bended knee like Jesus falling for the third time, before rising and finally taking his place. A smaller knot of young people and, somewhere in the middle of them, Ferrucci's mother followed. Everyone seemed to be talking, and there was a great deal of movement around the sides of the church as groups formed, dissolved, and moved on, and people decided to move to places closer to or farther from the coffin. No one came to sit beside Blume.

A scuffling and scurrying seemed to be coming from below his pew, and Blume watched in horror as a dog-like creature with Pernazzo's face leapt casually onto the pew beside him, and sat there, cool as a fucking cucumber. Blume knew it was not real, but he still felt he should warn the people in front.

He felt himself falling and grabbed onto the seat. The dog thing was gone, the church had become quieter, and the priest was speaking about the supreme sacrifice of Officer . . . Ferruzz—he corrected himself, Officer Ferrucci. Ferrucci, he repeated, to show he knew who he was talking about. Marco.

Eternal rest grant unto him, O Lord. He shall be justified in everlasting memory, and shall not fear evil reports.

Blume could smell the formaldehyde. He had caught a whiff as the coffin went by, but it had not registered. Now the smell was carried back to him on the steam of the incense the priest had released into the air. Beneath the harsh taste of camphor and cloves, he detected the sweet, familiar smell of death. It came in through his mouth and was swirling in his stomach.

My soul is deprived of peace, I have forgotten what happiness is;
I tell myself my future is lost, all that I hoped for from the Lord.

Someone slid into his pew, but he found it too painful to turn his head to see who it was.

The favors of the Lord are not exhausted, his mercies are not spent;
They are renewed each morning, so great is his faithfulness.

Blume felt himself tilt back into blackness again. No one would notice him at the back. He tried to breathe through his nose rather than his mouth, but heard himself let out a sudden rude snore, loud as a fart. People turned around to stare at him in disapproval. Pernazzo stood three rows ahead, laughing. Blume jerked himself awake, ready for action, but Pernazzo resolved himself into a sovrintendente from the Corviale district.

Ferrucci's sister, more girl than woman, tears streaming down her face, had just finished saying something about when she and her brother were little, and was now being accompanied back to her seat by her boyfriend or husband. Or was there another brother? She staggered back to her father, who still shook as if in silent mirth. The mother with the short black hair stroked her daughter's face. The policemen in sunglasses sat immobile in their pews as a song, which was not religious, began to play from the speakers. What was it she had just told them about this music? The song Marco had tried to teach her to play on guitar, "Everybody Hurts." True enough, thought Blume, but not everyone sings about it in such a whiny voice.

Blume could see the priest sitting off to the side in his purple vestments, not liking the profane music. Blume didn't like it either. For one thing, Ferrucci had been too young to be listening to the likes of REM. He suspected the sister had chosen it for herself. Her brother was beyond hurting now.

A cool hand on his forehead, and a woman's soft voice. "Hello, Commissioner," said Kristin, quietly. "I thought at first you were ignoring me, but you're not well, are you?"

Blume turned too quickly and was rewarded with a searing pain in the side of his neck.

"Easy, now," said Kristin, as if to a large dog. "I've seen you black out twice. You should be in the hospital."

"I know," said Blume. "But I had to be here."

"It's almost over," whispered Kristin. "Communion soon."

"That means we're near the end?"

"Yes."

"Are you a Catholic, then?"

"Lutheran. And you?"

"I have no idea. My parents forgot to tell me," said Blume. "What are you doing here?"

"I came to pay my respects. It's not the first time I have been to a policeman's funeral, nor will it be the last. Also, I knew you'd be here."

"You knew that? I didn't even know it myself until a few hours ago."

"I phoned the hospital. They put me on hold and after fifteen minutes told me you had gone. I figured this was where."

For a moment, Blume was not sure if Kristin was any more real than the creature he had seen sitting on the pew. At the front of the church, people were shuffling to and from the altar rail receiving communion. A lot of them were policemen.

He reached out his hand and she touched it for a moment. "Are you here in some sort of official capacity?" he asked.

"You seem to want to distinguish between official and genuine," said Kristin. "I am here as a representative of the embassy, and I am here because I care. Official and genuine at once, same as some of the senior policemen at the front. I am also here for you. I think you are somebody who cares. I think you'd like to help me, keep in contact."

"Contact with you, yes. I didn't agree to be a . . . what is it I am supposed to be?"

"It's not a formal thing. Make up your own name for it. Adviser, consultant, liaison officer, technical collaborator. Another ear on the ground for the embassy."

"I wouldn't have to provide confidential information?"

"Of course not. You wouldn't get paid a cent, either. It's a good citizenship thing. A friendship thing."

"Let me think about it," said Blume.

Applause broke out at the front of the church, and increased in intensity as the pallbearers made their way back up the aisle carrying out what they had carried in. The priest followed, swinging the censer, filling the air with Catholic novocaine. Blume and Kristin rose, and she applauded, too, while he stood there with his arm in a sling.

Paoloni did not come to him as requested, so Blume had to leave Kristin and go in search of him. He made his way over to a knot of policemen with a hard look in their eyes as they sucked on their cigarettes and exchanged monosyllables. He knew that vengeful look. He detached Paoloni from the group.

"I need you to do something."

"Is it to do with Ferrucci's killer?"

"No," said Blume. "It's to do with Clemente's."

"Oh, right." Paoloni shuffled his feet and looked back at the group of policemen. Paoloni was a different person from the penitent of a few hours ago. It was as if Paoloni had been infused with new purpose. It may have been the emotional effect of the funeral mass or—a thought occurred to Blume.

"Have you had any tip-offs about Alleva?"

"Have I had any tip-offs about Alleva? When could I have got a tip-off? When we were in church?"

"You could have got one just now. When you were outside here with the others," said Blume.

"No, I have not had any tip-offs about Alleva. Is that what you wanted to ask me?"

Blume was not sure how much longer he would last in the heat. He needed to lie down. "No, Beppe. I need you to deal with some business I left unfinished."

He gave Paoloni Pernazzo's address and told him to get there.

"If you can't arrest him for something, just stay close to him. I'll get you the authorization you need."

"Can't you get it now, send someone else?"

"No, Beppe. I can't get it right now, and why do you want me to send someone else—have you got better things to do? Also, aren't you forgetting something? You, me, this morning's conversation?"

Paoloni glanced quickly behind him, then nodded. "I remember." Then he looked at Blume in surprise. "Are you OK? What are you doing?"

"What do you mean?"

"You're leaning sideways."

Blume realized he had placed his full weight on one leg. He tried to rebalance, but his knee buckled and he found himself overbalancing left-ward, and he could not put out his arm to steady himself. He pivoted on his foot and pushed backward, and ended up falling on his ass, watched by mourners and policemen.

Kristin, behind him, spoke in English, "You got some nice moves there, Alec. Teach them to me sometime, huh?"

"Sure."

Kristin and Paoloni helped him back to his feet, but he felt like his head was full of helium and his chest full of lead.

"We're leaving here right now," said Kristin. "You're coming with me."

27

K RISTIN DROVE, AND Blume slept. He thought she would need directions to get to his apartment, but once he gave her the address she nodded and set off. She knew her way around the city.

He awoke as they reached his street. Kristin found a parking place and said, "I'll come up, make sure you don't die before you get there."

Blume was going to protest that he felt fine, but then thought better of it. For starters, he did not feel fine. They rode the elevator in silence, and Blume wondered what his conversational approach should be once they got inside. He hoped his apartment was tidy.

Blume sat on the sofa in his living room and decided they could talk about the funeral. Fifteen seconds later, he was asleep.

He felt like he had been asleep for only a few minutes when he was woken by the sound of his home telephone ringing. He heard Kristin answer. She walked in to him and handed him his cordless handset.

He was expecting Paoloni to call about developments with Pernazzo, but Paoloni had never called him at this number. Then he remembered his cell phone was dead.

"What time is it?" he asked as he took the phone.

"Twenty-five past ten."

"*Pronto?*" he said into the phone expecting the familiar wary pause and throat clearing with which Paoloni began his conversations, but it was a woman's voice.

"Commissioner Blume?"

"Yes, speaking." It took him a few seconds to place the voice.

"This is Sveva Romagnolo . . ." She allowed a few beats to pass and too late he realized he was supposed to say something. "Arturo Clemente's widow. We spoke last Saturday."

"Yes, I know who you are." That came out wrong.

"I'm glad you remember. Perhaps we could talk again about the progress made in the case?"

"Yes, we could, only—"

"Only you have not made much progress, have you?"

"I wouldn't say that. These things take time and—"

"I was told I would be kept abreast of developments, but this was not true, was it?"

Since her tone was rhetorical, Blume said nothing, to allow her to get to the point. Kristin disappeared into the kitchen.

"The director general of RAI 2 is a personal friend of mine. This morning he invited me to his office, and together we watched a documentary made by a man I thought was my friend, or at least my husband's friend."

"Are you talking about Di Tivoli?"

"Of course I'm talking about that worm. Who else could do a thing like this?"

"A thing like what?"

"Make a documentary like this. But you know what else annoys me?"

"What?"

"If Di Tivoli knew all this, then so did the police, and I was not told."

"All what?"

"What's in the *documentary*," she said giving a sing-song lilt to the last word to underscore his stupidity. "It airs in five minutes. I tried to call earlier, but you were not in, and the cell phone number you left with me does not work."

"You don't like what's in the documentary?"

"Not at all."

"So your friend in television wasn't such a friend that he could stop the documentary from going out?"

"I would not have dreamed of asking him. If it's the truth, then it's the truth and must be seen. I am not Berlusconi."

"But the man who made the documentary is a worm for making it?" Blume wasn't trying to score debating points off her, he just did not want her to realize how little he was understanding of the conversation.

"Di Tivoli was always a worm."

Blume saw no point in pursuing this further until he had seen the show she was talking about. "And you say it starts in five minutes?"

"Less now. I thought you might have seen it already."

"No. No, I haven't."

"Well, will you watch it now?"

"Yes, of course I will," said Blume.

Finally, Romagnolo's tone softened slightly. "I realize you were injured in the line of duty and lost a colleague. That was in connection with my husband's murder, wasn't it?"

"I can't really tell you that sort of thing. At least not like this on the phone."

"Well, I know it was, because I have my sources, and your colleagues Gallone and D'Amico report to them, as I am sure you know. Have you turned on your television? The documentary starts after the ad break."

Kristin reappeared and Blume pointed at the TV and mimed turning it on with a remote control. She came over, bent over him, and removed it from behind his back. Blume held up two fingers, and she turned on RAI 2.

"I have it on now," he told Romagnolo.

"Good. I'd like us to meet tomorrow. Do you think you can manage that?"

"Maybe not tomorrow."

"Well, it had better be soon," she said and hung up.

The ads ended, and Taddeo Di Tivoli's face appeared on-screen.

"La TV Di Tivoli" was the name of the show. Tonight's episode, Di Tivoli promised his viewers, was going to be a scathing report on cruelty to animals and the failings of Italian law enforcement. The title of this week's episode was "*Una vita da cani*," A Dog's Life.

"Are we going to watch this?" asked Kristin, taking a seat in the armchair rather than, as he had been hoping, on the sofa beside him.

"Yes. It's to do with a case I am, or was, involved in. Well, you know, don't you?"

"More or less," said Kristin. "What I'm interested in now is the widow and the possibility of political fallout."

"Political fallout?"

"If there is any. Then I can put it into a report from the country team, flag the report for the DCM's attention. It'll make me look good. You, too."

"Who's the DCM? The lead singer in this country band of yours?"

"Yes. Deputy Chief of Mission. He's OK."

"Well, I may be meeting her tomorrow," said Blume. "In the morning." It was hardly enough to get Kristin to stay the night, but it was worth a try.

Di Tivoli had added blond highlights to his mop of ginger and gray hair since Blume last saw him. He looked slimmer, too. He reused plenty of footage from the show that Blume had watched days ago with Ferrucci.

Once again, he saw the pictures of dogs with torn bloody ears that had so upset Ferrucci. Then back to the studio to see Di Tivoli shaking his head sadly, before brightening up a little and announcing that there were people and organizations dedicated to fighting such horrors. The screen filled with a photograph of a younger version of Clemente. It dwelled on the face for some time, as Di Tivoli did a voiceover describing Clemente's unstinting commitment and fundamental sense of justice. The report described the founding of the Anti-Vivisection League in 1977, when a group of like-minded individuals inspired by a sense of duty and compassion banded together to defend the defenseless. This was also the year in which the infamous Magliana Gang embarked on its blood-fueled exploits, Di Tivoli said. Blume watched some footage of young animal rights women answering phones. Then back to the picture of Clemente and Di Tivoli's voice: *On Friday, August 26, Arturo Clemente was brutally knifed to death in the safety of his own home.*

"Your case," said Kristin.

"As far as it goes. The crime scene was compromised, too much time has passed, and other even more serious things have happened, but, yes, it's still my case."

A red script imitating the style of a rubber stamp slammed the word "*Assassinato*" diagonally across Clemente's face, which then dissolved into nothingness to reveal Di Tivoli with grim demeanor standing in the studio, one hand resting on a desk. He wondered who murdered Clemente, and why. He ran his hands feelingly through his hair, and asked whether the killer would ever be caught. Sadly, he held out little hope for justice, given that the criminal investigation conducted by the Rome police had been unprofessional, incompetent, slapdash, short-lived, and inaccurate.

"Is this reporter some sort of enemy?" asked Kristin.

"It looks that way," said Blume.

From the screen, Di Tivoli wanted to know why the police had completely failed to follow the most obvious lead. Why was he, a mere reporter, able to discover a vital witness who—he paused, turned ninety degrees to his left to address a different studio camera—might even be a suspect, a person the police had never even interviewed? An image of Manuela Innocenzi filled the screen. She was at least ten years younger in the photo than when Blume had interviewed her. Even then her hair was carrot-colored.

Who is this woman, and what is her connection with the Clemente case, demanded Di Tivoli. The answer, he promised, was deeply disturbing, and was coming right up, after the break.

Di Tivoli spent three minutes outlining the first half of the show. Then up came the picture of the woman again. As Di Tivoli said her name, it appeared with a ticker-tape effect below the photograph: *Manuela Innocenzi, 41 years of age.* Fund contributor and card-carrying member of LAV.

One of the last people to see Clemente alive, noted Di Tivoli, Manuela Innocenzi was seen by him three nights before the murder. The pale-faced girl with black glasses from Clemente's office appeared on-screen and confirmed this. She had seen them leave the LAV office together on the Tuesday before the tragic event. Had she told the police this? Yes.

Who is Manuela Innocenzi?

The scene cut to old footage of gunshot victims in cars, lying on the street. *Magliana, Rome, 1986,* said the caption. Local crime is converging with high politics, said Di Tivoli, and these are just some of the victims of the spiral of violence caused by the power vacuum. More shots of dead bodies, most of whom, Blume reflected, had got what was coming to them. The political-criminal nexus started unraveling and the police struck decisively at the power structures and key figures, culminating in the successful Colosseo operation. Blume remembered that.

Now a new type of apolitical criminal leadership emerges, said Di Tivoli, slipping comfortably into the historic present. They break the political ties, limit their areas of operations, and scale down the killing spree by striking an agreement on territory and areas of operations. The triumvirate, as they became known, gain a reputation for "moderation." Di Tivoli, still standing in front of his desk, gave the word an ironic inflection, then added, "But it is a peculiar term to use, 'moderation.' Some might call it stalemate, or compromise, or corruption, or the defeat of the rule of law. For a quarter of a century, the police have not disturbed the criminal status quo in the districts of Magliana, Tufello, Ostia, Corviale, Laurentino 38, Tor Bella Monaca, Tor de' Schiavi, Pietralata, Casalbruciato, and Centocelle."

Di Tivoli stood before three photos of aging men: two jowly, fat; one thin with combed back white hair, resembling an osprey. He introduced them to his audience: Gianfranco D'Antonio, Fabio Urbani, and the thin one, known as "er falco," real name Benedetto Innocenzi, father of *the woman Clemente was last seen with*!

The rest of the show was repetition and filler. As the closing credits were rolling, the cordless rang again.

"I need to recharge my cell," said Blume.

"I'll do it," said Kristin, standing up. "I saw the recharger in the kitchen."

Blume answered the phone.

"Did you just see Di Tivoli's effort at investigative journalism?"

It was Principe.

"He's decided to force open the case again," said Blume.

"You and I are still off it, and we can be thankful," said Principe. "The widow phoned me earlier to complain about the show and its maker. Di Tivoli had the gall to tarnish the image of the heroic husband by revealing his tryst with that Innocenzi woman. Now, when she goes back to parliament, she's going to be the wife of the guy who was fucking the daughter of a gangland boss. Bad PR. Makes her look stupid, or even complicit. Di Tivoli hasn't done us any favors, either. He phoned me today, too."

"What did he want?" asked Blume.

"He was more interested in that Nicotra case. The sex scandal. He did the journalist thing, pretending it had nothing to do with him, really. But when I didn't give him any information, he started getting nasty, then asked what it feels like to be an incompetent prosecutor directing incompetent policemen," said Principe.

"It occurs to me that Innocenzi is not going to be pleased with the latest developments."

"Di Tivoli pretty much laid the blame for Clemente's murder at his door," agreed Principe. "That's . . . I don't know. Reckless, suicidal, brave even, in a creepy sort of Di Tivoli way. You don't go around accusing Innocenzi of stuff like that."

"Especially when it's probably not true," said Blume.

"I was going to ask you. You're still convinced it was that . . . I forget his name."

"Angelo Pernazzo," said Blume. "I am waiting for news on him from Paoloni. When I get some, I'm going to come back to you, get you to do something."

"I told you, I am no longer directing the investigation," said Principe. "What that means, apart from my career if I ignore an order, is that any evidence we gather will be inadmissible, any actions we take will be illegal."

Blume ignored this. Principe was right up to a point, but there were ways of getting around orders, especially for a magistrate who could cite any one of hundreds of contradictory sections of the *Code of Criminal Procedure*. Principe did not need a legal justification, he needed convincing—and he needed to be interested. Keeping his tone casual, Blume decided to go in for some speculation.

"Have you thought that Di Tivoli may have something to do with it?"

"Di Tivoli? No. How would that work?"

Kristin, who had returned and was leaning against the back of the armchair, hand on chin, looked interested.

"Well," said Blume, gathering his thoughts, "Di Tivoli obviously despised Clemente. You saw the show. It was like he was dancing on his grave. Di Tivoli knew about Clemente's affair with Manuela. Why did he not use it before now? It seems to me like Clemente had something on him. Maybe Clemente knew something about this Nicotra sex thing?"

"If you're asking why Di Tivoli did not use this knowledge of Manuela before now, I can think of many reasons. Maybe because they were friends. Maybe it just took him until now to turn his knowledge into a scandal show. Maybe he didn't know about it, or he had better things to do, or because it doesn't matter, or because his friend Clemente was not dead yet," said Principe. "If you're trying to get me to pursue a new line of inquiry, you're going to have to do better than that."

"For a friend, Di Tivoli has dragged Clemente's reputation through the mud."

"He's a journalist, Alec. That's what they do. And Clemente is way past caring. Only one who cares is his wife. Maybe Di Tivoli is doing the opposite, getting back at the wife on Clemente's behalf. Whatever the case, I don't see any connection with the Nicotra sex scandal, and neither do you. You just want me to get back into the case, but I told you, I can't."

"OK. What about Innocenzi, then?" said Blume.

Principe sighed. "What about him?"

"I don't know," said Blume. "Just a thought."

"So you're giving up on the idea that it was this Pernazzo character?"

"No," said Blume. "Maybe Innocenzi used Pernazzo to kill Clemente."

"Innocenzi decides not to use anyone from his army of killers, and sends in a first-timer, a slasher, someone who was going to leave trace evidence everywhere and would probably not know any better than to confess to everything and implicate Innocenzi when caught? Is that what you're trying to say, Alec?"

"All right, what about Alleva? Maybe Alleva hired Pernazzo. Alleva gets people into debt, makes them do things."

28

A BEEPING SOUND woke him up. By the time he reached the kitchen, he had registered that his phone was recharged and ringing, and Kristin was gone. He felt as if he had been drinking cheap grappa for a week. His bandaged arm throbbed, and as he reached out for the phone, he felt that the movement would snap his neck like a dry stick. As he touched the phone, it stopped trembling and beeping.

Blume swayed over to the refrigerator, yanked it open, and gazed at the desolation within. He removed a blue lemon and a black onion, and dropped them into the plastic bag below his sink. He carried the half-finished carton of milk with him into the bathroom, poured the yellow and green slop inside into the toilet bowl then pissed on top of the swirling mix. He stood there fascinated for a while, before flushing, washing his one functioning hand and returning to the kitchen for a breakfast of dry Rice Krispies. He had never noticed how salty they were without milk.

Caller ID had been withheld on the last call. Blume looked through the menu, but found no trace of any communication from Paoloni. He put down his cereal spoon and thumbed in Paoloni's number which he knew by heart, but got a message saying the number was unavailable and offering to send a text message to tell him when it became available again. In Blume's experience, this service had never worked, but he keyed in the digit 0 as instructed. Telecom Italia thanked him.

The salty cereal gave him enough energy to find more food in the house. After several boiled eggs, two pots of coffee, and four *friselle* steeped in olive oil, he felt better. Still no text message to say Paoloni was available.

Blume phoned the office, asked to be patched through to wherever Paoloni was, but was told Paoloni was on leave. They tried the same number Blume had been using, with the same result.

Although he didn't like to have to ask, Blume said, "I don't suppose you heard anything about a guy called Pernazzo getting arrested, did you?"

The sovrintendente at the desk had Blume repeat the name. Blume could picture him shaking his oversized shaggy head and blinking his two pin-hole eyes as he tried to think. "No," he said eventually. "No Pernazzo got brought in. I heard nothing. Maybe he was brought to a different *commissariato*?"

Blume thanked him, and was about to hang up when the sovrintendente seemed to be struck with a bright thought.

"Do you want to talk to the vicequestore?"

"He's there in his office?"

"No. But I can connect you to his cell phone if you want."

"No, it's OK. Thanks," said Blume.

"No problem."

Blume hung up, opened the dishwasher to put his plate in, and found it was full of clean stuff already. Rather than empty the dishwasher, he washed his plate and cereal bowl, using his one hand at the kitchen sink, and soaked himself. Fine. He needed a shower anyhow.

He waited for the water to warm, then stood beneath the dribble seeping out from the lime-encrusted showerhead, and lathered shampoo into his scalp. The phone rang again.

As he reached the kitchen, naked and dripping, it stopped. Once more, caller ID had been withheld. Paoloni was probably calling from an unregistered phone. Or maybe it was a call from behind a switchboard. Then it could be Kristin, calling him from her office in the embassy. He sat down at the kitchen table to dry out and wait for the next call.

Ten minutes later, the phone started ringing, slightly freaking him out since he had just then been staring at it and willing it to do exactly that.

It was Sveva Romagnolo. She wanted to see him now.

Blume said, "Your caller ID is hidden."

"I know. I'm not sure how to change the setting. Why? Is it a problem?"

"I suppose not."

She asked where they should meet.

"I don't know," said Blume, annoyed. "You're the one wants to meet. I didn't even say I would meet you today. You decide."

"I need a place where I won't be seen."

Blume said, "So this is to be a secret meeting?"

"Not secret. I just don't want to bump into anyone I know. I prefer it that way."

"Do you know anyone on Via Appia Nuova?"

Not that she could think of, so Blume made an arrangement to meet her in an hour at a bar five minutes from his house. If she wanted to go somewhere she wouldn't be known, she may as well come over to his zone of the city, to where he liked to hang out at breakfast, eating some mighty fine pastries with pistachio filling. He checked his appearance in the mirror and detached the whiplash collar, tossing it on the hall table. It made him look like an idiot.

When Blume arrived the bartender was putting out trays of lunchtime sandwiches. The pistachio pastries were long gone. Blume had two donuts and a sandwich while he waited. He hoped she would arrive before the lunchtime crowd did.

She came in the door at the same time as a crowd of workers from the Banca di Agricoltura next door, but unmistakably not part of them. Blume found it hard to work out how certain women did this. They stood out from others without seeming to wear clothes that were particularly different, in this case a yellow silk blouse with a Chinese collar, a fawn skirt, strange sandal-shoes of the same color that looked like a child might wear them, a shoulder bag. Not too much makeup. Clean, unfussy, simple, and somehow visibly wealthy. Maybe it was the way she moved.

She sat down on a chair opposite him that he had already had to defend twice as the place filled up. The noise level rose as the bank staff took their seats, joshed with each other.

"Can I get you anything?" offered Blume.

"No."

"Bettino might send the bartender round to ask for your order. You're occupying a place at lunchtime."

"I meant to get here earlier. It took me some time to find it. Well, it took the idiot taxi driver some time," she said. "What happened to your nose?"

"You mean my arm?"

"Well, that, too. I'm sorry. It was a stupid question. I know you were injured in that terrible attack."

"You wanted to talk," said Blume.

"Yes."

As Blume had predicted, the bartender came up and stood expectantly beside Sveva. She ordered a grapefruit juice, and turned back to Blume.

The barman duly noted down one grapefruit juice, then asked what she would be having for lunch.

Sveva looked at him with revulsion. "I don't want to *eat*."

"Yes, you do," said Blume.

"No, I do not."

"Look, I come here three or four times a week. I stay on good terms with them. Choose something."

"You choose," said Sveva.

"She'll have the *panino con la coltellata*," said Blume.

"*Scusi?*" said the barman.

Blume repeated himself. "*Panino con la cotoletta. Cotoletta alla Milanese.*"

The bartender nodded, then moved off. Blume noticed that Sveva was looking at him strangely.

"I'm not going to order just for appearances," he said. "When it comes, I'll eat it. A nice bit of fried meat will do me nicely."

"That's not what—I just thought you said—never mind. Tell me about the investigation."

"I can't. I mean, I wouldn't anyway, even if it was still my case, but seeing as it's not, I can't."

"Why do you think they took the investigating magistrate off the case?" she said.

"I have no idea," said Blume. "You're the politician."

"I don't consider 'politician' as much of an insult as your tone implies, Commissioner."

"My phrasing was neutral," said Blume.

Sveva's grapefruit juice came, and she pushed it as far away from her as she could till it sat balanced on the edge of the table.

"Sometimes everything is wrong," she began. Blume waited for her to continue, but she seemed to switch her line of thought. "Did you watch that documentary?"

"Yes," said Blume. "What was that all about?"

"That's what I want to ask you."

The *cotoletta* arrived and Blume motioned the bartender to put it in the middle of the table.

Sveva looked horrified as he cut into the meat. Maybe she didn't eat meat, either, like her dead husband. He realized he was not being polite, but he was hungry.

"Di Tivoli made that documentary out of spite," she said. "He is attracted to me. He's attracted to many other things besides me, but he's always had something special for me. Or so he says. Ever since university. But I am not in the slightest bit interested in him, also because he is, well, sexually ambiguous. He used to court me, then turn up with some boy he'd picked up on the Oppio Hill. That was not bad, back then, because back then Di Tivoli was a boy, too. Now he's older. He told me about Arturo's infidelities years ago. In fact, he even told me about them before they could be counted as proper infidelities. Di Tivoli seemed to think ratting on friends attracts women."

"You didn't mind your husband having affairs?"

"Yes and no. That's not really what I want to talk about."

"Fine," said Blume. "But tell me this, did you know about Manuela Innocenzi?"

"No." She was emphatic. "That I did not know. I knew he was seeing a woman, and I knew she was not so young, but I had no idea she was like that."

"Like what?"

"Well, ugly, to begin with. But the criminal connection. I mean, come on."

The last sounded like an appeal to her dead husband.

"So, like I said, Di Tivoli's trying to embarrass me, and he's doing a good job. First he drags our name into the dirt, then he makes me look like a fool for not knowing, and to end it all, he seems somehow to imply that I want a cover-up, or that I'm not interested in the truth."

"It's a good thing you did not try to stop the show from airing," said Blume. "That would have given him credence."

"I know." She paused to allow Blume time to finish his meal. "So what about this Innocenzi woman?"

Blume shook his head. "I know that communications in the force are like a game of Chinese whispers, and the farther a message has to travel down from on high to someone as low as me, the more garbled it becomes. And I know that nobody ever really knows what's going on . . ." Blume decided to cut short the rest of the diplomatic preface and went straight to his main point, "But I thought you were happy with the idea that your husband was killed by or as a result of Alleva."

"Happy? You thought I was happy?"

"You know—satisfied. Convinced. The point is, I got a pretty clear message—go get Alleva—because that's the word that's come down from on high."

"Convinced is the right word. They convinced me. Gallone, the people at the Ministry, some of my party colleagues. My uncle, too. He's the undersecretary for internal affairs. As for me, I never said that or anything of the sort."

"You never expressed any wish to see the case shut with Alleva as the guilty party?"

"I want whoever did this put away. I don't care who it was."

"What about your political career?"

Sveva paused, not to think, but to make sure he was watching her face closely as she spoke.

"That's important. I won't say it isn't. But I don't want a cover-up of any sort. If this Manuela Innocenzi is behind it, then have her arrested. I can deal with the embarrassment. Sooner or later everyone gets connected to a criminal family in this country. Everyone in Parliament, anyhow."

"The message I got was clear," said Blume. "Pick up Alleva. And because we rushed things, a young policeman got killed."

"So did my husband!"

She raised her voice enough to cause a slight click of silence in the hubbub around them. One of the bank tellers was still looking at them.

"But you sort of led separate lives, didn't you?"

Sveva pushed herself back from the table, causing the glass of juice to totter. Blume caught it just in time with a quick diagonal jerk of his good arm.

"I can see that I don't engage your sympathy. Maybe it's my politics, my background, I don't know. It's true Arturo and I led separate lives most of the time. He started it with his dumb betrayals, and I let him. Perhaps you think I should have spent more energy trying to keep hold of him? Made him feel better about himself? Is that my sin, here?"

"I'm not thinking of sin."

"Yes, you are. You've got the same angry, frustrated look as he had. Men like you . . ."

"What about us?"

"You never find the woman you're looking for, and you hate the rest of us for not measuring up."

"This may apply to your husband, but as for me . . ."

"You live alone, don't you?"

Blume said, "You looked that up. You've got access to files. It's not hard to find out things like that."

" 'Yes' was all you needed to say, Commissioner. And I didn't look it up."

Blume drank her juice and grimaced. He didn't like grapefruit.

"The crime scene," she said, her tone more conciliatory. "It was messed up. Mainly the fault of Gallone and D'Amico, wasn't it? I called the investigating magistrate, Principe, and he told me the first phase had been mishandled. Too many chiefs and not enough Indians, was how he put it."

"Good way of putting it."

"I admit it's mainly my fault for calling Gallone instead of making a normal emergency call. I hardly even know Gallone. I mistook length for depth. Just because we used to hang out a bit at the university a long time ago. Even then he was always a bit removed, always calm, priestly."

"We call him the Holy Ghost."

"I heard that. It suits him. He and the people in the Ministry—they never cared about forensic evidence. They just wanted to show their masters they were in direct control, and could steer the investigations. And you think I'm one of those puppeteers, but I'm not. My uncle may be, but I am not. My party does not want a scandal, the so-called Center-Left does not want a scandal, the government does not want a scandal. So they sent in D'Amico and Gallone to micromanage. I'm just caught in the middle."

"So now you want the truth," said Blume.

"You still don't believe me."

"You phoned Gallone straightaway. You wanted the micromanagers in first, experts in second. You got your wish. Including a half-ruined crime scene."

"I made a mistake. I was in a panic. You think if I was really panicked I would have called in the police on the emergency number, but I did what a politician does: I tried to regain control. I called Gallone, a friend on the Justice Commission, my party leader, my uncle. I wanted to be back in command. But not at the cost of the truth."

Blume shook his head, then suddenly stopped as a searing pain shot through his neck and upper spine. He exhaled heavily.

"You still don't believe me? My son was with me. You remember that? You remember it was he who found his father's body?"

"Yes," said Blume. "I remember. I am sorry he had to see that."

"Are you? Have you any idea how he must feel?"

"Perhaps a little," said Blume, fingering the back of his neck.

"You know how he feels?"

Blume tried to find some purchase for his aching arm on the table. "Well, he must miss his father terribly . . ."

"No. That's not really how it is with him. Not yet. You know what form his trauma is taking? Do you know how he's living this?"

"No," said Blume. "I don't."

"He thinks his father is still hurting. He can't stop seeing the slashes and the cuts. He keeps telling me that the wounds are hurting his father. I tell him bluntly and brutally that his father is dead, and can't feel anything anymore, but Tommaso is convinced Arturo is somehow still feeling the cuts of the knife. He's so insistent and certain that I sometimes begin to think he may be right. He's woken up every night and he says to me, 'Daddy's still bleeding,' like he was a reporter coming back from somewhere with the undeniable facts. I tell him it's just a dream. Then the other day—when was it? Monday. On Monday afternoon, Tommaso went into my mother's kitchen—that's where we are staying now, in the house in EUR that you saw—and he took a steak knife from the drawer and ran it across the inside of his palm. He pushed it in deep, too. I was out, and my parents had to take him to Bambin Gesù. They say he narrowly missed a tendon. Tommaso said he wanted to know what just one cut would feel like. He told the doctors that his father had lots of cuts like that, almost as if he was boasting. But he wants to know the precise number. He keeps asking how many times they cut his father."

Her lower lip trembled. She stopped to regain control of her facial muscles.

"The best thing I can tell my child is that his father is turning to dust and no longer bleeds. My mother's religious, but she's no fucking help with her dripping sacred hearts and bleeding Jesuses. I can't think of anything else to tell Tommaso. Where's the comfort? Where is it to be found?"

"There is no comfort," said Blume.

"Well, where's the justice, then?"

"It's in our minds," said Blume. "That's the only place you'll find it."

She nodded. "All I want you to know is that if that woman Innocenzi is behind this, I want her punished. Maybe I will end up doing some politics to keep my name out of it as much as I can, but I want her to be caught. Is that clear? If it was Alleva, fine. Better, at least for my image, but don't let her get away with it."

"I doubt she had anything to do with it," said Blume.

"So it was Alleva or his henchman after all?"

Blume stayed silent.

"Well, tell me. I need some sort of closure. I have to be able to tell my child something definitive someday, stop his father from bleeding."

"I will tell you this," said Blume. "There is no such thing as closure. In the end, it doesn't matter if the person is caught. I have yet to meet anyone who really felt better for seeing so-called justice done. Not even revenge works."

"That is palpably untrue," said Sveva.

"Don't talk to me like we were on a televised debate," said Blume. "I know what I'm talking about. I know you've seen them and heard them on TV, in books, on the news, all these people who rejoice that the person who murdered their child has been caught or even killed, but after a few months, it all comes back again, every bit as bad as at the beginning. They are no better off. What's lost forever is lost forever, no matter what you do afterwards. If the perpetrator is dead, it's often worse. The survivors have no one left to hate, so they turn to hating themselves."

"You're a policeman, and you say it makes no difference who's caught. Great."

"Nobody likes hearing it," said Blume. "A lot of cops know it, but they can't say it out loud, because it means almost all we do is too little too late. Unless we catch a perpetrator beforehand. That feels good. It only makes a difference if it prevents another victim."

Blume glanced at his phone on the table. Still no call from Paoloni.

"Are you expecting a call?" asked Sveva.

"I was. Now I'm beginning to wonder."

"Has it to do with my case?"

Blume hesitated.

"It has, hasn't it? Even though you've been taken off the investigation, there's still something you're waiting for. What is it?"

"I can't say," said Blume.

"Why not?"

"Do you know how many levels of hierarchy I am skipping by talking to you like this? Suppose I had an idea, and gave it to you, then you tried to impose it from above—have you any idea what sort of a mess that would make of my already static career? You're sort of outside the hierarchy, but you're above it, too."

"Do you have an idea who killed Arturo?"

"Yes," said Blume. "I do, but I could be wrong."

"And you can't give me a name?"

"No."

"And you've been taken off the case."

"Right."

"And there is no way I can get you put back on the case without everyone thinking you went behind their backs, which would screw your good reputation and career."

"Good reputation and career are inversely related. Let's just say my reputation."

"And you maintain it won't make any difference to me who killed my husband."

"Not in the long-term, no. The pain will be the same."

"I'm still not sure about that last part. Maybe you're talking about someone specific. Someone who doesn't feel any better for knowing."

Blume shrugged, and discovered that that hurt, too.

"And yet, despite all you have said and all that you profess to believe, you're still going to try to get the real culprit, aren't you?"

"Yes. And there's nothing I need you to do to help me," he said. "Except maybe stay clear of me, just so there are no misunderstandings."

Sveva Romagnolo stood up, and held out her hand. Blume half stood up, too, and took it.

"Thank you, Commissioner," she said. "Good luck with your unofficial investigation."

"Thank you, Senatrice," said Blume.

She left him sitting at the table, wondering if he had just made a promise. Ten minutes later he went to settle the bill, and Bettino handed him fifty-four euros.

"What's this?" asked Blume.

"Your change. The lady you were with left a hundred-euro bill to pay for lunch. Have I seen her on TV?" When Blume didn't answer, he said, "You don't want the change? I'll put it in the book as credit, if you want."

"I don't have a tab, Bettino."

"I can make you one now, Commissioner. Let's make it fifty-five euros credit, a better number. OK, now you're in credit with me, and in debt to her."

29

BLUME CALLED AND waited all day, but got no word from Paoloni. Principe was in court and unavailable for calls.

Back in his kitchen, Blume started calling around the police stations of Rome, seeing if anyone called Pernazzo had been brought in. He began with the station nearest Pernazzo's house and worked his way out in a spiral. Staying inside the city limits. He kept his tone casual. None of them had heard anything.

After wasting several hours in this way, Blume figured his casual inquiries would have been noted by now, so he phoned the Office of Questura. After repeating his number and qualifications to diffident desk sovrintendente, Blume was finally connected with a commissioner-in-chief willing to share a little information. None of the stations in the entire Province of Rome had reported an arrest with that name, he was told. Not that that necessarily meant anything. The updates were not always updated, as Blume no doubt knew.

Blume did. He waited expectantly. The commissioner-in-chief had given him the *quid*, now he would be expected to return with the *quo*.

"So what's the investigation you're working on, Commissioner Blume?"

Blume had a choice here. He could tell the truth. It would make it harder for Gallone and the Ministry to ignore the Pernazzo angle. But throwing suspects' names around like that, phoning in an unofficial capacity. It was stuff that could come back and bite you.

"It's a secret investigation," he said. He felt like a twelve-year-old making things up.

His interlocutor was unruffled. "All investigations are secret, Commissioner. Has this anything to do with that politician's wife? That was in your district originally, wasn't it?"

"It was," said Blume.

"Not the wife, the husband. It was the husband who was murdered. And you didn't correct me. Is this Pernazzo somehow involved? Has he anything to do with the people who shot the policeman?"

"No, no. It's a completely different case," said Blume.

"Indeed?"

"Yes. Check the reports from our office. My name's not even on them anymore."

"So this Pernazzo has nothing to do with any of that. They've put you on a new case, then?"

"Yes."

"I thought you were on leave. You were injured."

Did this bastard know him personally? Blume wondered.

"A minor thing. We're completely understaffed here. I'm just doing a bit of light work, making myself useful."

"We could do with more people with that sort of work ethic," said the commissioner-in-chief.

"Thank you," said Blume. He hung up.

The tiredness had crept up on him again. There was no point in going to the station now, and Paoloni had gone underground. He did this occasionally, but he always told Blume beforehand. Maybe Paoloni was watching Pernazzo. But he doubted it.

He could not think up an adequate excuse for phoning Kristin, and so he watched a Hitchcock film on television and fell asleep in front of it.

FRIDAY, SEPTEMBER 3, 9 A.M.

This time the call that woke him was from Kristin, which pleased him, though he would have preferred Paoloni.

She wanted to know if he had met Sveva Romagnolo, and whether he felt there might be political repercussions. Blume said he had no idea about political repercussions.

"Not anything big. Ripples in the rockpools, people changing places, networks tightening and loosening. It's only for a report."

"If you come over here, maybe we can talk about it," said Blume, feeling quite sly.

"OK," she said. "Right now?"

Blume felt like he'd just lost a game of speed poker.

"I don't really have anything to tell you, Kristin."

"So maybe later. I'm sure you have something I could make use of." She hung up before he could work out whether she intended any ambiguity.

The agente at the desk nodded and looked slightly embarrassed as Blume walked stiffly into the station.

"Welcome back, Commissioner."

"Thanks. I'm going to my office, in case anyone's looking for me."

Blume made it all the way to the second floor without encountering anyone else. They really were ridiculously understaffed here.

The door from the corridor led to the windowless antechamber with the desk and computer where Ferrucci had worked, and a second door led into his office. Blume went over to Ferrucci's desk and stood behind the chair, looking at his own dark reflection in the blank computer screen. Then he went into his own room and sat behind his desk, listened to the sounds of the station and stared out the window across rooftops at the back of the Church of Santa Maria sopra Minerva. He ran his hand over the patina of dust. It felt like years since he had been here last.

He picked up the receiver of his desk phone, placed the handset on the desk as he dialed the Tuscolana center. He had himself patched through to the IT department, and asked for Giacomo Rosati, another of the many people who seemed to be avoiding him.

"Jack, it's Alec." He winced at using Rosati's corny anglicized first name. He hardly knew the man. Small, elfin type with a pointy beard. He waited a beat, then added, "Blume."

"Commissioner, you don't catch me at a good time. A lot to do here to-day. Maybe I can call you back later?"

"It'll only take a second," said Blume. "Did Investigating Magistrate Principe ever get in contact with you about tracking an IP address?"

Rosati seemed to be having trouble remembering. Eventually he said, "Yes, yes. I remember. It was an unofficial lead."

"Right. The thing is, I was expecting you to call me back," said Blume.

Who did this guy think he was not calling back like he was supposed to, then coming over all self-important? Sort of IT midget it was faster to step over than go around.

"I thought I was to let you know only if we came up with a negative,

Commissioner. That is, if we found that the subscriber's number had not been assigned an IP at that time in question. But there was an IP assigned, so, yes, the subject was online."

"I see," said Blume. "Well thanks anyhow."

More wasted time. Pernazzo still had an alibi of sorts.

"You're welcome. Uh—" said Rosati.

Blume caught the monosyllable. "What? Were you going to say something?"

"No. Well, yeah, I suppose I was, but it's like so obvious I don't need to say it."

"Let's pretend I'm really stupid," said Blume.

"Everyone knows this, but having an IP number assigned to your line doesn't prove anything. I mean he could just have left his computer connected. I leave mine on for days, sometimes."

"Right," said Blume. "But this guy says he was playing an online game. Did you check that out?"

"No, I wasn't asked to look into the sites he was visiting, just whether he was connected. I mean, like, you need a magistrate to subpoena the owners of the Web site the subject was visiting to check whether he was really there," said Rosati. "Or you could just try to persuade the Web site owners to quietly release the IPs of users at the time you're interested in. You'd still need the backing of a magistrate, though."

"Which makes it difficult," said Blume. "But let's say we checked out someone and he was online and playing at the time, that would make a pretty solid alibi, wouldn't it?"

"Definitely," said Rosati. "Of course it could be anyone playing the game at that address, but if the IP matches the subscriber line, then we at least know someone was there at the time playing whatever the game was."

"Poker," said Blume. "Thanks, for the help."

"Poker?"

"Hold 'em Vegas or something," said Blume. Pernazzo was shaping up to have a good alibi, if it checked out. Now he would need a subpoena on the Web site, which meant going back to Principe, or a different magistrate. It meant a lot of paperwork and the end result would probably be to strengthen Pernazzo's alibi. There would probably be a financial record of some sort if he was winning or losing.

"If that's what he was playing, then he could have been using a bot," said Rosati.

"A bot?"

"A program that plays for you. It's called a bot, as in robot. Robot—bot. See? It's like an abbreviation . . ."

"Yes, I get that bit," said Blume. "Let's pretend I'm not stupid anymore."

"Yeah, well. It simulates a real player. You connect, start the program, and then go and do something else. That way you can play all night without having to stay awake. You can play lots of poker tables, and a decent program will beat beginners and pull in a small amount of profit. The casinos try to crack down on users who have bots, but since they deploy them themselves, it's impossible to immunize their systems."

"So you could use a bot to keep playing, and you're not even there," said Blume. "Where would you get a program like that?"

"You can buy them ready-made, they're not illegal or anything. Or you could use C++ programming and build one yourself. But you'd need to know something about computers to do that. Does the subject know anything about computers?"

"Yes," said Blume. "He does."

"This is interesting," said Rosati, who seemed to have forgotten that he was too busy to talk. "Using a bot as an alibi. I'm sure it's been done before, but I've not come across it. It would be hard to prove. I'd be interested in hearing how this works out. Let me know, would you?"

"Sure thing," said Blume. He felt an adrenaline rush. He was on to something.

Blume hung up and turned on his computer. For the next forty minutes, he queried the public records database, seeing what he could find about Pernazzo. Serena had been his mother's name, and she had died a year ago.

Pernazzo had a driver's license on which he had lost two tickets, an ID card, residence at the address where he lived. His declared income was pathetically low. His tax code corresponded to his given name. He now had a brief entry in the courthouse records as a result of his arrest at the dog fight. He had no convictions. His birth certificate was dated 1978. His mother was registered as unmarried, the name of the father as "not given" and paternity "not acknowledged."

Blume thought about the name plaque on the door. Pernazzo and T. Vercetti. He looked up Vercetti in the public records database, and was surprised to get zero results. He checked again, typing carefully with his one good hand.

No results found. Zero. Vercetti was a nonexistent name.

Blume tried "Vercelli" and found thirty-three entries for the municipality of Rome. But the name he saw had not been Vercelli. He tried Vercetti again, and again got no results.

Blume logged off the police intranet and went to the Google home page. With his middle finger, he slowly tapped in the name "Vercetti" in the search box and hit return. He leaned forward so quickly to look at what came up on the screen that he felt a pain shoot across his neck. *Showing 1-10 of 765,000 results*, said the page. The very first in the list displayed the name Tommy Vercetti. T. Vercetti. The name Pernazzo had on his door plaque. Blume clicked on the link, and read:

> *Thomas "Tommy" Vercetti (voiced by Ray Liotta) is a fictional character in the Grand Theft Auto video game series. He serves as the protagonist, anti-hero, and playable character in Grand Theft Auto: Vice City, where he emerges as the crime lord of his own syndicate . . .*

Not just elves and sorcerers, then. Pernazzo liked to play other games. Blume read about Grand Theft Auto, or GTA as everyone seemed to call it. By the end of the article, he had the feeling that he might be the only person in the world not to have heard of it before.

The idea was to shoot as many people as possible and rise in the criminal underworld.

He turned off the computer. Even if he could not ask anyone or get an investigating magistrate to give him a warrant, Blume was going back to Pernazzo. But as he stood up, the door to his office opened, and in stepped D'Amico.

30

A WEEK IN complete charge of the PR surrounding the stalled Clemente case had left D'Amico looking neater than ever. The whiteness of the French-cuff shirt peeking from under the shimmering gray of a finely cut high-buttoned jacket with peaked lapels was, frankly, a triumph. Blume suddenly felt everything he owned was dirty and old. He sat down again.

"There you are!" said D'Amico, with the voice of an adult who has been playing hide-and-seek with a child. He stepped across the room to behind where Blume was sitting, and folded his arms on the swivel chair, so that he was looking down on the crown of Blume's head.

"Maria Grazia is the investigating magistrate in charge of the Clemente-Ferrucci case. We're treating it as one thing now," he told the back of Blume's head.

Blume half-turned backward toward D'Amico, but it hurt his neck. "Move. You're making me nervous back there."

D'Amico came back around the desk, took the chair opposite Blume. "You're making people nervous, too, Alec."

"Am I?"

"You come in here in a parlous state, start reworking the case which you are no longer on. That makes people who lack your commitment look bad. I just tell them that's your American work ethic. But then you go and give them a real reason to be nervous by meeting Sveva Romagnolo. It looked like a secret meeting, too."

"You were watching?"

"Of course not. I am still your ex-partner, Alec. I don't spy. But she was being watched over."

"Watched over or just watched?"

D'Amico made a gesture with his hands as if releasing an invisible bird into the air. "It comes down to the same thing. I don't know. Really, I don't. I don't even think they were cops. Trainee domestic spies, probably. SISDE operatives sent in by the uncle. The orange-faced minister in Forza Italia. Looks like a squirrel monkey. Same surname."

"I know who you mean. But somehow the SISDE guys reported to you."

"No. This is just stuff I heard. I did have some doubts about the story or your meeting her. Now I don't. This investigation is doing your career no good, Alec. Leave it alone. You used to know when to leave things alone."

"I just need to get this one person, then I'll back out. You can handle it however you want, give the credit to whomever you want," said Blume.

"Why do you care so much, Alec? You had pretty cynical ideas about justice when we were partners. It's one of the reasons I quit the flying squad."

"The suspect I have in mind . . . I think this guy will kill again," said Blume. "I should have hauled him in the moment I clapped eyes on him."

"Why didn't you? It would have been easier then than now."

"I don't know. I didn't have enough evidence. I was alone. I had been told to go after Alleva instead." And, he thought to himself, I had my first date with a woman in eighteen months, and I was not thinking straight.

"Ah," said D'Amico. "That's not good. Well, I suppose we'll have to find a way of getting this guy. Have you got good evidence now?"

"Not as such. But fingerprints, DNA, it'll match."

D'Amico frowned. "We need to go through the magistrates for that."

"I know. In the meantime I sent Paoloni after the guy."

"Paoloni is on leave of absence. That's what the Holy Ghost told me. When did you send Paoloni in?"

Blume paused as if to think. He had suddenly noticed that D'Amico had not even bothered to ask for Pernazzo's name. "A short while ago."

"Has Paoloni reported back to you?"

"Yes," said Blume. He could play the disinformation game, too.

"Really? That's good, because Paoloni seemed to have disappeared from sight. The Holy Ghost has been invoking his safe return to the fold. He took leave, then vanished. I'm glad you're in contact. Where is he?"

"No idea," said Blume.

"Well, did he find your guy—what's his name by the way?"

"Vercetti."

"Did Paoloni find him?"

"Yes," said Blume. For all he knew, maybe he had.

"Again, no arrest? It seems to me like getting the suspect might be harder than you have allowed for. You need a magistrate to direct inquiries, here, Alec.".

"I know."

"And you're not going to get one if it's connected with the Clemente case. So you had better leave it completely, or leave it with me. I'll see what I can do. Pass the evidence to me, I'll make sure it goes to the right people. Get Paoloni to contact me, too, would you? We'll organize something."

"Right. I'll send the evidence over this evening."

"Great." D'Amico stood up. "You should rest, Alec. Not come in looking for work."

"What the hell is the sense in staying at home?" said Blume.

"You need family, Alec. Everyone has some family. You never visited mine when we were partners. Even Paoloni's got a son."

The door opened, and Vicequestore Gallone appeared, holding a yellow file folder.

Gallone did not welcome Blume back. He simply closed his eyes and nodded gently as if receiving a confession, and said, "Yes, yes," in response to a question no one had asked. Then, with the air of a man anxious not to wet his shoes in a dirty puddle, he stepped into the room, reached over and placed the folder on Blume's desk, and announced: "Road rage incident. A family man by the name of Enrico Brocca, shot dead outside a pizzeria after an argument over a minor car accident. Seeing as you're so anxious not to let your excellent police skills rust, I can assign the two men I put on the case to other duties, leave it to you. When you require manpower to move the investigation forward, you will come to me, with the paperwork filled out." He turned to D'Amico. "Good morning, Commissioner."

D'Amico smoothed an eyebrow with his thumb. "Good morning, Vicequestore," he said.

Looking at the two of them side by side, Blume was reminded of an old tailor fussing over a model. To Gallone he said, "This road rage case. Who's the magistrate in charge?"

"Your friend Principe," said Gallone. "You'll spend the rest of the day

reading the reports. There are no witnesses in this case. We are still looking. Maybe you could find us some witnesses. Contact the magistrate, inform him that you are on this case, and await instructions. I expect he'll
want you to go out tomorrow and interview the widow of the murdered
man."

Blume opened the file, not wanting to look at any of them. "Fine,"
he said.

Gallone glanced at his watch. "So I'll phone up the Office of Public
Prosecution, tell them the case has been assigned to a detective, shall I?"

He left without waiting for a reply. D'Amico lingered.

"What?" asked Blume. "What do you want?"

"Nothing. I no longer have any reason to be in this *commissariato*. I'm
going back to my office in the Ministry."

"Good-bye then," said Blume, opening the folder and beginning to
read. He did not glance up when he heard the door shut.

The report was an exercise in minimalism. The bare essentials of time
and place, a ballistics conjecture. There was a statement from the teenage
daughter regarding a moment prior to the murder in which one of the
aggressors appeared to search through the victim's wallet, the contents of
which had been sent to the lab for analysis. No witnesses Crowds are
made up exclusively of cowards.

There had been no real follow-up. Blume looked at the police sketch of
the gunman. It looked like it had been done by an abstract artist. The image
was as unhelpful as it could get. It was possible to project almost any face
into the almost blank outline. The chin tapered a little, maybe indicating a
thin face. The eyes were small, and the nose, too, as if the artist did not want
to commit himself to grand statements. The mouth was small and seemed to
have been made to look slightly puckered, or else to indicate incipient hair
on the upper lip. It was by no means clear. The accompanying notes explained that the children and the widowed wife had not been able to describe the killer in any detail. They had averted their eyes. But the report
also said that they had had two occasions to see the killer. Surely a better job
could have been made of it than this?

His cell rang and Paoloni's name appeared on the display.

"Beppe. Where the hell have you been?" said Blume. He went over to
his office door, checked no one was around, then returned as Paoloni gave
one of his typically laconic answers.

227

"Unfinished business. Then I had to fade a bit into the background. I'll tell you about it when we meet."

"What about Pernazzo?"

The one second of silence that followed this question was all it took for Blume to realize that Paoloni had not followed up.

"I got a more important lead. I was following it up. But it came to nothing."

"I told you to go get this Pernazzo," said Blume. "You said you would. Are you still the same person who was beating his breast and blaming himself for the death of a colleague, or are you back to your normal truculent self?"

"I'm definitely the person who cares about his colleague's death more than anything," said Paoloni. "Which is why I didn't make Pernazzo a big priority."

"You came to me and asked for help, I gave you something to do, and you didn't do it. And what's with the leave of absence?"

"I got injured, remember? Same as you."

"Are you still on leave now?"

"Prognosis was fifteen days. I had my first day yesterday. You want, I can go get your suspect now."

"You are on leave. I'm not sending an off-duty cop to a suspect's home."

"It doesn't have to be by the book," said Paoloni.

"It doesn't have to be absolutely against all the rules in the book either," said Blume. "What's with the sick leave, and the switched-off telephone, and now this attitude?"

"I need a break, Alè. I just need to get out of this world of killers and cops and cop-killers for two weeks. I'm sorry if I didn't do what you asked."

"What I ordered," corrected Blume. But it had not been an order, because he did not have the authority to give an order to arrest a suspect like that. Paoloni was right, it had been a request, which made his refusal to comply worse.

"Are we still OK?" asked Paoloni. He sounded more resigned than hopeful.

"I don't know," said Blume. "Come back on duty. Waive your sick leave and report straight to me. In an official capacity. Look contrite when I next see you."

Blume hung up. Paoloni had sounded different. Flatter, less scoffing, less explosive than usual. Something was up there.

Blume glanced at the photo of the murdered man. Killed for a parking place, according to the report. Jesus Christ. He laid the image aside and called the courthouse, got Principe on the line.

"I see we got fobbed off with a road rage incident," he began.

"What do you mean 'fobbed off'?" said Principe. "This is one of several important cases I am working on, now that the Clemente affair is in more capable hands."

"And you want me to follow it up?"

"Not high-profile enough for you, Commissioner?"

"What's with the tone, Filippo?"

"What tone? It's just sometimes I get fed up with the way some cases get the red carpet treatment, others get kicked into the long grass. This was a family man, murdered in front of his children on his wife's birthday. You don't think that's worthy of your notice?"

Blume hesitated, unsure what to make of Principe's attitude. "Of course I do," he said.

"I want you to stay focused on this case, and on this case alone. Is that understood?"

Blume was perplexed. First Paoloni going quiet, now Principe blustering like this. Principe continued, "Because it's the only one you'll get, Commissioner. Leave the Clemente case alone."

Blume began to suspect Principe was speaking to the gallery. His tone was too rhetorical.

"Have you read the report, Commissioner?"

Calling him Commissioner three times like that was a sort of code. Principe was not on his own in his office. They might even be on speakerphone.

"Yes," said Blume. "There's not much to it. An unknown assailant, possibly to do with a fight over a parking place. No witnesses."

"Get to it, then," said Principe.

Blume put down the receiver and rubbed his ear as if a small white grub had crawled down the line and into his head, and left the office wondering what the hell had gotten into Principe. Even with an appreciative audience, there had been something too manic in the magistrate's tone. A road rage case. Pathetic assignment.

31

GIULIA SAT IN the middle of her bed. Blume felt huge in the child's room.

He had spent the rest of the previous day going over the report and talking to the two policemen who had signed off on it. The involvement of forensics had been minimal. Even Principe, who had sounded so high-toned on the phone, seemed to have lost interest. The previous evening Blume had made the appointment to interview the widow of the victim, and now he found himself talking to the daughter instead.

Downstairs, a policewoman, Inspector Mattiola, newly arrived in the department, was doing her level best to get the woman to say something. Blume had brought her along to talk to the child, but he soon realized getting any sense out of the mother was impossible. So he left her to the new policewoman. He figured she needed to learn the hard way how unhelpful most interviewees usually are.

Not this child, though.

"Wouldn't you prefer to go downstairs, Giulia?" he asked her.

She shook her head.

"OK." The bedroom had one armchair. It was covered in her clothes. Blume stood there trying to figure out what to do.

"You can put them on the floor," she said.

Seeing no alternative, he hooked his good arm around a pile of jeans, underpants, small bras, socks, and shirts, and put them carefully on the floor beside the chair, then sat down.

"I'll be moving into his study soon," said Giulia. "A few months ago, he promised me that if I started helping around the house a bit, he would surrender his study and turn it into a bedroom for me. He even bought a portable computer, and started working in the kitchen, to get used to the idea. Now I'll get his room, anyway."

Blume pretended to examine the room with his eyes. Eventually he had to bring them back to the small grown-up sitting cross-legged on a child's bed.

"Giacomo could get this room," continued Giulia. "It's bigger than his, but he doesn't want to move. He's like my mother."

"I'm sorry," said Blume.

Giulia cast a skeptical look in his direction. "It's not as if you people did much. This is, like, the third visit."

"This one's different."

"You mean now you're going to catch whoever it was?"

Blume wished he had not spoken. "I can't say that."

"So it's not really a different sort of visit, is it?"

"No."

Giulia pulled a pillow from behind her, and arranged it against her back.

"At least you look sad. The others looked like they didn't care. If anything, they treated my mother like she had done it."

"It's the police way."

Giulia shrugged. "No wonder nobody likes the police much."

"What age are you?"

"Twelve. What happened to your arm . . . and your nose?"

"I crashed a car. It's only sprained, not broken. There's nothing wrong with my nose."

"If you say so."

Blume steepled his hands, hid his nose behind it, and said, "When I was seventeen, I lost both my parents. They were shot dead in a bank raid."

"That's sad. Did you catch the person who did it?"

"I wasn't a policeman then."

"Did the other police catch him?"

"No."

"So he is still out there?"

"No, he died."

"How do you know he died if you didn't catch him?"

"Someone told me later."

"Someone in the police?"

"I'm not sure. I suppose so. But what I want to say is back then, and it's not really all that long ago, the police I met helped me out."

he police were better in your day."

ad help," said Blume. He may have misread Principe, but
ead him like a book putting him on this case. Five minutes
interview and he had pledged his soul to the girl, whose suddenly
widowed mother sat dumb, helpless, and closed downstairs.

Their outing to the pizzeria, Giulia told him, had been to celebrate her
mother's fortieth birthday. Her father, who was two years younger, kept
teasing her mother about being old. Giulia could tell she didn't really
like him to make jokes, any more than he appreciated being called "Mr.
Smooth" in reference to his baldness. Her mother had said something
about pizza being all they could afford, and her father had looked hurt.

"She did that quite a lot," said Giulia.

"They argued a lot?"

"Not really," said Giulia. "But now she's hurting so much for all those
things she said. She keeps mentioning them."

"Tell me more about that evening," said Blume.

They were going to a pizza place. Giulia didn't know the address, but it
was near a hospital. Blume knew it. He had checked the address in the file
and driven slowly past the site of the killing before proceeding to the
apartment.

On that evening, Giulia said, they walked out of the house just as a loud
clap of thunder burst overhead, and it started bucketing down.

It was almost ten o'clock when they arrived, and the parking area was
full. This started another sort of argument about whether he should drop
them off outside the pizzeria or not. Her father didn't want to give any
money to the gang-operated parking attendants, her mother said he was
going too far away from the restaurant. She said they would get soaked
again, even though the rain was already easing off.

All of a sudden, her father braked and pulled over because he had seen a
place, but on the wrong side of the road. The traffic did not let up for ages.
Finally, with a quick shout to Giulia to double-check through the side window, her father lurched into a rapid U-turn. The road was just wide
enough to accommodate the turning circle of their small car. Revving the
engine a little, Giulia's father straightened up and set off in the opposite
direction. The herringbone parking rendered the gap invisible from that
side of the road, and they were already practically upon it before they spotted it again.

"Hah!" cried her father, swinging the car out a little to get a better angle of approach, and standing on the brake.

The screech, the swish of tires not quite gripping the wet tarmac, the sudden blare of the horn from behind, and the water-filled light of the headlights coming through the back window and filling the car with a bluish light made her think she was going to die, so that when the actual rear impact came, Giulia couldn't believe how soft it was. Just a slight bump, that pushed her softly forward in her seat, and a crack and a tinkle of the car's taillights fragmenting.

Her father stayed outwardly calm. She knew he was faking it, but he continued the maneuver, and edged the car into the gap.

The vehicle behind had wheels that seemed to go as high as the door handles on theirs. As Giulia, her brother, and her mother all got out, Giulia saw the driver of the car behind open his door and jump down onto the road, just like that, without even looking, even though he was practically in the middle of the road. Her father never allowed them to get out on the traffic side. The man was lucky no one was coming behind. Also, he left the driver's door wide open, blocking the whole lane.

The passenger door opened, and another man, a far smaller one, jumped out on the safe side, covering his head against the rain.

Her father had bent down and was looking, she imagined, at the broken taillights, and shaking his head. Her mother called to him in half-warning and half-pleading tones. She was worried about a fight. Giulia remembered her father saying, "We're in the right. He rear-ended us."

Giulia watched the two men. They did not come forward to look at the car, nor did they even bother to look at their own. They simply stood there, in the spotlight of their own headlights. As her father approached them, the large man leaned over slightly and glanced at the side of his vehicle.

They frightened her. They frightened her mother, too. She could feel this in the way her mother pulled her away onto the sidewalk and propelled her and Giacomo toward the bright windows, crowded tables, and loud happy sounds of the pizzeria. She glanced back and saw her father standing in front of the large one while the other seemed to be searching through her father's wallet. She thought he was being robbed, right there on the street, but ten minutes later, her father, tense but smiling, was sitting beside her, helping her choose a pizza.

She asked for a Coke, not because she wanted one, but because she knew he disapproved of sugary drinks and would give one of his little lectures about the targeting of children by multinationals. And when he had finished, he would allow her to have one, laugh at his own weakness, and not feel so bad.

Her mother had said he was wrong not to call the police. She said they would probably slash the tires. Her father drank four tall glasses of beer. He didn't usually drink so much beer, but her mother didn't seem to mind tonight.

"Just remember, I'm driving," she had said.

They left the pizzeria about an hour later, maybe less. There was a small scene when her father paid for the meal using his Bancomat card. Her mother asked about cash, and he said he had left it at home. As they came out, Giacomo was swinging like a monkey from his mother's right hand, and, for once, her parents had linked arms. Giulia went to hold her father's left arm, but realized the sidewalk was not broad enough and she would get bumped into by people coming from the opposite direction.

So she was three steps behind when she saw her father and mother stop and unlink arms, and her mother slowly and gently beginning to push Giacomo's face sideways with the palm of her free hand, as if something had already happened that he should never see. Then her father took a step forward on his own, and Giulia saw the same two men again. The large one had a blue mark on his neck. The smaller one had his arm outstretched. At the end of his outstretched arm, he held a gray-barreled piece of weaponry such as Giulia had only ever seen, or thought she had seen, in her brother's toy box.

The large man looked surprised. She remembered that. And then the small one shot her father.

"What sort of mark on the neck?" asked Blume, mainly to distract her mind from the images it was now replaying.

"Like four triangles pointing into each other. Blue, same color as veins," said Giulia.

"A very big man?"

"Bigger than you, even," said Giulia.

"There was no police sketch of him," said Blume.

"They never asked for one. It took so long to do one of the man who shot my father . . . And they didn't seem too happy with the result."

"I am not too happy with them," said Blume.

"They're right, sort of," said Giulia. "I couldn't describe him properly to them. It's hard to picture him. He was small and horrible and I see him in my sleep, but I can't see his face. It's like it was blurred. As if the rain had washed his face off of him."

"Close your eyes. Listen only to my voice. I know this is an awful place for you to go, but I know you go there anyway, and I know you stay there reliving it. Only this time, I'm accompanying you. Maybe that might help a little? Now whatever you see in your mind's eye, I can see, too. Like we are there together. Relax your shoulders a little, that's it. Now don't worry about the face. Just tell me some other details. Can you see his feet, for instance?"

A minute passed, which Blume used to get her to relax her arms, legs, hands. Finally she said, "No."

"No problem," said Blume. "I can see them. Ugly feet. Now think of his arms. Especially the arm that he used to murder your father."

"I can see it," she said. "It's thin. More like my arm than yours. Wait, he was wearing a bracelet, too. Silver, with a chain."

"The sleeve was what color?"

"White."

"A shirt?"

"No, tracksuit top, underneath he had a V-neck and nothing under that."

"Move up a little. What about his chin?"

"Sharp. Small mouth. No, it's sort of wide, too. He smiled afterwards."

"Any hair on this face, a goatee, beard, mustache, sideburns?"

"I can't remember. I can see the mouth with a little mustache, and I can picture it without one. Both sort of fit."

"What color was his hair?"

"I can't remember. Not dark, not blond. Mousy. His skin was white. As white as his tracksuit."

"That blue cross . . ." said Blume.

"No, that's on the other man, the large one."

"Yes I know. It's just . . . never mind. Did they touch the car?"

"I don't think so. Mommy pulled us away quickly. Then afterwards, they were waiting outside the restaurant. The police took the car away. I don't know where it is, and my mother's not interested in finding out. But we're going to need it again next week when school starts."

Nothing of any use had been found on the car. Blume had read the report. Why had they not given it back? Some bureaucrat who could not give a damn that his lethargy caused suffering.

Blume eased Giulia back out of the memory, and spoke to her a little of a recollection he had of himself, crawling on a long gray beach by the Pacific Ocean. A memory from when he was three, which they said was impossible, but he had it all the same. Giulia seemed to remember a day she had spent at Villa Borghese, and she could have been no more than three at the time. Her father had pushed her all the way from the house in her stroller. Hours of walking. He brought pasta in a thermos and they ate that and watched some horses. She was almost asleep as Blume stole out of the room.

He left the house charged with anger for what had happened, and anger at the way his own force had treated the family. The policewoman followed meekly behind. She had got nothing out of the mother. So now they had two follow-up interviews, no reports on progress, even if only to say there had been no progress and never would be.

"Is this one of those hopeless cases, Commissioner?"

Blume looked at her. Young, dowdy, and a bit sad-looking in her uniform. She had been working in immigrant affairs before this. If he remembered right, she had asked for a transfer.

"All homicide cases are hopeless," he said.

"I meant for solving." It surprised him she had the nerve to come back at him with a reply.

"Inspector . . ."

"Mattiola," she supplied.

"I knew that. Look, we will do our best. You didn't see what the girl was like. A life force. She's holding the family together."

He was going to make sure the technicians did their job properly. He would demand resources. He might even go to the press. He would show Principe a thing or two about caring for ordinary people. He would devote his entire being to resolving the road rage case. He owed it to the child.

His phone went, and he waved the inspector away, telling her to write up a report on the non-interview. The call was from Sveva Romagnolo.

"Hello. Commissioner Blume?" she sounded edgy. "It would not surprise me if someone were listening to this conversation, but we have nothing to hide, have we?"

"Insofar as we have nothing, yes, I agree," said Blume.

"It has been brought to my attention that I am being followed. For my own safety."

"So I hear. I have nothing to do with that. I'd love to have the resources to do things like that," said Blume.

"I know they're not your men. I wish they were. I wanted you to know that less than an hour ago I received the nastiest and most abusive phone call you can imagine."

Blume, forgetting his arm was in plaster, instinctively tried to bring his finger up to his other ear to close off the sounds of the street.

"Who?" he said, looking for a silent area in the street.

"I was called a bitch, whore, slut—lesbian, too. I deserved to die instead of my husband. I was going to die, I needed to watch my back."

Blume leaned into a wall to hear better. "This was a woman saying these things, wasn't it?"

"So you know who it was. She said she knew who killed Arturo. Said she'd have them castrated. She said she had a cop in her pocket, and she used your name."

"Did she ever actually say who she was?"

"No. I didn't understand for the first minute or so, then it became obvious. She just went straight at it. Said Di Tivoli was a dead man walking for insulting her like that. Then when I asked her if she was Manuela Innocenzi, she started up again. Don't use my name, bitch. My name on your cocksucking lips . . . that sort of thing. So you know what? I'm glad those idiots from SISDE are supposed to be watching me, and I hope they're recording this, too. Manuela Innocenzi, I'll repeat the name just in case it gets lost in transmission. Someone's got to stop her."

"I don't think she's really going to do anything," said Blume. "Not to you. That's not how it works."

"Her father is . . ." began Sveva. Blume could hear the fear in her voice.

"Organized. Her father is organized. Careful, low-key. You're not in danger. She's not going to persuade him to do anything like that."

"Can you be sure?"

"Yes," said Blume. He hoped he was right.

"Can you maybe go and talk with her?"

"Well . . ."

"I mean as soon as you can. Like now. It's hard enough already. You need to get her away from me. That's all I care about now."

"All right," said Blume, "I'll deal with it."

"Thank you," said Sveva. "I won't forget this."

When Blume reached the car, an Alfa Romeo, Inspector Mattiola was standing there.

"I thought I told you to get back—oh, right, we came in the same car."

He had even allowed her to drive him. He loosened his sprained arm from the sling.

"I can manage on my own. You call for a car to come and pick you up."

Inspector Mattiola nodded slowly as if finally understanding something. She had nice features. And she was quiet, which was good.

Blume got into the driver's seat, turned on the engine, winced as he used his damaged arm to turn the wheel, and pulled out, leaving Mattiola standing on the curb.

32

MANUELA INNOCENZI LET Blume in as soon as he identified himself. As he entered the apartment, she was pulling up her hair with both hands. She let it go and as it cascaded in ringlets down as far as her shoulders she said, "Hello Alex."

"Alec," corrected Blume.

"I prefer Alex," she said.

"To whom?" asked Blume.

He walked into her living room, and glanced around to make sure they were alone, before settling among the fat cushions of her favorite Roche Bobois armchair, next to her second favorite dog, a golden retriever called Mischa.

She invited Blume to say hello to Mischa, but he refused.

"What happened to your arm and nose? It must have been the crash," said Manuela.

"My nose is fine," said Blume. "What the hell was that call to Sveva Romagnolo about? You think you can get away with threatening people like that?"

"Yes. And we follow up on threats, too. It's where our power comes from."

"She's a senator of the republic. They are probably monitoring her calls. Don't be fooled by the party she belongs to. If push comes to shove, she can and will draw on more muscle than you. Especially since you're not really anything except your father's spoiled child. So you can forget this 'we' and 'our power' shit."

"She's a slut. And she's a coward. I scared her. She won't sleep easy for nights."

"She already doesn't sleep so well, what with her son having nightmares about his father."

"She never looked after the child. Arturo did that."

"Well, she's looking after him now. Let me ask you, do you feel good about what you've just done? I mean, leaving aside the fact that you've compromised your father's position and made threats to a member of Parliament and shown yourself for the ugly bullying drab that you are—do you feel good now?"

"Yeah. I do. Apart from little Tommaso. I wasn't thinking about him. Anyhow, it got you here, didn't it?"

"You and Clemente together," said Blume. "I just can't see it. I've read up on him. I saw his house, his handsome successful wife, with her exquisite taste in clothes. Clemente was a good guy: educated, polite, cared about people and animals. You, I see you as better suited to petty bosses, shooters, shylocks, building speculators, drug runners, the sort of people whose women also use Botox, peroxide, gym lessons, and purgatives to keep the looks they never had to begin with. People like you. Know what I'm saying?"

Manuela was intent on stroking her dog, repeating its name soothingly, caressing the creature's forehead with her thumbs, no longer looking at Blume. Eventually, her eyes still on the dog, she said, "I'm the real widow in this case. And you know it. That bitch will be married within the year to a wealthy politician or something. And you are a cold bastard. I bet you have no one waiting for you at home. And if you do, I wouldn't want to be her."

"I wouldn't want you to be her either," said Blume.

"You know something? You have it all wrong about me." She finally looked at him, and he noticed her eyes were more green than blue. "The men I've had, they've been like you."

"Cops?"

"Very funny. I meant English, American, Australian."

"It's not as if we're all the same," said Blume. What was that she had just said about getting him here?

"Something about English makes you all a bit similar," said Manuela.

"Clemente was Italian. You must have been slumming it."

"Arturo was a good man."

"Like I said, not your type. How did you meet him?"

"Before him, I was with this guy called Valerio."

"Another Italian," said Blume.

"He was my type of man, according to you. He liked to say his job was 'damage maximization.' That's what he called it. He thought that was really witty. He talked a lot of soccer, played five-a-side with his buddies, and always ended up having a fight with someone on his own team. Anyhow, one evening, he picked me up, said we were going someplace different. Which to me meant we weren't going for a pizza and a night in a bar in Testaccio. I was not all that curious about his surprise, even when he headed out of Rome with me in the car. I only started asking questions when he drove off the road and across a strip of field, but by then we had practically arrived. It was a dog fight."

A cell phone started shaking on a lacquered table next to her. She picked it up, listened for a moment, said, "Yeah. No. No problem. Fine," and hung up.

"Who was that?"

"Just someone," said Manuela. "Nothing to do with us."

"Where was that dog fight?"

"Out by the Ponte Galleria, in an abandoned warehouse. So when I realized what sort of a place he had brought me to, I refused to leave the car. He left me there, took the car keys. Then after half an hour, I decided to go in, get him to drive me home, break it off. When I went in, a pair of Fila Brasileiros were savaging each other. There must have been a hundred people there. I couldn't see him. And I couldn't stop myself from watching the fight."

Manuela paused. She had turned pale. "Anyhow, I ended up vomiting, and someone must have told him to get me, because next thing he was there leading me back to the car. He was talking all the time about a bet he had made on an Argentine Dogo. Then—get this—he asked me what drug I had taken to make me sick like that. He even wanted to take me to a hospital. Well . . . Anyhow, it ended that night."

"So you joined LAV as a result of that experience?"

"Yes. The following day."

"You phoned them? How does it work?"

"I looked up the offices and went straight in and asked to talk to the man in charge."

"Who was Clemente."

"Yes. They didn't want to let me talk to him, so I said I had some very important information about a dog-fighting ring."

"You told him about the meets?"

"He knew all about it already. Turns out he had been campaigning all along, and reported the fighting every month to you useless bastards. The best he got was one raid and about three changes of venue."

"That was the Carabinieri, not us," Blume specified. "They probably didn't have the manpower, what with all the organized crime and stuff. What extra information did you give?"

"None. I just said that to get in to see Clemente. The idiot asked me if I'd hand out leaflets. Said the campaign was to change people's attitudes, sometimes to get the law changed, institute a special police division, the *polizia veterinaria*. I offered him a donation of seven thousand euros."

"Is your father in any way involved in the dog-fight business?"

Manuela paused, as if she were listening for a sound from outside. Eventually she said, "He's involved, but at a very remote level. When he heard I was frequenting antivivisectionists, he asked me to stop because it was upsetting some of the people he does business with."

"And you said?"

"I said no. He threatened to cut my allowance. I still said no. It was a question of principle." She crossed her arms and stared defiantly back at the memory.

"The people who were upset, they included the person who ran the business, Alleva?"

"Sure. Alleva, that's the guy who ran it, had threatened Clemente in the past—or got one of his henchmen to do it. He definitely wasn't happy to see me with Clemente. It was a bit awkward for me, too."

"How?"

"You know, being with a man who kept reporting to the police, or the Carabinieri, same difference. And the press. Still, it wasn't such a big deal."

"Did your father warn Clemente off?"

"I don't think so."

"Would Clemente have told you if he had been warned off?"

"He would have."

"Could Clemente have told you, and you're not telling me?"

"My father had nothing to do with Clemente's murder."

"Could your father have warned Clemente not to open his mouth to you?"

"My father had nothing to do with Clemente's murder."

"Could your father maybe have helped Alleva arrange the killing?"

"My father had nothing to do with Clemente's murder. And that's something he wanted me to pass on to you. That's a message from him."

"I see. OK, message received. Clemente . . . You liked him."

"Yes, I liked him a lot. I really did."

"He liked you?"

"Yes."

"He wasn't ashamed of you?"

"You don't have to keep insulting me."

"I'm not interested in whether you feel insulted. I want to know: Did Clemente introduce you to all his friends?"

Manuela bent down to fondle the dog again, allowing some of her orange hair to fall down and obscure her face. "No. He introduced me to no one."

The doorbell rang.

"Get that, will you?" said Manuela, the wistful tone that Blume had detected evaporating as the chime faded. "It's got to be those real estate people. Flash your badge at them, make them go away. I'll fix us a drink."

Manuela sprang up and disappeared out of the far door leading, he imagined, into the kitchen. With his arm in a sling, it took Blume so long to extricate himself from the yielding cushions of the soft armchair that the doorbell rang again before he got to it. Annoyed, he yanked it open.

An old man with no ears wearing a white linen jacket over a pink T-shirt was standing beside a young man in a half-unzipped tracksuit. He had just begun to register something funny about the old man's face, when the young man stepped in and shoved the barrel of a small-frame pistol hard against the underside of Blume's chin.

33

THE GUNMAN KEPT Blume's head tilted awkwardly back, preventing him from getting a look at him. The older man, who smelled of after-shave, ran his hands expertly across Blume's stomach and waist, up and down his side, back, and front, then patted him gently as if he was a big baby with wind. Then he hunkered down on a single knee around Blume's calves, before standing up again, to extract Blume's wallet and cell phone from his front pants pocket with considerably more ease and speed than Blume himself had ever managed, even when two-handed. Then he gently raised the sling holding Blume's plastered arm, and slid his hand across the sweaty patch below on Blume's polo shirt. Blume was fascinated by the man's earless head.

"Clean," he said at last.

"I don't like that," said his younger partner, releasing some of the pres-sure on Blume's chin.

"What?"

"*Clean.* Don't say *clean.* That's what cops say."

"Yeah? What do we say, then?"

The young man withdrew his tiny pistol entirely from Blume's face to gather his thoughts and think about this.

Free to move, Blume turned his eyes to the older man. Where his ears should have been were two crumpled pieces of pink flesh that resembled the @ of an email address. They looked infantile and out of place perched behind his aged face. He wore two thin pendants around his neck, one of which, a golden horn amulet, had slipped out from below his T-shirt. Tufts of hair rose from below the neck.

"The fuck you looking at?" said the young man.

Blume ignored the question.

"I said . . ."

"Shut up, Fà," said the older man. His overtanned face fissured into countless lines and wrinkles as he concentrated on a plastic-covered card in his hand.

"This is your badge?"

"Can't you read?"

"I can read just fine."

Blume said, "Because I thought maybe at your age, you'd need reading glasses, though I can see how wearing them might prove difficult." Blume broke off as the young man, smelling mockery in the air, shoved his pistol back into his face.

The earless one remained calm. He was old. He must have heard them all by now, and if he was still alive in this business at this age, then he must have some self-control. At least Blume hoped so.

"Fà. Get rid of it," he told his partner.

The young man lowered the weapon again.

"Commissioner Alexsei Blum-eh?"

"More or less."

He slipped the card back into the wallet.

The young man made the pistol vanish into his velour top. The other handed Blume his wallet and phone back.

Blume took them wordlessly, and glanced behind him. No sign of Manuela. The dog slept on.

"Step out?"

It was phrased as a request, but the young man moved slightly behind Blume. Blume chose to step out of the door, and the two followed. Neither of them had a weapon in evidence. Blume thought about making a break for it, and felt the muscles in his legs throb. He imagined hurtling down the stairs, lurching into the banisters with his sprained arm.

The young man pressed the elevator button. All three stepped in.

"I suppose 'clean' is all right," he said as the doors slid shut. "I can't think of another way of saying it."

The older man poked Blume in the back.

"You're really Commissioner Blume?"

"My fame precedes me."

"You're not a journalist?"

"No."

"Good. There's something I want you to know."

"Tell me."

"This isn't abduction."

Blume turned around and said, "No?"

The elevator stopped and the doors opened. A woman with a small boy and some shopping bags was waiting to get in. Blume went to help her, then remembered his arm. The youth pushed past them, then stood outside the elevator. He reminded Blume of a pouting soccer player who played for Juventus. Almost good-looking, except for the mouth.

"It's OK," said the older man, "I got it."

He helped the woman get the bags into the elevator. Blume, feeling useless, stepped out of the way and watched. Although the mother was saying thank you, Blume could see from her face she was uncomfortable with their continued presence.

Blume smiled at the boy, who was clutching a handful of small Japanese action figures. The doors slid shut just as he began to smile back.

Glistening from the effort of helping the woman with the shopping bags, the older man came up to Blume.

"This is not an abduction. I want to make that clear. Up there, in the apartment . . ."

"Yes, what shall we call that?" asked Blume.

"A precautionary search."

"I am a police officer."

"Yeah, we know. We had to check. Now anything you do from here on out is of your own free will."

"Like if I walked away?"

"Even that. We might follow you."

"If I pulled out a phone, called up a car to have you arrested for assault of a police officer with a deadly weapon, aggravated ab—" Blume stopped. He could see a look of genuine boredom in the old man's gray eyes. "So, you want me to come with you?"

"That would be by far the best solution. But I want to emphasize that this is something you are doing of—"

"My own free will. So you said."

The tracksuit behind him moved impatiently. "Can we get out of here? People can hear things."

"Good point, Fà." To Blume he said, "If you came with us, it would make things easier. You get in your own car, there's no telling who you might call. Maybe you'd take a wrong turn, spend the next hour trying to find us again, especially since you would be driving with one arm."

"I have an automatic transmission in that car. But you have persuaded me. Where am I voluntarily going with you?"

"Mr. Innocenzi's."

Blume thought about it. "OK. I wanted to talk to him anyway."

"Happy coincidence."

The three of them walked out under the midday sun and climbed into a double-parked Cherokee. The older man sat in the back with Blume. They drove north along the quays of the Tiber, then turned right to head into the center. A traffic policeman began flapping a red-and-white stick shaped like a lollipop at them as they entered the blue zone. They slowed down to let him see the permit on the windshield. The traffic policeman signaled at them to go on.

They crossed the center. As they drove up Via Veneto, Blume's reluctant captor pulled out a cell phone and told someone they were almost there.

They arrived at their destination, on Via Po, in the embassy district of the city. The driver pulled the car up to the curb.

"There. The house with the green door. Just one bell. Ring it."

He opened the car door and Blume stepped out.

34

PATIENCE, THOUGHT BLUME. He would take a small kudos loss on the way he had been brought here. Another youth in another velour tracksuit, zipper undone to reveal a hairless shining chest, opened the door before he rang or knocked. The youth stayed by the door as Blume walked into a hallway lined with framed motion picture stills of Alberto Sordi, a stylized picture of Mussolini, and a futurist poster of fast red cars.

From the far end of the corridor, someone said "He was great, wasn't he?"

Blume looked down, his eyes adjusting to the dimmer light, and saw Innocenzi. He had seen him in plenty of photos and even on TV. He was wearing a green silk shirt, white cotton pants, a pair of Chinese kung-fu slippers.

Blume said, "No. I hate Sordi. Hate his movies, hate his voice. All that Romanaccio shit."

Innocenzi seemed taken aback. "Wow. You're the first person I have met to take that attitude. Maybe you need to be a true-blood Roman instead of an American to appreciate the man. But he's gone now, may his great soul rest in peace. Also, I was talking about Mussolini."

Blume reached Innocenzi, who held out a hand in greeting. Blume thought about it, then took the proffered hand, which was as hard as a seashell.

"Great," said Innocenzi. "In here."

He left the door ajar as he followed Blume into the room, which was furnished as if a teenage hippie from the 1970s had moved into the drawing room of a spinster from the 1920s and simply added stuff without ever taking anything out.

A lava lamp sat on lace draped over a mahogany dresser, a huge old-fashioned stereo with yellow lights sat blinking on a polished flat-topped wooden trunk. A small shrine to the Sacred Heart was attached to the far wall. A few LPs were fanned out over the floor: Led Zeppelin, Bob Dylan, Cream, Lucio Battisti. Silver candlesticks, cigarette papers, a green plastic clock, and a cigarette rolling machine were reflected in the large oval mirror of a vanity to Blume's left. Hanging on the wall behind was an old poster with a stylized dove symbol.

Slightly off-center was a square card table topped with green felt, marked with burns and with stains from the rims of glasses. Innocenzi pointed Blume into a chair, pulled one up himself, sat at the opposite end of the table and said, "You've been paying visits to my daughter."

"Yes."

"Even though you're not on this case?"

"Yes."

"You're something else, know that?"

Blume didn't feel like he had any explaining to do, so he sat silent. Innocenzi, who seemed to be lost in contemplation, did the same. Innocenzi's breath smelled of garlic and mint. The stubble sat on his face like grains of wet black sand. His age was most visible from two creases running diagonally from his high cheekbones down the side of his face, giving a triangular and simian shape to the area between his upper lip and nose. He still had plenty of hair, but he kept it too long at the back, and too black for his sixty-eight years. It was high time, Blume felt, the Italians came up with their own word for mullet.

A chandelier with bulbs missing hung from the ceiling. The light from the window was muted by half-closed wooden shutters. A sofa made from extruded aluminum and hard plastic upholstery sat in the middle. What the hell did the boss spend his millions on?

After a while, Blume said, "If we're not going anywhere with this, I may as well go."

Innocenzi made a slow chopping movement with his hand. "No, no, no. Stay there. I was just getting to know you in person, and maybe I have something to tell you about your cop-killers, Alleva and Massoni."

"As you said, it's not my case."

"You want me to give someone else the information?" Innocenzi sounded disappointed.

"That's not what I said."

"Well, as it happens, I already did. I told Inspector Paoloni where to find

Alleva and Massoni. I told him—let me see—on Wednesday, was it? Whatever day the funeral was. I can tell from just looking at your face that this is news to you. I can also tell that you've been betrayed. You know what people do when they've been betrayed? They wrinkle the top of their nose. And with your nose, it's very easy to see. So Paoloni didn't tell you?"

"What did he do to them?"

"You're not in the picture at all, are you? Good. I like to break news. So Paoloni turns up at the address I gave him, in an unmarked car. He waits for a bit and three other cops, one from your place, two from Tor Vergata, or so I heard, meet at the bottom of the street, around one o'clock at night."

"Have you got the names of these cops?" said Blume.

"Serenity and patience, Commissioner. I've got more than that, as you'll find out if you let me finish my story." He waited to see if Blume wanted to interrupt again, then continued: "We've got a few people watching. They were there because I trust them and wanted to reward them with some light entertainment. One of the cops from Tor Vergata had a battering ram. The others have weapons which I don't think are standard issue for you people. Colt revolver, one had. Scared of dropping shells, I suppose. No masks or balaclavas, just upturned collars. So they burst into this apartment and scare the living Jesus out of a foolish bartender who thought he could skim on the poker machines we installed in his premises. My people said the bartender and his wife squealed like two pigs when they burst in."

"What did they do to them?"

"Your colleagues? Nothing. They wanted Alleva and Massoni, didn't they? They just got out of there as quickly as possible. You should have seen the looks on their faces."

"You were there?"

"No, no. I saw the video. My men were there for entertainment value, but also for a purpose. All four faces. It's clear that Paoloni is the leader. We also have a recording of me giving him the false address."

Blume glanced behind him. The door to the room was very slightly ajar, and he could just make out the immobile figure of someone standing outside.

"No. We're not videoing this," said Innocenzi. "Not that you have any reason to believe me." He made a scissors movement with two fingers and pulled something out of his breast pocket. "Here. Have this. I am still amazed at how small these things are. Technology never stops, and, to be sincere, I cannot keep up with it. Apparently, all the footage is on this."

It was a small memory card. Blume took it. There was no point even in asking if it was the original.

"By the way, Alec, why were you with my daughter?"

"Just some loose ends. Don't use my first name."

"I'll call you what I want. Have you gathered them up yet, these loose ends?"

"Well, I was getting there. Then I got interrupted by a man with no ears and a doped-up youth who could easily have shot me by mistake."

"Sorry about the youth. He's an apprentice. They have to be broken in, you know? You think it's moral to go to my daughter's house like that, just to satisfy your curiosity?"

"She needs to be more careful. She could get herself and you into trouble. Anyhow, it was a setup. She forced me to visit, and your men were there waiting."

"*O la Madonna*, listen to you and your suspicious mind. It was not like that. My daughter, she can be impulsive, but she means well. I keep an eye on her. You were seen arriving, and the decisions afterwards were mine. She likes you, Alec. She phoned me to get assurances that nothing bad would happen to you. She explained that you had a good reason to be with her. She told me about her call to that woman politician."

He pulled out a pack of Chesterfields, lit one, dropped the pack on the table, pointed to it.

"No, thanks," said Blume.

Innocenzi blew a stream of smoke out his nose. Blume noticed it came out of his left nostril only. A silver crucifix hung from a chain around his neck.

Innocenzi jabbed the cigarette in Blume's direction. "OK, let's do it like this. First thing, you're free to walk out of here anytime you want, and you won't get grief from me now or later. Second, I'm going to say a few things to you, then watch your face to see what effect I'm having."

"Faces don't tell as much as you think," said Blume.

"You know, I think you're wrong there, Alec. Or maybe I'm wrong. Hey, humor an old man. What happened to your nose, by the way?"

"My nose is perfectly fucking fine."

"Aha, calm down. Are you ready or not?"

"What? Now I'm supposed to take on a stony expression?" Despite himself, Blume set his face to expressionless.

"Perfect. That's the sort of face I want. Now, I think that if Alleva and Massoni were to turn up dead, you would follow another lead before coming after me."

"That's what you think?"

"Good. You're not showing too much expression yet. So that's what I think, and that is why I'm going to tell you where Alleva and Massoni's hideout is."

Blume felt himself tense a little.

"Fantastic!" said Innocenzi. "You can't deny a flash of interest in your eyes there. Faces don't lie. I've always been right about that."

"You just gave me a film of Paoloni falling into the same trap."

"Except that was Paoloni and you are you. I needed some more leverage on him, a bit of compromise power. Evidently Alleva knows compromising things about Paoloni and probably the other four policemen, or maybe they were just there to avenge a colleague. And now Paoloni is even more compromised than before. It's divine justice, and I love it. Anyhow, here it is. Alleva's real hideout. It took far longer than I thought possible to find this out. Alleva's a slippery bastard." Innocenzi pulled a grubby piece of paper from the same pocket that had contained the memory card, and placed it on the felt between them. Blume glanced at it, saw an address.

"Not in Rome," said Innocenzi. "Near Civitavecchia. Now all you have to do is go there, and then get an extradition warrant, because by now he'll not be long gone. In Argentina, trying to build a new life, bless him. It will be easier for us to find him there than here. Isn't that paradoxical?"

"Why should I believe this is the address?"

"Make an act of faith, Alec. Why should it not be the real address? I trust you not to go there with a death squad."

"And why should I think that you haven't already made a visit?"

"If I or someone representing my interests had visited Alleva and Massoni, it might have ended badly for them, in which case I could be giving you the address to a crime scene that points back to me, which I would never do. I want you to ascertain that Alleva has indeed gone, that I have no involvement in his actions, especially as regards the killing of the young policeman, may God grant his soul everlasting peace."

Blume did not touch the piece of paper.

"I am steering well clear of this, Alec. Dead policeman. Dead dog lover. I don't have it on my conscience, and I don't want it on my mind either. I'm handing it over to you. Do you want that address or not?"

"You just gave it to me. I can remember an address."

"Take the piece of paper; it's more symbolic that way."

"Fine." Blume snatched the piece of paper, put it in his breast pocket. "I don't think Alleva had anything to do with Clemente's murder. But we are going to get him for what he had done to Ferrucci."

"Poor kid," said Innocenzi, touching the crucifix on his neck. "You're doing a fine job, Alec. Unlike your superiors. Even the man's faithless wife seems to accept that it was Alleva. That's what her so-called friend in the Questura is telling her."

Blume said, "That's the line they're taking."

"Yes. The guy in the Questura, the person the widow is taking advice from?"

"What about him?"

"He's the same guy your former partner D'Amico works for. I forget his name. I can look it up if you want." Innocenzi paused to measure the effect of his words. "I can see that was not much news to you."

"More of your face-reading. I don't need the name of D'Amico's boss," said Blume.

"Yeah. He's a total irrelevance. What's he to us? But now this Di Tivoli. What do we make of him? He appears on our television screens and opens twenty-five cans of worms on air. I hate to judge another man—but what can be expected from a queer such as Di Tivoli?"

"Is that all you got on him? That he's gay?"

"It is an utter abomination, and a detestable act," said Innocenzi.

"Doesn't bear thinking about," said Blume. "But is that all?"

"Transvestites, transsexuals, ladyboys. Also, when it comes to age of consent, he skates on thin ice. Barely legal."

"But legal?" said Blume.

"What are you, his lawyer?"

Blume said, "Di Tivoli has always followed Sveva Romagnolo around like a lost dog. It sounds to me like he swings both ways."

"Merciful Jesus." Innocenzi raised his hands to his ears. "That makes it even worse."

"How about this theory?" said Blume: "You had Clemente killed for what . . . outraging your daughter or getting in the way of dog meets. That's what Di Tivoli is implying."

"I've been talking to people who were upset on my behalf at that scandalous documentary. Di Tivoli is not going to make up any more stories like that."

"Did you know Manuela had been with Clemente to Di Tivoli's house in the country?"

Innocenzi closed his eyes and nodded slowly, like a stoic receiving his death sentence. "I knew that. She is so vulnerable it breaks my heart. And your eyes are filled with sympathy, too. You are a good man, Alec. I am happy to be able to do you this little favor with the address."

"I don't want to be beholden to you."

"Wonderful! That's the spirit," said Innocenzi. "This is the sort of relationship that we should have. I like a neat distinction of roles. I gave you the address because I want nothing to do with all this. You check the place out, you'll find no connections leading back to me."

Blume said, "Tell me about Alleva and how he worked with you."

"Alleva's trick was to come up with new ways for doing stuff that wasn't so important. Not so big as to make people jealous. He didn't trespass on other people's turf. He avoided building up his own group, though maybe he could have done better in his choice of personnel."

"You're using the past tense," said Blume.

"Alleva cannot operate anymore now. That must be clear. He has gone from the scene. Pity. He was not a saint. Few of us are. But he had some integrity."

"What's wrong with his personnel?" Blume asked.

"He never found good men. That guy, Massoni, he kept around? He was always going to get Alleva into something stupid. I'm only surprised it took so long."

"How long have they been together?"

"Ten years. Maybe more. They go back some. Before the dogs, Alleva used to sell slimming pills on TeleCapri, then he moved into selling those anticancer pills invented by that doctor from up north. The one who died from a tumor?"

"I remember that," said Blume.

"The dog thing—it wasn't really anything to do with me. Personally,

I don't mind dogs. We were all happy to allow him to organize it, then reap rewards for his efforts, share out his proceeds, wink at some of his tricks, because he was not always up front with us. You know how it is, a man who deals in honey licks his fingers. But after Clemente got himself killed the other day, I had a serious chat with Alleva. I looked deep into his face. He said he had nothing to do with Clemente's murder, and I believed him. But he doesn't always keep control of Massoni, so he couldn't be sure."

"You didn't talk to Massoni himself?" asked Blume.

"No. I was planning to have a chat, when, bang, all of a sudden Massoni starts a shoot-up with the police and the two of them disappear. It'd make you wonder."

"So, you want me to find Massoni, because maybe he killed Clemente. Won't he be in Argentina, too?"

"I don't think Alleva would have allowed Massoni to come with him. Alec, my friend . . ."

"Don't call me that."

"I consider you a friend nonetheless. Alec, perhaps Massoni killed Clemente, but perhaps he did not. You see, Massoni knew who Manuela was, and, let's be fair to the man, I don't think even he could have been so criminally negligent. Can you imagine, murdering my daughter's partner, illicit or not? It almost scares me to think of the consequences. But let's say Massoni thought of getting someone else to do it. Well then. I would not have considered him the subcontracting type, but you never can tell."

"Why not find him yourself?"

"Conflict of interest. I can't get remotely caught up in this now that a policeman has been killed. I would appreciate Massoni being kept alive, though. Your moral integrity offers me better guarantees in that respect than Paoloni. And perhaps you'll share any ideas you might have about the person who did this to my daughter's . . . I don't know what to call him."

"Her lover," said Blume.

"Please," said Innocenzi. "This is my daughter we're talking about. Anyhow, your cooperation would be really appreciated."

"Don't count on it," said Blume.

"Manuela says you are to be treated as a friend now, so I forgive your attitude. Unfortunately, when talking to her friends, Manuela confesses all sorts of things she should keep to herself. She's very open. Did she perhaps tell you about losing her dog when she was a kid?"

When Blume nodded, he continued, "She always tells people that story. Poor child. She tell you about losing her mother, too?"

"Yes."

"See?" said Innocenzi opening his arms wide as if making his point to a silent circle of onlookers. "That was a bad time in our lives. There were uncharitable people at the time. Losing my wife wasn't enough for them. They wanted to crucify me, pin the murder on me, too."

"People?"

"An investigating magistrate in particular. A bitter devil of an old man, nearing retirement. Never did anything with his useless little life, wanted some fleeting fame before going to meet his Maker. I heard afterwards he had succumbed to a heart attack after a road accident." Innocenzi smiled, revealing two long canines, "Luckily, the assistant prosecutor of Foggia was an intelligent young man, bright future in front of him, knew how to run an investigation, knew what made a real case and, more importantly, what didn't. Thanks to his intervention, the investigation finally moved off in the right direction."

Blume said, "The perp was never caught. The investigation hardly went in the right direction."

"It was the right path. But the right path does not always lead to the result you wish for," said Innocenzi. "No one was charged for her murder. That happens sometimes."

"Happens a lot," said Blume.

"Yeah. Must be frustrating for you," said Innocenzi. "That young magistrate, he's older now, of course. I hear he operates here in Rome. Maybe you've even worked with him? He's called Filippo Principe."

35

When innocenzi pronounced Principe's name, Blume felt as if some invisible noxious gas had seeped into him.

"Principe? Maybe it was another . . ." He stopped.

Innocenzi circled his finger over the green felt of the poker table. "Do you know what *kompromat* means?"

Blume was thinking of how Principe had assigned him to the road rage case, and did not answer.

"*Kompromat*," repeated Innocenzi.

"Sounds like a type of cash card or a place to wash your clothes or something," said Blume. "Maybe it's a Russian word?"

"It is Russian. How did you guess?"

"I'm good at languages."

"You are very gifted. The Russians are making inroads. Lots of Russians. Albanians, too, of course. Can you imagine that? Back in my Fronte Gioventù days, I used to think Russians were naturally Communists. Turns out I was wrong. The Russians are very hierarchical, organized."

Blume began to refocus. "So are you."

"Not as much as people think. The 1970s and 1980s. Those years were a step back. Politics got in the way, and groups started organizing them into cells like they were terrorists. Started acting like terrorists, too. Manifestos, political programs, and—" He waved his hand in exasperation. "There was no central authority, no one to turn to, no respect, no way of settling disputes. A disaster. Then things started improving, we went back to the old ways, threw out the politicians, dropped the ideologies. Just in time, too. A few years later the Russians arrived."

"So now you're organized?"

"Things are much better than they were, Alec. Everyone appreciates this. More hierarchical, as it should be. There is a separation of roles. Politicians and ideologues are now kept at arm's length."

"I feel comforted."

"You should. It's why we can talk like this. *Kompromat.*"

"I still don't know what it means."

Innocenzi said, "Suppose I confess a secret to you that allows you to destroy me, what would you do?"

"Destroy you."

"Don't try to be funny."

"Who says I was joking?"

"I say you were. That's how I'm going to take it."

"Fine. So what should I do instead?"

"If I know you can destroy me, I'll destroy you," said Innocenzi. "You think it's good to gain knowledge, but once you have it, you realize you were far better off without it. But there is no going back. So what do you do now? What you do is you hedge the risk. You tell me a secret that would allow me to destroy you. That way, I have less reason to fear what you might do. Intense fear leads to intense violence. If you spread the risk, you lower the violence."

Blume said, "People have lots of secrets."

"The more of their secrets I know, the less worried I am about what they are going to do, and the less inclined I am to treat them as enemies. Seeing as we live in decadent times, I get plenty of material. Even on people who think they've nothing to hide. People like Paoloni or Di Tivoli, say. The Russians have a word for that, too: *poshlost.*"

"Do you know much Russian?"

"I have Russian friends now. How times change," said Innocenzi. "Sometimes, just to remind the politicos and administrators and reporters and police and magistrates and all the others that I'm watching, I let slip a little something. A story appears in a scandal magazine about a certain politician in the company of a whore, the hidden interests of an anticorruption campaigner in property development. You remember Di Pietro and that gift Mercedes, made him stop going after Berlusconi? That's *kompromat* at work."

"And do people have things on you?"

"Sure they do. Even you do."

"How?" asked Blume.

"You know I am vulnerable through my daughter."

"Most fathers are."

"You know my daughter is a gossipy, vain, aging woman who had an illicit affair with a politician's husband."

Blume said, "That's not much."

"It is still something. Gives you some leverage, some *kompromat* power. Maybe you should balance things out, tell me something about yourself."

"You'll have to find that out for yourself."

"Alec, maybe I know things already. But the situation is this. You were taken off the case, but you went to interrogate my daughter in her house. I give you the address of the culprits. I invite you here, treat you well. The way I see it, it's time you reciprocated."

Blume crossed his arms.

Innocenzi said, "It's not corruption. I want you to reciprocate by doing what you were going to do anyhow."

"Which is?"

"Continue working the case. Put it back on track."

"To get the heat off you? You have the situation pretty much under control. Anyhow, I am not totally convinced you're not behind it."

"Yes, you are," said Innocenzi.

"I don't get it. You want me to stop talking to your daughter, fine. As far as I can see, you've got plenty of ways of making me stop, anyhow."

"Sure, I have, Alec. But I want you to act of your own free will in the matter. My daughter, who has a strong sense of retributive justice, had grown very fond of that dog campaigner, Clemente. I didn't approve of it, but, hey, peace and love, no?"

Blume waited.

"So when he got himself killed, she was very upset, came to me, asked what had happened, who was responsible, whether I might not be able to do something. We asked around. I personally spoke with Alleva, like I told you. The man had no idea what I was even talking about. He had nothing to do with it. I called in some favors, checked out the thinking of the authorities—nothing, except for reports that you and your friend Paoloni had reached the same conclusion as me, which was that it was random and could not be solved through the normal channels. Oh—Paoloni tipped Alleva off, you know that?"

"Yes."

"I'm not convincing you, I can see that. Sometimes I can't convince my own daughter. Manuela. She doesn't believe me. She half thinks I had something to do with it."

"Like she still has doubts about how her mother died," said Blume.

Although Innocenzi did not change position, the comfortable posture he had been using was suddenly gone. The creases in his face seemed to smooth as he stared at Blume. He had blue-green eyes, like his daughter. He held his gaze on Blume just long enough for Blume to understand that he stood no chance of staring him down.

"I don't understand that, Alec. Now why would you say a thing like that? My dead wife. I don't know. It has to be a cultural thing, you being an American. You can't have thought it through before you spoke. Wow, what a thing!"

"All right, it was . . . irrelevant," said Blume.

"And you're not even apologizing. Amazing. What is relevant is for you to catch whoever killed Clemente."

Blume felt his finger move and his brow furrow before he had a chance to stop himself, and Innocenzi caught the gestures.

"I see you're surprised, I think I know why, too."

"No. You're over-interpreting," said Blume.

"No. I am not. You are surprised I don't already know who you are looking for. I know you have a theory of some sort that no one else does, but try as I might, I can't get Paoloni or anyone else to give me the name of your suspect. It's your thing, he says. Nothing to do with him. See? Paoloni is faithful as well as faithless. We humans are a mass of contradictions. Now, I'll tell you what would be really fantastic, is for you to go and get this person who killed my daughter's dog protector."

36

INNOCENZI ACCOMPANIED BLUME back to the Cherokee, said something to the two men inside, then touched his elbow, shook his hand.

"My men say you go around unarmed," said Innocenzi. "Is that wise?"

"Sometimes I carry, sometimes not."

"I think you should have a weapon. Especially with that arm. You're very vulnerable, Alec."

"I'll be OK."

"Oh yeah? *Ma 'ndo vai se la banana nun ce l'hai?*" said Innocenzi.

His former abductors drove him back to where his car was parked outside Manuela's apartment building. From there he drove back to the office.

Sitting alone at his desk, Blume looked at the address Innocenzi had given him. He felt aggrieved at not being able to trust even Principe. He made the first of several phone calls.

Ten minutes later, the door to his office smashed open, banged against the wall, and ricocheted halfway closed again. The threads of wire in the rippled glass stopped the pane from shattering.

"Sorry, it was a bit stiff," said Paoloni. "I signed back on duty like you asked. What do you want from me?"

"This is simple enough," said Blume. "You're going after the two who killed Ferrucci. Only this time, I don't want you to go there in secret with a death squad. Oh—and this time, I don't think Innocenzi will be filming you, either. He's got more footage than he knows what to do with. He even gave me a copy, though I haven't seen it yet. I'm not sure I want to."

Paoloni hit the side of the door with the heel of his hand.

"Yes, caught on film, Beppe. When I told you to come back in, I didn't know about this yet," said Blume. "All I knew was you were not being straight with me. OK, I can take that because I have learned over the years to trust you only so much. I thought you would help me keep tabs on Pernazzo, then when I realized you weren't, I found I wasn't so shocked after all. But I didn't take you for a murderer."

"They killed our colleague. We were going to teach them a lesson."

"No, Beppe. You were going to kill them. Off duty, at night, with untraceable weapons. Alleva knew too much. You tipped him off, but more than that, you were on his payroll, and I'm pretty sure now there was other stuff. How much was he paying you?"

"Not just me. Everyone. People like that pay off everyone. I was not acting just to save myself. And they killed a cop. Most of what I got from him I recycled to pay for more information. It's how it works."

"You will have plenty of time to explain all that. Maybe Alleva himself will do the explaining for you if this address turns out to be accurate, and if he's still there."

"You're sending me to pick him up now? That doesn't make sense."

"You're not going there alone, Beppe," said Blume.

"I get it. You're coming with me."

"Not me. A small team of officers is being picked right now."

Paoloni's face was still a strange mixture of yellows from the bruising. He looked battered, defeated. "Who's doing the picking?" he said.

"The Holy Ghost himself. By the way, I said you got the tip-off. I prefer it that way. I don't think you're in a position to challenge me."

"You want me to accompany Gallone to Alleva's hideout?"

"Gallone and his team. I think he's called in the press and the forensics, in that order. It should be quite a *scampagnata*."

Gallone appeared at the doorway. He was in full uniform and smelled of aftershave.

"Vicequestore, sir," said Blume. "Chief Inspector Paoloni is ready as soon as you are."

"I have been ready from the moment I received your phone call," said Gallone. "I have already settled jurisdiction complications with the local prefect and Questura in Civitavecchia. But I need to know where this information comes from."

"Paoloni can explain all that on route," said Blume. "As for me, I've got to get back to the case you assigned me."

Paoloni shot Blume a questioning look and Blume understood his dilemma. He needed to know if he had any leeway left, if he could try to spin more lies, find his way out of the trap. Blume could have simply informed on him, or ordered him to confess, but he did not want to use evidence from Innocenzi against a colleague, no matter how rotten. And he sort of knew about Paoloni anyhow, if only he had admitted it to himself. So Blume returned his glance with a blank stare. He had not decided yet what he wanted to happen to his second-in-command.

After they left, Blume went to pick up his desk phone and call in for the files on the road rage incident when he noticed that the voice mail light was flashing. He picked up, keyed in the voicemail number, and listened to the message. A voice belonging to an unknown youth told him to call Chief Technical Director Dottor Alessandro Cantore at the crime labs on the Via Tuscolana. Blume noted down the number, called, and waited patiently as his call was answered and he was passed from one person to the next.

He had seen how the scientific unit handled their calls. A few cordless phones lay around on the Formica tabletops, and whenever a call came through, whoever was not busy and happened to have a cordless lying near at hand would pick it up and then wander around the lab looking for the right person.

After five infuriating minutes, someone handed the chief technical director the phone.

"Yes?" The important *dottore* made no attempt to hide his annoyance at being interrupted.

"Blume," said Blume matching the unfriendly peremptory tone.

"No, wrong number," declared Cantore, and hung up.

Blume replaced the receiver with exaggerated care. He placed his left palm flat on the table, closed his eyes, and breathed deeply.

Blume was beginning to calm down when his phone rang.

"Yes?"

The same youthful voice explained that Chief Technical Director Cantore had just remembered that Blume was returning a call. He wanted to know if they could meet in half an hour. Blume said they could not, since it would take him at least forty minutes to get to the labs. He was not going to put a flashing light on his car and drive fast with one functioning arm, and he was not sure he wanted to request a patrol car. If this was about Clemente, he preferred not to draw attention to himself. The youth sounded worried, went away, came back and asked if Blume could meet Cantore in an hour.

"Talking on the phone is beneath the great man, eh? Is this helpful to the Clemente or the Enrico Brocca case?"

The youth did not understand.

"Get him on the line."

The phone went thunk as it was put down on a table again. Eventually the voice was back to tell him that Cantore did not want to talk on the phone, because it was a confidential matter.

What the hell. He had promised Giulia he would find her father's killer. This was part of the price to be paid.

37

ALESSANDRO CANTORE WAS in the farthest, most inaccessible, and darkest part of the lab, as if he was trying to avoid Blume. He was powerfully built, his bulk exaggerated by his proximity to a very young and wispy girl who was looking into a microscope. Heavy hands clasped behind his back, he was slightly bent over her and seemed to be peering into the waves of her thin hair with the same intensity of interest with which she was gazing at whatever was wriggling under the lens. He straightened up slightly as Blume entered. Although Cantore's big face and square spectacles, which resembled a pair of old TV sets, were fixed on him, Blume was not entirely sure that he had been noticed. The Scientifics all had a haunted, white, and slightly absent look as they stared intently at their samples of blood, dust, semen, skin, hair, soil, spit, and poison.

Blume leaned against a table scattered with chemicals, litmus paper, and a Gordian knot of electric wires leading to various blue and infrared lights, and waited to be acknowledged.

The director had a booming Venetian accent. "Are you Bellun?"

"Blume," he corrected in a neutral tone. They had met three times before.

"Ah, that's right." Cantore tottered on the edge of an apology, but held back. "Come into my office, we can't talk here." He nodded significantly at the slip of a child looking down the microscope. She did not seem to have heard a word. She had not, in fact, moved at all.

Cantore barged past Blume and led the way through the middle lab, ignoring the startled looks of two whey-faced interns sloshing a liquid around in a reagent tray.

"In here," he instructed, pointing at a pale green door that looked like a utility cupboard. He opened the door with his shoulder.

Blume followed, expecting to find himself in a claustrophobic hole.

Instead, the office was roomy. It had space for two bookshelves, and Cantore's desk was the size and shape of a ping-pong table. It was piled with papers and books, and someone, presumably Cantore himself, had been using plastic petri dishes for ashtrays.

Blume sat down on a chair so low that his eyes were just level with the surface of Cantore's overflowing desk. Cantore busied himself stacking the piles of paper, cups, and ashtrays into even higher mountains. With a final grunt of satisfaction, he positioned himself carefully in the center of the frame, sat, and glowered down his paper canyon at Blume.

"Clemente case," said Cantore. "I hear you're off it. Pity. I was looking forward to more dog hairs."

"That's what must be so good about your job, Professor," said Blume. "A dog hair this week, who knows what treasures next week will bring."

Cantore clapped his hands twice, either celebrating Blume's sarcasm or marking the end to the opening formalities. "I think I remember you now. Awkward foreign bastard," he said.

"I'm investigating a new case," said Blume.

"There was tons of evidence!" shouted Cantore. "Not in your new case. I'm talking about the Clemente case. Positively tons of it. Either the killer was an idiot . . ."

Blume waited. "Or?" he said eventually.

"Or nothing. The killer was just an idiot," said Cantore, and burst out laughing. "So what we have here"—Cantore thumped at the desk as if indicating a photograph, but Blume couldn't see anything—"is a bar of soap with a great big perfect thumbprint, three fingerprints. The same prints were found on the body, on the wall, on the bathroom mirror, in the wardrobe, on the front door, on a box of shopping, everywhere we looked."

"And they belong to Clemente's killer?"

"Not all the victim's friends were cooperative in giving their prints, and we've still got some unaccounted for, but, yes, let's say they belong to the killer."

"But you got no result from the AFIS database," said Blume.

"I sent them to Guendalina—you know Guendalina?"

"No."

"Nice girl, Guendalina. She manages the AFIS database. Always helpful. Lovely woman. Really very . . ." Cantore lowered his voice so suddenly that Blume missed the rest. Then, returning to full volume, he continued:

"So anyway, I told Wendy—that is to say, Guendalina—what the case was, and she told me she had heard it was very important, and was being much talked about up there in the corridors of corruption."

"And?" prompted Blume.

"She got nothing. But you know this."

Blume asked, "Why did you call me?"

Cantore hoisted two plastic bags above his head with an air of triumph. One contained a torn pink booklet that Blume recognized as an old-fashioned driver's license, the other a green and red credit card. "Enrico Brocca's driver's license." He glanced up at his other hand. "And his credit card," he added. "Your new case."

Blume looked at him uncomprehendingly.

"We got prints on them," explained Cantore.

"You're only getting around to that now?"

"No, we got these prints ages ago. Level two friction ridge identification, but the print on the license is excellent."

"Great," said Blume. "And you ran them through the AFIS database?"

"Yes. But we got no match," said Cantore, settling back in his chair, and disappearing for a moment behind the papers.

Blume leaned forward to bring him back into view. He did not understand what Cantore was saying. He asked, "No match? I already knew there was no match on the AFIS. If there had been, we'd have arrested someone by now."

"Well, if it interests you, the no-match will become a definite match when the AFIS database is updated." Cantore smiled revealing a row of square teeth the color of tea.

"I'm not following you anymore," said Blume.

He heard a click, a shuffle sound behind him, and turned around to see Principe entering the room.

"The prints from the Brocca murder scene go into the database, obviously, though we can't associate them with a name," continued Cantore. "Filippo, I'll get someone to bring you a chair."

"It's all right Alessandro, I can stand," said Principe from behind Blume. "I see you've almost finished explaining it to him."

"I have finished," said Cantore.

"No you haven't," said Blume. "The no-match on the driver's license . . ."

"And on the credit card," chimed in Cantore.

"And on the credit card," said Blume. "They are no-matches. What the hell good is that?"

"I didn't say they were a no-match," boomed Cantore. "What would I call you all the way down here to say that for? What I said was they don't match on the AFIS, because the AFIS has not been updated to include them."

Principe stepped from behind Blume until he was on his left side. Blume stared down the desk at Cantore, who had stopped speaking and was looking at Principe with a "you-explain-it-to-him" sort of look.

Principe explained: "What he means, Alec, is that there will be a match as soon as the AFIS database has been updated with the fingerprints from the Clemente crime scene. The reason is that the unidentified fingerprints from Clemente's house and the unidentified fingerprints on Enrico Brocca's credit card and license are one and the same. The same person did both killings."

Blume eased himself around to face Principe. "You knew this?"

"The connection between the two cases, yes. Now you have to use it."

Cantore bellowed some clarification from behind the desk, "It depends on which time frame you choose to use, Inspector Bellun. It is self-evident that Public Minister Principe and I knew of the connection before you. But we have not known about it for long."

"Alessandro, it's Commissioner, not Inspector, and Blume with an *M*. Let's use first names and 'tu' here."

"If you say so," said Cantore.

"Dottor Cantore informed me of the match two nights ago," Principe told Blume. "I got the road rage case assigned to me, then put you on it. I could not be explicit over the phone."

Cantore suddenly heaved himself out of his chair. "I am not interested in hearing these details," he said. "I just thought you should know about the fingerprint match."

Principe said, "I appreciate it. Do you mind not mentioning it to anyone for a day or two?"

"Why would I mention it ever again?" said Cantore. "In fact, I don't even see why I should be here. I have too much to do as it is. You're welcome to use the office, though."

Cantore passed Principe and gave him a friendly thump on the back, then stood before Blume, a massive form filling his entire field of vision. An enormous doughy white hand emerged from the bulk. "Commissioner Bellum . . ."

They shook hands and he left.

As soon as Cantore had slammed the door, Principe said, "I was not able to be forthcoming on the phone. There were people in my office." He gave Blume an appraising look.

"I thought I detected something in your tone," said Blume.

"That was for appearances."

"I understand that now . . . It's a busy place, the Prosecutor's Office, especially in Rome. Where were you before you got transferred here? Foggia?"

"Foggia, that's right," said Principe. He took a sheaf of papers from his inside pocket, and prepared to read.

"Any interesting cases when you were there?" asked Blume.

Principe lowered the papers in his hand, peered over the top of his glasses at Blume, and said, "Alec, it sounds to me like you're trying to say something."

"I was talking to Innocenzi earlier today," said Blume, watching Principe's face closely.

"You got to talk to him?" Principe looked surprised. Then Blume saw his mouth open in a tiny o of recognition, and then form a pained smile. "The murder of Innocenzi's wife. That's what this is about."

"Yes, that."

"Innocenzi works like that, Alec. Divide and rule, sow seeds of distrust, know more than everyone else or pretend you do."

"I know, he explained it to me. He calls it *kompromat*."

"What does that mean?" asked Principe.

"It means he's got something on you."

"He's got nothing on me," said Principe. "There was no evidence against Innocenzi at the time. Many people thought he had arranged the murder of his wife, but there was nothing to prove it."

"What did she do? Betray him?"

"I don't know, Alec. Maybe she did nothing. Motivation was one of many things missing."

"People kill with little motivation."

"Sure," said Principe. "I know that. But there was no evidence, no clear

269

motive, just suspicion. The case would never have stood up in court. And if it had, then it would have required a hell of a lot of fabrication on our part. That's what the chief prosecutor wanted. I didn't."

"You managed to persuade him."

"It wasn't that hard. The magistrate in charge was old, ignorant, corrupt. The case was never going anywhere. It was easy to terminate his line of investigation. A lot of people were happy to see me force a change of direction."

"And you were happy to do as they asked?"

"Sometimes the wrong people want the right thing for the wrong reasons. This was one of those cases." Principe looked directly down at Blume. "You have known me for eleven years. It took—what? Half an hour in Innocenzi's company to undermine that? Decide what you think, then tell me."

Blume remained silent for a full twenty seconds. Principe settled back on the desk and waited.

Finally, Blume said, "Sorry. I should have thought it through."

Principe nodded, apparently satisfied.

But Blume could not quite tell what he really felt. He was angry with himself. If he had stopped Pernazzo, stayed on him instead of keeping his date with Kristin, the child's father might be alive. Bad enough though it was, he kept this thought in the foreground, because underneath was an even worse one, which was that he had somehow goaded Pernazzo into murder. He had called him a loser, a failure, and so Pernazzo had gone out to kill, while Blume was trying to make Kristin feel sorry for him with talk of his parents.

"Pernazzo's got an alibi that I don't think is real," said Blume, and told Principe about his conversation with Rosati.

Principe unfolded the sheets of paper he had taken from his pocket and began to read. "I hate it when there's computer stuff involved. It's all above my head. But the main point is we now have another way into the Clemente case through the unfortunate Enrico Brocca. Or you do. But we may have to use the child as a main witnesses."

"It wasn't road rage, it was part of a game," said Blume.

"A psychopathic game, you mean?"

"Yes. But not just that. Have you ever heard of World of Warcraft, Grand Theft Auto, EverQuest . . ." Blume could see by Principe's face that he hadn't. "I'll get Pernazzo to explain once he is in custody," said Blume. "And now it's my turn to surprise you: Innocenzi gave me the location of Alleva's hideout near Civitavecchia. The Holy Ghost is flitting down there as we speak. Along with Paoloni. And God knows how many others."

Principe set aside the papers. "You sent them . . . Good move, I suppose. I wish I had known first, of course. What do you think they will find there?"

"An empty house, trace evidence. I don't know. Too little too late, that's for sure. Nothing that allows us to step back in time and prevent any of the killing."

"If we could go back in time to prevent murders, we'd both be out of a job," said Principe. "And how far back would you want to go? To Cain and Abel?"

"I'd settle for last week," said Blume. His cell phone started ringing. "Or maybe some time before they invented these things."

38

HAVING REMAINED DETACHED and efficient while killing Clemente, and having successfully battled down an onrush of nausea at the scene, Angelo Pernazzo was disappointed that he threw up as soon as he arrived home. It was the tension, especially on the drive back, he decided. He wiped the toilet rim with some paper, filled the bath with tepid water, and lay in it for an hour until the water was cold and gray. Then he put all his clothes in the washing machine, poured in bleach and detergent, and set it at the highest temperature. Whatever did not survive, he would throw out. He put on a pair of elasticized gray tracksuit bottoms, a pair of cotton espadrilles, and a red V-neck Roma soccer shirt. He ate some Ringo chocolate cream cookies, drank a Diet Coke, and felt better.

He wiped down the knife with a rag soaked in pink denatured alcohol, enjoying the smell and the glint. Then he put it on his desk next to his computer. That is where he had always kept it since he bought it at a martial arts store outside the train station in Ostia, nine months ago. He had impressed them, walking in out of the rain, ignoring all the shit on display, asking for a Ka-Bar Tanto that he knew they would have to order from Japan.

Exactly on time, he took his scheduled twenty-minute sleep. When he awoke, he climbed off the sofa with the same sort of feeling he used to get on his birthday morning, when he knew his mother would be waiting in the kitchen with precisely whatever gift he had asked for. The last gift she had given him was a silver bracelet with his name inscribed on it. This was his first birthday without her, but if Massoni came through on his promise, today Pernazzo would finally get himself a pistol.

He had asked for a Colt Python, but Massoni had laughed at him. Eventually Massoni agreed to get him a Glock, in exchange for which he wanted Pernazzo to do him a little favor, which was to go to Clemente, tell him to back off, stop disrupting the shows.

"You want me to take him a message from Alleva?" Pernazzo had asked.

"No. Just tell him to back off. Don't say who the message is from."

"I could say it was from myself."

"And how would that work, Angelo? Are you going to threaten the man? Just deliver the message. No source, just a warning. Think you can do that?"

Once Pernazzo had done this favor, Massoni promised, he would get his gun. For fifteen hundred euros. Angelo knew it was five times as much as it was worth, and Massoni knew he knew.

Pernazzo's first real contact with Massoni had been a fist in the stomach. That was eighteen months ago.

His mother was still dying in her bedroom, and the doorbell had rung. He answered to a massive man with a blue tattoo on his neck. Massoni asked Pernazzo to identify himself and, when Pernazzo did, punched him directly in the solar plexus.

Pernazzo had never received a punch like that. As he lay on the floor, all he could think of was that he needed to breathe in, but couldn't. The blow had scrambled his thoughts, which re-formed into a single imperative: breathe. His brain started screaming the command, his limbs began to thrash as he tried to obey. Perhaps the worst of it was that he could not make a sound. He lay there jerking, mouth open like a fish, agonizing in total silence. No one had hurt him physically before. Then, finally, the air came whooshing in, making him hoot, gasp, and hoot again. By the time he had finished hooting, he could hear his mother's anxious voice from the bedroom asking if that was him.

Massoni had taken apart the living room, the bedroom, kitchen. He had done it professionally and quietly. Pernazzo saw he had looked in several places where he had hidden money in the past.

"Where is it?" Massoni had asked without even turning around, as Pernazzo staggered in behind him.

"I haven't got it. You said to have it for this afternoon. It's still morning."

"If you don't have it now, you won't have it in the afternoon."

"Yes, I will. I was paid for a Web site. Bank transfer the other day. The money's in the bank."

Massoni went over to the door leading into Pernazzo's mother's bedroom. As he reached it, he paused and turned around to look at Pernazzo.

"What's in there?"

"My mother."

"And maybe the five thousand you owe Alleva? Five thousand eight as it now is."

"No, it's not in there. She's very old. She's dying."

Massoni stepped back a little from the door.

"She could have heard that," he said.

"She's too doped to know, too much in pain to care."

Massoni leaned over and practically plucked Pernazzo from the ground. "We're going to the bank together. I hope for your sake you were telling the truth."

Pernazzo had been telling the truth. He had been paid five thousand for a Web design, five thousand more for some JavaScript that wasn't even very good, and a few hundred from another client for some style sheet templates. His bank balance was eleven thousand euros, of which he owed twenty-two hundred in VAT immediately, and around four thousand more in taxes, payable in a few months. After paying off his fifty-eight-hundred-euro gambling debt to Alleva, he would be unable to cover his tax bill. Unless his mother died first.

Pernazzo came out of the bank that day with sixty-three hundred-euro notes. Massoni was waiting for him. He handed him fifty-eight notes. Massoni counted them three times. Pernazzo allowed him to walk away a bit, then called out. Massoni stopped, walked back over, fists clenched. As he reached him, Pernazzo deftly inserted five one-hundred bills into Massoni's hand.

"That's for not going into my mother's bedroom. I appreciate it."

Massoni looked at him, closed his fist around the money. He smiled contemptuously at Pernazzo.

Pernazzo smiled back. Massoni could be bought. It took longer than he expected, and he had to pay Massoni off a few times, but eventually, Massoni told him the underdog trick, and together they laid out a plan for placing a large bet against Alleva. Massoni said he would get some other friends involved.

He sat by the phone and waited. After an hour and ten minutes, it rang.

"Did you take the message?" said Massoni not wasting time with preliminaries.

"I did," said Pernazzo. He felt a catch in his throat, and wondered whether he was going to vomit again. But then he realized it was joy rising from his chest. He did not want to vomit: he wanted to sing, roar, laugh. Pernazzo hugged himself in glee.

"Did he say anything?"

Pernazzo thought back. Had Clemente said anything? He could only remember grunts and gasps and those wet sounds at the end.

"No."

"Shit. If he brings journalists again we'll have to cancel for months."

"I don't think he'll bring any journalists to the dog fight tomorrow," said Pernazzo.

"Did he say that?"

"Not exactly. This is shit you can't explain on the phone."

He left the phrase hanging there, but Massoni ignored it. "You got the money?"

"Yes."

"OK. I'll be around in an hour."

Pernazzo sat waiting. Listening to the radio. There was no news of Clemente's murder. He was scared of what Massoni might do if he found out, but he was dying to tell him, too.

39

MASSONI SAT DOWN on a wooden-slat chair near Pernazzo's desk. The chair let out a sharp crack. Massoni stood up, looked at it, and sat down more slowly. The chair held its own. He put a plastic bag on the floor, and lifted out a gray Puma shoebox, about to give way at the sides.

He slid the box across the floor toward Pernazzo, who had settled on the sofa. It hit something sticky on the floor, fell over, and lost its lid. Inside, partly enveloped in a lint cloth, was a colorless Glock 22 that looked like it was fashioned from prison soap. Pernazzo bent down to retrieve it. Massoni did not move a muscle.

Basically, Pernazzo was disappointed. The weapon did not look impressive. It did not even look real. He really did not want to part with fifteen bright green hundred-euro notes for this thing.

He picked it up. It was even lighter than he had imagined. With a sudden sense of panic, he wondered if it might not be a fake, and Massoni was brimming with silent laughter right now, dying to tell his friends about selling a toy gun for one and a half grand. Casually, he checked it. It looked real enough. He had read that all you had to do with a Glock was pull the strange double trigger.

"The money's there, on the desk," said Pernazzo. He watched as Massoni looked over, saw the envelope, and beside the envelope the magnificent knife. Now there was a real weapon. "Be back in a moment."

Pernazzo took his gun, went into the kitchen, and examined it more carefully. It was real. He exerted tiny pressure on the safety catch and trigger mechanism, and felt it begin to travel back. That's all it would take. Then he opened the refrigerator, came back in with two tumblers and a one-and-a-half-quart plastic bottle of Fanta, his favorite drink.

"Want some?"

"No," said Massoni.

Pernazzo twisted open the top, enjoyed the hiss and the gassy orange whiff, then poured himself a full glass. He put the glasses on the desk. The money was gone; the knife was in a different position.

He drank down his glass, holding the Glock by his side, in a natural way. He put down his glass, picked up the plastic bottle, and carried it over to the sofa, and crammed it into the corner so that half of it was protruding from below the velveteen brown cushion. He leaned over, placed the barrel of the pistol right against the plastic, and, as he had read he was supposed to do, squeezed rather than pulled the trigger.

The gun went click.

"You didn't like your Fanta?" said Massoni.

Pernazzo kept his back turned. He could feel himself beginning to shake. He tried to modulate his voice, but the words came out vibrating with emotion. "The gun you sold me doesn't even work!"

"It's not loaded," said Massoni. "Look."

Pernazzo had to turn around now. He set a look of indifference on his face as he did so, but the grin on Massoni's face almost made him lose it.

Massoni was holding out both hands. In one was a magazine clip, in the other a red and gray box.

"Bullets," said Massoni. "Here." His huge hand beckoned Pernazzo to give him back the pistol. Pernazzo thought about it, then surrendered the weapon.

Massoni popped out the magazine, inserted the new one, shook the box. "These are forty-caliber cartridges." He opened the box, plucked out snub-nosed bullets, and began pressing them into the empty magazine with his fat thumb. "Like this. Easy, see?"

"Just put them on the desk."

Massoni did as asked, and said, "You've got to tell me what that move with the Fanta was about."

"Give me back my gun first."

Massoni held out the weapon, and Pernazzo snatched it. He let it hang in the air for a few seconds, its square-shaped barrel pointing causally toward Massoni's crotch, kneecaps.

Eventually Massoni noticed, and said, "Careful."

Pernazzo went back to the sofa. The weapon in his hand felt better balanced.

"Why do you want to shoot the bottle?" insisted Massoni.

"I want to test it."

Massoni scraped his neck tattoo with his forefinger.

"Test what?"

"The Glock!"

"Against the Fanta, it is going to win."

"The bottle is a silencer. You put the barrel up against a full plastic bottle and fire, it muffles the sound."

Massoni pulled his head back in disbelief. "Who told you that?"

"None of your business."

"You want to shoot that bottle on the sofa?"

Pernazzo began to raise the weapon slightly so that it was aiming at Massoni's barge-like shoe.

"Yeah."

"You'll cover the whole place in fizzy orange."

"That's obvious," said Pernazzo.

"Yeah, but you'll blow a hole in the sofa, too."

"So?"

"I don't get it. Those are forty-caliber cartridges. You'll probably smash a hole in the wall or floor, too, and the noise would be just as loud."

"No, it won't. The bottle will silence it."

"No way. Not a forty-caliber in a closed room. You ever used a pistol in an enclosed space?"

Pernazzo looked at the large shape of Massoni, colorless against the bright window. His hand ached in sympathy with his imagination, which foresaw the Glock in his hand and himself standing in front of Massoni sprawled on the floor as he retrieved the money.

Massoni shrugged, "Whatever you want to think. Tell me about Clemente. Did you tell him we were watching him, his wife, his kid?"

"Yes."

"Did he say anything?"

"No."

"I don't even believe you went to his apartment," said Massoni. "He probably wasn't even in. Or maybe you chickened out when he answered the door. It doesn't matter. We'll find a proper way of persuading him."

"I killed him," said Pernazzo. "I got in and I killed the bastard. With that knife on the table, the one you just touched."

Massoni moved away from the window, and the sunlight struck Pernazzo between the eyes, disorienting him and giving a strobe-light effect to Massoni's movements. One moment he was at the window, the next moment he seemed to have got across the floor in a single jerking movement and was standing in front of Pernazzo. He balled Pernazzo's shirt in his fist, drew their faces together, then relaxed and said, "No. You're kidding. In your dreams you killed a man."

"That's his bag there," said Pernazzo pointing to the gray backpack near the desk.

"What's in it?"

"Nothing. I used it for my clothes."

"No, you didn't. This isn't some fantasy game."

"I killed him. You'll hear. It'll be on TV and the radio."

"No way," said Massoni. "I was just messing with your head sending you there. You think we need you as messenger boy?"

"You couldn't afford to go there yourself. It was too risky, so you sent me."

"If we wanted to harm the guy, we'd have sent a real person. Jesus, you're serious? How did you get in?"

"The building door downstairs was open, then I just knocked on his apartment door. He opened."

"And you—what—you burst in and stabbed him?"

"A guy was delivering groceries. He had gone upstairs, left two boxes there. When the dog lover opened, he thought I was the grocery boy. Made it easier. Except I had to wait till I was sure the real grocery boy wasn't going to knock on the door."

"He was on his own?"

"Yes."

"Thank Christ for small mercies. Do you know whose daughter he's fucking? That's why I couldn't do it . . . Have you any idea what you've just done? What was so hard about dropping a few hints, like I said? I should—I should shoot you right now."

But Massoni made no move to extract a weapon. Maybe he was not armed. Pernazzo tightened his grip on his own.

"I need to phone Alleva," said Massoni. "This is unbelievable."

"So phone him. It's about time you and he started taking me seriously."

Massoni pulled out a small folding cell phone, and stared at it doubtfully.

Pernazzo wondered how he managed to push fewer than ten buttons at a time with his sausage fingers.

Massoni eventually made his call. "Yeah, I know, unbelievable," Pernazzo heard him say. He used the word three times.

When he had finished, he looked at Pernazzo and shook his head slowly from side to side—a gesture of admiring disbelief, Pernazzo felt.

"Are we going to see Alleva?"

"No. First, we check that this is true. You stay here. Don't move from this house."

"What about our bet for tomorrow night—the underdog fight?"

Massoni ran his hand through the hedgehog hair of his head. "You expect the dog fight to go ahead? After Clemente has been killed? The whole operation will close for months now."

"Shit, I hadn't thought about that," said Pernazzo.

"Alleva's going to hold you responsible for lost income. But that's the least of your worries now."

"We can do the underdog bet some other time, then," said Pernazzo.

"Sure we can, Angelo. Sooner or later you're going to be a big winner."

"And you. You get thirty percent."

"How could I forget?" said Massoni. "Stay in, remember? Answer the door to visitors. It'll be me or maybe Alleva."

He left.

Pernazzo spent the rest of the day monitoring the news. At eight, he took a scheduled twenty-minute nap and dreamed about his mother, as he always did ever since the night he helped her to die. He dreamed about Clemente, and he dreamed about the girl with the sleek hair running barefoot. He had met her in Second Life, or when he was in primary school. He couldn't remember.

When he woke up, his eyes would not open and his body would not move when he commanded it, not that he wanted to. He felt as if his body were made of heavy metal, and the bed was magnetic but soft. He wished he could stay immobile and relaxed like that forever.

He thought he was awake because the radio was playing, but then he noticed it was talking about Clemente and Alleva, so he figured he must still be asleep. Then it was talking about the weather and a storm front making its way down south. Pernazzo sat up and realized he was back in real life.

He left the radio on while he worked on a new style sheet for the Web site of the local government offices of Genzano. It was pathetic. He knew Perl, and could make the deadest Web site interactive in a few days, but no one cared about quality. They would pay him two hundred euros. The plaque on the door had cost him a hundred fifty. It was meant to be an in-joke for a planned real-life meeting at his place with two Blood Elves, but they never showed up. Both made pathetic excuses that night when he met them online.

The radio did not mention Clemente again, so it must have been a dream.

Friday had become Saturday, and Saturday had unfolded hour by tedious hour and done nothing to celebrate Pernazzo's new status. Meanwhile Pernazzo's Uberman sleep schedule was going to hell. It was the tension of waiting and hearing nothing. Finally, at five in the evening, the radio reported on the killing of Clemente, husband of a respected Green Party MP. He hadn't known that bit about the wife and was pleased. It enhanced the prestige.

At ten to nine, the intercom buzzed and he went to answer it.

"Pernazzo?" said the voice.

It wasn't Massoni. He did not recognize the voice. "Yes?"

"Angelo Pernazzo?"

"Yes. What do you want?"

And then the voice said, "Police."

40

ANGELO PERNAZZO FELT slippage in his stomach when the voice pronounced the word "police." He ran to the table in the living room, where he had set down the Glock, picked it up, then ran back. But if there was more than one of them, it would be pointless trying to shoot his way out. The intercom button buzzed again, loud and long. The effect was to turn his fear into anger.

"I'm still here, fuck it," he told the impatient cop.

"Did you hear me? I said police."

"OK," said Pernazzo. He buzzed open the door, and went into his bedroom, and slipped the Glock and the Ka-Bar under the mattress.

The buzzer sounded again. He answered for the third time. "What!"

"Which floor?"

"Third."

"OK. On my way," said the voice. It was still a lone voice.

When Pernazzo opened the door, the cop was alone. "*Permesso?*"

Pernazzo halted his retreat down the corridor. A policeman about to arrest for murder does not come alone, then ask for permission to enter. He turned around and checked out the visitor, sizing him up, looking for his weak points.

He was a tall man, forty-ish, heavily built. Similar to Clemente, but not as soft. Except the cop seemed like he'd be more ready for an unexpected attack. He bent his face forward slightly as he examined Pernazzo.

Over the next half hour, this policeman invaded Pernazzo's life, derided him, took over the apartment, inspected things, touched objects, expressed disgust, suspected everything, reviled him as a loser. Pernazzo felt seasick with nerves and rage. Then the cop took the peanut butter label.

He could have gone to his bedroom, returned with the knife, and stuck the fucker there and then, and he wanted to, but he remembered some words of wisdom written on a message board by a champion gamer at a guild meeting: You can never isolate and kill a cop. Like careful mountaineers, they always tell other people where they are going.

Pernazzo needed to join Alleva as quick as he could now. He needed to be part of a gang. He needed to work fast.

Before leaving, the visitor handed him a card. Commissioner Alec Blume, it said. The commissioner had laughed out loud at the underdog story, called him a dupe. Alleva used to be a con man, he said. Pernazzo had not considered this possibility.

But if it was a con . . . Massoni, who knew his mother had died and left him some money. The big bet on the underdog. Maybe there was no such thing. Maybe underdogs just lost.

Ten minutes after the police commissioner had left, Massoni buzzed, told him to come downstairs. They were going across town because Alleva wanted to talk.

"I'm being watched," Pernazzo whispered into the intercom.

"What? Can't hear you."

"I'm being watched," said Pernazzo. "The police are out there watching me."

"Get down here, you paranoid little fuck," said Massoni. "No one's watching you. You think I don't know how to spot police surveillance?"

Before he left the house, Angelo stuck the Glock into the back of his pants. He put on a belt to hold it in place. It was uncomfortable, it was not easily accessible, and he had a cringing feeling in the small of his back and in his anus for fear that the weapon might go off. But he was no loser. He had demonstrated that yesterday. And he would prove himself again, as soon as the opportunity presented itself.

41

Massoni drove a BMW X5. Everyone drove an SUV nowadays, except Pernazzo. That was something else that was going to change. Massoni drove fast over the wet roads, one hand on the steering wheel. He seemed to be trying to send a text from his phone. At San Camillo Hospital, he did something that must have canceled all the hard work of the last few miles, because he braked, cursed, and hurled his phone on the floor in front of Pernazzo.

As the phone hit the floor it flashed and began to vibrate, and Antonello Venditti started singing, "Grazie Roma."

Massoni held out his right hand. "Give it back."

Pernazzo stole a look at the screen before placing the phone in Massoni's palm, but all he saw was a number.

Massoni flipped open the phone, cutting off Venditti's anthem. "Yeah?" he said.

Massoni knew how not to reveal too much on a cell phone. After a series of monosyllables, he snapped the phone closed and announced, "We're not going to Alleva."

"What?"

"We're not going. He says he doesn't even want to see me, not till things have calmed down. He told me to take you home."

Pernazzo mustered all the authority he could and said, "Keep driving in the direction you were going."

Massoni ignored him.

"He's fucking us over, that's what he's doing," said Pernazzo.

"What's with this 'us'? He's not meeting you, is all."

"Think about it, Massoni. He wants you to stay with me while he gets away. You got to learn to think for yourself. Make him need—Brake!"

Massoni had already slammed his foot onto the brake pedal half a second before Pernazzo managed to shout. Pernazzo could feel a shuddering from beneath his feet as the antilock braking system locked and released the wheels in rapid cycles, and he could hear the wash of the rainwater spinning from the tires.

Massoni bashed the horn with his fist at the stationary car in front. They were going to make it.

Almost.

The SUV eased its way into the back of a small family car that had stopped dead in the middle of the street. The impact was negligible.

"Look at this guy!" said Massoni as the car they had just hit swerved out of sight and into a parking place to the right. "Causes a crash, then just finishes his parking."

He opened the door and hopped out. Pernazzo waited a second, then followed suit.

Massoni walked around to the front of his car, bent his head, and examined the damage. Perhaps there was a slight dent in the fender, it was hard to tell. The other driver was arriving, white-faced. Water droplets from the large-leafed plane trees above splashed on his bald head. Massoni executed an elegant sweeping movement with his hand in the direction of his fender, like he was selling the car. A woman, presumably the wife, hurried away with two children. The woman had a fat ass. The girl had long sleek black hair that shone in the wet. Nice. Pernazzo watched them as they made for a pizzeria. The husband half-turned and followed them with his eyes, said something, then turned back to Massoni, and said in a loud voice, "If you want, we can call the police."

Massoni said something that Pernazzo missed. He moved in closer and heard the bald man say, "Is that a threat?"

Evidently it was. Massoni grabbed the man's lapel and yanked him in front of the car, pushed his head down, made him look at a scrape that Pernazzo couldn't see.

The bald man said, "My car's damaged worse. You're at fault. Driver behind is always at fault."

Massoni looked over at Pernazzo and gave him a can-you-believe-this-guy sort of grin.

"I need you to give me two hundred euros," Massoni told the man.

"I don't have two hundred euros."

"Too bad," said Massoni, "because that's what the damage to my car is going to cost. You're lucky I know a panel beater does discounts."

"I don't have that sort of money."

"Listen to him. That sort of money. It's exactly the same sort as what you have in your wallet."

"I don't have that much."

"How were you going to pay for the pizzas?"

"They wouldn't cost two hundred."

Massoni reached out, pulled the guy toward him. "Just give me your wallet, see what's in it."

The man shook his shiny head, but when Massoni spun him around and yanked his wallet out of his back pocket, he did not put up much resistance. Massoni pulled out two fifties and a twenty, rubbed them between thumb and forefinger, folded them into his pocket, tossed the wallet high in the air between Pernazzo and the bald man. Pernazzo was faster, and leaped slightly to snatch it.

"Give me that," said the man, finding his voice as Pernazzo opened it.

Pernazzo pulled out a supermarket points card, dropped it on the ground. "There you go," he said.

He pulled out a Visa card, a San Paolo ATM card, glanced at them, then flicked them to the ground, one by one, first to the left, then to the right. He pulled out a pink driver's license, read out the name.

"Enrico Brocca. Pleased to meet you, Enrico." He ripped the license in two, threw one piece leftward, the other rightward. Then he emptied the whole contents on the ground. Coins, cards scattered on the road. The man moved back and forth, almost on his knees, as he retrieved his belongings.

Massoni pulled back his leg and made as if to deliver a kick. The man covered his head with his arms, and Pernazzo laughed. "You're lucky we've got places to be, Enrico," he said.

The man walked slowly away toward the pizzeria. Just before he reached the front door, Pernazzo saw him bend, brush the wet from his pants, take a deep breath, raise his head, steady his walk.

Pernazzo and Massoni climbed back up into the car and sat there.

"You handled that pretty well," said Pernazzo. "But there's something missing in your method. You're reactive only. You need to become more of a protagonist."

Massoni spun the steering wheel and made a U-turn, shaking a fist at the motorists coming from both directions. "I didn't see you being much of a protagonist just now, standing there like a wet rat watching me."

"Where are we going?"

"I'm taking you back home."

They drove in silence for ten minutes. Then Pernazzo asked, "Where do you think Alleva is now?"

Massoni shrugged.

"Let me ask you something."

Massoni drummed the steering wheel as he waited for a light to change.

"Have you got anything on Alleva?"

Massoni switched on Radio DeeJay, and after listening to the music a bit said, "I know that song. Robert someone. Sang it at Festivalbar. Good song."

Pernazzo reached over and switched off the radio.

"You're not listening to me."

Massoni switched the radio on again. "You want me to break your fingers?"

Pernazzo left the radio on and spoke over the music. "The way I see it is this. You break fingers, hassle people a bit, but you haven't done anything really important for Alleva. I'm not saying you've never killed a man, but you've never done it for Alleva, have you? I'm right, aren't I?"

"So what?"

"He hasn't let you see him do anything really bad, either. Right? That means you can't compromise him."

"Yeah. We're still working together. So it's good."

"Not good. Bad."

"I don't become his enemy or a danger."

"You are something he can walk away from. You've no leverage. Me, I've just given myself leverage on him by killing Clemente. Right now, he's trying to figure out who I am. That's what he's delaying for."

Massoni flicked on the windshield wipers to brush away some droplets.

"I was just thinking, he might cut us out of the loop," said Pernazzo.

"There you go with that 'us' again."

"He's excluding you, too. You're not indispensable to him. You need to forge a bond that he can't break even if he wants to."

Massoni pushed his shoulders back into the seat, preparing to drive again. "I don't know what you're talking about."

"I can show you how. Right now."

"Show me what?"

"How to get Alleva to respect you and need you."

"He said he's not meeting you."

"We don't need to meet him. Just drive back to that pizzeria where that guy dented your car."

"Why there?"

"You want me to show you or not?"

"No."

Massoni turned up the music and accelerated back in the direction of Pernazzo's house.

"Are you sure there were no police watching my house?" said Pernazzo after listening through two Carmen Consoli songs back-to-back.

"Those are great, great songs," said Massoni. "She's a genius. Beautiful. The police don't have the manpower to keep watch on important operators. You're not even below their radar. You're . . . further below their radar than a . . . You're like an insect to them. Know what I'm saying? Hey, this is Ligabue, listen to this one." He turned up the volume even higher.

"Commissioner Blume," said Pernazzo. "He said he'd be coming back. He found stuff at my place. I think he can connect me to the killing."

Massoni turned down the volume. "There's a commissioner who's visited you already? He knows about Clemente?"

"He knows something. His card is in my wallet."

"Give it to me."

Pernazzo gave Massoni Blume's card.

"What does this guy have on you? How did he get to you so quickly?"

"I don't know. But he's got nothing on me. Nothing unless I tell him."

"If you bring my name into it, or Alleva's, you're dead, you get that?"

"I get that."

They had reached Pernazzo's house. Massoni turned off the engine, then said, "Turn off the radio, Pernazzo."

Pernazzo turned it off. When he turned around, Massoni was pointing a black pistol straight at his forehead.

"There is one way to make sure you don't talk."

"There is another way," said Pernazzo, his voice rising to a squeak.

"This is the best way I can think of," said Massoni.

"Not if I've written a full confession, naming you."

"You're bluffing."

"No. I thought this might happen."

"We'll tear your place apart before the police get there. We'll find it first," said Massoni.

"It's a blog on the Web. So far it's an inactive blog without public access. They'll take a while, but if I get killed, sooner or later the police will check my Internet activity and find it. That's something you can't do, no matter how many people you intimidate."

Pernazzo closed his eyes tight and counted to three. Nothing happened. He kept counting. When he had reached seventeen, Massoni said, "So what's your idea?"

Pernazzo opened his eyes again. "It's not really an idea. It's a trust thing. We're warriors, right? We need to team up. Drive back to the pizzeria, and I'll show you how."

"If I drive you back there, what'll you do?"

"Trust me. You'll see."

"What about this policeman and the confession you've put on the Internet?"

"Then we deal with that. It's all part of the compact we have to make."

Massoni shrugged. "I don't know what you're talking about." But he turned the car around.

10:45 P.M.

A quarter of an hour later, they were back at the scene of the accident.

"OK. Double-park sideways, on the road, but not in a way that blocks the traffic."

"There's a free space there," said Massoni.

"No, double-park: it's better."

Massoni, finally, did as he was told.

"Now," said Pernazzo. "Wait here. I'll be back in a second." He hopped out of the car, scuttled across the road, disappeared into the pizzeria. Two minutes later, he was back. He rapped on the driver's side, and Massoni rolled down the window.

"OK. Let's stay here five minutes."

"What are you doing?"

"You'll see."

Massoni rolled up the window, turned up the music on the radio, and left Pernazzo outside, standing next to the car.

Pernazzo allowed slightly more than five minute to pass, then signaled to Massoni to get out. "Come on."

Massoni followed Pernazzo across the road, onto the sidewalk. Pernazzo stopped, moved in against the wall. Massoni stopped, too, and stood in the middle of the sidewalk.

"You're kind of noticeable," hissed Pernazzo. "Stand to the side."

"Noticeable for what?"

A group of seven people left the pizzeria and walked right past them chatting. Not one even glanced at them.

"You're right," said Pernazzo, easing himself away from the wall. "We just look like we're waiting for a table. Ah!"

A woman and a man were walking out, arms linked. Massoni recognized the man as the one they had had a bit of fun with earlier. A child was trying to swing on the woman's free arm. The silky-haired girl was behind. The four turned left, in their direction, and Pernazzo walked out in front of them.

Enrico Brocca and his wife unlinked arms. She was already moving backward, putting her hands over the child's face, leaving her husband standing there alone.

Pernazzo raised his arm and fired his new Glock point-blank into the bald man's heart.

As the man fell backward, Pernazzo fired into the middle of the egg-shaped face. The bullet came out the back of his skull like an exploding aerosol, so that when his head hit the concrete it was almost with a splash. Pernazzo went over to the inert form on the sidewalk and fired into the lower abdomen, releasing a faint smell of beer.

Then, instead of retreating in the direction they had come from, Pernazzo continued in the same direction, passing by the wife, who was shielding her silent children's eyes.

"That's how you do it," said Pernazzo over his shoulder. "Now you and me, we got a bond of trust we can't break."

Massoni stuck his hands in his pockets, put his head down, and walked quickly away from the scene.

Pernazzo had no time to savor it. People were arriving. Someone made a swallowing noise nearby, and he turned to see the woman, still huddled with her children, resolutely not looking at him.

He thought of the policeman, then spat on the barrel of his Glock and rubbed it to make sure it wasn't too hot to go back into his waistband. He wove his way through hissing traffic on the slippery tarmac, scampered down a narrow alleyway, eyes agleam, and was soon lost to sight.

42

DRESSED IN A new T-shirt with cutaway sleeves, low-slung jeans, and sunglasses, Pernazzo sat at the dining table, unpicking his mother's crocheted doily. He wondered if Commissioner Blume would return as threatened. Thanks to his hypersleeping, the police would never catch him napping.

At eight in the morning, he went into the bathroom and cut the sides of his hair very short, then took a razor to what remained. He looked at himself in profile, which is probably the angle the photographers would have when they took shots of him.

From eight until midday, he played online. At eleven he had boiled two hot dogs and an egg in a pan and, as he ate them with ketchup, began to wonder if he wasn't being unduly pessimistic. Police raids took place in the morning. The commissioner had maybe been bluffing.

At midday, he left the apartment, caught a bus down to a place in Porta Portese, and inquired about getting a tattoo on his upper arm. It would cost a hundred and twenty euros. Shortly after he came home, he went for a scheduled nap of twenty minutes, but woke up after only ten.

He spent an hour writing the confession he had bluffed to Massoni about, and posted it, limiting reader access to himself.

At two o'clock in the afternoon, he held Blume's card in his hand and thought about calling him up and saying, *Well, dickhead, are you coming to pick me up or not?* Or, *Hey, cop . . . I thought you said you were . . .* Or maybe he could be ironic—formal. *Am I speaking to the commissioner who paid an invasive visit . . . ?*

At three o'clock, he reevaluated the evidence against himself and decided that, as long as they didn't take DNA samples, it didn't amount to much. He had no idea what his rights were regarding the surrender of fingerprints. Nor could he work out how the cop got to him so quickly.

Maybe he needed a lawyer. He could phone the notary who had handled the transfer of the property deeds from his mother to him. Maybe the notary knew a lawyer.

At four o'clock, he was listening to Radio DeeJay and heard about an incident in which a policeman had been killed and two others injured. They gave the name of the dead policeman, but not the injured ones.

On the six o'clock bulletin, they gave the names of the suspects as Alleva and Massoni. They warned that both men were armed and dangerous and asked the public to keep a lookout. There was no further mention of Clemente, already yesterday's news. Later, on RAI 1 television news at eight, the two cases were linked. The fugitive cop-killers were wanted for questioning in connection with the murder of an animal rights activist. A magistrate standing on a flight of steps refused to comment on any of the cases. Pernazzo boiled himself another two hot dogs, opened a can of tuna, and drank some long-life milk. It looked as if he was not a suspect, after all. Part of him felt some disappointment.

He put aside his anxiety and enjoyed a good night's gaming, faction versus faction. He outfought and outplayed everyone, and a few players remarked on his phenomenal stamina and gameplay. The only bad moment came when one of his so-called companions disagreed with him about the value of an Arcanum of Focus.

"You pull down way too much hate, you die overmuch, and your mana pool is the smallest," Pernazzo warned him.

"Dont knock js cuz u so stoopid u dont get it."

Pernazzo stayed calm, gave the kid some sound advice. "Smooth it out with stat gear and balance your pve. You need hp REAL bad as a +dmg lock whos thrown out most of their stm gear that +200 is total worth it. Evrybdy know +dmg tunnelvision instead than stats is unkorrect if u R planning high-end attx."

But the crackhead wouldn't listen. Pernazzo almost logged out in his frustration. The policeman did not come that day.

43

JUST BEFORE NINE o'clock on Monday morning, Pernazzo was sitting on the toilet playing white-water rafting on his cell phone when he received a text message from an unknown number.

Change SIM call bk now.

Pernazzo was so excited he forgot to flush.

He went straight out to his local Vodafone center, and bought himself a new SIM card. He produced ID, showed it to the teenager in the red jacket behind the counter, then filled in the forms using an invented name and address. The youth didn't even glance at what he had written, just gave him the SIM. Pernazzo put it in his phone and called the mystery number back.

It was Massoni. Pernazzo felt a thrill that went from the back of his throat to his balls. A wanted man calling him. A RL cop-killer. But no sooner had the thrill run through him than it began to fade, and the disappointment that had been sitting at the base of his stomach rose up and flooded his mind. He was disappointed at the sheer inevitability of it. Who else was it going to be?

Massoni began their conversation by unraveling a long string of obscenities. Eventually, Pernazzo began to pick out other words but he could not make sense of them. Massoni was talking about standing in the sun, dying of thirst, and being eaten to death by insects.

Finally, he made sense. "I need you here now, as quick as possible. But you need to make sure you're not being followed. Go to where we held the last dog show. Go past the prefabricated huts and across a field to where there are dog cages. You can't see them till the last moment. If anyone is following you, they'll have to come across that field and you'll see them. There is a white Renault Kangoo there, with the keys lodged under the back left wheel. You can get there by taxi, then take the Renault, come out here."

"Why should I do this for you?"

Massoni paused, then said, in the calmest tone he had used yet, "There's a lot of money in it. Alleva is doing bank transfers. I need someone who knows about computers. Besides, he sent me to get you."

"Get me?"

"Take you to Innocenzi, have you explain yourself."

"Who's Innocenzi?"

Massoni couldn't fucking believe this and said so. Not only had Pernazzo killed the man Innocenzi's daughter was sleeping with and sent shit flying in all directions, he didn't even know he'd done it.

When Pernazzo finally understood, he felt powered up. "So why didn't you do as Alleva said and take me to this Innocenzi person?"

"Drive into Rome with every cop and Carabinieri looking out for me? I would never have made it as far as your house. It was a setup. Alleva must think I am really stupid. What he needs is to buy time so he can get away, and he was going to buy that time with me."

"You mean he'll have told the police you were coming in?"

"Sure."

"Wow. That's so sneaky."

Massoni told Pernazzo how to reach the dog cages. It took him some time to explain it to his and Pernazzo's satisfaction.

Pernazzo went home, picked up his portable, two USB keys, and his Glock. He dropped them all into Clemente's backpack, then called a taxi from his cell as he came down the stairs onto the street, and the taxi picked him up just a few minutes later.

Pernazzo told the driver to head down the Via della Magliana. The taxi driver, unlike the ones Pernazzo had seen in movies, was not happy just to drive: he wanted to know the exact destination.

"I'll know it when I see it," said Pernazzo, which was the truth. The taxi driver muttered something about time-wasters, but drove. When, on the city outskirts, Pernazzo told the driver to stop where there were no buildings, signposts, or intersections, the driver continued on for two hundred yards, until Pernazzo had had to raise his voice: "Stop right here!"

Yeah, in the middle of nowhere, he told the disbelieving taxi driver. Yeah, he knew what he was doing. Yeah, yeah. He thought of pulling out his Glock and shooting the driver in the face. Instead, he didn't tip, and the driver burned rubber as he took off, cursing.

Pernazzo now stood in an open field, phone in hand. Massoni was on the line.

"There's hornets everywhere here," said Massoni. "Big black and yellow bastards. And I'm thirsty."

Pernazzo reached over and stripped a handful of bay leaves off a bush and crushed them. It was nearly lunchtime, and their fragrance reminded him he was hungry. He was sweating as he crossed the field. He could see a white vehicle in the distance. "You said the van was white?"

"Yes. You there yet?" asked Massoni.

"No. Not yet. So Alleva is trying to betray you," said Pernazzo. "Told you he would. How far are you from the house?"

"About half a mile."

"He can't see you, can he?"

"No, he thinks I'm on my way into Rome to you."

Pernazzo tried to picture the scene. "Alleva's in the house now, with no transport?"

"I've got the only car," confirmed Massoni.

"It said on the news you made a getaway on motorbike."

"We changed for a car. Dumped the bike."

"He's got a phone, though?" asked Pernazzo.

"He's got lots of phones. This is one of them."

"You had better stop any vehicles. Taxis. That's how he'll get away."

"I worked that out for myself, thanks," said Massoni.

"Just out of interest, Massoni, why did you shoot that cop?"

"I don't want to talk like this on the phone."

"We've both changed our numbers."

"Even so. The cop didn't look like a cop. He could have been someone Innocenzi sent."

"What? You thought he was one of Innocenzi's soldiers or something?"

"I didn't think too hard. He looked like he wanted to stand in my way, so I removed him. Are you at the dog cages yet?"

"Almost," said Pernazzo. "Why would Innocenzi do something like that?"

In front of Pernazzo lay a bright field, flat and manicured enough for a professional soccer match. It looked to him like England or Ireland or one of those perfect places with horses and church spires. At the far end of the field, Italian squalor reasserted itself in the form of crumbling out-houses made mostly out of corrugated sheets of aluminum that could be seen through a thin curtain of tall reeds and sedges. It was becoming hard to walk and talk in the heat without gasping. Pernazzo stopped on the edge of the perfect field.

"I am out near Civitavecchia," Massoni informed him. "Take the high-way all the way to the end, call when you come off it," said Massoni. "Al-leva has passports, money, accounts. A thing for printing or something. I saw the stuff. He pretends the two of us are going to get away to Ar-gentina together, but there's no photo of me in any of those passports."

"So you've parked out of sight from the house?"

"Yeah, and I'm dying of the heat here."

Pernazzo said, "So get in the car and turn on the air-conditioning."

"Can't. Can't see the lane properly from inside the car, and I need to be able to hear any cars coming."

Pernazzo hung up and entered the field. Halfway across, he suddenly felt he had entered an invisible gas chamber filled with the powerful and repelling stench of the dogs. He paused to get used to it, bent down a little to reset his senses.

He reached the end of the field, which sloped down into a ditch con-taining a small canal that was supposed to carry the brackish water away to the sea. But the canal had been dammed by the plastic and rubble thrown into it, and sat stagnant, feeding the vegetation that screened off the outhouses and the cages containing the dogs.

The smell of the dogs had been growing stronger, but he had been accustoming himself to it. He scampered down the embankment, hopped over the ooze of water, and ran up the other side to peer out from behind a clump of sedge grass.

In front of him, fifty yards away, sat a row of about thirty iron cages, deep brown with rust. Every other cage contained a dog, or at least no two dogs were placed in adjacent cages. The long row was protected from the sun by an asbestos roof supported at either end by concrete walls and intermittently propped up by metal pylons. It looked like the gable end of an old factory or warehouse.

Pernazzo could not see from the shade of the sedges into the shade of the cages, but the dogs seemed mostly to be prostrate. To his left, the orange car-cass of a stripped-down bus was subsiding into the earth. Someone had boarded up two of the windows with plywood, and the next one was curtained off with a dark tartan blanket that swayed gently. It looked as if a tramp had made it his home. Outhouses constructed of wood, plastic sheets, and corrugated iron were collapsing into each other on the right.

Glancing on both sides of him, he emerged from the hedge and started making his way across the abandoned lot toward the dogs in the cages. A rolling growl indicated that his approach was being watched.

The guttural sounds from the cages began to rise in pitch and spread among the dogs. One of them was on the verge of barking. He felt his Glock, still attached to his belt, still in danger of slipping. When all this was over, he would get himself a nice holster.

Suddenly a Tosa Inu rose majestically in its cage and, overcoming the exhaustion of hunger and heat, roared its disapproval of the furtive figure approaching. It was the command the other dogs had been waiting for. At once, they all began to bark and snarl, though an American bulldog decided to howl and yelp instead. Pernazzo froze. He could smell the breath of the dogs, and they smelled his fear, which he was now converting rapidly into aggression. It felt like the very earth was shaking. He could feel it vibrate, up to his thigh.

Shocked by the sudden uproar from the dogs, it took him a few seconds to realize the vibrating and singing was coming from his phone. He yanked it out. The sun was too bright to read the screen. He pressed a finger into his ear to drown out the dogs.

Massoni was shouting. "You in the van yet? I've turned back a taxi. I'm standing dying in a field in the sun. If you don't do it, I'll just go back, kill Alleva myself. I'll kill him twice."

"Wait, Massoni. We can do better. You'll see. Stop the taxis. Taxis are good. Much better than accomplices. Pay them if you want. They like being paid when there's a no-show. Don't make them go to the police or anything. Pretend you're the one who called. Car broke down but is OK now. If you kill him now, you won't get his money or anything else he has on the computer. If I was him, I'd have hotels, plane tickets, houses abroad—everything lined up and ready, saved in virtual space."

"Hurry. I'm going insane here. Insects." Massoni hung up.

Pernazzo found a good strong stick, held it in his left hand, and walked by each cage banging on it and roaring at the animals. He got the best reaction from a Doberman pinscher.

He held the pistol in his right hand just in case a lock was faulty. The animals had worked themselves into a fury, except for a black-and-white mongrel, with a lot of German shepherd genes that just stood there, baring its thin and sharpened teeth. He tried to goad it by poking the stick between the bars. It didn't react.

"Are you the underdog I was supposed to bet on?" Pernazzo asked the beast. He walked back toward the cages. Some of the dogs were already getting used to his presence and had stopped barking in the hope of food.

Tucked into what looked like a field latrine several yards from the cages were three refrigerators powered by an external generator exuding diesel. A new aluminum covering and generous use of masking tape protected the wiring and the generator from the elements.

He opened the first one and stared in fascination at the heaving pink mass of horsemeat packed into plastic bags squeezed into every corner. The sweet smell of the meat, fat, and blood was so strong that he thought for a moment the refrigerator must have broken down, but then he realized that if it had, he'd have known the difference. The second refrigerator contained more of the same, though the meat in this was whiter, less pungent, and wrapped in paper. The third contained strings of meat on bones and three bottles of Peroni beer with twist-off caps.

Lying next to the refrigerator was a long white pole with a twisted bit of cable coming out of one end and a hoop at the other. He pulled on the cable and watched the hoop at the other end tighten.

Pernazzo drank a beer, which tasted a bit oily. He tossed the bottles at an abandoned trailer, aiming at the windows and missing. He thought he saw something moving beneath. A rat, probably. A large one, from the shadow it cast.

He grabbed a handful of meat, and went directly to the mongrel's cage and threw it at the bars. About a third went in; the rest wrapped itself on the bars and fell outside. The dog took what had arrived, and ate it calmly. Other dogs growled and some barked, but there was a lot more whining this time. He risked putting his hand near the cage and picking up the dropped bits, which he inserted between the bars. The dog soon ate those. Pernazzo tossed him more and more meat, which the animal ate with equanimity.

Then he fetched the long pole with the wire noose and held it in front of him, unsure what to do. A small pulley system allowed the front bars of the cage to slide up, like a portcullis. Pernazzo reckoned the mongrel was small enough, and risked opening the trapdoor a third of the way. The animal meekly poked its head out, and Pernazzo slipped the steel cord over its neck, then pulled the lever on the pole. He dragged the animal sideways across the gravel, keeping a good distance with the pole, and then opened the trapdoor of a cage containing the Tosa Inu. His courage and skill now increased, he performed the same operation with the Doberman, feeding it, holding it down with the control pole, and maneuvering it into the same cage, so that all three dogs were enclosed in a space so tight that it reminded him of a cartoon. The underdog whimpered and tried to squeeze its way out between the bars. The other two tried to stand up, but they did not have sufficient space. They crouched, legs bent outwards, and bared their teeth at each other. He waited five minutes, hoping to see the two larger dogs go for each other or turn on the underdog, but the animals seemed determined only to growl. Pernazzo resolved to come back after three days to see what the result was.

A zinc sluice-trough ran lengthways through all the cages. It entered through a narrow aperture on one side of the cage and out the other side to the next, and so on down to the end. The trough sloped slightly so that the water flowed down as far as the last cage. It was done so that the dog nearest the faucet got first go at the water. The water flowed just fast enough for some water to reach all the way down to the last animal. Pernazzo turned the faucet off.

He made several trips back and forth to the refrigerator, gathering the gobbets and hunks of meat, which he placed outside the dogs' cages, just out of their reach.

44

PERNAZZO WAS DRIVING past the turn-off to Santa Severa when his phone started playing the Black-Eyed Peas.

"Where are you?" demanded Massoni.

"On the way. Past Santa Severa. Fifteen minutes tops."

"I've turned back three taxis. The same guy came twice, can you believe it? Says Alleva raised a real stink on the phone."

Pernazzo turned on RAI Radio 2. Francesco de Gregori and Fiorella Mannoia were singing "L'Uccisione di Babbo Natale." He listened all the way through, but didn't get it. Two DJs came on and cracked a series of jokes at each other and howled with laughter. He phoned Massoni. "Right. I'm near Civitavecchia, now what?"

"Wait till the divided highway runs out—have you got any water with you?"

"No. The road runs out. I can picture that. I know where you're talking about."

Massoni said, "I've just been thinking about Ferrarelle, waterfalls, icy streams, melt water, Sprite."

"Directions, Massoni."

"Clock exactly five-point-three miles, turn off to the right. Go thirty yards. You see a green gate to an abandoned house on your left, you're on the right road. If not, go back to the main road, take the next turn to the right . . . Dust . . . Another fucking taxi!"

Pernazzo hung up. He was less than ten minutes away. He found the road as Massoni had instructed, and didn't need to look for the gate, because as he turned into it, a taxi pulled out. He drove four miles over a red dirt track.

Suddenly a large powdered figure emerged as if from nowhere and stood in the road in front of him. Pernazzo stopped and Massoni rapped on the driver's window with hairy knuckles.

"You sure you've no water? Some Sprite maybe? A beer would be good," said Massoni when Pernazzo rolled down the window.

"No. Let's move. You'll get water when we get back to the house. How far?"

"What?"

"Are you listening, Massoni?"

"Sure. It's the heat. Can you say whatever it was again?"

"OK, but listen. We drive back toward the house, slowly so that he doesn't hear the vehicles approach. How close can we get before they become visible from the house?"

Massoni slapped himself to get rid of insects. His mouth was open and his tongue protruded slightly.

Pernazzo said, "Picture yourself in the house. You are inside looking out. How far before we become visible?"

"About thirty yards. If he's inside looking out, but if he's outside the front door he'll see us from a distance."

Pernazzo said, "He probably won't be outside in this heat. Unless he's getting nervous, which he probably is. Anyhow, let's just get on with it."

He outlined his plan again.

Massoni got into the SUV, turned it with some difficulty, then drove slowly back toward the house. A minute later, he pulled onto the shoulder and Pernazzo did likewise.

Massoni got out and, ducking slightly, made his way into the fields to his left, and circled around the back of the house. A small olive grove afforded him protection at the back, but it still took him a full ten minutes to arrive at the front of the house. He went down on his hands and knees to get past the front window, and then stood up right next to the front door. Then he waved to Pernazzo, who gave three short blasts of his car horn, then got out to watch.

In the distance, Pernazzo saw Massoni stiffen as the door to the house opened. He saw Massoni step out in front of the figure that had emerged and deliver a massive blow with the flat of his hand sending him sprawling on all fours to the hard-baked earth. Then Massoni delivered a series of accurate head kicks to the prostrate figure. He climbed into the van and drove toward them.

Massoni hauled his boss into the house, pulled a chair out from under the small table in front of the kitchenette, pushed him down into it, then jerked him up by the hair, told him to sit straight, put his hands on the table where he could see them. Alleva did as he was told, placing his palms down flat on the yellow plastic tablecloth like a drunk preparing to leave for the bathroom.

Even the few seconds during which the door was open had been enough to allow in a group of flies that went straight to the middle of the small room and began circling. A bluebottle shot through the room and banged off a cupboard, and a massive carpenter bee hovered on the other side of the window glass, as if planning a break-in.

Massoni sat down on the chair opposite. Pernazzo appeared in the doorway.

"I bet you're Angelo Pernazzo," said Alleva, a slight slur in his voice. They were the first words he had uttered since he had been brought down outside the front door.

"Very unimpressive now that I'm here," said Pernazzo. "Maybe you should have kicked him a bit more," he said to Massoni.

Alleva's face was swollen on the left side. Pink blood dripped from the corner of his mouth, red blood from above his eye, and he was coated in dust that looked like paprika.

Pernazzo walked to the head of the short table and looked down at the two men seated opposite each other. "Am I the only one who finds the crackling of the grass insects hard to bear?" he said.

"It's the heat," replied Massoni. "I'm just going to get myself a glass of water." He made to stand up. He lifted up his enormous hand to reveal a small stainless-steel revolver with a barrel stretching hardly any further than its trigger guard. "He had this on him. He's not armed now."

Pernazzo held up a hand, "You sit where you are, Massoni. I'll get you your water."

He came around the table, passing behind Massoni, and stepped behind the counter that separated the living space from a kitchenette. He opened the refrigerator, looked in.

"Levissima," he said. "Melted glacier water. Tastes of nothing, but quenches the thirst just great." He took out a clear plastic bottle with a blue label. "Where do you keep your glasses? Oh, here they are. Nice little place, this. Well-equipped. Very small. What was it, an animal house or something once?" He took out two glass tumblers, which clinked together as he clasped them between thumb and finger. He carried the bottle and the glasses over to the table, going behind Alleva this time, and placed them on the table. Then, reaching behind into his pants, he pulled out the Glock, tilted it slightly at Alleva's temple. Alleva flinched, started to say something, but Pernazzo tapped him on the ear with the piece, and he fell silent.

Pernazzo said, "Pour me a glass, too, Massoni. It will taste all the better for the wait."

Massoni had wrenched the plastic cap off the bottle, and had almost been about to tilt the bottle straight into his mouth. Displaying unexpected breeding, he stopped himself in time and put water into the glass farthest from him first, and then into his own.

Massoni took the tumbler in his clumsy hand, brought it to his parched lips, and Pernazzo shot him in the face.

Massoni's head snapped back. The glass slipped onto his chest, rolled over his stomach, fell onto the floor without breaking. Pernazzo swept his hand across the table and scooped up the small pistol in his left hand.

"Jesus!" shouted Alleva, bringing his hand up to his ear.

"How do you think that happened?" said Pernazzo. "The glass not breaking?"

Massoni's left arm twitched.

Pernazzo said, "Looks as if he's still alive, what do you say?" He walked around the table and looked at the back of the skull. "Yuck. Looks pretty bad from here."

"Jesus," repeated Alleva, cupping both hands over his right ear. "You've burst my eardrum."

"Must have been a nerves thing. Like frog legs twitching when you put a current into them."

He walked around the table, stood slightly behind Alleva's left. "You can hear fine with this one, right?"

Alleva nodded.

Pernazzo said, "So how am I doing for a noob?" He tapped Alleva's good ear with the warm barrel.

Alleva hunched his shoulders, leaned forward. Pernazzo pressed harder, and using the pistol as a pivot, described a semicircle until he was next to Massoni's slumped body. He unzipped Massoni's top, then pulled back for a few seconds to double-check. Massoni seemed too warm to be dead, and there wasn't that much blood either. Carefully he slipped his hand in and pulled out a two-tone pistol with a silver slide and black frame.

"Nice. What sort is this?"

"I can't see," said Alleva.

Pernazzo released some of the pressure and Alleva unbowed his head.

"A Sig Sauer I think."

"And this little one you had?"

"A Davis P-32."

"I'm still learning," said Pernazzo, pocketing Alleva's pistol. It fit nice and neat. He pushed Massoni's Sig Sauer down the back of his pants. It was very uncomfortable. "Where were you planning to escape to?"

"Argentina."

"This evening?"

"What?"

Pernazzo raised his voice. "This evening?"

"Starting from this evening."

"Any more taxis on their way?"

Alleva hesitated a second, which was all Pernazzo needed. "I see. Phone up the taxi people, tell them you don't need them anymore."

"I have to stand up, get the phone out of my pocket."

"Just so long as you sit down again, and don't turn around."

Alleva stood up, took the phone out.

"Give me the phone." Alleva backhanded it to him. "Last number you called?"

Alleva gave a weary nod. Pernazzo pressed the green button twice, listened to see who answered, then stuck the phone at Alleva's good ear. The man on the other end did not seem happy.

Alleva finished with, "You can send out who you like, but no one will be here." Pernazzo hung up for him.

"I'm not sure I like that. They could still send someone," said Pernazzo.

"What was that? I can't hear."

Pernazzo brought his mouth closer to Alleva's left ear, "Better?" he whispered, and huffed some moisture into Alleva's earhole.

"I can hear you, if that's what you mean," replied Alleva.

"I said they might still send someone."

"You want to talk to them?" asked Alleva.

"No. I want you to talk to me, Renato. That's your Christian name, Renato, isn't it? Let me see . . . I suppose we can begin with where you keep your money, and how you're going to transfer it to me. Massoni thought he needed my computer expertise for this. I even brought my portable, just in case. But why Massoni there didn't just beat it out of you is beyond me."

"Massoni was incapable of turning on a computer. He thought you needed to be good at math to operate one."

"So he'd have gotten me to do the transfers, then killed both of us?"

"Probably not you," said Alleva. "He would have needed your help again. He'd have killed me, no problem."

A fly had settled on Massoni's blood-speckled forehead and was crawling downward.

"Tell me, this underdog thing . . . Were you in on it, or was it Massoni's idea?"

"Underdog? What's that?"

"You know what it is," said Pernazzo.

"What was the idea? That some unlikely dog would win in combat?"

"Yeah, that's the general idea," said Pernazzo.

"I didn't even know he was setting you up," said Alleva. "I didn't think he had the imagination, though this underdog sounds like a variation on an old con trick. Feed people false inside information; let their greed do the rest."

"He thought I would bet all my mother's inheritance."

"How much was that? A bet over ten thousand euros had to be approved by Innocenzi, who gets twenty percent. Massoni would have had to tell me about it then."

"It was eight thousand. That's what I told him. I was just stringing him along, really."

Alleva took his hand away from his ear and fingered it gently, feeling for damage. Pernazzo felt a tickling on his own hand and glanced down. A hard-shelled brown and white insect was sitting in the soft spot between thumb and index finger.

"How stupid did that dead man there think I was?" He pointed to a portable computer on the countertop separating the kitchenette from the table where Alleva now sat. "I'm taking it that Compaq notebook on the counter works."

"It works," said Alleva.

"You can't have broadband out here, though. Too far from the digital exchange."

"No, just a TIM GSM dongle. It's slow."

"No broadband, no neighbors, nothing at all out there except hidden Etruscan tombs," said Pernazzo. He moved over to the counter and opened the computer.

"Password?"

"Sirius69."

Pernazzo typed it in. "Aww . . . Now look at that. Nothing in the browser history, all your cache cleared. You are a careful man. This means I'm going to have to trust you to open all your online accounts. Now, how can I be sure you're going to do that?"

Alleva said, "They only let me transfer to another account that is in my name and that I have already activated. If I transfer into my account, it'll take a few days before I can transfer from there into yours."

"You think I would make you do all that work? All I need are the numbers, codes, any electronic keys they gave you. I'll do all that hard work of transferring the money."

He placed the notebook in front of Alleva. Then he gave him a pen and a piece of paper. "Start writing down your passwords, and show me that they work."

After half an hour, Alleva had opened three accounts. They were all he had going, he said.

"Your balances amount to less than three hundred thousand? That's not so good for a life of crime."

"There were overheads. And this is an emergency escape. I didn't have much planning time."

Pernazzo put his Glock to the back of Alleva's head and pressed hard, really hard, as if the gun was a knife that would eventually penetrate. He nodded in the direction of a closed door. Judging from what he had seen outside, this had to be the only other room in the place.

"What's in there?"

"Bedroom."

"And?"

307

"Floor safe."

"Let's go."

Alleva's knees wobbled slightly as he walked and Pernazzo eased the pressure slightly. Alleva pushed a camp cot aside, knelt down, opened a floor safe. He pulled out a wad of green hundred-euro notes, which set Pernazzo's heart racing. Three passports and—

"Hold it! Put that stapler thing down, slowly."

Alleva did so. Pernazzo picked up and held aloft a shining metal object with a lever. "Weighs a ton."

"It's an embosser. For the passports," said Alleva. He dug his hand into the safe again, Pernazzo stood directly behind, as if he was pissing down his back. Alleva took out five shiny metal circles contained in clear plastic discs. Pernazzo stooped, picked them up, and rattled them.

"And these?"

"Those are the dies. For the embosser. For the passports, after the photo, you emboss, country seal, official, relief . . ." Alleva, unable to get enough saliva into his syllables, stopped talking altogether.

"I saw credit cards on the kitchen counter in there. Are they clones or original copies?"

"Neither. They're legitimate."

"OK. Give me the name and the numbers of your main account in Argentina. Don't say you don't have one. Do you have something to write on?"

"I don't need to. Banco Galicia e de Janeiro," he said. "My account name and the codes are on the inside page of that book on mushrooms in the other room."

Pernazzo walked over to the one shelf in the room, pushed Alleva back into the sitting room and, keeping him under steady aim, pulled out a tall book with damp, powdery pages. He opened to the first page and looked at what he saw written there.

"If I check these numbers now, find they're no good . . ."

"They're good," said Alleva.

"It all ends here, as far as I can see," said Pernazzo looking through the numbers and nodding in approval, as if he could already see they would work. "I've just had one hell of a time these last few days. Maybe I'll leave the country, go to Argentina instead of you. I see my life as a vast prairie under a rolling sky. I feel good. So what's it to be?"

"What's what to be?"

"The manner of your death, Renato. How do you want to die?" Pernazzo reached behind and pulled out Massoni's Sig Sauer.

"I don't want to die," said Alleva, his voice low.

Pernazzo transferred the Sig Sauer to his right hand, the Glock to his left, then pushed it into his waistband.

"I'm sure I won't want to either when my time comes," said Pernazzo. "But I'm giving you a choice. A head shot like I gave Massoni, or . . . I don't know . . . a shot through the heart? But if you want, we could fight to the death, just you and me. Single combat."

Alleva began to say something.

"But you have so much more experience than me. Just to make it even fair, I'd have to incapacitate you further. A bullet into each kneecap, ankles, elbows, too. And that would just make it fair. But then I'd have to do more to make sure I win."

"What sort of a choice is that?"

"I'm giving you a chance to fight and be aware of life and its light in the final moments. I think I'd like that myself."

"Want to swap places?"

"Sorry, that's against the rules," grinned Pernazzo.

"You said you'd make sure I couldn't win," Alleva's voice became clearer as it rose in anger.

Pernazzo said, "That's right. I'll give you a chance to fight, not a fighting chance."

"That's no choice at all," said Alleva.

"Of course it is. You can't win against death anyhow. I'm giving you the choice. In some ways you're luckier than most."

"I don't feel very lucky."

"I can appreciate that. But time to decide."

"I don't want to decide."

"What have you decided?"

"I haven't," said Alleva. "Don't do it. Please."

"I am going to do it, you know that. You're not allowed special favors."

"Wait," said Alleva, his eyes fixed on the black hole of the barrel. "I haven't decided."

"Trust me on this."

Pernazzo took the Sig Sauer in both hands, working his thumbs up and down both sides of the grip trying to find and disengage the safety.

"No! I do. I would prefer to fight. I've made my choice."

"It has just occurred to me that a fight would complicate the crime scene I am about to build. I should have thought of that before. My bad."

He gave up looking for the safety, and started to pull the trigger, hoping it would turn out to be a two-stage pull like his own Glock. But the trigger seemed specially made for Massoni's heavy fingers, and he had to squeeze really hard so that when the round exploded with a harsh crack, the whole weapon bounced upwards toward the ceiling. He cursed and yanked the weapon down from the air, ready to fire properly, but Alleva had gone. Pernazzo looked in surprise at the empty space, then realized that he had just heard Alleva make a sound like an owl and a gentle thud as he fell backwards from his chair.

Alleva lay on the floor, arms thrown back, which was not what Pernazzo wanted. He had envisaged Alleva and Massoni lolling dead in their chairs on either side of the same table. But this would do.

Working slowly and methodically, he wiped down the Glock on his T-shirt and fitted it into Alleva's hands. He took hold of Alleva's floppy right arm, then, like an instructor with a pupil, held his hand and squeezed off another shot in Massoni's direction. Good. Then he gave Massoni back his Sig Sauer, aimed at where Alleva had been sitting and began to pull Massoni's fat dead finger on the trigger. This time, however, the movement was smooth and fast, and the weapon fired immediately, making him jump. He preferred his Glock, and was sorry to leave it in Alleva's hand.

Pernazzo then removed every book, magazine, and piece of paper in the house, and placed them in the van; the cash, the passports, embosser, mushroom book, and Alleva's laptop went into the backpack. He flicked through one or two books before picking them up, but found nothing. He went into the bedroom, closed the floor safe, twirled the dial, wiped it with a bedsheet.

And now Pernazzo needed a nap. There was one armchair in the room, upholstered in synthetic orange with black ridging. He set his digital watch, leaned back into the slightly damp material, and slept.

When his beeping watch woke him up twenty minutes later, he went to drink the plastic bottle of water he had given Massoni, but it had turned warm. He stepped into the kitchenette and turned on the faucet and drank. Then he left, double-checking he had pulled the front door closed.

45

WHAT SEEMED TO be bothering Paoloni most were the flies. "The flies, maggots, the heat, the smell. You have no idea." Paoloni paused, then hammered out the syllables as if to a simpleton to get his point across. "You. Have. No. Fucking. Idea."

Alleva was dead, Massoni was dead, and Blume could hear exhilaration in Paoloni's tone. Revenge and reprieve all at once.

"Have you called the forensic team?"

"Sure."

"How long have the bodies been there?" asked Blume.

"I don't know. I'm not a medical examiner, thank Christ. With this heat. Maybe four, five days."

"Wait, I'm putting you on hands-free." Paoloni had no right to feel exonerated, but Blume still felt it fair to warn him: "Prosecutor Principe is here with me."

Blume set his telephone on the desk and pressed the loudspeaker. ". . . appreciate it," Paoloni was saying.

"This is Prosecuting Magistrate Filippo Principe. Have you made a positive identification?"

"Yes, Giudice," said Paoloni. "Alleva and Massoni. Not so as you'd recognize them, but they had their wallets."

"What killed them?"

"It looks like gunshots. Both have gunshot wounds to the head. I didn't notice wounds anywhere else on the body." Paoloni paused. "They may have shot each other. That's what it's supposed to look like. Each has a pistol in his hand."

"But you don't think they shot each other?"

"No, I don't. The forensic pathologists will say for sure."

"What's wrong with the scene?" asked Principe.

"Two people killing each other at exactly same time with head shots? Two simultaneous lethal shots? They pulled their triggers at exactly the same moment? I don't think so."

Principe nodded at Blume, who nodded back as if to say, yes, Paoloni was a good investigator.

"What else?" asked Principe.

"One cadaver—Alleva—has this cute little baby belt holster, but the gun in his hand, a Glock, is too big for it. The place is cleaned out. There's nothing here, like someone else lifted it all. Also, one of the casings was in the wrong place in the room. I saw two near the table, which is fine, but Zambotto found one near the wall. It could have bounced or something, but it's a strange place for it to end up. The number of shots fired seems wrong, too. You'd need to be here to see. By the way, there's a bedroom with a closed floor safe. Maybe there's something there. But we had to get out so as not to contaminate the scene."

Blume asked him what sort of place he was in, whether there were neighbors.

"The last house we passed on the way was about three miles away, though maybe there's another house on the other side. But the place is isolated. You can't see it from the road. Also, a car is sitting in the driveway. A big Beamer. Model X5. Nice car. We haven't looked inside, thought we'd leave that to the technicians."

"Good," said Blume. "Any signs of other cars, other traffic having been there?"

"You mean tracks on the ground and stuff? The forensics are arriving, along with patrol cars. Looks like it's about to get very busy. Carabinieri, too, from the looks of it."

Principe said, "Inspector Paoloni, if the killer wanted it to look like a suicide or reciprocal killing, let's make sure we are seen to be thinking along those lines. Make sure no one mentions the possibility of a third person."

"Vicequestore Gallone might," said Paoloni.

"You'll have to stop him," said Principe. "I'll talk to him myself later."

"OK." Paoloni hesitated, as if waiting to hear from Blume. Then he hung up.

Principe looked at Blume and said, "Well?"

"The first thing to say is it does not make sense for Innocenzi to kill them and then tip me off."

"Agreed."

"And if he sent someone to make it look like a suicide pact or a simultaneous murder, he'd have sent someone who knows how to do it right," said Blume.

"Agreed."

"And if the setup is amateurish, well, you know where I'm going with this."

"You can go there, but I'm not sure I'll follow," said Principe. "You want me to believe Pernazzo is responsible for this, too?"

"Yes," said Blume. "We know Pernazzo killed Brocca and Clemente. Right?"

"Know is a strong word," said Principe, "but let's assume it."

"So we know Pernazzo can kill. Clemente campaigned against Alleva and Massoni, and Pernazzo attended their dog fights. Then we have a sighting of Massoni and Pernazzo together when Brocca got killed."

"We do?"

"We will," said Blume. "Once I talk to Giulia again. And if we start looking more closely, I'm sure we'll find more connections."

"But you are not accusing Pernazzo of killing Ferrucci?"

"No."

"It doesn't make sense. Why would Alleva and Massoni reveal their hideout to someone like Pernazzo?"

"Maybe he did computer work for them. We'll find out. Pernazzo has no record. That's all it takes. No record. If everyone was DNA-fingerprinted at birth it would be a different story."

Principe looked doubtful. "DNA fingerprinting? That's a bit—you know. Infringes personal freedom."

"No such thing," said Blume, moving briskly toward the door. "Let's go catch ourselves a killer."

Blume turned around to see Principe still leaning against the desk. "You won't help?"

"Remember Article 55 of the *Code of Criminal Procedure,* Alec? As a policeman, you can act preventatively. I don't have the same scope, especially in this case. At the risk of sounding like a lawyer, I'd prefer not to know exactly in advance what you're going to do. Do you trust your own judgment?"

"Not always."

Principe clicked his tongue like a teacher who had received a wrong answer. "I mean in this case, do you really trust your own judgment?"

"Yes. Angelo Pernazzo is our man. I am sure of it. It's time I brought him in. It's way past time."

Principe straightened up, walked over to Blume, gave him a friendly half slap on the cheek. "Then trust your own judgment on this."

He opened the door and, before Blume could reply, was gone.

46

BLUME RETURNED TO headquarters. After some haggling, he finally managed to get a squad car and two policemen called back in to take him to the crumbling house on Via di Bravetta.

The two policemen who arrived in the squad car couldn't have made up his age between them. One of them couldn't take his eyes off Blume's plastered arm, as if he had never seen anything so strange or exotic in his life, which was possible.

They exchanged glances with each other as Blume clambered into the backseat of the car. Superior officers never did that. The backseat was for junior officers and criminals. But Blume had had enough of front seats for now, and his arm hurt.

The stores had closed for the night and the traffic on the streets was beginning to flow again as they left. It took only twenty minutes to reach their destination.

Leaving the driver in the car, Blume and the other young policeman, whose name he never even asked, got themselves buzzed into the shabby apartment block by an old woman to whom they simply declared "police" when she asked who they were. No wonder criminals had such an easy time.

The elevator mechanism smelled of old oil and grease, and the cage took an age in coming. They stepped into the narrow space, and ascended to the third floor in silence, trying not to breathe all over each other, before stepping out into a short hallway with three doors. Angelo Pernazzo's with its plaque dedicated to a virtual killer was the middle one. Blume walked up to it, raised his fist to thump at the door, then lowered it.

"Hold it," he said.

The young policeman, who had not been on the point of doing anything at all, looked confused.

An image of Ferrucci sitting at his desk, tapping away at the computer, eyes moving back and forth as he eagerly awaited a command or simply some attention came into his mind. A sense of fatigue overwhelmed Blume, and he felt his confidence drain from him as he realized what he had been about to do. He was right about Pernazzo, a person who had killed at least four people. And here he was on the point of confronting a killer, with a single, unprepared rookie cop as backup.

He was going to have to call in help. Trusting himself did not mean doing it himself. On the contrary: it meant being confident enough to risk what remained of his reputation by ordering a full-blown raid. If Pernazzo turned out to be the wrong person, he might as well apply right now for a job guarding a bank.

"Ring the door on that side," he ordered, indicating the apartment to the right of Pernazzo's. "Show your badge, speak quietly. Ask if they think Pernazzo is in. I'll do the same here."

Blume pressed the button, and heard a sharp buzz from immediately behind the door, but no one answered. On the other side, meanwhile, the young cop was speaking quietly to an old man wearing wide shorts, a yellow shirt, and thin white socks pulled up to his knees. The old man had opened the door fully: another easy victim.

Blume knocked and waited. Still no one. He tried the buzzer again. Nothing. The young cop finished his talk with the old man. Blume motioned him over, made a quick downward bye-bye motion with his hand to warn him to speak quietly.

"Says he doesn't know," said the young cop. "Says the son keeps to himself, was never one to have friends. He used to know the mother, but she died a year ago. Nobody in that one?"

Blume slapped the neighbor's door with the palm of his hand, "Doesn't look like it."

"Are we going to try this middle door?"

Blume looked at the unwrinkled and uncomplicated face of the young man in front of him and thought of Ferrucci.

"No. I've changed my mind. We're going to call in backup, and we're going to get a warrant to get in there."

The kid looked annoyed, like he had been told he was too young for a fairground ride. "But we haven't even tried."

"Nor will we. Let's get back to the car, radio from there," said Blume.

But he could not help himself from trying to peer in through the security peephole. The killer could very easily be right there. He might have heard them ringing next door and be looking out, looking directly into Blume's eye. Blume considered telling the young cop to point his Beretta directly against the peephole, see if that produced a panicked scuttling from behind the door.

Blume sidestepped out of the radius of vision of the middle door and positioned himself in front of the old man's door. Then he hunkered down and tested whether he was able to keep his balance with his arm in a sling. He could, but only just. On bended knees he made his way back, below the scope level of the peephole, or so he hoped, and pressed his ear to the door. The elevator behind him clunked and whirred, and moved down. From behind the door, he thought he heard a scuffling sound. He could also hear a Mulino Bianco commercial playing on a TV, advising people to eat healthily. It could have been from another apartment, but he doubted it. The apartment next door was empty, and he did not remember TV noise getting any louder when the old man had opened the door.

Then he heard it. A sniff. That's all it was. The sound of someone sniffing from the other side of the door. Still crouching, he took five painful sideways steps out of the range of vision, but the effort was too much and he slowly keeled over onto the floor, on top of his sprained arm, his knees locked in pain. He bit his lip to stop himself from shouting out. Eventually, he struggled back into an upright position. The young policeman, unable to work out a coping strategy for insane superiors, was staring down the stairwell.

Blume was physically exhausted from his exertions. His ribs felt as if they had pierced his lungs, his arm throbbed. Even his teeth were paining him. He pressed the button for the elevator.

The elevator took a long time, and seemed even slower going down than it had been on the way up. But as they made their slow descent, Blume's pain was subsiding and his confidence rising.

They got out into the courtyard. Blume caught a glimpse of a figure walking fast out the gate, head bowed. There was something slightly strange in the gait. The world was full of people fearful of the police.

Blume stopped and told the young cop, "I'm staying here outside the main door to make sure our man doesn't leave the building. You go back to your partner, call in backup, then wait for them to arrive. Just say you're acting under my orders, and anyone wants to know, they can talk to me. I'll see about the warrants." He felt confident.

47

ANGELO PERNAZZO SLOWED to a walk as soon as he came out the apartment building, not so stupid as to draw attention to himself. He managed only a few steps before he had to bend down and adjust his cotton-and-rope espadrilles, which were threatening to trip him up. He had almost lost them completely in his rush down the stairs to beat the two idiot policemen in the elevator. He pulled up his foot, crooked his thumb, and snapped the fabric back up over his heels. He hefted Clemente's gray backpack onto his shoulder, and turned sharply as he heard the front door to his apartment block snap shut again. He saw a cop in the car across the street looking straight at him, but not really seeing him.

He heard footsteps behind. They were after him. He chanced a backward glance. A uniformed policeman was following him. Walking, not running. Now the cop cut diagonally across the street to his partner in the car, ignoring Pernazzo. No sign of the commissioner who had tried to look the wrong way through the peephole.

Pernazzo had prepared the backpack after seeing Di Tivoli's documentary on Wednesday night. In went the cash, his knife, the embosser, the passports, Alleva's little gun, and Clemente's wallet, which still had his ID papers and credit cards. Alleva's mushroom book, bank codes. A perfect compact escape kit. What was in there was enough to take him away from Italy to anywhere he wanted. On Thursday he visited a photo booth, took twenty-four pictures of himself for the passports, and added them to the kit. He spent the afternoon looking at Google Earth images of Argentina, then called Tecnocasa and announced he wanted to put his apartment on the market. They said they would send someone around the next day.

No wonder Commissioner Blume had not returned. He had to be busy collecting evidence against Innocenzi. But even as the credits were rolling on the documentary, Pernazzo began to feel frustrated at the continuing failure of recognition. He needed to talk to Di Tivoli about this. Give Di Tivoli the full story, then make good his escape, maybe.

Or he could kill Di Tivoli. That would be interesting, because then everyone would be convinced it was Innocenzi revenging himself for the exposé about his daughter.

He'd play it by ear.

Pernazzo did a phone directory search for Taddeo Di Tivoli from the Virgilio Web site, and there he was. Journalists like being contacted.

On Friday night, for the first time ever, Pernazzo got bored with his online gaming. All of a sudden, it did not seem real. He logged out of World of Warcraft, played a bit of EverQuest, with the same result. Later on, he found he could not sleep when he wanted, and when he did, it was for far more than the twenty minutes that Uberman allowed.

When, that Saturday, he heard the noises on the landing outside his apartment and seen the police through the peephole, he almost brought up his dinner from shock. Time to run.

He stayed still, staring out, unable to move in case Blume noticed a flicker in the light. Then the cops, who could just as easily have been killers sent by Innocenzi, took the elevator down. Pernazzo seized his one last chance, grabbed the backpack, and ran headlong down the stairs, only realizing he was wearing cotton-and-cord slippers when he slipped on the first landing. As he picked himself up, the slowly descending elevator drew level with him. He hoisted the bag onto his shoulders and took the stairs four at a time, gaining on, overtaking, and leaving the old elevator, Blume, and the policeman behind.

Pernazzo's Opel Tigra was parked two streets away. He hoped the traffic would not be against him. He drove as fast as he could, releasing some of the tension. He considered going carefully, stopping when lights were yellow, touching the brake pedal every few seconds like his mother used to do—she even signaled to go around double-parked cars—but there was no point. No policeman in Rome ever pulled anyone over for reckless driving. They considered it demeaning.

It took him thirty-five minutes to reach Di Tivoli's house. He found a parking place less than five minutes away and walked as quickly as his slippers allowed.

It was now past ten and quite dark. He had fifteen minutes before he needed to hypersleep. He took Alleva's Davis P-32 out of the backpack, slipped it into the back pocket of his pants.

The front door to Di Tivoli's apartment block was closed. He pressed the intercom button below Di Tivoli's. A woman answered.

"Who is it?"

"Signora, I have some materials here from RAI to deliver to Dottor Di Tivoli, but it seems that either he is out or the buzzer is not working. The thing is, I have to get other deliveries of urgent news tapes done and so I'd like to just drop them off outside his—"

The woman got bored with listening and buzzed open the door without a word.

Pernazzo called the elevator. With just three floors in the building, the stairs would have been quicker, but he preferred not to walk by the door of the woman on the second floor in case she was watching. The marble in the building gleamed under the lights. The elevator was old, wooden, large enough to take a bed. It was suffused with yellow light from a series of low-watt bulbs and smelled of beeswax.

Pernazzo stepped out, closed the brass gates, and beat softly with his fist on Di Tivoli's thick door.

"Di Tivoli! C'mon, open up. Open. Hurry up," he said in an urgent whisper. He kept hammering the door, softly but incessantly. Eventually he heard footsteps.

"Who is it?" said Di Tivoli, but opened the door before waiting for a response. As soon as it was open a crack, Pernazzo dropped his bag into the gap. The metal embosser made a louder thud than he had expected. He would have to be careful about the noise, given the presence of the woman in the apartment below. Then, with the bag acting as a stop, he squeezed himself in with such speed that Di Tivoli had to turn around before he realized who had just entered.

"What?" said Di Tivoli. "Who are you?"

Pernazzo saw a look of disgust and contempt on Di Tivoli's face, but then he caught the gratifying whiff of fear.

"Are you alone?" Pernazzo asked.

"Yes . . . That is to say, no. I'm expecting someone . . ."

Di Tivoli could not think whom he was expecting. Pernazzo moved over to a bookcase, leaned against it, and waited as Di Tivoli's eyes looked him over. The pistol sat squat and safe inside his pocket. No need to brandish it about.

Speaking from the hallway, Di Tivoli said, "I want you out. I don't know what you think you're doing. I just got back . . . I am very tired."

Pernazzo lifted his bag, moved into the living room, and said, "The police are looking for me."

Di Tivoli followed. He was wearing a silk dressing gown with a gold paisley pattern. "Well it's hardly my doing . . . Have I seen you before?" He dipped his hand into a square pocket, trying to be master of the situation, lord of his own house.

"There's only one reason I can think the police are after me," continued Pernazzo. He moved his hand behind his back, and enjoyed the spectacle of Di Tivoli trying to monitor every micro-movement while retaining a casual demeanor.

"And that is?"

Pernazzo said, "You put them onto me."

"I don't know what you're talking about, or who you are."

"I know. You see, I'm Angelo Pernazzo. I am the person who killed Clemente."

Di Tivoli paled, then sat down slowly in an armchair. Even more slowly, he picked up a remote control.

"What are you doing?"

"Turning up the air-conditioning," said Di Tivoli. "You killed Clemente?"

Pernazzo watched him carefully as he pointed it at an air-conditioning unit with a winking green light above the window.

"It's fine. Leave it," said Pernazzo. He did not like the idea of Di Tivoli holding anything in his hand.

Di Tivoli dropped the remote into armchair cushions behind him, made a steeple out of his fingers, and arched his eyebrows. His forehead was wet. He said, "You don't have to tell me any more than you want to, but how do you figure I put the police on you? I don't even know who you are."

"I worked it out. The police found my name because I was detained when the Carabinieri raided a dog fight, and the only reason they raided the dog fight was because TV cameras were running. Yours."

"The raid was Clemente's idea," said Di Tivoli. "I'd have just filmed the fight, no police or Carabinieri."

"And, like I said, I've dealt with Clemente."

"Arturo was . . . He was all sorts of things, but he was also my friend," said Di Tivoli.

"You did a hell of a job on his reputation with your exposé about his affair. For a friend."

"He's dead now. It makes no difference."

"His widow probably didn't like it."

"No, she didn't, and she told me. Also, I risked my life with that program. I exposed a connection with the most powerful criminal family in Rome."

"That was brave."

"I am a journalist," declared Di Tivoli. He brought his hands together as if considering a proposition. "It is my job to tell the truth, to speak truth to power."

Di Tivoli's voice had become louder and clearer. Pernazzo reckoned the man was gaining in confidence, so he snapped the pistol out from behind his back and pointed it straight at Di Tivoli's stomach.

Di Tivoli's steepled fingers interlocked, and he brought his hands down toward his groin. "Can you not point the gun at me, please?"

Pernazzo lowered the pistol. He wasn't going to use it, anyway. He tucked the gun back into his pants.

Di Tivoli assumed a slightly less slumped position on the armchair and said, "You should leave now, Angelo. That's your name, isn't it? Make a break for it. The police still think Alleva had Clemente killed. They won't be looking for you."

"I just told you they were."

"Probably not for the murder—you don't mind me using that word?"

"It's the right word. And if they're not looking for me, how come that commissioner was at my house this evening? He called in a whole raiding party."

Di Tivoli asked, "What commissioner?"

"His name is Blume," said Pernazzo. "He took a real dislike to me the moment we met."

"Blume?" Di Tivoli's voice lifted slightly. "He's not on the Clemente case now."

"You know a lot about what's going on."

"I have my sources." Di Tivoli made his first attempt at a smile, but it did not come off.

"Well your sources are wrong. Because the commissioner came to my house just now."

"I'm telling you, Blume is not working your case. The police don't know anything about you."

"Sure, they do. And now so do you."

"I don't get it," said Di Tivoli. "They found Alleva and Massoni. The dog-fight organizer and—"

"I know who they are."

"Sorry," said Di Tivoli. "I hear they've been found dead. So maybe the case will be closed now."

"That's what you think?"

"Gangland slaying. Those guys, they sure don't mess around, do they?" said Di Tivoli, his voice taking on some of the syncopated rhythm of a hard Roman accent. "Maybe Alleva was skimming the bosses, and they whacked him. What do you think?"

Pernazzo tapped himself on the shoulder and smiled. "I did that to them. It was me. It's something . . . I don't know. I've gained strength, learned from my mistakes, but I don't have my own style yet. And I don't know where to go from here."

Di Tivoli opened his mouth as if to say something, but only managed to suck in a stream of air that caught at the back of his throat.

Pernazzo pictured him dead in the armchair. What would it look like? A few days after an exposé of Innocenzi, TV show host found dead in home, from . . . He'd work out the details in a moment. Unnatural causes. They would have to look into Innocenzi, forget about him. Maybe all the killings could be pinned on Innocenzi.

Pernazzo turned around to look at the bookcase behind him. "You know, since I came in here, that thing has been staring at the back of my head. What is it?"

"It's an Etruscan head," said Di Tivoli.

Pernazzo reached up, took it in his hands, and holding it, walked over to him. "This is wood? It feels like steel. It's so heavy. This head is bigger than mine." He held it aloft, and Di Tivoli began to move forward in his seat. He lowered it, then made as if to throw it at Di Tivoli, who flinched and flung his arm up protectively.

Pernazzo laughed.

"So is this like one of those household gods? A protector?"

He walked behind the armchair on which Di Tivoli sat. "Do you believe in that sort of thing?"

"Not really . . . Look . . ." Di Tivoli began to turn his head.

"No, stay looking forward. So, has this mean-looking bastard protected you?"

"Yes. Until now," said Di Tivoli.

"Right. Until now."

Pernazzo held the bust aloft in both arms like a trophy. He put so much downward swing into the blow that his feet slipped from under him and he toppled halfway over the back of the chair. The impact as the scowling wooden face hit the back of Di Tivoli's skull jerked the bust out of his hands. It bounced against the back of the armchair cushion, tumbled down the arms, dropped onto the Persian carpet on the floor, and rolled a little farther with a dull rumble.

That and the crack of impact were almost all the noise.

Di Tivoli had made hardly a sound. Just a sort of farting noise came out of his mouth.

Pernazzo picked himself up. The back of Di Tivoli's head was visibly caved in. Di Tivoli was bent forward as if examining his navel, and a steady bright stream of blood was rolling off the side of his face, dripping onto the armchair cushions and darkening there.

It had been far easier than he had imagined. And far quieter than a pistol. Pernazzo went over to the matching beige sofa opposite the armchair, lay down, and slept.

When he awoke twenty minutes later, the Etruscan head was watching him from the floor. The nose was chipped, and Pernazzo wondered if he had done that. Di Tivoli was in precisely the same position as before.

Di Tivoli's car keys were easy to find, but he could not find the man's wallet anywhere. When he found himself opening kitchen cupboards at random, he stopped. He went back to the bedroom, which he had already searched, checked the bedside table again, slid his hand under the mattress, slid open the mirror-fronted wardrobe, and looked for clothes that might have been recently worn. Still no wallet. Di Tivoli had a small room dedicated entirely to shoes, but the man had feet like canal barges. Pernazzo tried on a few pairs, but he simply stepped in and out of them. He continued to hunt, hurling the shoes out of the alcove into the bedroom. He came across a few pairs of women's shoes. They fit him, but had high heels.

Then he had an idea, and went over to Di Tivoli's bent body. He inserted his hand into the dressing gown pocket, and found the wallet. Not only that, but it was stuffed with cash. Pernazzo counted 950 euros, including a 500-euro note. He had never seen one before. He put the wallet into his own pocket and went into Di Tivoli's study. It had the same color scheme as the living room: beige, white, gray. Pernazzo appreciated the style. It was like an expensive hotel for executives. Three widescreen monitors sat next to each other on a buffed steel desk with a matte black finish. Pernazzo wondered for a moment if Di Tivoli had been a hardcore gamer, then remembered he worked in television. He did not bother switching on the machine. It would be password-protected, and he did not have time to hack.

In the hallway, Pernazzo found keys to the apartment and another bunch on a ring. They included two short padlock keys and two long, old-fashioned rusting keys that might be used for a garden door. If Di Tivoli had a place outside Rome, he could go there, lie low for a day, while the investigators concentrated on questioning Innocenzi.

He went back into the living room. Another impressive bank of technology. He switched on the massive TV and channel-surfed for a bit, familiarizing himself with the large remote control.

"You got Sky satellite," he told the slouched figure in the armchair. "Doesn't that count as helping the competition? But, hey, there's nothing good on RAI anymore."

Good surround-sound effects, too. Speakers all over the room. Not so obvious, either. Great plasma TV. Pity he couldn't just take it all home with him. He checked the cables at the back and saw the screen was hooked up to a small-format computer.

The computer seemed to be on. Pressing AV on the remote control gave him a screen with Windows XP Media Center. He had never seen the Windows logo so large. Nice. Even if it was Mickeyware. A Red Hat OS was what was needed here. There was the recorded TV menu. He could not find the remote control for this, and hunted around. He found a Daikin remote control for the air-conditioning.

Wait a minute. He went over to the armchair and pushed Di Tivoli's inert body sideways. Di Tivoli's head lolled over the side of the armchair, and the blood worked its way around so that it now seemed to be dripping from his ear onto the floor. Pernazzo felt for the remote control Di Tivoli had shoved behind the cushions, and pulled it out. He looked at it.

"You sneaky fucker," he said. He pressed a button and looked at the on-screen menu.

Di Tivoli had been recording. The microphone was right in front of him. So obvious that it was invisible.

Pernazzo stopped the recording, saved it as a file, which he named "deleteme." He rejected the suggested ".wav" ending and added an .xls suffix instead. Then he deleted the misnamed audio file and emptied the trash. It would not stop anyone who knew what they were looking for, but it would hide the file for long enough. In two days, he would be in Argentina.

He ran through the menus and a file name caught his attention: 08_28_Blume.wav. He opened the file.

From behind him, Di Tivoli said: "This heat is killing me."

Pernazzo spun around and ran backwards at the same time, almost crashing into the TV. Di Tivoli still lay slumped on the armchair, blood now dripping onto the floor.

"Nice place you've got here," said a voice he recognized. Commissioner Blume. "You know, we're practically neighbors. I live on Via La Spezia. Know it? On the corner of Via Orvieto, the one with the fish market?"

The clever bastard had recorded the cops as they interviewed him. There was another person, a Neapolitan. Presumably another cop.

Pernazzo sat on the sofa and listened through the entire interview. Then he went back to the start. Blume was saying, "You know, we're practically neighbors . . ."

48

P ERNAZZO DID NOT leave the apartment until half past three in the morning.

He put his things into the backpack, including the unused pistol. He closed the door softly behind him and, to minimize the noise he made, slipped silently down the stairs without calling the elevator. His car was parked nearby, and he considered whether he should move it. The police would be looking for it by now. He decided against it. A legally parked car was almost invisible. The police would probably not find it for months.

He had the key to Di Tivoli's car, a Range Rover, and was looking forward to driving it. A second key with the FAAC trade name embossed on it was attached to the ring. A steep ramp to the left of the building led down to the basement and garages, and was closed off by an automatic gate. Pernazzo inserted the key and turned. He stood nervously in the shadows as two orange lights started flashing, but the gates swung open noiselessly. He made his way down the ramp and into the garage. He pressed the electronic key, and Di Tivoli's Range Rover whooped and blinked.

Pernazzo clambered aboard and drove up the ramp, turning the lights on to full bright to break through the blackness. He felt tall and heavy and important in the car. It had a TomTom SatNav device, and he turned it on. The screen mapped out a route to Padua. He pressed a button and another route leading out of Rome to Amatrice appeared. The address was the same as he had found on the scrap of paper in Clemente's wallet. Stop one, Amatrice. Stop two, Bari. Stop three, Patras. Or maybe he'd go north, exit Italy by way of Slovenia or Austria.

He found the large car difficult to handle. Concentrating on driving the vehicle, he got confused in the streets that lay in the shadow of the

Tangenziale, the raised highway that led to the city beltway. He stopped by the side of the road, and got the TomTom to show him where he was.

The navigator directed him to an access ramp that was blocked off with red and yellow road barriers. A sign that looked like it had been hanging there since the early eighties told him the closure was temporary. The TomTom seemed to know nothing about it.

Pernazzo had to turn around several times. There were few cars on the roads at this hour, so it was not a problem. But he could not find an alternative way onto the Tangenziale. He decided to drive until the TomTom finally came up with another idea. The dashboard clock said quarter to five. He was going to have to postpone his next twenty-minute sleep.

He pulled onto Via La Spezia and realized the TomTom had let him come too far. There was still almost no traffic, but to his left he saw lights. He could smell saltwater and fish from the market. He felt hungry. He could murder a cappuccino and a cornetto with apricot jam. The rules of polyphasic sleeping prohibited coffee, but Pernazzo was beginning to find Uberman's sleep schedule tiresome. He would give it up once he reached Argentina. No, he would quit it the moment he got off Italian soil.

He pulled into a parallel street and found a parking place large enough for the oversized vehicle he was commanding. He hesitated a moment, then decided to leave the backpack with its weapons and money under the driver's seat. He took some cash from Di Tivoli's wallet and put it into his own.

The bar was an all-nighter for bus, tram, and train drivers. It was over-lit, and the counter was uncomfortably high, but the cappuccino was as good, perhaps better, than he had imagined it. The cornetto, too.

It was time for another twenty-minute sleep, but Pernazzo was too buzzed with caffeine, sugar, and a new sense of purpose. It was surely no chance he found himself on this street.

He climbed back into the Range Rover. In one of the buildings opposite him, the police commissioner was fast asleep. He did not know which one, but there were only two gates opposite the fish market, as the commissioner himself had said.

Pernazzo knew he had to get to sleep now, or he would be unable to operate later. The coffee had been a terrible mistake. Something subconscious had been going on there. He'd think about it later. He reprogrammed the Amatrice route into the TomTom. Finally, it came up with another route.

Pernazzo relaxed; the failure of the SatNav had been stressing him out. Now he felt able to lean back into the beige leather seat and drift.

He overslept by a full hour and awoke with a spasm from a dream about Etruscan warrior tombs. Dribble had whitened the corner of his lip, and his mouth was dry as a thistle. Outside it had gotten bright, and Via La Spezia had filled with traffic. There was no air in the car. Pernazzo cracked open the window and checked his watch. It was six thirty, Sunday morning. He decided to wait until half past eight. He had had a bad sleep, and felt like he had been smacked around the head, but one essential question had been resolved. At some point during the night, he had decided to wait for the mocking policeman to come out of his house.

49

Blume felt he had never slept so well. When he awoke in the morning, his mind was clear, his body perfectly relaxed, his sore arm no longer so sore. Kristin was a quiet and still sleeper. He touched the hollow of her back with his hand. Her muscles tautened, her spine arched slightly inward, and her legs straightened She was also a watchful sleeper.

He had decided to call Kristin the evening before as soon as he realized his operation was going to fail. If he could not catch Pernazzo, he would make something work out right that evening.

The failure owed much to "upstream issues," as Gallone might have put it. The way this worked was that the upstream people pissed into the water, and the downstream people like Blume had to drink it. The upstream people decreed that no technical team and not even one detective were available. Blume stood in front of Pernazzo's house and cursed.

A prosecutor, sights set on political glory by the time he was in his forties, had issued an order to clear out a housing project of all its Senegalese inhabitants. Dozens of police were spending the evening as temporary prison guards. The best Blume could get was a very reluctant promise from the Arvalia station to keep Angelo Pernazzo's apartment under guard. Even for that, the Arvalia commissioner wanted a direct order from a magistrate within the hour or, he told Blume, he would pull his men out.

When the agente scelto came up carrying a battering ram in a canvas bag, Blume ordered him to break down the door. This took longer than expected. Eventually, the woodwork splintered, the elderly neighbor with spindly legs opened his door again, squinted out, and asked if they needed any help. The cop with the battering ram yelled at the old man to step the fuck back into his apartment right now, and he did.

Then they were in, but the suspect was not. Blume realized he had just entered very dubious legal territory. He took a cursory look around the stinking apartment, ignoring the looks of the other policemen that he felt radiating up and down his back like three electric heaters.

He put a guard on the door and went downstairs, and it was then he decided to call Kristin. As for the rest of them, including Principe, he would drag them all here personally in the morning. Stick their faces in the evidence. All of a sudden, every injury sustained in the accident was making itself felt.

He phoned Kristin without quite knowing what he was going to say. When she answered, he asked would she mind giving him a ride home. He gave her the address. She said, "Sure," and hung up.

Feeling energized again, Blume took the stairs to the third floor, told the agente scelto from Arvalia not to let anyone in for any reason. He went downstairs again, stood in front of the house, and tried to interpret the tone in which Kristin had said "sure."

As he stood there, it occurred to him that he should have posted someone at the front door before going up to the apartment. It was part of basic training, but Blume could no longer even recall the clarity of first principles and the strict rules he thought were observed everywhere when he first joined the force. At the back of his mind, but oozing forward as an undeniable truth, was the idea that he was not skilled at the tactical side of things.

Kristin picked him up half an hour later in a ruby Alfa Romeo 159 with a radiator grille that looked like it was grinning at him. She winked the lights and he climbed in, correctly guessing she would not ask what he had been doing or why he had called her.

Her driving style made no concession to the fact he had recently been in an accident. She accelerated through a yellow light onto Via Silvestri, squeezed around a bus that had decided to merge no matter what, and said, "I'm going back to the States."

Blume stopped struggling with his seatbelt. "When?"

"In a couple of weeks."

"When you say couple . . ."

"I mean two."

"Because most people don't mean two when they say a couple," said Blume, "unless they're referring to people."

"I know, but I do." Kristin managed a right-angle turn without touching the brake.

Blume surprised himself with his next statement. "I could come with you. Get my broken back teeth fixed. Americans are good at dentistry. Teeth are important there."

She turned and smiled. "You could."

"I've got a lot of saved vacation time. Sick leave, too, if I choose. I just need to finish this case."

"How's that going?"

Blume finally clicked his seatbelt into place. "Almost there. All we have to do is catch the person responsible."

"That's all?"

"That's all. But I think everyone is more interested in closing the case as it is. I don't think they want to believe in my killer."

"Your killer. That's an unlucky way of putting it." Kristin accelerated as a light turned yellow, then thought better of it and braked hard. "So what d'you think of the wife? It's almost like not catching her husband's killer is a favor."

"It's complicated. Well, the thing itself isn't all that complicated. The people are. People are complicated."

"Corrupt, you mean."

"That, too," he agreed. "Where in the States?"

"New York, then Washington, and then Vermont."

"I used to be from Seattle," said Blume.

"Used to be. You don't feel American?"

"Sometimes I do."

"Can you understand me if I say I am happy to be American?" Kristin emphasized her happiness by blasting the horn at two youths who were jaywalking their way across the road.

Blume said, "Happy? I thought we were supposed to be proud to be American. Happiness is something we pursue. Like criminals."

"The sort of people who go around saying they're proud to be American are embarrassing for those of us who have reason to be."

" 'An idea is not responsible for the people who believe in it,' " quoted Blume.

"Very good. That's Don Marquis. America used to have a lot more people like him in it."

"I didn't know who had said it," admitted Blume.

"Now you do."

"Not really. I still don't know who Don Marquis was."

"He was a Midwesterner."

"Oh. Don as in . . . Don. Not a priest then."

Twenty minutes later, Kristin parked. She got out with him, accompanied him across the courtyard. When they arrived at the front door of Blume's building, she remarked, "You look like Jacques-Louis David's Napoleon with your arm like that. Your nose helps, too. Maybe you want to have it seen to?"

When they reached the apartment, Blume hurried into his parents' study and leafed through their LPs. He put a scratched copy of *Wavelength* on the old Ferguson turntable, Van Morrison sang "Hungry for Your Love," and she appeared in the frame of the door.

Kristin smiled. "You're supposed to seduce, then abandon, not the other way around."

She walked in, sat down beside him on the old velvet couch his mother used to like. *Words alone are certain good*, he thought, then couldn't think of any. He and Kristin sat in the study studying one another. Her glances seemed tinged with hostility, but her knees were inches from his. Blume wanted to bury his neck and his breast and his arms in her bright hair.

"I don't like this shrine," said Kristin.

"What shrine?"

"This place. Your parents' undisturbed study. I don't like it."

"Oh."

Kristin crossed her legs, brushing the side of his leg. She was wearing a simple black cotton skirt, and Blume felt his groin, stomach, and chest twinge and pulse as he glimpsed the inside of her thigh. He could see the underside of her calf tauten and relax as she circled her foot.

"You have a big, lost, lonely, angry face."

She said it gently, without contempt.

"No. I'm OK. I've been here a long time. I'm not lost anymore." Blume switched to Italian, bringing out his Roman accent to the full: "*Pure tu, però, non c'hai nemmanco l'ombra di un'accento se non vuoi.*"

She touched the side of his face with the back of her hand. "I thought you'd prefer it if my Italian sounded a bit more beginner's level, bring out your protective side. But, yes, I'm pretty good. I do a lot of interpreting for Italians who think they can speak English. It's amazing how many of them believe that."

"You interpret into Italian, too? You can do that?"

Kristin replied in perfect Roman dialect: "*Er mestier mio è a fa' capi' fra loro du' persone che parleno lingue differenti; e così ripeto a tutt'e due quello che je farebbe comodo d' ave' detto.* I'm a diplomat."

"*Ammazza,*" said Blume. "You still look American, though." He lowered his gaze to her ankles and the faded geometry on his mother's thinning carpet, and said, "You said you were a legate. Do you carry an FBI badge around?"

"What do you think?"

"I bet you don't."

Kristin stood up, undid the bottom button of her green silk blouse, and put her hand into the waistband of her skirt, briefly exposing her navel. Then she pulled out what Blume at first took to be part of the inner lining of the skirt, but turned out to be a black silk bag.

"It's not some special-issue FBI thing," she said in response to his stare. "It's a perfectly ordinary Eagle Creek money belt."

"I wasn't looking at the belt."

She unzipped the bag, pulled out a plastic-covered ID badge, and tossed it to him. He could feel the warmth of her body on it. He cupped it in his hands, then examined the gold-and-blue emblem.

"Fidelity, Bravery, Integrity," he read out. "The FBI seal is the same as the European Union flag."

"Here." She held out her hand, and he put the card into it.

Her green blouse still hung loose, and the silk money bag sat on the sofa between them like a discarded undergarment. Blume felt suddenly parched.

"I'm going for a glass of water. Can I offer you something?" Blume moved over to the door.

"No, thanks."

When he returned to the study holding a glass, Kristin had stood up and was standing in the doorway. The slight breeze flowing from the kitchen window rippled her blouse.

"It's stuffy in there."

"My shrine, as you called it."

He set down the glass and kissed her. A fractional thought or phrase crossed his mind, something to do with lips sucking forth his soul, but flew completely out of his mind when he felt her mouth part under the pressure.

All thoughts drained out of him, to be replaced by a single, all-embracing sense of joyful disbelief. With his one functional arm, he fumbled at her blouse. The straps of her bra felt rough and tight against her skin. He pushed and she walked backwards into the room. He guided her feet over the creases and furrows of the Persian carpet without allowing her to fall until they reached the sofa. He labored at unbuttoning her blouse, then pulled down her bra until it was below her breasts, plumping them up. Kristin held up a warning finger, sat up and deftly released the fastener at the back while Blume gazed transfixed by a whirl of light freckles running down from her right shoulder. He started pulling at her skirt. It bunched and folded and rose, but he did not seem to be able to reach the end of it. Frustrated, he pulled his arm out of its sling and tried to get a better purchase on the sofa.

"Wait." She stood up and stepped out of her skirt as if it were three sizes too large. Then she held out her hand to him. "Not in here," she said. "Let's go into your room."

Blume checked the clock. It was already seven forty-five. He should have gotten going earlier. He got up, showered, and dressed, then went into the kitchen, wondering what he could offer her for breakfast.

He was standing at the open window of his kitchen, staring down at the street below, when Kristin touched him on the back.

"It's noisy in here," she said, raising her voice above the traffic noise. She folded her arms across her breasts.

"I know," roared Blume as an ambulance went whooping by.

"Why have you got all the windows open, then?"

"Because of some rotten kitchen that was in the chicken fridge."

"What?"

"Other way round. Rotten chicken in the kitchen fridge." He closed the window. "I opened the fridge to get some milk for my coffee. The smell is pretty foul. Also, there's no milk."

"Any other food in there?"

"Not so as you'd recognize it."

Kristin wrinkled her nose. "How about we go out for breakfast?"

"Good idea," said Blume. "You get dressed, I've got some calls to make."

Kristin left to shower and dress, and Blume phoned Principe, who answered, sounding like he was still in bed. Blume said he needed to get a team into Pernazzo's flat. Circumstances had changed, he said, even though they had not. Before Principe could raise any objections, Blume gave him the address and said he'd meet him there in ninety minutes. That way, Principe would have time to prepare the warrants or his excuses, and Blume would have time to have breakfast with Kristin.

Then, at twenty past eight, they left the house together.

50

PERNAZZO WAS ON the point of turning on the engine and driving away when his target, arm in a sling, appeared in front of the apartment building. Pernazzo took Alleva's Davis P-32 out of Clemente's backpack and climbed out, but held back to calculate line of sight, distance, and pace. The front door of the building opened again and a woman stepped out. She fell in beside the target and linked her arm through his good arm. The woman was an unforeseen element, but as she was blocking the commissioner's only means of defense, her presence was almost certainly an advantage.

He would simply walk up behind them and plug the two bullets into the back of his head, and plant the third one in his face if he came down backward—at the top of his spine if he went down forward. The woman would scream. Maybe two-two, one-one would be the best combination.

Clack-clack, then people would look round in mild surprise and hear a soft pop, then another. He'd see the stupid looks of puzzlement on the faces of the passersby, like when he did that idiot outside the pizzeria. There would be disapproving frowns at the two people suddenly lolling on the sidewalk, then a gradual reappraisal and alarm. Some would even smile, as if recognizing something.

Pernazzo stayed on the opposite side and allowed Blume and the woman to remain thirty paces ahead. Outside cell telephone stores and take-out pizza outlets, entire committees of early-rising Sunday time-wasters loitered on the sidewalk.

He glanced up and down the street and made a rapid count of the people he could see. Apart from the targets, he could see a pair of girls walking toward them and him, five people standing outside or ready to enter their apartment buildings, four or maybe five people behind him.

The bright marble statues of Jesus and John the Baptist poised on the top of the facade of San Giovanni were visible at the end of the street, their arms raised as if in gentle appeal to the traffic below to shut the fuck up just for once.

Pernazzo crossed over to the same side of the street as his two targets and picked up his pace. A small knot of bus and tram drivers in blue stood on the sidewalk, for no visible purpose, and he passed them by rapidly. A fat man with a small dog stared at Pernazzo as he hurried by. Pernazzo stared at the dog, which was crapping right in the middle of the sidewalk. Four people, now five as a man with a plastic case came out of an apartment building, turned, and walked out of the scope of his vision. Twenty paces away now. Four people were between him and them.

Pernazzo skipped slightly as he increased his pace, closing the gap to ten paces, then flapped out his shirt, and slipped in his hand beneath. He felt the grainy polymer grip, at body temperature. He was close enough now to hear them and noticed they were speaking English.

The commissioner with the broken arm was on the left. He had placed his good arm lightly against the small of the woman's back, as if ushering her into a room.

Trying to keep the movements fluid and leisurely, he extracted his firearm, cupped the grip with his left hand, and raised his arms, his finger already tightening around the trigger. It was a head shot from three paces. Blume would go down, the woman would half-turn around, and he would blow a hole through her temporal lobe.

The moment he felt the blow under his wrist, he knew it was the woman who had hit him. He knew it because it was the lightest of blows, no more than a tap, but she had somehow managed to push his shooting arm up. As he brought it down again, adjusting his aim to shoot her first, her arm flashed out again, and made contact, harder this time, again with his wrist. It hurt no more than the last one, but to his intense surprise and rage, he felt his fingers jerk open and release the pistol. He tried to catch it with his left hand before it hit the ground, but even as he bent down slightly, he heard the blank clink of the Parkerized metal hitting the sidewalk. In the split second he was standing there with his left arm dangling stupidly between his knees groping for the pistol, she hit him twice. Even now, she was not inflicting any pain. It was as if she had stroked his face with the back of her hand. Pulling himself up again to full height, he found that the lumbering cop had finally maneuvered himself around and was now staring at him, a look of amazement on his face. Then she stuck her fingers into his eyes and the commissioner's face was replaced with triangles of blinding pain. With a roar, he flung himself at her, ready to bite if need be, but came to a total standstill when she punched him in the throat, then pushed the flat of her hand into his nose.

His pistol was lying on the ground, and she would probably get to it first. It was a lost fight. He stepped back, just in time to avoid taking the full brunt of another white elbow in the throat. Her hair collected the light as she stepped forward after him and delivered a punch to the side of his head, which he managed to parry with his left hand with the result that his hand bitch-slapped the side of his own face.

A flash of red to his left warned him of another attack, and he realized she was preparing to use her leg this time, while the cop was now coming at him straight on, struggling to get his arm out of its sling.

Pernazzo saw his chance. Dropping his right shoulder, he wheeled his left leg around and smashed it into the cop's right ankle. The impact caused Pernazzo's cotton espadrille to fly off. As the cop staggered to re-gain his balance, waving his broken arm in a narrow useless circle, Pernazzo jerked upright out of his crouch and back-smashed his elbow into the side of the cop's face, sending him lunging sideways into the woman. Then he ran straight off the sidewalk and diagonally across the road, losing his second espadrille. A car whipped by him at high speed, inches from his feet and stomach. A horn blast sounded in his ears, and behind the horn, he heard a shushing noise and someone's tires failed to find purchase on the asphalt. As he reached the other side, a scooter horn squawked at him, and the driver seemed to swerve with the intention of running him down.

Kristin stayed Blume's sideways fall to the ground, but she allowed him to hit the concrete nonetheless. She jumped over him, landed, and hunkered down without losing sight of the pistol, which lay next to a piece of pink bubblegum. She snatched the pistol off the ground, tossed it to her other hand, and drew a bead on the small white head of the assailant before it ducked into the traffic.

Blume made an exclamation and she swiveled around, fearing he might be under attack from some other quarter, but realized he was referring in some way to her handling of the weapon. She snapped her head and shoulders back again to take aim, but she had lost vital seconds. She could not fire into the traffic. She held her aim, watching as the assailant ran almost headlong into a speeding car. Had she fired, the bullet could easily have hit the vehicle. Serve the asshole right for driving like that in a built-up area. The assailant was now on the other side of the street and running parallel to the old Roman wall. A missed shot would bury itself into ancient Roman history rather than straying into a passerby, she reflected. She moved the pistol fractionally upward. If the traffic let up, she would have a clear shot, and she would not miss. If the traffic let up. He had put thirty-five yards between them. She saw the breach in the walls to which he was headed. It was maybe seventy-five or eighty yards away and required a leading shot against a moving target. It was beyond the limit of a handgun of this type. Even so, she realigned. As she did so, a red and gray Number 85 bus heaved into sight and stopped on the far side of the road.

"Kristin!" Blume was standing beside her now. She lowered the weapon, and turned to him. A semicircle of shocked pedestrians had come to a halt several yards away, and was bunched up in a group, afraid to go near the English-speaking couple standing in the middle of the street brandishing a weapon.

Casually, in full view of everyone, Kristin wiped the gray metal against her blouse. It left a dark stain. She placed the weapon on the ground.

"His fingerprints," he protested.

"We know who that was," she replied.

Blume placed his foot on the pistol, and said, "*Polizia. Siamo della polizia.*"

"*Polizia!*" Kristin yelled out in a clear voice. "Goddamn it, what a nation of rubbernecks," she said to Blume.

Blume shouted out again, turning as he did so to trace an exclusionary arc around himself and Kristin as more people were drawn toward the commotion.

"Kristin, listen," he said. "You may want to walk away from this. Just walk away. Whatever you want. But decide now, because a patrol car is coming up behind you. Do you want to be a character in the story I am about to tell the patrolmen?"

"No. It would be easier if I wasn't."

"I agree. Will you meet me tonight?"

"OK."

"It's possible I won't make it. Depends how this pans out. I'll let you know. Also, can you avoid going home?"

"I need to change."

"Pernazzo might know where you live," said Blume.

"I don't see why. And too bad for him if he does."

As she turned to go, one of the patrolmen yelled out: "*Signorina! Non si muova!*" but he had no real authority in his voice. She heard Blume's voice ordering the two young policemen away, telling them not to enter the crime scene, to call for backup, to clear the crowd. The gawking file of people on the corner opened ranks to let her through. She was calm. She was smiling.

51

PRINCIPE LOOKED OVER his half-moon glasses at Blume. It occurred to Blume that the glasses were a sort of stage device. Like the piles of folders, barely held closed with ribbons, they formed a necessary but also a theatrical part of the public prosecutor's paraphernalia.

The two men were seated in Principe's office in government-issue armchairs, knees up, almost touching. It was already past lunchtime, and as far as Blume could see, nothing had been done to catch Pernazzo.

"Alec, I know what you're thinking," said Principe, frowning over the steel frames.

"You're psychic? Maybe you should book a hall, get out of the business of directing murder investigations, because . . ."

"That will do. You're thinking you should be out there hunting down the man who tried to kill you and your woman."

"What woman would that be?"

"We can come back later to the question of the two officers and several witnesses who saw an imaginary woman with you, but just because you're not out there yourself doesn't mean all investigative activity has ground to a halt. There is a warrant issued for Pernazzo . . . Also, there have been some developments."

"What developments?"

"Di Tivoli."

"What about him?"

"He was found this morning by one of his young friends. His head smashed in by a heavy object—Wait!" Principe slammed his hand down as Blume cursed. "I only found out about it shortly before you arrived in the back of a police car. A team is already there."

"I need to get there, too," said Blume.

"The call was not assigned to us and they have an investigating magistrate already on the scene. Anyhow, you already know who it was."

"I seem to be the only one."

"No. It was Pernazzo. At least that's what Di Tivoli said."

"Wait, I thought you said Di Tivoli had had his head . . ."

"Di Tivoli is not dead, though I hear he's in a very bad way. He keeps repeating the name Pernazzo, or did until he fell unconscious again. He might not make it."

"When was the attack?"

"Seems like it was last night," Principe replied. "It looks as if Pernazzo tried to kill Di Tivoli and then you. The magistrate on the case is a good guy, used to work as an assistant with me. He's got a team searching Di Tivoli's house."

"Check Di Tivoli's computer for recordings."

"What?"

"He records things. He's a journalist and a Craxi-era socialist. You don't get trickier than that."

"OK," said Principe. "If you say so."

Blume didn't like the tone. "I do say so."

"I'll pass on that information to the investigating magistrate in charge of the case."

"And I'll tell my colleagues," said Blume.

"And you'll tell your colleagues. But I will pass on the information, and the magistrate is reliable. He's already ordered a search of the neighborhood, and they found Pernazzo's car."

"Did they look inside it, too?"

"Yes. Nothing important yet. Let me finish, would you?" Principe waited for a signal from Blume. "So the next thing the magistrate did was to start looking for Di Tivoli's car and—this I just heard—it's missing from the underground garage where he parks it."

"So Pernazzo is driving Di Tivoli's car. Now we have the make and license plate. Maybe we'll get lucky, though it didn't do much good when Pernazzo was driving around the city in his own car."

"We might," said Principe. "Di Tivoli has a Telepass device on his vehicle. RAI pays all travel expenses, you see. Including highway tolls."

"Good to know that my license fee contributes to his free travel through toll gates," said Blume.

"Maybe you'll see it as money well spent in a minute," said Principe. "Every time the vehicle goes on or comes off a highway, it is electronically logged. That means once Pernazzo takes a road out of the city, we'll know, and we'll also know which one," said Principe. "The ICT unit in Tuscolana is monitoring the numbers now."

"Immediately? The vehicle passes a toll point, they see the ID flash up on their screens and call you?"

"No. It takes almost an hour to process the numbers. It's not us that's slow, it's the mainframe to which the electronic toll gates are connected. But I've also alerted the highway police."

"I didn't know you could get a vehicle ID from a Telepass device," said Blume.

"You can't," said Principe. "But the device has to be associated with a credit card or bank account number. In this case it's a bank account number held by RAI. We checked with RAI, and they were able to associate the device ID to Di Tivoli's expense account."

"We?"

"Me, then. It was my idea."

"That was good. But suppose he doesn't take a highway?"

"Then it won't work," said Principe. "But he has to take a highway sooner or later. It would make it easier if we knew where he was headed. Have you any idea?"

Blume shrugged. "He should be trying to get out of the country. If I were him, I'd be driving toward the sea."

"We checked to see if he has any other properties he might try to use as a safe house. Nothing in his name, or his mother's name. No brothers or sisters. Some cousins in Australia. We've been looking through his apartment, but the guy's best friends seem to be computer avatars, gambling sites, Helen Duval . . ."

"Who?"

"A porn diva. I was certain you'd have heard of her. Also, we've already checked Alleva's place in Rome, and Massoni's, just in case he thought he could hide out there."

"You've connected Pernazzo to that crime scene already?"

"No," said Principe.

"But you think it was him?"

Principe hesitated. "Half an hour ago I got a phone call from Innocenzi."

Blume stayed silent. There was something inevitable about hearing the name again.

"What did he tell you?"

Principe ran the palm of his hand up his face, finally pushing off his glasses, and said, "He didn't tell me anything. He asked questions. Asked if the police know the probable whereabouts of the man who had killed Clemente."

"The concerned citizen," said Blume. "Do you think someone has tipped him off?"

"That we're looking for Pernazzo? Maybe. Where Pernazzo is, no. We don't know that ourselves yet," said Principe.

"No, we don't," said Blume, an idea beginning to form in his mind. "So everyone is coming around to my idea that Pernazzo is the person we want?"

"Sometimes you act as if Alec Blume is the only man in town who knows where the bad guys are," said Principe. "I can maybe find a good legal argument for coming in the window after being thrown out the front door on the Clemente case, but the finest argument won't do me or anyone any good if the whole thing collapses into a heap of recriminations."

"But you think it will collapse? With all this evidence?"

Principe sighed. "It's messy. But if we don't step on anyone's toes, then we'll get Pernazzo for Brocca's murder at the pizzeria. We don't need Pernazzo for the Clemente case."

"Yes, we do," began Blume, but Principe held up a calming hand.

"I said we don't need Pernazzo for the Clemente case, not that we don't need the Clemente case for Pernazzo."

"You've lost me."

"The Clemente case is still off-limits for us. In the end they'll have to convict Pernazzo, but that's up to them. Maybe they'll have to recognize his responsibility for the killing of Alleva and Massoni, but we get him for the killing at the pizzeria, and now for trying to kill you. Is that OK by you?"

"I don't want him getting off for anything."

Principe lowered his voice, "All the rest will come out during the trial. I guarantee it."

"Why not now?"

"The wheels of justice turn slowly. The case will take a long time coming to trial. By then, interest will have died down. And a general election held."

Blume touched a new bruise on the side of his face. "There is nothing political about Pernazzo. He's psychopathic. We never get dumped on for psychopaths. If anything, it's the opposite. Everyone suddenly remembers they need the police and the magistrates. Even the politicians have to pretend to appreciate magistrates for a day or two. Society rallies around and remembers it exists. Everyone's happy."

"With Pernazzo out there killing people, Clemente becomes a random murder. Before Pernazzo appeared on the scene, it looked like Clemente died for an ethical cause. Your version of events makes it less clear-cut."

"That's nice: my version," said Blume.

Principe relaxed his shoulders and looked directly at Blume. "Alleva's role as the main bad guy was helped a lot by the fact he, directly or indirectly, got a cop killed."

"I get that," said Blume.

"But when you complicated the story with talk of this new person, Pernazzo, it was almost as if you were exonerating Alleva in some way. That's one reason you were not getting the full support of your colleagues. It is as if Pernazzo was somehow your problem. I know that's not the case, but there is a psychological element at play here. Especially after the death of Ferrucci. I am not condoning this, and as the magistrate in charge of the investigation into the random killing of Brocca, I shall do everything in my power to bring the perpetrator to justice. What I cannot afford to do is insist on investigating Pernazzo for the Clemente case. That will come out eventually, but it will be the decision of the judge in charge of preliminary inquiries, the chief prosecutor, the court, even the magistrates' council. But it is a decision for other people to take later."

"He tried to kill me . . . and my woman."

"Ah, so she was there, your woman."

"Fuck it, Filippo, stop playing games. She was there. She saved my life. But she prefers to be left out of this."

"Fine. Are you so sure she's 'your woman'?"

"What that's supposed to mean?"

"An irrelevance," said Principe. "Pernazzo. He's—how can I put this— he's like a leftover piece from a completed jigsaw puzzle. It would be good if we could just throw out the extra piece. If someone were to get to

Pernazzo first, then the full truth would never be known, but I suppose justice could be achieved nonetheless. Also, I'd say your efforts were due some recognition."

Blume's cell rang. He looked at the screen to see who it was, but the ID had been withheld. He answered anyhow.

"Aha! My favorite American policeman," said Innocenzi's voice. "I was on this side of town, and I thought I'd pick up a few pastries from De Pedris for after mass." He dropped his voice, low, confidential. "Better a day-old De Pedris pastry than a fresh one from the rat hole near my house." He continued, "When I realized where I was in the city, I wondered if by any chance business might have brought you to the courthouse, which I can see from where I am sitting. By happy coincidence, I catch you there. De Pedris does this fine coffee with hazelnut foam—know it? You deserve one after the shock you had this morning. Also, there's a thing I was wanting to ask you. Just you, mind, and no one else."

52

Blume checked the time on his phone and walked with his head down, not saluting anyone in the corridor. It was quarter to two already. If Angelo Pernazzo had been in Di Tivoli's apartment the night before and taken Di Tivoli's car . . . When he reached the elevator, he suddenly turned on his heel and marched back the way he had come and straight into Principe's office without knocking. Principe was on the phone and covered the mouthpiece as Blume entered. Then without even saying anything to whoever it was, he hung up.

"Filippo, listen to me," said Blume, speaking rapidly. "Di Tivoli had—has—a second home in Amatrice. I just remembered Manuela Innocenzi mentioned it. There's a damned good chance that's where we'll find Pernazzo. Find out as quick as you can. Get the address. If Di Tivoli has more than one property outside Rome, give priority to whichever is nearest, but I'd bet on Amatrice. If Di Tivoli's vehicle is logged going in that direction, then we'll have him."

Blume left again, and walked quickly down the corridor again and out of the Halls of Justice. He hurried across the broad avenue and headed in the direction of Via Cola di Rienzo. A platinum blond woman with black made-up eyes and puffed-up lips eyed him contemptuously from a café table. Mutton dressed as lamb.

Blume pulled out his phone, called Principe, and got a busy signal. Only four minutes had passed, anyhow. Calling like that would just slow things down. But he could not allay the feeling that Innocenzi was ahead of them.

Two youths in red and yellow tracksuits sat outside the café, neither of them drinking anything, both of them smoking. They side-watched Blume as he walked in. Innocenzi was seated alone at one of the four tables in the café, reading *Il Messaggero*. There was no sign of the pastries he was supposed to have bought.

Innocenzi folded the paper as Blume sat down opposite him.

"What do you want?" said Blume.

"Coffee, thanks, Alec."

"Very funny."

"Calmness and control, Alec. If you're not offering, then I'll get the coffees."

This entailed raising his hand in a languid salute. The bartender was beside the table as if teleported there. Innocenzi ordered. The coffees arrived. They drank them in total silence. Innocenzi curled his little finger in the cup, covering the tip in a sludge of coffee and undissolved sugar, which he rubbed like cocaine on this gums, then sucked his finger.

"I see you, and I feel a sort of admiration—you know? Like a singer who won't compromise his style or politics to sell albums. Like Lucio Battisti, Gino Paoli, Neil Young, you know?"

"No," said Blume.

Innocenzi laughed. "That's it. Just that sort of bolshie attitude. So what can I do for you?"

Blume wiped his mouth with the back of his hand. "Nothing. You said you wanted to tell me something."

"I heard about your trouble this morning."

"Who told you? D'Amico?"

"I don't betray people who tell me things. That's how come I'm the last one standing. Are you all right?"

"I am fine, and very moved by your concern."

"Will they get the person who tried to do this?"

"We will get him, yes."

"When?"

"Soon."

"Excellent. What a bitch you having a sprained arm. Otherwise you'd probably have got him there and then."

Blume said nothing.

"Lucky for you, you had such a good woman to defend you. Kristin is a girl who knows how to fight."

Blume may have blinked, but no more than that. He should have been ready for that. How much Innocenzi knew about Kristin was anyone's guess, which is just how he wanted it.

"I heard extraordinary reports of a man running barefoot from the scene," continued Innocenzi. "Probably an exaggeration, but you have to wonder. No professional would have made all those mistakes. A professional would have got you both. You, then Kristin. That's what a professional would have done. You'd never have seen it coming. I often wonder, do you even have time to hear the sound of the last shot. But this guy?" Innocenzi tapped the coffee cup as if it had turned into the person he was talking about. "He's a bad joke. An embarrassment. He kills people like Clemente, who my daughter says was a very good man. I finally squeezed the name out of the department. Angelo Pernazzo. His apartment is being searched."

"Pernazzo is the subject of inquiries," said Blume.

"Now I hear Alleva and Massoni are dead, may they rest in peace. I don't suppose you have any idea who did this?"

"It looks like they killed each other," began Blume.

Innocenzi held up a restraining hand. "Please. Reciprocate some of the respect I have shown you. You're not a good bullshitter, anyhow. Not Italian enough. Play it straight, like an American."

"That really stirs my national pride," said Blume. But Innocenzi was partly right. He saw no point in temporizing just for the sake of it. "OK, maybe Pernazzo had a hand in this killing, too," said Blume. "It seems clear he was in regular contact with Massoni. You realize that if he's not the one who killed Alleva, suspicion will fall on you?"

Innocenzi flicked at an invisible piece of dirt on his wrist to dismiss the idea. "You realize that Alleva was under my protection. And even if he wasn't, you can't have debtors killing creditors, customers murdering entrepreneurs. The whole system would collapse. I take it you have heard what happened to our poor friend the television host?"

"Yes."

"Pernazzo again?"

Blume half nodded.

"This is becoming embarrassing."

Blume's phone rang. He pulled it out. It was Principe. Blume had been right. Di Tivoli had a house near the village of Amatrice.

"What now?" asked Principe. "Shall I send out units to the place?"

"What about tracing the vehicle? Wait for that," said Blume. "I'll call you back in five minutes." He closed his phone, slapped it on the table.

Innocenzi leaned over, gave him a playful push on the side of the shoulder. He looked almost pleased. Now it was his turn to pick up his phone. He keyed in a number, holding up a hand as if to stem a flow of inconsequential chatter from Blume, who remained tense, mute, and watchful.

"Fifteen minutes tops," Innocenzi told whoever it was had picked up on the other side.

Blume's phone danced on the tabletop. He grabbed it.

"Di Tivoli's vehicle was logged three hours ago leaving the Strada dei Parchi highway. He should be at Amatrice by now. I'm giving the order to move in."

"OK," said Blume. "Tell them to approach with caution. Remember they're country policemen you're dealing with." He closed the phone. "Let us suppose," he said to Innocenzi, "we were both looking for the same person at the same time. Who do you think would find him first?"

Innocenzi did not hesitate. "Not the authorities."

"You don't think the authorities are on the right track?"

"They could be rushing to the spot, Alec, as you and I sit here at one remove from all that is going on."

Just to make sure, Blume said, "Rushing to the spot where this common enemy now is?"

"That's how I would picture it."

"And, based on your past experience, do you think the authorities would make it in time?"

"Let's say a magistrate were to place a call through to the local police in Amatrice right now. I still think it would already be too late."

"Damn!" Blume hit the table. "Manuela tells you everything, doesn't she?"

Innocenzi touched his lips. "I don't like hearing you say things like that, Alec. It's almost as if you're saying that if anything happens to this man who tried to kill you, Manuela's responsible. See the problem there?"

"It's no problem if nothing happens to him."

"If nothing happens to him. You want that?" But before Blume could reply, he continued. "You don't want it. You just gave us five minutes' warning. If something bad happens to him, it's because you wanted it that way. You're setting him up."

Blume pulled out his phone, hit redial, got Principe. "Go for it. Get as many units to that address as you can. Do it now."

Innocenzi watched him. "It will still take about fifteen minutes before the first local cop gets there. It is now five past two. Want another coffee? Something stronger? We've got a few minutes to sit here serenely together, see how things pan out."

"With me playing alibi to you," said Blume.

"I don't need alibis, Alec." He raised a finger, the waiter appeared. "A Crodino for myself and . . ."

Blume said nothing.

". . . the same for my friend."

The waiter returned and Innocenzi watched as he poured the fizzing orange drink from the dinky bottles into two small glasses. Then he said, "Do you remember Gargaruti, your landlord? The one you had after your parents died?"

Blume knocked back his Crodino in a single gulp, pouring half of it down his air passage.

Innocenzi leaned over and gave him a thump between the shoulder blades. "I see you do. Now I'm not going to pretend I know all the details. Let me give it to you as I got it at the time. Gargaruti owned at least twenty apartments, which brought him to people's attention. Twenty apartments and you become visible. If you don't want to get shot at, you need to declare yourself, strike a deal. Right?"

"I suppose," said Blume, his eyes still watering. He suddenly felt as lost in the world as when he was seventeen.

"Also, Gargaruti was already paying a *pizzo* on his *rosticceria*, or so they say. I wouldn't know. So he was known. He needed persuasion to generosity. One of those guys who must've been worth millions but preferred to spend the whole day in a dirty apron sticking spikes up the asses of chickens and serving fried potatoes with rosemary. In his spare time, he spent the evening screwing rent from his tenants. You want to hear the story?"

Blume did. He had to.

"One day a request came through to me to have someone lean a little on Gargaruti, just to give a poor American kid a break. The reason I came to hear about it in person is that the request came from the cops. We have a sensible rule that says no one except me is allowed to do deals with the authorities. All contacts with the police had to go through me, and still do. I always have to meet the policeman in person. Just to keep things honest. So I talked to this cop and his partner, who was a woman, which is something I don't approve of, but they were both good people, and they told me the story about an American kid, lost his parents in a bank raid. It seemed like a good thing to do, and it was fun to get at Gargaruti that way, and so this kid's rent just suddenly and magically went away, and we were all happy to feel a bit like heroes. You'd think this American kid would have wondered about it. But he didn't. Instead, he went to college, and then—guess what—joined the Polizia di Stato, bought the apartment at a knockdown price, not asking too many questions why, and became the purest policeman in the entire world. His career isn't up to much, but he's totally uncompromised. I like to think I contributed to that story of success."

Blume gripped the table hard, anchoring himself in the present. He was thirty-eight years old, no longer a lost child. His feet were flat on the floor, and his body had weight and substance. He would not allow Innocenzi to be the one to guide him back.

"You think I'm polluting your memories?" asked Innocenzi. "I helped you, my friend."

"You're not a friend," said Blume.

Innocenzi fingered the crucifix under his silk shirt. "That's up to you." He made as if to get up.

"You are not a friend," repeated Blume, gathering his thoughts. "So I want to know why you decided to help me."

"An exchange of favors. It happens all the time. I think it may have just happened now between us."

"The two police officers weren't senior enough for you to do them a favor."

"I make no distinction in rank. One of them's pretty senior now, so maybe I saw in advance . . ."

"No. That's not it. Who killed my parents, Innocenzi?"

Innocenzi put the palm of his hand against the side of his face and pushed the loose skin folds below his jowls, causing the skin of his face to crumple. "It was not my doing."

"If you remember the name of my landlord after all these years, you can remember the murders in the bank, and you know who did it, and why."

"Maybe someone has already told you who did it," said Innocenzi.

"The grave number of the killer that got sent to me? That was you?"

Innocenzi nodded.

"Was that another favor?"

"Yes. That was a favor. But it came with no strings attached."

"Who were those two in the bank that day?"

"They were nobodies. The robbery—it wasn't even for the money. It was an invasion of my turf, a challenge to my authority. A *sfregio* from my rivals. It led to . . . some terrible things. Pointless cruelty, and it helped the Calabrians get a foothold. When two fight over a bone, the third gets the meat."

"You knew who killed my parents."

"The killer was my enemy, too. I had nothing to do with it."

"Had you anything to do with the death of Pietro Scognamiglio?"

"Was that his name? I'd forgotten."

"I haven't."

"No, you never forget a thing like that."

"Did you have him killed?"

"If I did, would I say so? Maybe in this context, speaking to you as a son, not as a cop, I would. But no, it wasn't me. We couldn't touch him—part of a truce agreement we reached after a few months. I think his own side got rid of him eventually. Not my concern. When I heard, I thought you'd be interested."

"You think I should be grateful for this? You think I don't blame you? They were killed because of you, because of the division of Rome into fiefdoms. Because of you and your drugs and racketeering and protection and gambling and prostitution and extortion and theft and your exploitation of the weak and your miserable fucking low-life turf wars."

Innocenzi stretched his arm across the table and tapped his index finger against the side of Blume's nose. Blume made to grab his finger, but Innocenzi pulled it away. The rectangle of light at the front of the bar dimmed slightly as Innocenzi's two minders, smelling tension, filled the entrance.

"No, don't touch. That would be a really bad thing for you to do, Alec."

Blume leaned back, and tried to control the pounding anger in his head.

"Listen to me, Alec. Rome has always been this way. Since the Middle Ages. Since before then. Since always. Who do you think the Colonna were? The Orsini, Farnese, Borghese, Chigi, Pamphili? All those big palazzos in the center, with their barred windows and thick walls, what are they there for? Each family controlled an area, and they fought and killed each other, and so it goes on. And now you, a half foreigner, think you can come here and tell me about how this ancient city, the greatest on earth, *caput mundi*, should be run. Fuck off back to where you belong, and get some perspective."

"So my parents just got caught up in the historical cross-fire. That's it?"

"That's it. Like they were in Lebanon or somewhere. I tried to make it up to you, and now I think we're about even."

Innocenzi got up and left. Blume sat at the table rereading his past.

53

THE FEAR PERNAZZO felt as he ran was physical. An invisible finger was stealing through the air and prodding him gently in the back where he imagined the bullet would enter when the woman with red hair fired. He switched direction to the right, and the finger seemed to follow, now pressing at the back of his neck. Then he rushed parallel to a brick wall for thirty yards and onward, under an aperture in the old Roman fortifications, across a ribbon of grass, past teenagers sprawled on stone seats, and across another avenue, this time with hardly any traffic apart from a tram visible far in the distance. Still no side street offered itself. He crossed two more avenues, both of them leading down to the basilica with the marble statues. If any cars had been called out, they would have no difficulty running him to earth in this area. He continued his beeline flight until finally a side street appeared on his right. He ducked into it, only to find that it led straight back to another broad avenue and afforded little hiding room, but at last the steely fingers receded.

Pernazzo slowed his pace, and, by the time he left the short street to emerge near Santa Croce di Gerusalemme, he was able to affect a casual stroll past a group of clergy gathered outside the basilica. He finally registered that his slippers had fallen off his feet. He stopped at a trash container and, glancing round, pulled out a plastic bag of garbage. It was slimy on the outside, and smelled powerfully of ketchup and cabbage, and he thought he felt something move inside it, but it was only the pulse in his wrist and the sweat running down his arm. Carrying his bag of trash, he walked on, keeping his head bent down. As he reached the avenue in front of the church, he saw the first patrol car.

It was eighty yards away and moving in his direction, but traveling too slowly to be responding to a call. Either it was simply cruising or a bulletin had already been issued. He drew level with a green garbage container, and hoisted open the top, obscuring himself from the car, the car from him. He threw in the stinking bag of garbage, wiped his palms on the front of his pants. The patrol car drove on.

With exaggerated care, Pernazzo crossed the road to reach a bus and tram stop, and stood among a group of university students, who tried to avoid staring at his blackened bare feet. Thirty seconds later, a tram trundled up and they all got on. Two stops later, back roughly in the direction from which he had fled, he got off again. He could hear sirens. They all seemed to be converging on him.

Pernazzo squeezed into a doorway and observed Di Tivoli's car from a distance. Finally, he moved out of the doorway toward it. His foot slipped on something soft. A few yards later, something sharp inserted itself between the toes of his other foot. He did not look down, but kept his eyes fixed on the car. He made it. He climbed into its safety. He could smell leather, the volatile plastic compounds, his own body. He looked over at his gray backpack, snug on the floor. He switched on the TomTom SatNav device. He keyed in the address of Di Tivoli's country villa in Amatrice.

Working the car pedals barefoot was uncomfortable and difficult. The clutch was the worst. He passed two police cars going in the opposite direction. Looking through the rear-view mirror, he saw no sign of them slowing down as they passed him. It looked as if no one had discovered Di Tivoli yet. He had time.

The soothing SatNav voice told him he was leaving the city limits by way of Strada dei Parchi. She repeated the name, in case he had missed it. He opened the window to let in the warm smell of gas and oleander.

He brushed his hand over the steering wheel, and leaned back into the seat. He would get an SUV in Argentina. He would cruise the boulevards of Buenos Aires in his car, living the life Alleva had planned for himself. He had heard it was a city like Paris. He had checked it out on Google Earth, and seen the trees.

The highway was almost empty, and he gave full rein to the power of Di Tivoli's engine. He closed the window and brought the car up to 85 mph before starting to slow down. The road looped around the outskirts of L'Aquila. He did not like moving inland like this, away from the sea, but in a few days, he would be standing on the wharves of Buenos Aires watching the ships arrive.

He left the motorway and drove for 70 or 80 miles on a winding country road before, and, following the gentle advice of the navigator, turning right onto a white gravel road that cut through the fields like a bandage.

The house was two miles from the road, and one and a half from the first house he had seen. The land was richer, heavier, and greener than that near Alleva's hideout. It was cooler, and the cypress trees cast long shadows.

He reached a two-story villa made of brown stone with a red slate roof, and the SatNav assured him he had arrived. He sat there waiting to see if anyone would come out, ask what the hell he thought he was doing. No one did. The place looked empty.

He drove around the house, bumping his way over a patch of field, to park the car out of sight in an overgrown yard, next to a rusted swing. Just as he was about to turn off the engine, he caught a slight flicker of gray movement from the bushes at the far end of a plowed field that started where the garden ended. He instinctively grabbed the steering wheel, then relaxed his grip a little as he recognized the gray outline of a wild boar, which turned and trotted away into a thicket.

He cracked open the car door, put one foot on the grass, and checked for any other wild animals that might be about. He could hear scuffling and crackles in the thickets, whispers in the trees, and the wash of river water over gravel, but nothing human disturbed him. He looked down the field toward the area where he had seen the piggy eyes looking at him a few moments before. He got out. The grass felt good on his aching insteps.

Staying at the back of the house, keeping his head slightly down all the time, he crept up to a window and peered in. He could make out heavy rustic furniture, an old rug on a red floor. He moved over to a backdoor, tried to open it with Di Tivoli's keys, which didn't fit. He had no wish to venture around the front and be seen. The next window was small, frosted. It would lead into a bathroom. He stood with his back to it, and hit it with his elbow. But at the last moment, he pulled his elbow back, afraid of what the shards of exploding glass might do. He located a muddy rock, and hurled it at the glass. He thought he heard a crack, but the rock bounced back. He tried again. This time the window disintegrated. The noise scared him a little, and he stayed still, listening to the trees and fields. Carefully he picked the deadly triangles of glass from the side of the frame, felt around to the latch, opened the window, threw in his bag, then climbed in after. He moved quickly through the house to the entrance hall. He opened the front door, looked out, saw nothing. He double-checked that he had pulled the front door closed. To his right was a small panel of circuit breakers and the main switch for the electricity, which he snapped on.

The living room was large and open-plan, fronted by a broad, crystal-clear rectangular window that looked out over a sloping mound and gave a good view of the sky. It reminded him of the field on the Microsoft desktop. There was a thick and expensive table in the center of the room, magazines and books scattered on it. But the window made him feel too visible, and he crept upstairs.

He found what seemed to be a child's bedroom at the end of the corridor. He carried his bag over to the corner of the room and dropped it on the bed, over which lay a faded Spiderman bedspread. He lay down on it, and breathed in the earthy smell of mold, liking it. He had lost touch with his sleep schedule, but reckoned he was due for another hypersleep. He closed his eyes.

An hour later, Pernazzo awoke from one of the deepest, most dreamless, and calmest sleeps he had had in years.

He got out of the bed, unzipped the bag, and carefully set out three blank passports: one Italian, one Argentine, and one Greek. He chose the Greek one.

He searched an old closet. Many of the clothes had black patches of dry rot and damp on them, all of them had a musty odor. But he found an old shirt that fit him. He got down on all fours and hunted around the bottom of the closet emerging with several pairs of shoes. He found socks. An old-style pair of All-Star basketball shoes with a high ankle turned out to be his size. Things were looking up.

He found a pair of blunt scissors in the top drawer of a child's study desk painted in several colors not on the market since the 1970s.

He cut along the edges of the photos, the scissors making a thunk-snip sound as he walked them across the white spaces. He chose the most perfectly cut one, and inserted it into the framed area of the Greek passport. From the same desk drawer he took out a small, old-fashioned bottle of glue, but it was completely dry. He thought for a moment, then went into the corridor and opened a door to his left, which opened into another child's room, and then one on the right, which led into a bathroom brightly tiled in yellow. He found some toothpaste, carried it back into the bedroom, and squeezed some onto the back of the photo. He pressed the photo firmly into place, then tested it with his thumb. It held without sliding, which was all he needed.

Now he took out the metal embosser. He disassembled the head and inserted the die with the Greek emblem that Alleva had prepared for himself. When he had inserted the relief die, he thumped the embosser arm to make sure it was set firm. The sound of the slam echoed back at him from the other side of the house. Then he fixed the recessed die in place, slipped the photo and paper between them, and pressed down hard, making a gentle thud that almost sounded as if it had come from below. The wooden desk creaked. The Greek-cross embossing and surrounding lettering came up fine. The effect was excellent, especially since no one was going to examine Greek lettering with any real knowledge. It would look even better once he had applied the laminated strip of cellulose acetate, which would require the use of an iron.

But that could wait. In the meantime, he would prepare the Argentine and Italian passports and get dressed, maybe even wash. He was beginning to enjoy himself. Tomorrow, he would be taking an Italian ferry from Naples to Sardinia or from Bari to Greece. The possibilities were many. The day after, he would land in Paris. Then he would use his Greek passport to book a flight to Argentina. Maybe he would spend a few days in Paris. He had never been there. Maybe he could even spend a day at Disneyland. He looked at his handiwork again, and suddenly was worried that the photo did not look like him. The face he saw seemed too yellowish. But he had taken it only the other day. A second worrisome thought struck him. The photo was too recent. The issue date on the passport was from three years ago. The photo was from three days ago. Would they notice?

He picked up the toothpaste and went back, passport in hand, to the bathroom to look at himself in the mirror in the cabinet door. He felt light-headed and unreal. He had not eaten. He leaned over the sink and took a few breaths. Then he looked back up at his reflection and screamed. An old man with no ears was standing behind him.

54

S TAY THERE," WAS all the man with no ears said. Then he called downstairs. "Will someone come up here and take a look?"

"Coming." A woman's voice.

Pernazzo considered hurling himself at the man in the doorway, but he felt rooted to the spot. The man with no ears and bored eyes looked impregnable. Then he stepped aside and Pernazzo saw a raw-faced woman with peroxide hair who chewed gum as she studied his face. He had seen her somewhere before.

"Are you Pernazzo?"

"No."

On Di Tivoli's documentary show. That's where he had seen her. Manuela Innocenzi.

"Yes, you are," she said, then turned around and walked out.

Pernazzo made a half movement after her, but the man with no ears stepped to close off the door. There was at least one other person in the corridor.

"Hey. Wait a minute," said Pernazzo. "Maybe there's been a mistake. Who do you think I am?"

No reply.

Surreptitiously, he felt around the sink for the scissors, but then remembered they were in the bedroom, and they belonged to a child and were small and blunt.

He heard the sound of someone shuffling slowly across the landing and into his bedroom. Again, Pernazzo considered rushing the man with no ears, but found his feet would not respond.

"Come here," ordered the man in the doorway. "Come on," he added in an exasperated and half-cajoling voice when Pernazzo did not move. "I don't want to have to drag you out by the ears. In there," said his captor.

He gave him a gentle push into the bedroom and stood by the door. Sitting on the bed, leafing idly through the passports, was the woman again. Pernazzo felt his sweat soak through the entire back of his shirt. He had to try to gain a negotiating position. He nodded at the passports, and tried to fix a knowing smile on his face, but she did not glance up.

"Pretty good, aren't they?"

She threw a glance in his direction, as if checking to see where the unexpected noise had come from, then put down the passports and pulled out some Transcend memory sticks from the bag.

"Ah, now those. Those are special," he tried, but she had already lost interest, and was now peering with one eye at a circular metal die contained in a transparent plastic disc.

"That's the relief die for a passport. The recessed die is in another case," he offered.

Manuela Innocenzi put the metal circle down on the bed, and picked up one of the five sheets of numbers.

"That's just backup. In case something goes wrong with the memory sticks, which could never happen. With these numbers I can reconstruct bank account numbers and telephone contacts."

She took out the Ka-Bar Tanto, and examined its hilt. She took it out of its sheath, and turned it back and forth as if looking for blemishes on the blade. He realized he should never have kept that knife, no matter how important it was to him.

Pernazzo stared at a Star Wars bedside mat on the floor beside the bed. C3P0 had his hand raised in greeting.

"How did you find me?" All at once, this was all he wanted to know.

She ignored the question, but spoke at last. "You had no reason to do all these things. You had a choice. I was born into it, and I tried to move above, without hurting my father's feelings. Arturo was my last chance to change. I would have made it, too. I'd have got away. Escaped into goodness."

Pernazzo had no idea what the ugly woman was talking about, but he was in no doubt of her power.

She said, "You killed Arturo with this," and gently waved her hand to forestall any protests. "And you kept it because you are proud of what you did. Arturo and I had a deep sense of justice. Know that? It's what we had in common."

Pernazzo felt a shadow move down his head and body as hope drained away.

This backpack was his. I remember he used it to bring a packed lunch. He was always walking or cycling, always had this bag. He kept a book for identifying flowers in it. Not just flowers. He was enthusiastic even about weeds, grass."

Pernazzo looked at a world map on the bedroom wall. It curled at the edges. The Soviet Union still existed. Argentina was green, Brazil orange, Chile pink. His feet were cold.

"How did you find me?"

"We all get found out in the end."

Pernazzo found himself in the corridor, the earless old man behind him. He moved down the staircase as if it were an escalator. At the bottom of the steps stood a youth in a white tracksuit, who looked hardly older than a child. He had a butt-fluff mustache, a hairless chest, and doe-like eyes. He was also holding a pistol and pointing it casually at Pernazzo's heart. It was an elegant model, like Massoni's.

The kid seemed nice enough. Pernazzo looked slowly to his right. The raw-faced woman had sat down, her big feet pointed in his direction. She was twisting something in her hands and staring at him with her small blue eyes, never taking them off him, all the time working the gum in her jaw. The old man's phone rang, he pressed it to his mutilated ear, murmured something about five minutes, put it away.

"Move," commanded the boy. They left by the front door, and the boy suddenly gave him a hard shove, as if the house had kept him polite and he was only now coming into his element. Pernazzo slipped on the grass, went sprawling forward, and considered breaking into a sprint, but the boy was just behind him with his long-barreled pistol. Pernazzo saw two four-by-four vehicles parked in front of the gate. How had he not heard? They circled the house, and he was in the back yard again. There was the broken window, the shining glass shards.

As they approached the thicket at the end of the yard, he tensed, ready to make a break for it, but though the top of his body felt light and ready to burst into flight, the lower part seemed to be wading through water. The youth whispered "Stop," and his voice was so close that Pernazzo felt the hairs in his ears tingle.

Pernazzo walked on a few paces, wondering whether his mother could see him now.

"I said 'stop.'" There was no annoyance in the soft voice.

Using the energy surging through the upper part of his body, Pernazzo bent down and grabbed a broken elm branch, but it was as light as cork. He spun around, stick in hand, but the kid was five paces behind and out of reach. He didn't even seem to have noticed Pernazzo's weapon.

"Wait a minute!" said Pernazzo. He raised the rotten stick above his head. "This is too light. I need . . ."

"What?"

But Pernazzo could not think of anything to say.

The kid shot him through the right elbow. When he heard the crack, Pernazzo thought the wood had exploded over his head. And, then, suddenly, the pain was so bad he wanted to tear off his right arm with his left.

The next bullet buried itself in his kneecap and did not come out. As he went down, he felt vomit rise from his throat, and when he hit the ground he sucked it all back in again and couldn't breathe. He wriggled over onto his side and dislodged enough to be able to gasp for air. Something infinitely strong and merciless grabbed his shattered arm and pulled, causing the agony to move from his elbow to his entire body. Far above him stood the darkened face of the young man and above him a blue sky with clouds like faint chalk marks.

Pernazzo had not planned for the pain. It left him no chance of clarity. Most of all, it was not fair. He had no chance, lying there. A distant idea was beginning to form in his mind, somewhere behind the pain. He would need some time to work it through. Time to recover. It had something to do with change. He was sure it was going to be a beautiful idea.

"Wait," said Pernazzo, "I think I may . . ."

The young man in the white tracksuit shot Pernazzo twice in the forehead, putting an immediate end to the thrashing movements. He used his foot to push the scrawny corpse over and, never one to take a gamble, delivered two more shots to the back of the head.

55

WHAT ABOUT THE dogs?"

The speaker was Sveva Romagnolo, and Blume couldn't believe her question. He had just finished describing the discovery of Pernazzo's body at Di Tivoli's country villa in Amatrice, and this was her idea of a suitable response.

"The *dogs?*" He took the phone way from his ear and looked at it as if it were responsible for the ludicrous question. His main concern now was what to do about Paoloni. He could not come to a decision.

"I know it may sound like a strange question after all you have been telling me, Commissioner, but you see, I've already heard all about what happened to Pernazzo. Your boss Gallone was very pleased to be able to give me every detail, along with assurances that he would handle the media. I don't want to hear any more. Not for now. And it's the very first thing Arturo would have asked. So now I'm asking for him."

"Ferrucci said he would look after that," said Blume. "But after he got . . . well . . . it got forgotten." Whatever he did, he would not report Paoloni to the authorities. Paoloni could do that himself.

"You know where the creatures were kept imprisoned, don't you? The details were in Arturo's files."

"Somewhere near Ponte Galleria, I think," said Blume. He had been working with Paoloni for seven years. Until now, the differences of style had not mattered.

"And no one has gone to rescue them yet? In all this time, no one thought to rescue the dogs? That's . . . It's unspeakable."

Blume brought his mind back to the surreal conversation he appeared to be engaged in. "Ferrucci wanted to do something, I remember. The dogs will be dead by now, I suppose. Unless someone was giving them water. I hadn't really thought about it."

"Well, think about it now."

"If they're not dead, they'll have escaped and they'll be feral," said Blume. He needed to confront Paoloni now.

"Get a team and go there," said Sveva.

"It's the responsibility of the municipal police or the local health board," said Blume. "Not a matter for the murder squad."

"So call them. Call someone. Then call me back, let me know."

Blume had just sent the last of the case files to the Halls of Justice. It would take the best part of the day to get the files back, find Clemente's notes on the whereabouts of the damned dogs . . . Unless.

Blume looked up the number of LAV on his computer and called Clemente's office. The doleful secretary answered. She remembered him, without much fondness, but seemed to soften a little at Blume's unexpected display of humanity. More to the point, she was able to suggest a place where the dogs might be caged. He could do that, then deal with Paoloni who, wisely enough, had returned to sick leave.

Just under an hour later, Blume stood in the middle of a field, head bowed in an effort to get his nose out of the wind and away from the smell it was bringing with it. About 250 yards in front of him, set among collapsing prefab huts and rusting vehicles, were silent metal cages. He could just make out inert lumps and dark shapes in them, and he was not moving a step further. He kept his head down and examined the knotty grass growing out the sand, mud, and crushed seashells.

Blume stayed like that for ten minutes until a four-by-four with the letters *ASL* and the Lazio coat of arms came rolling over the field and a three-man squad from the Health Service arrived with blue-and-white overalls, orange protective gloves, and an armory that included not only restraining poles and a narcotizing projector but also a shotgun. They all wore masks. They seemed to think it was his task to take them all the way to the cages.

"Not without a mask," said Blume. One of them went to the van and came back with a mask. It was impossible to talk with the mask on, so they walked the last stretch in silence.

It was already evident from fifty yards that every dog was dead. Some of them, those at the far end, were already mummifying. The ones nearest the closed off water faucet were almost invisible behind the swarms of flies. One cage seemed to contain one dead dog and the ripped remains of two others. The rest contained one dog each. One of the team handed his companion his dart gun and pointed a fogger machine between the bars. Blume moved back from the billowing white smoke toward a broken-down shed, avoiding an incongruous refrigerator, also crawling with insects, and leaned against a decaying trailer propped up on three cinder blocks. The ASL team could deal with this foul mess themselves.

The fumigation fog seemed to have gotten into his mask, or maybe it had steamed up inside. Blume pulled it off, got hit by the stench, and put it on again quickly. That was worse. He could see nothing. He leaned down and pulled it off again.

As he did so, he thought he saw a small amber light flicker on beneath the trailer. He hunkered down to check what it was. As he registered the presence of another amber light, he felt a prickling of danger run up to his hairline from his neck. They were not lights; they were eyes. Then he heard it, a growl, and before he had time to stand up again, two canine fangs appeared in the blackness and a huge, heavy, stinking black shape rushed from under the caravan and hurled itself on top of Blume, sending him crashing to the ground. As he fell on his back, he could see the civil protection team twenty yards away, enveloping themselves in smoke, oblivious behind their masks.

Blume shouted, then instinctively brought his arms up to his throat, but the animal did not attack him there. Its tactic seemed to be to use its weight to immobilize him before tearing at him with its teeth. The beast opened its huge mouth over Blume's damaged arm. He could feel its tongue and breath on his hand, and tensed as he waited for the jaws to shut and sever his fingers. Blume started thrashing about, and realized the animal was not as heavy as it looked. He punched with his good arm and connected with the animal's cold nose. It barked and took its weight off him completely. Scrambling to his feet, Blume delivered a massive kick to the flank of the animal, which shuddered and yelped. He kicked it again, and it rolled onto the ground, assuming almost the same posture as Blume had been in a few seconds ago.

Blume brought his foot up, ready to strike with his heel this time, but the big black dog just lay there, breathing fast. A muffled yell came from behind, and Blume turned to see the men running toward him. One shouted something from behind his mask, then ripped it off and shouted again: "Stand back!"

One of the team, still in a mask, was pointing the shotgun, the other a tranquilizer gun. Blume started to step back, and the one with the shotgun was the first to step forward. Blume stepped back to where he was.

"Get away! That's a Cane Corso. It can rip out your throat with a single bite."

His companion with the shotgun took off his mask to observe, "A bit small for a Cane Corso."

"It's young. Also, it's badly malnourished. But don't let it fool you."

Blume looked at his bandaged arm and hand. The animal had covered it in saliva.

"Stand back, Commissioner."

The dog had had plenty of opportunity to bite his arm off. But it had not used its teeth. Even as he had thrashed about and hit it, the animal had done its best to continue licking his hand. That's all it had done. He realized now that he had managed to smash his fist into the dog's nose because it was trying to nuzzle him. Blume moved a little closer, and the animal thumped its ugly cropped tail back and forth, then closed its strange tigerish eyes.

"What are you going to do with it?" asked Blume.

"We'll put it to sleep with this." He slotted a feathery red dart into the light rifle.

"Then what? He gets put down?"

"Phenobarbital overdose. If I had to choose a way to die, I might just choose that. Very peaceful."

Blume hunkered down and stretched out his arm. The dog lifted a mud-caked paw and made a sort of whinnying sound. Blume patted the muscular neck, still sleek and clean.

"Can we get him some water?" he asked.

56

"DID YOU FIND the dogs?" asked Sveva Romagnolo as she answered the door to Blume later that evening.

"Yes." He was not sure he liked doing this woman's bidding, but being here postponed his meeting with Paoloni to another day.

"They were all dead, as you said they would be, weren't they?"

"Mostly."

"Not all of them? I suppose they had to be put down immediately. Fighting dogs can't live in human society. All they know how to do is kill. Arturo always said that, you know. Everyone thinks that loving dogs is an unconditional thing, but he was tough, too. He would have banned certain breeds entirely. It is an act of gross irresponsibility to keep certain types of dog in the company of humans. You may have noticed he had no dog of his own. Anyhow, thank you for coming."

Blume stepped into the apartment. The doors to the terrace were open, and a warm night breeze was blowing in.

"Let's go out on the terrace," she said.

Blume sat in the same wickerwork chair as last time and described his meeting with Pernazzo. He told her about the computer games, the gambling, the connection with Alleva, the murder of Enrico Brocca outside the pizzeria.

Sometimes she winced, more often she nodded as he spoke. At no point did she display much anger, though her features were indistinct in the half darkness.

When he had finished, she said, "And do you have any idea who killed Pernazzo? Your boss Gallone will only tell me investigations are ongoing, and none of my other contacts seem to have any idea . . . or interest, really. The important thing was for me to react well, which I did. The case itself is unimportant to them."

"If I tell you who I think killed Pernazzo, you won't insist on my going public with it?"

"No. Of course not."

"And you won't advance the hypothesis in my name, even when you see the investigation peter out without anyone being brought to justice?"

"I won't use your name. I may make a fuss, though."

"It was probably Manuela Innocenzi. Eventually you'll hear this from other sources, too."

"That . . . woman?" Now he could hear anger and disgust in her voice. "Have you any evidence?"

"More likely, she asked for it to be done. I don't have direct evidence, but I got a call from Benedetto Innocenzi the other day that points in that direction. He called a few other people, too, to give the same message, which was not to think of importuning his daughter or there would be reprisals, and, above all, compromising revelations."

"I will insist on a proper investigation."

"You are within your rights," said Blume, then instinctively ducked as an orange-and-white soccer ball bounced off the back of his chair. He turned around to see a child with long hair and a babyish face scowling at him.

"Tommaso!" said his mother. "This is Alec Blume. He's a policeman."

The child continued to stare at Blume. It was a hostile stare, but it contained no real malice.

"You play soccer?" said Blume. There, that was precisely the sort of inane thing that grown-ups said. Quite rightly, the boy ignored the question and went to retrieve his ball, then began slapping it on the tiles directly behind Blume, canceling out any hopes of conversation, while his mother smiled apologetically not at Blume but at the child. Time to go.

Blume stood up and watched as the boy bounced the ball too high and lost control of it again.

"You're not very good at that yet," said Blume.

Sveva Romagnolo stared at him in outrage.

The child retrieved the ball, tucked it under his arm, and said, "I am good."

"Not yet. I think maybe it's because of your hair. It's too long. It gets in your eyes."

"Tommaso has beautiful hair," said Sveva. "You were leaving, Commissioner?"

Tommaso bounced the ball five times in succession, then said, "You believe I can do it faster than that?"

"I do. I think you might be a natural, but you need to practice. A lot. And when you can bounce it all day using your hands, then you have to learn to do the same with your feet. It takes ages, but, like I said, you look like a natural to me. Get someone to cut your hair, see if I'm right."

"Commissioner Blume! Tommaso, say bye-bye to the policeman."

"Bye, Tommy," said Blume.

"Tommaso. Not Tommy," said Sveva.

She strode across the living room, thumping her bare heels against the floor.

Tommaso followed as far as the French window, and called out, "If I learn to do more than a hundred will you come back and watch?"

"Sure, I will," said Blume.

Sveva stopped dead in her tracks and looked at her son, standing framed in the doorway, holding the ball above his head. Then she looked at Blume.

"That is grossly irresponsible of you. Suppose he really does want you to come and watch him. What then?"

"Call me, and I'll come over," said Blume. "And cut his hair. He's not a girl."

"I realize my son is not a girl. But I like long hair on a child. Arturo was like you: he wanted to give him a haircut," said Sveva.

"That's why you should do it now. Don't pretend nothing has changed for him."

57

THE FOLLOWING MORNING Blume, finally off duty, gave himself the luxury of staying in bed until ten. He had breakfast in his local bar, running down some of the credit left by Sveva. He phoned Paoloni and got no reply. Here we go again, he thought.

So he phoned Kristin in the embassy and was surprised when she invited him to her place for dinner. Seven o'clock. Blume figured he should arrange to meet Paoloni at around four. The pain of the meeting would be lessened by the prospect of seeing Kristin immediately afterward. But first, he had two other important appointments.

After breakfast, he drove down to Via Tuscolana to the vet and asked about the dog he had brought in the day before. The receptionist, whom Blume couldn't help thinking of as a nurse, told him to wait. He sat beside an elderly woman with a cat in a cage. The cat had three legs. The woman narrated events as they happened.

"And here is a nice man come to sit beside us, Melchior," she told the cat. "He's hurt his arm, just like you hurt your leg. Though of course, his arm is still attached, isn't it?"

Luckily, he did not have long to wait.

Blume looked in dismay at the animal that stood in front of him. Somehow, being cleaned up made its head and shoulders seem even larger than it had last night when, with the dire warnings of the ASL unit, he had transported it back in his car.

"He's unusually small for that breed," said the vet. "A bit of a failure as a Cane Corso, really. When I first saw him, I thought he was young and had more to grow. But he's fully mature. You can see that from his teeth. Some are loose, by the way. Let's hope he doesn't lose them. He is undernourished, and suffered dehydration. But he must have got food from somewhere. Perhaps there was some available in the place you found him?"

"There seemed to be some scraps of meat near the cages," said Blume. "I hope that's what he was eating. I do not like the idea that he might have eaten other dogs."

"Not this guy," said the vet. "Look at him. Does he look like a cannibal to you?"

Blume said he could not tell.

"Exactly," said the vet. He touched the animal on the side. "Bruising on the flank shows that some bastard gave the poor thing a kicking very recently, and he cows easily, which suggests he was regularly beaten in the past. But basically, he's in good shape. Probably got worms from polluted water sources, though. He seems to be good-tempered. Definitely a quiet dog. Don't leave him unattended with children, though. In fact, don't let him off a leash, and just be careful. He could change. You need to feed him small meals four times a day for the next month. Plenty of phosphorous, potassium. Let me see . . . magnesium, Omega-3 and -6 fatty acid supplements. You look bewildered."

"I'm supposed to do all this?"

"Someone has to do it. Big dog, big responsibility. Don't worry about the diet, I'll write it all down for you. You'll need to walk him a lot, too. Make a return appointment for next week, then every two weeks after that for the next two months. You can pay by check if you like."

Blume had planned to leave the creature there for a few days, but when he learned that the vet charged more for overnight stays than the hotels Blume went to on vacation, he changed his mind.

The dog sat in the back, its breath on Blume's neck, eyeing his driving. Blume made a visit to a pet shop for a collar, a retractable leash, a food bowl, vitamin supplements, cereal, assorted cans, and antiparasite powders. It came to €112.15. He was shocked at the total. The store owner asked him if he had €2.15 in change, and Blume conducted an awkward one-handed search through the coins in his wallet. Sitting in the middle of them was the tiny memory card Innocenzi had given him. He had still not watched the video. His computer didn't have the right kind of reader, anyhow. He balanced it on his finger, almost flicked it away, then returned it to his wallet.

When he got back to the car, an attractive young woman seemed to be waiting for him, hands on hips.

"What sort of a monster are you?" she demanded.

Blume felt this was a bit strong. "Sorry. I don't usually double-park."

"What are you talking about? Open the windows of that car immediately. That creature could die in there. Have you any idea how hot it gets inside a car? An animal that size uses up all the oxygen. Open, damn it!"

Blume did as he was told. He explained to her that he was new to this, that it wasn't his dog. She gave him a lecture on animal welfare and let him go on to his second appointment.

Blume drove over to the Brocca household. He put the collar on the dog, which seemed none the worse for having been baked in the car, then spent a while fitting the leash to it. Then they both got out and went up to the apartment.

Giulia's mother answered. She looked better than before, and managed a weak smile, which vanished when she saw the dog. She seemed to be on the point of saying something when her daughter appeared behind her.

"Alec! You have a dog," said the girl. "What's his name?" Her mother stood aside to let them in.

"He doesn't have a name, Giulia, and he's not my dog," said Blume. "It's a temporary thing. Look, he hasn't even got a tag."

Blume looked around the living room. It was tidier than when he had been there last. Giulia's mother sat down in an armchair and motioned Blume to sit on the sofa opposite. He sat down without relinquishing the leash. Giulia sat near Blume on the sofa. The dog stood between them, and blocked their view. He yanked on the lead a few times, but the dog tautened its neck and threw him a bored-walrus look.

"Is your son here, Mrs. Brocca?" inquired Blume, leaning his head back to see over the dog.

"No, he's with his grandmother. I don't want him to have to listen to this, even if nothing will be worse than what he saw."

"Did forensics send your car back?"

"Yes, thank you."

"Sit!" shouted Giulia suddenly, but the dog remained where he was. She stood up and walked over to it, and Blume tightened his hold on the leash. The girl was only a little taller than the animal. Her whole head could fit in its mouth. "Lie down!" She pointed to the floor. The dog lay down.

Blume showed them pictures of Pernazzo, whom they identified immediately. He showed them pictures of Alleva and Massoni. Giulia remembered Massoni, her mother did not. Then he began by telling them that the man who had killed their father and husband was dead. They nodded. They knew this already.

He stumbled over a few condolences, not sure where to begin the narrative they were waiting for because it really began the day he walked into Pernazzo's apartment and failed to arrest him.

Not only had he not arrested Pernazzo, he had insulted and goaded him, then rushed off to meet Kristin, leaving Pernazzo to reassert his virility by killing Enrico Brocca and ruining this family. He quickly glossed over the details.

But Giulia was ready for him. She pulled up her legs onto the cushion, turned to face him better, and said, "When you first saw Pernazzo, did you get a bad feeling about him?"

"Yes." He would not lie to her.

"But you couldn't arrest him then? You can't arrest people just because you don't like them. Right?"

"Right," said Blume. "I can't do that." He noticed the dog was drooling on the carpet.

Twenty minutes later, Blume concluded his version of events with the news that Pernazzo had been assassinated in a house in the country and that inquiries were continuing, but again Giulia was waiting for him.

"Who killed Pernazzo?"

"We don't know."

"Liar," said Giulia. "When you tell the truth you say 'I' and when you're lying, you try to spread the blame and say 'we.'"

"Giulia, you mustn't," said her mother, but her voice lacked all conviction.

"We have a right to know," said Giulia, looking straight at Blume.

"I think it was a woman called Manuela Innocenzi, but it is not likely to be proved." Blume realized he was going to have to explain who Manuela was, which meant filling in more details.

When he had finished again, Giulia said, "So my father was Pernazzo's second victim after Clemente? I think that was important enough for you to tell me right away."

"It didn't seem relevant to your case," said Blume. "Also, I suspect he might have killed his mother, too. It was probably what set him off, but none of that can be proved now. So your father would have been the third."

375

They sat there in silence for a while. The dog seemed to have fallen asleep.

Finally, Giulia said, "I don't feel anything. No, that's not right. I don't feel any different now that I know who did it and that he's dead."

"I think I do," said her mother. They both turned to look at her. Tears were flowing freely from her eyes, but her face seemed strangely composed, as if she was unaware that she was crying.

"I think I feel better," she said. "I have something to tell myself. I can say this thing to myself now, and . . . I can't explain. It's like I haven't been talking to myself. But this is something I can say to myself. You mustn't mind me, Giulia, when I say this, but I wish I had killed him. I wish I had strangled him with these hands." She held up her hands, which were small and finely shaped.

As Blume and his dog took their leave, Giulia followed them to the door and said, "Are you coming back?"

"Do I need to?"

"No. I don't think so." She held out her hand, but Blume brushed his hand over her hair instead.

"Bye, Giulia. Look after your mother and brother, but don't get trapped. You are still a child. Make sure you get looked after, too."

On the way back to the car, Blume sent a text message to Paoloni asking to meet. The dog whined and looked at him.

"You're hungry? That must be it. Are you planning on being hungry often?"

Blume went home to feed the dog. Paoloni had yet to reply to the text. The longer he took to reply, thought Blume, the easier it would be to withhold sympathy.

When he opened a can of meat and cereal and put them in the new bowl, the dog barked, nearly causing Blume to hurl something at it.

"Your bark is far too large for my apartment," he told the dog, which barked again, hurting his ears. Blume put the bowl on the floor. He had forgotten to buy a water bowl, so he filled up a shallow saucepan. When he bent down to put the water next to the food, the food was gone. The dog then lapped up the water in twenty seconds. Blume filled it twice more before the dog had enough.

He left the house at five, far too early for his date with Kristin. It would be his first visit to her place, and she was cooking. Blume had a strong suspicion that she would not be much good, but he was not visiting for the food.

There was no question of leaving the dog at home. It was just too big and too strange, and it had somehow sensed that he was leaving and placed itself by the door.

No sooner were they down in the street than the dog squatted and relieved itself, right in the middle of the sidewalk.

"Oh, Jesus Christ," said Blume, revolted. He remembered again how much he hated dogs.

"Hey!"

Blume turned around. Another outraged woman, older this time. She pointed to the mess. Blume apologized, but it wasn't good enough. After a while, he lost patience. "This entire city is covered in dog poop, litter, and graffiti. You Romans are the dirtiest people on the planet. So don't come on to me like we're living in Switzerland or something. You live here, deal with it."

He walked away, feeling bad. The woman was right, of course. There should be more like her. And what was all that about "you Romans"? It must be the prospect of meeting Kristin that was making him feel like an outsider again.

"As for you," he told the dog, "clean up your act."

58

BLUME MADE ONE more attempt to contact Paoloni, and this time the phone was answered.

"I've been avoiding you," said Paoloni. "But I've been doing some thinking, too. We need to talk."

"I know," said Blume. "But let's put it off until tomorrow morning. I'll call, you answer this time."

"OK, but call as soon as you can. I want to get this over with."

Blume thought he'd give Kristin a surprise and wait outside the embassy on Via Veneto for her. It took all of three minutes of standing outside the gates of the embassy with the dog before a car with three men inside pulled up and he was asked what he thought he was doing. Blume showed some identification, which they passed among themselves, looking at it carefully. One of them keyed the details into an onboard computer. Blume waited to be validated, and explained he had a girlfriend who worked in the embassy.

The man in the backseat said something, and the driver looked at Blume. "You're an American," he said in English.

"Yes," said Blume. "Originally."

"But you're an Italian police commissioner, too. How does that work?"

"It's a long story."

"I bet. What's your girlfriend's name, by the way?"

"Kristin Holmquist."

"Kristin? I know Kristin." He gave him a big smile, and suggested he wait for her across the road at the Palace.

"Too plush for me," said Blume. "But I'll get out of your way."

"Spoken like a real colleague. Nice dog, by the way."

In the end, he called Kristin, told her to meet him at a place he knew on Via Crispi. A small bar five minutes away that didn't mind his dog and charged the same for sitting as for standing.

"Alec! What a beautiful dog!" said Kristin as she walked up half an hour later. "That's a Cane Corso, isn't it? The Romans used them in battle. Did you know that? Who are you keeping it for? What are we doing here?"

"Change of plans. You like this dog?"

"I love him! He's not mature yet, is he? What's his name? I hope it's something totally Roman, like Pertinax, or Pugnax or—I can't think of any more, Domitian, Nerva, Aureliano." She sat down and crossed her legs.

"Those are all good names," said Blume. "Choose one."

"You mean he hasn't got a name yet?"

"No, no name. Perhaps you might give him one?"

"What do you mean?" said Kristin.

"I mean, you can have him. As a gift. You said you liked dogs."

Kristin slowly closed her eyes, then opened them, and seemed disappointed to see him still sitting there. "I don't believe you just said that."

"It was a joke," said Blume. "I was just kidding. Hey, c'mon, really. Would I try to hand a dog off on to you like that?"

"It was a joke?"

"Sure it was."

"So what are you really going to do with the dog?"

Blume thought, blinked a few times, then said, "I had not really gotten around to—"

She interrupted him. "You weren't joking at all, were you? You really thought I'd take the dog just like that."

"Half-joking, wholly in earnest. No, not even that. I mean, if you had said yes, that would have been cool . . . no, it wouldn't have. OK, let me tell you about how I found him," said Blume.

"I am not interested in that right now." Kristin was standing glaring down at him, her face obscured by the sunlight behind, her hair a fiery red. "You just thought you could dump an unwanted dog on me like that. Like I have nothing better to do? By the way, apart from the fact you already know I'm going to the States in a few days, how often do you think I have to travel there?"

"I don't know," said Blume, who had not been there in ten years. "Three times a year? Four?"

"I go back once a month. Just how in the hell did you think I was going to deal with having a dog . . . I don't even know where to start with this. You hate dogs. Right?"

"Well . . . Hate is a bit extreme."

"You hate them. It was practically the first thing you said to me. So now you are trying to offload something that is hateful to you on me."

Blume wished he understood his own psychology better.

"A dog is a living being, a responsibility, a thing you give in love, a sign of a long-term commitment. I was not even so sure about inviting you to dinner. I thought maybe it was too . . . domestic. That it might signal too much. Then you do something like this."

What he saw as a miscalculation of timing and tone was turning out to be a big mistake, one of those blunders he made that told women things about him that he didn't even know about himself. Blume had been here before, only with a different girl and no dog.

"Maybe you'd like to hear how I got this dog?" he tried.

No, it turned out she did not. Few things could interest her less. She brought up the subject of his parents' mummifying study, his immobility, his depressing home and whole attitude. "I think we're going to have to press the reset button, Alec. Keep it strictly professional."

Then she walked away, leaving Blume blinking blindly in the sudden sunlight.

59

IF KRISTIN THOUGHT his apartment was depressing, thought Blume, she should see Paoloni's. In six or seven years, Paoloni had yet to find time to unpack the boxes he had brought with him when his wife threw him out, and he had rented a place two hundred yards down the street, convinced she'd soon see the error of her ways. Paoloni's wooden chairs had once been used as weapons during a fight in a pizzeria. The owner donated them as a gesture of deep gratitude for Paoloni's help in restoring peace. The room also contained a heavy leather armchair of the type to be found in the waiting rooms of certain government ministries.

"That's a nice TV," said Blume.

"Yeah, thanks. It's full HD. You're supposed to be able to see the sweat on players' faces, the mud on the soccer ball, even the individual blades of grass," said Paoloni. "Except the screen's too big or my chair's too close, so you get a bit seasick watching it. To see it properly you have to stand at the front door, where you are."

"Right," said Blume.

"I was thinking," said Paoloni. "Let's go out. There's a sort of park and playing fields behind the church. We could go there."

"Sure." Blume had no problem leaving Paoloni's apartment, but if he had known they were going to a park, he'd have brought the dog. He'd closed it in his bedroom, but the beast could probably break down walls with its forehead.

Paoloni chose to sit on a bench near a chain-link fence behind which two teams of kids were playing soccer on synthetic grass. A few fathers were shouting instructions from the sidelines.

"Would you have killed them?" asked Blume, getting straight to the worst point first.

"I don't know. Probably. But I can't be sure. See, I know Alleva. He'd probably have surrendered immediately when he saw us come in. That would have made it hard to do."

"But you'd have done it? Put a bullet in him?"

"I'm not talking moral choices here," said Paoloni. "I only mean it would have been hard for me to get away with it. The other guys with me, they weren't there to carry out an assassination. If Alleva and Massoni resisted, they would not have asked too many questions about lethal force, but if Alleva surrendered immediately and I killed him, that would have been a problem."

"Come on, Beppe. You don't expect me to believe that. The four of you went with one mind and one intention. There's no point in protecting them. And you're all on film."

"Innocenzi gave me a copy," said Paoloni. "We look like idiots, don't we? Go there intending to revenge a colleague, leave there looking like the Marx Brothers."

"I haven't watched it. I don't think I will. So, you were with—who—Zambotto and . . ."

"Two other guys I used to work with in Corviale."

"Names?"

Paoloni seemed to be distracted by the soccer game.

"Names, Beppe." Blume repeated. "You think it's OK Innocenzi knows and I don't? Anyhow, it's all on film."

Boschetti and Castellani. They're sort of inseparable. Mean bastards both."

"I was protecting you, and you did this," said Blume. "What would you do now? Are you even listening?"

Paoloni was watching the game again. "I don't know what I'd do if I was you," he said. "Me, I'd look the other way, but that's the whole problem isn't it? I've looked the other way too many times. I've been doing this so long, I've gotten sucked in. There's no longer any real difference between me and them. But I wasn't on the take. Well, I was, but I used all of it—most of it—to buy information."

Blume thought of Paoloni's rented apartment and believed him. More or less.

"What happened to all that guilt about Ferrucci?"

Paoloni spat, lit a cigarette, and said, "That was real. That's still there. It's the main reason I wanted to get Massoni and Alleva."

"I don't think I can let this go, Beppe. I can't pretend this didn't happen."

"I know," said Paoloni, staring forward, eyes still fixed on the soccer players. "That's the difference between us. At the beginning, it wasn't like that. We were basically the same, but you never got streetwise. That's because you have always been . . ." Paoloni suddenly stood up, tossed his cigarette aside, and punched the air. "See that?"

"What?"

"That goal!"

A skin-headed youth with black lines tattooed down his arms ran up to the fence, pointed at his chest, plucked at his jersey. Paoloni gave him a thumbs-up, and shouted: "Brilliant header. Fucking brilliant!" His face bright, smiling, Paoloni turned to Blume and said, "That's my son Fabio. Lives with his mother. He's the best."

"You've been here watching your son play soccer all this time?"

"Yeah. Parish league quarterfinals, under-sixteens. That's Ottaviano they're playing against. Hey, I was listening, too," said Paoloni.

"You could have told me."

"I didn't think you'd be interested."

"You're not so good at telling me things, Beppe. You can't even come clean about wanting to watch your son play football."

"You might have said no. Anyhow, does it make a difference to what you're going to say?"

Blume looked at the teenagers running around in front of them. They almost looked like professionals, almost looked like men, except they ran around too much. All that energy and enthusiasm.

"I want you to quit the force. If you do that, I'll look after you from inside, make sure none of this comes out."

Paoloni said, "I thought that might be what you'd do."

"It's a favor, Beppe. A big one. And you will still owe me."

"I know. Maybe I needed to get out anyhow. Alleva and Massoni, they'd have been my first murders. Others would have followed. Once you start, you know."

"Yeah," said Blume. He took out his wallet, extracted the memory card, gave it to Paoloni.

"I don't need to see this. Destroy it. The fewer copies the better."

"Thanks." Paoloni slipped it into his jeans. "I destroyed my copy already. But Innocenzi will have distributed it. That's how he does things."

"If you're off the force, he won't have much use for it," said Blume.

They sat in silence for a few moments, both of them watching the game, Paoloni intently.

"That winger's fast," said Paoloni eventually.

"Yeah. But he crosses too wide," said Blume. "Your son's very good. He plays a lot?"

"More than he studies. Dumb bastard smokes, though. Cigarettes. Ganja, too. Pops a few pills on Friday night before he goes out dancing. Thinks I don't know."

The other team scored.

"We're all attack, no defense," said Paoloni.

"What are you going to do?" said Blume. "For money, I mean. It's going to be hard finding work at your age."

"That's OK. I have something lined up," said Paoloni. "Through a friend who quit a while ago. I've been thinking about it for the past few days, and now I've decided."

"What?"

"It's not a great job."

"Yeah, but what?

"I'm going to become a bank guard."

60

BLUME SPENT THE morning and early afternoon airing his parents' study, shifting out some of the more useless pieces of furniture, and sorting through their papers, many of which were infested with silverfish and dust. He had dumped a lot of paper, and his newly freed arm was aching from the effort.

Last week he had phoned Kristin to tell her he was cleaning out the study, and she didn't hang up. A few days later, she said she knew a good dentist near New York, if he wanted to come over to the States to have his chipped teeth seen to.

"It's not as expensive as they say. I'd be interested in seeing you back in context. Anyhow, you decide. The embassy books my flights, so if you're thinking of coming, you'll have to do it yourself."

Blume went straight online and booked a ticket to New York. He'd phone her from there. As he logged off, the dog padded into the kitchen in the hope of food.

"Oh, great," said Blume.

The smell of the dust in the study reminded him powerfully of something he couldn't remember. It was a frustrating sensation. Like when he tried to recall his mother's face, now fading fast from his mind.

The policeman and policewoman came back the following afternoon, hours after he had identified his parents' bodies. He didn't faint or cry or make a scene at the mortuary or there with them. He had invited them in for coffee, which felt like a grown-up thing to do. But they didn't want to come in, and they had no more information to give. He left the door open and went into the living room, where he had decided to do his school assignment because if his parents had been able to see this, they would have been proud of him, comforted to see him so maturely getting on with life.

The police came back in the evening. A policeman accompanied by two women. One was in uniform and wore too much makeup. The other had no uniform and reminded him of his geography teacher. She wanted to know who his nearest relatives were. He told her that his nearest relatives were his parents. Aunts, uncles, grandparents, she specified. Not that he knew of. Maybe an aunt on his mother's side. His father had been an only child, like him. His parents' parents were dead, like his were now. No, he did not have anywhere else to go.

"Still hurts?" asked Principe.

Blume sat in the magistrate's office scratching his arm.

"Not really. It itches like hell. It began itching when they took off the cast. I'm going insane."

"Don't worry about it. The itching is a sign."

"Of what? Liver cancer?"

"Healing, Alec. Which reminds me, did you hear about Manuela Innocenzi?"

"No. What?"

"She flipped her car. She must have been doing one hell of a speed. They could still smell the alcohol on her when they got there. She's in a bad way, apparently. No loss, I suppose."

"When did all this happen?"

"Last night. On Via La Spezia. That's near where you live, isn't it?"

"Yes."

"So you're leaving us for a long vacation? It's good for some."

"I've added vacation time to sick leave. I'm going to Rye first, then on to Vermont."

"RAI?"

"Rye," said Blume, and spelled it. "It's a place in upstate New York. Kristin has a dentist there. Says he's the best there is. The thing is, it means I've got to get rid of a dog."

"Get rid of it? As in put it down?" said Principe.

"It's a Cane Corso. Stupid, quiet, possibly dangerous around children, given to bouts of salivating. Do you want to look after it for me? I'll be gone for a month."

"Very funny," said Principe.

"See what I mean? No one wants a dog like that. The law says I was supposed to register it by today, ten days after taking it in. Officially, it was supposed to be put down anyhow. So, if I decide to—you know—there's no problem, or shouldn't be. I can't see any difficulties with the paperwork for its . . ."

"Execution?"

"I see no choice," said Blume.

"You know, Alec, I've known Kristin for about two years, though I can't say I know her well. She phones up sometimes, keeps up to date, angles for inside information, is greedy for gossip, hands out invitations to seminars in the States, organizes a few short conference breaks in lakeside hotels for prosecutors, policemen—all paid for, or else at special discount rates. The sort of legal, gentle corruption that drug companies use on doctors. She is a fine-looking woman, tough and terrifyingly intelligent."

"So what are you saying?"

"Keep the dog."

SATURDAY, SEPTEMBER 17, 9:30 A.M.

Flight AZ 645 bound for JFK banked suddenly over the sea above Fiumicino, sending a fairground thrill and nervous laughter down the aisles.

For a split second, Blume felt weightless. As he looked directly down at bright blue water and imagined himself falling in and slipping under, the back of his throat tightened. Then the wing of the plane came up again, and Ostia slid down the window behind it, into the shimmering dome of heat and smog that covered Rome.

Then the plane started to climb again and move north. After only ten minutes, the coastline of Tuscany was briefly visible. Blume sat bolt upright and craned his head so that he could continue to look back for as long as possible, causing the ache in his neck to return. He ran his tongue over the jagged edges of his soon-to-be-fixed back teeth.

He was chasing after a woman who did not admire him. Maybe there was something wrong with him. Behind him a murdered colleague and Paoloni's betrayal. The second was worse, though it shouldn't have been: potential killer, an unreliable partner, a corrupt cop, but—somehow—a friend.

Paoloni was quitting the force. Blume dropped by a few days later. He found his former partner alone in his flat, in a state of deep depression, and left him perhaps even more depressed, but no longer alone. Paoloni said he couldn't keep a dog for a month without knowing what to call it, and Blume told him he could call it by any name he wanted.

ACKNOWLEDGMENTS

I owe a deep debt of gratitude to several people for their belief in me, but none more than Dottoressa Donatella Uccella. I also extend my heartfelt thanks to Manuela, Luca, Fabrizio and Stefano for keeping me focused and on the straight and narrow, and to my friends at Casaletto. Grazie di cuore a tutti quanti.

I want to thank Cormac Deane for his meticulous and expert analysis of an early version of this book, and Ciaran Deane, who made several thoughtful suggestions about its structure and tone. I am very grateful to my editors Benjamin Adams and Michael Fishwick, the former for his care, patience and great professionalism; the latter for his enthusiasm, encouragement and inspired book-changing suggestions. I have been blessed with a very fine agent, Sarah Ballard, who kept the Blume project afloat in what turned out to be a very difficult period, and I have a wonderful foreign rights agent in Jessica Craig.

Finally, although neither wanted to be named in full, my thanks to Beppe and Mimmo of the Polizia di Stato for their advice and help.

KEEP READING!

Enjoy a sneak preview of the next installment in the Commissario Alec Blume serie

THE FATAL TOUCH

With the help of his associate Caterina, Blume is called to the scene of a death con
nected to a spate of muggings. Though the Carabinieri—military police—are tryin
to control the investigation, Blume has other plans.

When it becomes clear that the victim spent a career as an art forger, enemies—an
hidden treasures—begin to emerge. Relying on old friends and intuitions, Blum
hurls himself into the center of the mystery, risking his job, his neck, and just abou
anyone who trusts him. Brace yourself for another story of treachery, corruption, an
detective work, with a spectacular conclusion.

The new novel by Conor Fitzgerald

THE FATAL TOUCH

Hardcover U.S. $25.00
Bloomsbury USA
Available wherever books are sold

1

IN THE PHOTO on his desk, Antonio was smiling straight at the camera and holding up a gold medal with a blue plaque on which was written Manager of the Year.

He was struggling to replicate the smile now as he looked across his desk at a Chinese couple and two cops—one bored, the other hostile. The bored one, sitting farthest away, blended in with the gray wall. He looked like a spoiled priest and barely spoke. The hostile one seemed at first glance like he might be a great thinker or poet, thanks to his high forehead and early onset baldness.

"Tell those two fucking Jap monkeys that if they can't be bothered to come down to the police station to report a mugging, we're hardly going to give the loss of a Nikon camera top investigative priority. They're lucky we bothered turning up at all. No reported crime, no investigation," said the poet.

Antonio held up his hand. "Please, Agente . . ."

The policeman slapped the insignia on his shoulder angrily.

"I'm sorry, I don't know what rank those three Vs make you."

"Assistente Capo."

"Please, you're upsetting my guests."

"What, they understand me all of a sudden?"

"Your tone. Also, they are not Japanese. They are Chinese."

"That makes some sort of difference?"

Antonio smiled his whitest smile at the Chinese couple, who shrank back in their seats. He handed two neatly typed sheets of paper to the policeman with the big forehead, and said, "This is a statement declaring the time and place of the mugging, and detailing the items stolen. The description of the assailant isn't up to much, but they do mention he had a pointy knife."

"Oh, a pointy one?" The policeman tossed the papers back onto the desk. "If they want these to be valid, they need to go down to the station and report it."

It had taken Antonio two hours of cajoling and smiling and bowing and persuading, followed by an hour of painstaking translation of Sino-English into Italian. In the end, he had simply written up most of the report for them, as he had done before for others. He suspected the Chinese couple, or the husband at least, of exaggerating their losses. It was now eleven o'clock at night. It would be nice, he thought, if a hole opened in the floor and the policemen and the Chinese guests dropped with a scream into a fiery pit. Then he could insert himself between sharply folded hotel sheets and sleep.

The first mugging of a guest had occurred a year and a half ago. Tonight's made twenty-three, which meant the rate was more than one a month. He had even prepared a template for mugging reports and insurance claims on his office computer. The hotel was gaining a reputation as being in a bad area, which it wasn't. HQ had sent round a memo warning all employees to refrain from using the word "unlucky" in connection with the establishment. Bookings were down, and he had had to lay off three members of staff. His name was being associated with misfortune. Guests that get mugged go away unhappy, tell their friends, write letters, and, in one case, put all the details up on a very popular blog. Embassies had been informed. He was not manager of the year at the last award ceremony.

"My job is on the line," he said.

"Not our problem," said the cop.

"I thought muggings were a problem for the police," said Antonio. "By the way, what's your name?"

The great expanse of head turned red, and the cop stood up. "What sort of an asshole question is that?" he roared.

Antonio beamed at the Chinese couple and made a reassuring gesture with his left hand to indicate that all was dandy, and this is precisely what he wanted to happen.

"Just a friendly inquiry. I can't call you Assistente Capo all the time."

"So call me Capo. And don't bother us with this sort of shit." He picked up the report and flung it back across the table, but the pages wafted gently down in front of the Chinese man who said some word several times over, then reached for a pen, and scored out two of the items from the list of stolen goods.

Antonio breathed through his nose, and tried to enjoy his pearl gray suit and white shirt. Lone women in the hotel liked him. He had not made a million by age thirty, but expected to by the time he was forty. At least he was not a cop. When this streak of bad luck ran out, he would be snatched into the upper echelons of the hotel chain. Within two years he would have an MBA. He spoke fluent English, a language he loathed, Spanish, a language he loved, French, some German, a smattering of Japanese, and some Chinese, which had turned out to be far easier than he had dared to hope.

He turned to the Chinese couple, and spoke to them in English, throwing in a few Chinese honorifics that seemed to leave them cold. He promised them that everything was under control. The police were this very minute trawling the streets of Trastevere looking for the man who robbed them. They would not be billed the full amount for their room. The hotel would do all it could to make the rest of their stay as pleasant as possible.

As they left the room, the Chinese tourists gave him a look of disbelief that he had seen on the faces of the Korean, Japanese, Spanish, English, French, German, and American guests. It seemed humans had a universal expression to denote disgust with hotel managers.

He placed the failed mugging report in his drawer, and turned to the two policemen, giving them his best boyish grin and a what-can-you-do-with-these-people shrug.

"I am sorry about that. Can I get you anything to drink?"

The forehead creased and two gimlet eyes fixed themselves on him. "We don't drink on duty."

"Sorry, I wasn't thinking. Well, if you ever want, you know, refreshments, and by that I mean snacks, sandwiches, whatever, don't hesitate to pop in. Just mention my name, uh—*Capo*."

"Assistente Capo Rospo, and this here is Agente Davide Di Ricci."

Antonio longed to denounce the two troglodytes for dereliction of duty. But he would bide his time. He'd begin with security video footage of them eating and drinking for free. Then he'd gather more evidence and turn his staff into a stream of witnesses. Someday, he promised himself, when he was in charge of the entire Hudson & Martinetti Hotel chain in Italy, this fucker with the unfeasible head would receive a career-ending summons out of the blue. He smiled at him again, and said, "I really appreciate your being here."

The door to his office burst open. Rospo was on his feet, pistol half drawn.

Two young German tourists, a woman and a younger man, almost a boy, heads lolling, staggered in, and collapsed into the chairs just vacated by the Chinese couple. The woman seemed helpless with laughter. A smell of smoke and beer now joined the smell of policeman sweat and Chinese garlic that had already polluted his pristine office.

"*Wir haben eine Leiche gefunden! Einen Landstreicher,*" said the woman, then theatrically shushed the man who had not spoken yet, pointed to the policemen, and said, "*Schon? Italienische Gründlichkeit,*" and giggled.

The man, who had drunk enough to make his eyes shine rather than dull, pulled out one of the free tourist maps from the lobby, and showed it to Antonio and, speaking English, said, "I have circled the place. I think it is right. The police have been very fast to arrive here."

"I hate drunken northerners. What are these two fucking clowns saying?" demanded Assistente Capo Rospo.

"They seem to be saying they have found a dead body," said Antonio.